# fall into me

## CELINE L.A. SIMPSON

*First edition*

*ISBN (paperback): 978-1-7635659-5-1*
*ISBN (hardcover): 978-1-7635659-6-8*

*Editing by My Brothers Editor*
*Cover art by Celine L.A. Simpson*
*Illustration by Celine L.A. Simpson*
*Illustration by Chelly Rose (Character Art)*

*This book was professionally typeset on Reedsy.*
*Find out more at reedsy.com*

*For my dad.*
*For always being my safe harbor.*
*For giving me heights to aspire to.*
*For being the sort of person who doesn't give up and teaching me to do the same.*
*I love you; this one is for you.*

*(Definitely don't read this one, though!)*

*For those with tender hearts, that crave a peaceful life.*
*Being soft doesn't mean you are not strong.*

Won't you fall for me?
Won't you fall for me?
With my love as your garden
Won't you fall for me?
Won't you fall for me
From reality?
I am yours in the end
So won't you fall for me?

Fall For Me - Sleep Token

# Also by Celine L.A. Simpson

Standalone Dark Billionaire Enemies to Lovers Romance
*Just My Luck*

Standalone Reverse Grumpy/Sunshine Romance
*Convincing Florence*

Music to my Ears Duology (Interconnected Standalone Rockstar Romances)
*Music to my Ears (MTME #1)*
*All The Best Notes (MTME #2)*

The Lost Child of the Crown Series (Fantasy)
*Terraleise*
*Heir of Vaashaa*

# Content Warnings:

**Explicit Sexual Content**
**Stalking**
**Blood**
**Sexual Assault**
**Death**
**Domestic Violence**

# Prologue

**Before**

Everyone has an earliest memory.

Some people recall memories from age nine. Age ten.

Some people think they can recall memories from when they were in the womb. (They can't, because it's scientifically impossible, and I don't think I like those people.)

My earliest memories are from around five, and I remember thinking to myself that I was certain I could tell the most about a person by the way they laughed.

Every person has more than one, and I think that's why I loved that my brain could have that thought. There are so many types of laughs one person can have that I'm not sure you're ever really done discovering them. Not for yourself or the people around you.

There's something about getting to hear someone's laugh. This outward, crystal clear sign of joy. Of happiness. You can't hide it once it's happening. It's like this unspoken permission for you to unzip yourself for a little while.

What I remember most about growing up is how my house was always filled with laughter. There was so much of it in every corner.

It painted the walls of the kitchen, the living room, the dining room, and the den.

It painted the whole inside of the house and the outside. It was absolutely everywhere, all the time, and then when it faded, this incredible peacefulness was left in its wake.

Those are what my earliest memories are made of.

My dad's eyes crinkled at the corners, face split in two from a smile that made him look years younger. My mom with her head tipped back, nothing but a wheeze escaping her as she clutched her stomach in a desperate attempt to deter the cramps that ensued from the sort of laughter that made your eyes water.

I remembered looking at my little sister, who watched our parents with wide, dazzling brown eyes filled with unhinged adoration before she released a scream of her own. Clapping her hands and bouncing in her high chair, completely unaware of *why* she was suddenly filled to the brim with an overwhelming amount of joy, only certain in the knowledge that she *was*.

I remember thinking to myself that when I grew up, all I really wanted was for the walls of whatever home I had for myself to be splattered with laughter in the exact same way. I didn't want it to just start and end with the walls of this future, imaginary house, though.

I wanted to be covered in it. Head to toe. When I went to school. Out with my friends.

I wanted the inside of my very first car to be positively *defiled* with laughter.

I wanted it everywhere and on everything. In my hair, my eyelashes, between my toes like grains of sand that you could never get rid of.

It never occurred to me that anything could move over that belief like a blanket of clouds slowly taking over the sun.

Imagine seeing them in the distance, sweet and cozy.

You might want to stick your hand up into the heavens and pull a handful of those fluffy bastards down to take a big bite. They're scattered at first. The periods without sunshine at all are sparse and fleeting. Hardly enough to even start to notice the warmth leaving your skin.

But then they get more serious, and whether they break for the sunshine or not isn't up to you at all.

That's what I learned. That the sun was the laughter in my life, and the clouds had become something controlled completely by my heart. More terrifyingly, by the people—*the person*—who held my heart.

I heard his laugh first.

It wasn't particularly loud or brash. There's no reason it should have stood out among the others. No reason at all. I know for certain that in the moments after it had burst to life and filled the air of the bar around us, it had sought me out specifically. Like a string tied to one of my ribs. Tied to *all* of them.

I followed it right until I heard the sound again. The only real word I had for it was entranced.

Or drunk.

I was also incredibly drunk. But my eyes still worked, and I could see him where he sat right at the bar with someone who could have been incredibly famous or maybe he was just talking to a potted plant. I had no idea, and I didn't care. I paid them–*it?*– no attention.

Him, though. I noticed *everything* about him.

This rough-around-the-edges man with tattoos covering both his arms, all the way down to his wrists and peeking up above the neckline of his shirt. With hair that hit his shoulders and probably hadn't met a brush in its lifetime but in the sexiest way.

This man with eyes a blue so light they looked violet, even in the dim yellow light of the bar that was filled way past what I was sure was the legal limit for patrons.

I could imagine dipping a brush into his laughter and painting my life with it. I didn't remember ever wanting to do something so badly, maybe ever.

I'd been content in my bubble of imaginary invisibility, where I could stare openly at this other human being with no concerns at all about being caught. It didn't even really register when his eyes met mine, and he held them. Like we were forged. Tethered together, and something made complete and total sense in that split second that our eyes met.

Then he stood up from his table and started walking toward us, and my whole world screeched to a halt.

"Oh my god."

"What?" my roommate Angelika said, looking literally everywhere except at the giant, very firm-looking man walking directly at us.

"Jelly, talk to me. So it looks like we're speaking." I reached for her leg under the table and squeezed.

She swatted me away immediately. "*Ow.* What is wrong with you? How can I speak to you when you're not even looking at me?"

We had a…complicated relationship. I think I liked her maybe forty percent of the time. She liked me much, *much* less than that, and I was sure it was because I had the audacity to ask her (very politely and with no direct eye contact) to stop having sex so loudly in our shared dorm room after I'd been woken up for the third time.

"I *need*—" My words cut off as Violet Eyes stopped right in front of our table.

"Holy smokes. You're a whole lotta man." Jelly let out a low whistle, and I reached out and gripped her thigh again.

"Would you like to dance?" Oh, *oh.* His voice.

"Cali." A forceful shove was delivered to my shoulder.

"I…thank you." *I thank you?*

"She thanks you." Jelly's beaming, incredibly entertained smile was audible even as I sunk my nails into her leg. "Fuck me, Calista. You're going to hit an artery," she gritted out between her teeth, finally managing to unlatch my nails from her thigh.

I was still staring at the *whole lotta man.*

"You know," Jelly said, hopping off her stool. "I think I saw someone I'd like to meet outside."

"It's raining," I said, my eyes not at all on her.

"I guess we'll test your theory and see if I melt!"

And then she was gone.

Then there were two.

"Calista," he said. Pronouncing every letter of my name with intent, like every syllable held a taste. "I'm Fane."

"Calista." I introduced myself again like a moron. "My middle name's Rose." I shrugged like that information was useful to this hot stranger who was watching me while I tried to fit my whole foot right into my mouth. "So…Cali Rose. But, uh, Calista is fine. Better, even."

Holy *balls*. Kill me now.

"Cali Rose is pretty." He seemed to look glad to still be standing in front of me instead of horrified that he'd walked up to the world's most inept conversationalist.

I cleared my throat and opted to pretend the last minute never happened.

"I've never met someone named Fane before," I mumbled, undoubtedly dazed by this human stranger in front of me.

"Would you look at that," he said, holding his hand out to me.

"What?" The word was breathless and enthralled and hopeful.

"The first thing we have in common." He pulled me up to standing until I was eye to…pectoral?

"You are a very big man," I said, staring directly at his sternum.

That's when I heard it again.

His laugh. It just ripped right out of him. Head tipped back and body shaking with delight.

Completely and totally unzipped.

It was contagious, and I knew those breathless, enthralled, and hopeful feelings were all over my face.

When he asked me to dance a second time, I said yes.

I said yes to a first date, and a second, and a third.

It was the end of my second year of college, and immediately, I had no idea what life looked like without him in it.

I was consumed. Entirely. I had been covered in the sun shining warmth of that same laughter that had tied itself to every rib for two years. I couldn't imagine wanting anything else. I didn't think there was anything *more*. There was simply this person who controlled the clouds in my sky, and every single day was perfect.

Peaceful.

My god, that peacefulness. I didn't think there would've been something to steal my craving for the sunshine but Fane was total, utter peace. It was safe and strong and solid and in that, I had everything I needed.

Even when things weren't perfect, they were still *perfect*.

And then my mom got sick. She got sick, and it was like I could *feel* the laugh lines around my father's eyes smooth out for the first time in my life. That was the first time I realized what it was like to be heavy. The first time I *saw* someone else be heavy. Covered entirely in clouds without a speck of sunshine to be seen. It was *terrifying.*

So, I moved home.

There was never any other option for me. It had always been the plan to go back one day, and I couldn't help thinking that I was doing my part in making it that little bit better by bringing him home. By adding him to the fold of this safe, perfect place.

There was never any other option for me.

*For me.*

# 1

## Calista

**After**

For the last four days, my word of the day was one I'd neither heard of before nor been able to use in a sentence.

For some reason that startled me.

"When would I ever need to use the word flummoxed?" Maybe I wasn't the problem. Maybe it was the app on my phone. An app I currently paid for, might I add.

"Did you say phlegmy? Are you sick?" Gus yelled like we were on opposite sides of the room rather than separated just by the width of the coffee counter.

He'd forgotten his hearing aids again, and I tried really hard not to wipe the spit I could feel that just landed on the end of my nose.

"No phlegm here, Gus." I handed him his coffee in a to-go cup along with his change, which was the five-dollar bill he had handed me to begin with.

"Oh, well, that's good. You make the best coffee in town." He nodded at me in fierce agreement with his own statement.

"I make the only coffee in town." I quirked an eyebrow at him.

"Doesn't make it any less true." Gus was perpetually uncomfortable with giving compliments but handed them out like candy on Halloween. It meant that he was always rosy-cheeked and flighty with his eye contact.

I always do the same thing every day to soften his apparent discomfort because I really liked Gus. "You're just trying to butter me up for a free cookie." The first was free for everyone, but Gus didn't know that.

"Is it working?"

"Like a charm." I grinned at him brightly before sliding a still warm chocolate chip cookie into a bag. "Have a good day, Gus," I said, handing it to him.

"See you tomorrow, Cali." He harrumphed and dragged his feet the whole way out of the café.

Gus had been my first customer every morning of every day except Sundays for the last year and a half. He was also Santa Claus every year at the park in the middle of town since before I was born, and even in his retirement from community-based activities, he still looked the part.

In the plan that was my life…well, I hadn't really *planned* my life. Not with extreme detail. Not beyond my single, nonnegotiable: that I lived a life where laughter was always around every corner. I wanted the creases around my eyes and mouth to proudly show the evidence of it to people who knew and loved me. To people who didn't.

I guess if I unpacked it, that happiness was the coalition of a few things. Things that, if you'd asked me five years ago, were also baseline items.

Four walls and a roof over my head. Being able to wake up every day in Darling and its inherent warmth, its safety. This town was a bubble from the outside world, and almost everything good that had ever happened to me could be recounted and placed somewhere within the seven minutes and fourteen seconds it took to both enter and exit the town limits.

The last part of that baseline used to be someone to share it all with. Someone to depend on to help keep the clouds from impeding on the sunshine that was all the *good* that life had to offer. All the laughter.

But plans change.

The bell above the door to the café sounded just as I rounded the corner of the small kitchen tucked away in the back, a tray of fresh cookies in hand.

"There she is." My dad strode into the café with a grin splashed across his sun-kissed skin and rounded the counter. He dropped a kiss on the crown of my head before he grabbed two cookies right off the tray and his coffee off the top of the machine that I'd made at the same time as Gus's.

Dallas Grey had been my second customer every day except Sundays for the last year and a half.

"Hey!" I reached for the cookie contraband a second too late. "I'll tell Mom!" I gave him my most serious look, with a hand on my hip for emphasis.

"You know, you look just like her when you do that."

"Compliments will get you nowhere!" I yelled as he reached for the door.

Two seconds later, the bell rang again, and he reappeared. I rolled my eyes to hide my smile with zero percent success. "I'm not going to tell her, but you should know the amount of sugar, butter, and chocolate in those is enough to make you blackout for maybe a second."

"Then why do you make them?"

"Because they taste amazing."

"Well, see, that's why I take two. One to try, and—"

"One to be sure. Yeah, yeah." I crossed my arms and scowled at his still-smiling face. The smile that I'd inherited. I was my father's daughter, through and through. From the same hazel eyes to the wavy black hair. I was a copy and paste of him, whereas my sister, Abbey, was the spitting image of our mother.

"Don't be a smartass, and remember we've moved dinner to tonight at six because your mom's got to be at the hospital Thursday night. Don't be late, or you'll hear it from your mother."

I saluted at him. "But smartass is my middle name, as you've told me many times. And I know, no lateness here."

"Love you, kid. Best coffee in town."

"Love you too. And you have to say that. We're related."

"Have I ever lied to you?"

"I'm still waiting for Walter to get back from his 'summer camp,' so yes." Walter was my rabbit that I'd won at the Autumn Fair in town when I was eight.

He let out an exasperated sigh. "You never did let that go."

"You still haven't given me any other explanation." I grabbed a cup from the top of the machine as Maggie, my constant third patron for the last year and a half, slid past my dad.

"Morning, Dallas."

"Morning, Mags. How's Delilah?" he asked, wiping his hand down the front of his shirt, eradicating the last evidence of his contraband cookie.

"Oh, she's doing good." Mags took her regular seat right in the middle of the café. Most people craved the corners, or at the very least a wall to press their backs against. Not Mags.

"We meant to catch up the other day, but she never got back to me." I walked around the counter and set down her coffee and a cookie. We'd been doing that since I got back to town, playing a never-ending game of phone tag that resulted in a total of zero catch-ups.

"She had an unexpected visitor." There was a twinkle so bright in her eyes when she said the word "visitor" that I sort of wondered if the only person who hadn't expected them was Delilah.

"Oh?" I said it as casually as possible, but no one grew up in a small town and didn't develop a small taste for a little gossip. "Any ideas who?"

"Dylan Mason."

My sudden intake of breath was so aggressive I immediately began choking on my own saliva. My dad was there in a heartbeat, coffee in one hand and smacking my back with incredible amounts of force with the other.

"*Ow,*" I rasped, desperately waving him off in an effort to protect the integrity of my bones. "Dad, you're going to break a rib. Did you say *Dylan Mason?*"

"The very same."

"The one that, you know…" Holy shit, I really needed to call Delilah.

"Mm-hmm." Mags nodded her head, eyes still twinkling as she took a sip of her coffee and let out a grateful hum. "No one makes coffee like you, Cali."

"Keep your eyes on your cookie. This one's drooling." I pointed at my dad before ushering him out the door. "I'll see you tonight. Drive safe and be safe, please."

"Always do, always am." With a final kiss to the top of my head, he walked out the door, and I couldn't help the pressure that filled my chest. My dad was a firefighter, and it had always been my claim to fame when I was a kid growing up but the feeling of waiting with bated breath for him to walk through the front door every night hadn't ever shifted. Lodged in my heart like shrapnel.

Owning the café and being one of two employees, I was constantly run off my feet in a really non-aggressive way. Especially considering that Sammy and I only worked together on Saturdays.

I didn't have to worry about forgetting orders or customers growing disgruntled over a lack of available seating. The stream of people was reliable—just enough to keep me moving, yet never too overwhelming.

An empty seat? Filled within minutes.

A stack of dockets cleared? Time to put cookies in the oven or take them out.

The rhythm was predictable: walk out front, hand off cookies, take the next order, prep a sandwich.

So, no. I hadn't pictured my life in detail, but I knew it wasn't supposed to look like this.

And you know what? That was okay. Because now I knew what my days *would* look like. I knew the people who would fill them. The first person to walk through my coffee shop door. The second. The third.

I knew the cookie recipe by heart—reliable, unchanging. Just like the life I'd built here. It wasn't splattered with the laughter I'd dreamed of. The peace that settled after was fleeting, but the thin clouds above left enough light to get by.

It was four fifteen p.m., and, just like the day before, I started to close the café. The bell on the door rang, which was jarring for two reasons.

In the last year and a half, the bell had never rung at four fifteen p.m. The second was that in the brief moment when the street outside could be heard from the inside of the café, a chorus of voices trickled in.

The street in front of my café was usually quiet. The school run was done, and Mrs. Dellante had walked by with her five Pomeranians, stopping for almost exactly fifty seconds while they drank out of the dog bowl out front. That was why the chattering didn't make sense, because it hadn't existed before. Never at this time or on this street.

I leaned around the doorframe that led into the kitchen and noticed first the cars that had parked on the street. It would be a pretty good bet that I knew almost all the cars in all of Darling. A weird thing for me to have in my arsenal of things that may potentially impress you, but I saw them drive by my window every day. Sometimes several times a day, and I'd never seen these ones before.

Work trucks lined the street all with one thing in common: they all had 'Mackenzie Co.' on the side. The same logo was on the back of the shirts of the huddle of men that had congregated out front. It seemed stupid to me at that moment that the very last thing I noticed was the man, the strikingly *big* man, standing in the middle of my café.

I hadn't really thought about what would happen if this exact moment came to be. I think I did a lot to actively avoid it entirely, but it struck me as strange that so much and so little had changed about the person standing in front of me.

Was he *bigger*? Was that *possible*? Had he spent the last two years tracking down the exact location he more than likely already knew I'd be at?

I found all the above all at once too hard to comprehend because I had stopped waiting for Fane Mackenzie to show up at my door a very long time ago.

I wanted to blink and for him to disappear entirely.

"Calista."

The moment my name left his tongue, I could hear the way he laughed as if it were the bell above my door. I felt myself glitch, my world being smothered in too bright sunshine and then doused in heavy sheets of rain.

I wanted to take out my contacts and rub my eyes. I hated the finicky little bastards on the best of days, and this just felt like another reason why I should stop wearing them. The only sane explanation was that I had been given a pair that had the illusions of this man right on them.

The mop I was gripping like my only tether to the real world fell from my hands and clattered to the floor, and all I could think was that I was finally able to use my word of the day.

Flummoxed.

# 2

## Calista

**Before**

"Are you just going to stare at it, baby?"

It was a unique sensation, feeling all the blood rush to my face in the span of a single second, and it seemed like tonight was going to be full of new and unique sensations.

"I—What?" I pushed my glasses up my nose. The muscles in my throat were working overtime, swallowing in a nervous tic I didn't realize I even had until this exact moment.

"My hand." The smirk on his face told me everything I needed to know about how visible my blush was under the fluorescent lights of the bar.

"I'm not a good dancer," I said, still looking directly at his hand. "But you could sit and talk?"

He was quiet for a bit, and I could feel his eyes on my face while I kept mine on his outstretched hand. "I'm not a good talker…plus, this is my favorite song."

Fane's voice felt like every sensation I had ever experienced and loved, rushing all over me, all at once. I'd never heard a voice like his before.

Rough and smooth. Gentle and commanding. Soft and razor-sharp.

My brain couldn't figure out if I should be impressed by the fact that he had managed to make me ruin the pair of panties I had on with a total of two minutes of conversation clocked in or horrified and in desperate need of a visit to the doctor.

Or a therapist.

"This isn't the sort of music I thought would play at a bar like this," I said. The song currently playing was "Fall For Me" by Sleep Token, and the song before had been one by Lady Luck. The one before that was all screaming voices that made my throat hurt to even listen to it.

"And what sort of bar do you think this is?" His head tilted to the side, full of amusement.

I dragged my eyes away from him to the neon sign above the bar that read 'Heavenly Horns'. "Maybe like Bible study meets a fetish-based costume shop?"

Fane's hand was still extended between us when his other landed over his stomach, and his head tipped back in a throaty, intoxicating laugh. It rained down on me, settling onto my skin in a fine shimmer, making everything it touched luminescent.

"Well," he said, looking back at me, his smile heartbreaking. "Good thing I know the DJ."

"Who's the DJ?" It didn't matter, but I didn't want to stop talking to him. I was hanging on to every word he said, even more desperate for them now that I knew they were coveted things.

He pointed a finger at his own chest. "My playlist."

"You should add some country music. Maybe some Gracie Abrams."

"I'll consider it," he murmured, hand still extended.

"If I dance with you, will you keep talking to me then?" I was proud of the way I lifted my chin up and squared my shoulders like I was this brave and immovable woman.

That's not to say I *wasn't* brave and immovable. It was just more in a being-able-to-find-my-way-back-to-a-location-without-maps-even-if-I'd-only-ever-been-there-once sort of way.

"All right." Fane tipped his head in the sort of nod that told me everything I needed to know about whether or not he was a man who kept his word.

I slipped my hand into his. Rough and worn and warm, adding dimension to the person I was painting him out to be in my mind.

Touching him felt like something entirely new, and at the same time, it was deeply known by every cell in my body. The rightness of it all when I looked up into his violet eyes and followed him onto the dance floor.

3

## Fane

**After**

It honestly felt like I'd been tripping balls for the last seventy-two hours.

I hadn't slept at all for the first twenty-four, and everything after that was now too grimy to recall.

Cali looked at me like she'd seen a ghost, and then she started to blink rapidly. So fast it was kind of alarming.

I wanted to move toward her, but I doubted that would help. No, I *knew* it wouldn't.

When her eyes popped open, she reached up like she was about to rub them before stopping herself and clamping them shut again.

I cleared my throat and felt like I might be drowning. "Are you—"

"Mother of God," she gasped. "You're real." Her eyes flew open, one hand immediately landing at the base of her throat.

"Hi." Good fucking Lord. I had never been very good with words, but I had at least been able to stay away from being some sort of monosyllabic dickhead. Until now.

"Hi." Her brow furrowed as her head tilted to the side. The move was so familiar to me that I knew exactly what was going through her head. Even when I had no real right to anymore.

"Fane." She said my name like it had sat on a shelf at the back of her mind,

11

and she was blowing the dust off it. For one small, minute moment, I had no idea how this was going to go, and then she narrowed her eyes at me, and I knew I'd been wrong.

I was fully aware of exactly how this was going to go.

"What the hell are you doing here, Fane?" She was pissed.

"The sign out front said coffee." I gestured back toward the street to where the group of contracted tradesmen loitered.

"We're closed." She crossed her arms and took a single step back further into the kitchen.

There was a huge sign in the window of Cali's café that said, "We are open until 5!" I saw it when I walked in. I knew she knew it was there too, because I'd wager she was the one to put it there.

I took my time looking from her face to the clock on the wall on my right that showed four thirty p.m. before looking back at her face. And God help me, I tried, but I couldn't stop the way my mouth curved at the side because I knew she was full of shit.

Turns out, that was not the right reaction to have in the presence of a woman harnessing what I am sure rivaled the wrath of the devil.

"We're still closed," she bit out between clenched teeth, crossing her arms and jutting out her hip.

She was so familiar to me. And every single move she made, every second I could drink her in, my ability to breathe got easier and easier. It wouldn't last, this moment of peace I'd found. I knew that. But I'd be damned if I wasted even a second of it.

I opened my mouth to say something else, overcome with this sudden need to ruffle her feathers. I wanted to push her buttons. I wanted to see that flush I knew hid just under the collar of her shirt spread up her neck.

I hadn't seen Calista Grey in almost two years, and every single scenario that I had imagined, every moment that I'd played out in my head and memorized what I'd say, no longer meant a single thing in the light of seeing her in the flesh.

"Why are you *here*, Fane?" Her voice wavered, and I wanted to tell her exactly why I was there. I wanted to tell her where I'd been, too.

The thought of the last two years made me clench my fists. Made me want to crack my neck over and over and fucking over.

However, showing up out of the blue and saying, *"Hey, remember my dad? The one I hate, the one I swore I'd never be like? Well, surprise! I ended up working for him, and now he's got his sights set on Darling. Your Darling. And I didn't know what else to do, how else to stop it."* That didn't feel like the best approach.

Instead, I just said, "Work."

*"Work?* You're here for work? In Darling? You're here to work, here in Darling?" With every word that came out of her mouth, her eyes got bigger, and the bigger they got, the harder I clamped my mouth shut.

"Are you…are you *laughing?*"

"No, ma'am." I shook my head, knowing I should look away from her, but completely and totally unable to.

Everything. I memorized everything about this woman, and still it had not done her justice.

Closing my eyes had been a mistake the last time I'd seen her. When I opened them again, she'd been gone.

I watched now as her body went from rigid to mildly defensive. The way her crossed arms loosened, and her pointer finger reached up briefly to the bridge of her nose before she dropped both arms to her sides.

I felt it more than I saw it happen. The way she let her eyes wander over me. I could categorically list the things that she would pick up.

My hair was shorter. The last time she saw me, it was longer, so long I used to keep it up half the time. Now, it fell against my nape in a tousle of dark brown waves, long enough to tuck behind my ears but too short for anything else.

I could have imagined it, but it looked like her hand twitched like maybe she remembered what it was like to run her fingers through it. Just like I hadn't been able to stop doing, why I had ended up cutting it to begin with.

I knew she was taking note of the tattoos that hadn't been there before. The ones that covered my neck. My hands.

I didn't let myself take her in more than I already had. Even those few moments already felt like a mistake.

The woman in front of me might have loved me once, but she certainly didn't love me now.

It felt like a handful of minutes between then and when the door behind me opened. The bell above it was sweet and light, cutting the tension that had formed like a knife through butter. A glance at the clock told me I was wrong, and it was now five p.m. on the dot. We'd spent almost thirty minutes just…staring at each other.

"Kid? I saw your car was still here, and I…"

I let my eyes fall closed, giving myself a moment to *feel* the shit that I had so thoroughly stepped in before stepping to the side and turning to the man behind me.

Calista's dad.

"Hey, Dad." Cali's voice was a strangled croak.

I can honestly say that this was the first time I'd ever seen Calista Grey nervous.

It was night and day the way she went from doing her best to become a part of the wall behind her to taking the five strides to get her from where she was to where I stood.

Right fucking next to me.

"Fane?" Dallas Grey took his hat off and reached for my hand the same way he had the first time we met.

"Sir, nice to see you." I shook his hand back, but he didn't stop there. Instead, he pulled me into the sort of embrace that made you feel a part of something. Important. I couldn't remember the last time I'd felt like that and tried to keep the look of *what the ever-loving fuck was happening?* off my face.

That was a lie I told myself often. I could sure as fuck remember. I could remember it down to the day. Down to the *second*.

"I did not expect to see you here! Cali didn't say a single thing to us." He stepped back with a grin on his face and a light in his eyes. A light that had been there the last time I had seen him. One that meant I was a part of his family.

One that should absolutely not be there right now.

"Oh?" I was impressed that my voice came out sounding normal instead of the high-pitched squeak I had been expecting. Not that I'd ever squeaked in my fucking life, but if I were a betting man, I'd have bet it would've happened for the first time right now.

"No, well, you know." Cali slid a finger up the bridge of her nose again before flicking her eyes up to mine and away just as fast.

"It was a surprise for me too," she said, giving her dad what I used to call her *I want to cry* smile.

"I'm surprised you could get time off work long enough to make the trip," Dallas said, crossing his arms and leaning against the door he just came in.

I nodded, looking down at the woman next to me as if I could read what the fuck was on her mind just by wishing it. "Well," I started, clearing my throat and reaching up to rub the back of my neck. "The, uh, the—"

"Mines," she filled in for me, and I just stared at her while I collected myself because *what the fuck?*

I cleared my throat and looked back to her father. "The *mines*…"

"Are closed," Cali supplied, rather unhelpfully, and I felt my eyes almost fall out of my face. I clenched my jaw at the same time her grip on my arm tightened, nails digging in.

"The mines you worked at in Australia closed?" Dallas frowned at us, pushing off the door and looking for all the world like the concerned sort of father I always wished I had.

"To me," I added quickly. "Closed to me. As in, I no longer work there."

"That's right." Cali's head nodded so furiously it looked like it was about to come off, an unhinged sort of grin plastered on her face. "They fired him."

"Or." I knew she could feel my glare. "I quit."

"You know," Dallas shook his head, taking off his hat to run his hands through his dark peppered hair before replacing it. "You two are really made of sterner stuff. What's it been, Cal, a year and a half?"

"Almost two," she mumbled, and I still couldn't stop looking at her.

"Almost two years." He whistled low and long before clamping a hand on my shoulder and shocking me back into the conversation. Dallas wasn't a small man, but I had a few inches on him in height and width.

It had always felt weird, looking *down* at her dad.

"Yep." I nodded, reverting to the monosyllabic dickhead from before.

"Real happy for you guys." Dallas pulled Calista into a tight hug with a kiss on the top of her head. "Glad you can finally start your lives together."

"Thanks, Dad." Her voice was muffled against his shoulder.

"So, I'll tell your mom to set another plate for the table, but I'll let you surprise her. Sound like a plan? Six thirty sharp."

"What a plan!" Cali half raised her hands in the air like, somehow, it would help with making her sound less like she was in pain. Dallas just stared at us with a big grin on his face, like he was waiting for something. That's when she looped her arm through mine and leaned her head on my arm like her touching me wasn't a big deal. Like I hadn't thought of her every day, of every month for the last six hundred and fucking thirty-nine days.

"Great plan." I nodded at him as he delivered a double thumbs up and headed for the door, the little bell sounding too light and peaceful for the way my heart was thrashing in my chest.

Cali didn't move for the next handful of seconds, and I might have imagined it again, the way her fingers flexed on my bicep before she pulled away and turned to face me.

"So," she said, not meeting my gaze, "You're going to laugh at this." She sounded like she'd rather yell the words at me, but the situation demanded she at least attempt to be civil.

"Okay." My voice came out rough. Filled with everything I was feeling. Panic, curiosity, wonder, confusion, concern. A mild amount of hysteria. A fucked-up little bit of hope.

"When I moved home…" Her eyes flicked up to mine and then away, but it was enough for me to see the jagged edges of pain that still remained. "No one had expected me to show up alone."

I was glad she wasn't looking at me because she didn't see the way I flinched at her words. Every single one of them was like a knife she'd flung right at my chest. Not even needing to look to hit the bull's-eye.

"When they asked where you were…" My eyes darted from her face to her throat, and I watched the way she swallowed once. Twice. Then she shook her head and dragged her eyes from the floor to meet mine. It was like seeing a completely different person.

There was not an ounce of the pain I saw before. So much so that I was half convinced I'd made it up. Wanted it to be there so much, maybe I imagined it.

All I saw was…nothing. She looked at me with *nothing*.

"I wasn't going to break my mom's heart more than it already was, so I lied. I told them you were tying up some loose ends in the city. I thought they'd forget about it, considering my love life was nowhere near the most important thing going on right then. *But…*after a few months, my dad asked about you. Instead of breaking *his* heart, I told him you were in Australia."

"Working in the mines," I clarified, my heart still thrashing, my lungs burning. All while I was coming to the realization that if I was going to get through the next few months, I would have to seriously change my approach.

Cali didn't just feel *nothing*. I could see it, *feel* it. Right to the very center of me.

She hated me. She had every right to, I wasn't debating that. I just hadn't expected it to rip the air from me the way it had. Like the last little bit of hope I had just disappeared.

"I figured it would be a good reason to tell them eventually that it didn't work out, but…" She pushed her finger up the center of her nose again, and I finally figured out why she kept doing that. Cali wasn't wearing her glasses. "I could never bring myself to do it. So, here we are."

I nodded. Only because I wasn't entirely sure what else to do.

"Will you go along with it?"

My eyes were still on her throat. At her tone, they snapped up to meet her hazel gaze. She was glaring at me, but like she was trying hard not to. Like I had inconvenienced her by showing up and making her out herself in the lie she'd wrapped us both in.

"I don't know anything about Australian mines." I hadn't been able to take my eyes off her the moment she stood beside me. So, I did the only thing I *could* do. I matched her glare with my own.

Matched her *nothing* with my own.

It wasn't fair, but I reached for that kernel of rage that simmered deep in my soul that sparked to life when I woke up and found her gone. The one time in my life that I'd let myself fall into a deep sleep, an exhausted sleep, and my biggest fear had come to light. That I wouldn't wake up in time to stop something bad from happening. From losing someone I loved.

She had no idea what I'd done. What I'd sacrificed.

And it was all for her. There was no time to explain. She hadn't given me even a second from the moment she asked me to move home with her, and all that came out of my mouth was, "No."

And now, she didn't know the fucking half of what it had taken to get here. To be here for *her.* Like seeing her was easy for me. Like losing her wasn't the most fucked-up thing that had ever happened to me.

If Calista wanted to fight with me, I was more than happy to step into the ring with her.

"Yes, well, I'm sure you can Google it." She crossed her arms and kept her narrowed stare firmly in place.

"What's in it for me?"

"What?" Her face went blank.

"If I go along with it…" I enunciated every word like I was talking to a child. It was condescending and mean, and the way her nostrils flared in anger made something zap down my spine. "What's in it for me?"

Her foot started to tap on the ground. Brows drawing close while she pursed her mouth to the side. Calista wasn't just thinking. She was *panicking.*

"What do you want?"

"I'll let you know."

"That's not fair," she blurted. Her brows drew in further.

"Yeah, well, that's life." I let my stare turn into a glare. The sick sort of satisfaction I got when her eyes narrowed further was borderline sociopathic.

We were locked in a silent, unmoving battle. She, I was sure, was trying to think about all the ways she might get away with killing me. While I was still trying my fucking hardest not to step closer to her, to wrap my hand around her throat just to see what she would do.

I was caught between wanting to squeeze until she gasped in that way I knew she did and fucking begging her to put her hand back on my arm where I could still feel the burn of her touch on my skin.

Cali surprised me when she nodded her head, mouth still pursed and brows still drawn, but that was a nod of agreement nonetheless, and I felt like I'd just won the fucking lottery somehow.

"I'll—I have a new number now," she said, looking anywhere but at me.

"I know," I said. Saying more in those two words than I really meant to. The only way I'd know that was true is if I had tried to call her. Tried to text her. I had done both of those things. Many times.

Her face registered that, and then, like she'd made herself delete that bit of information, her face went blank again, and her voice went flat. "What's yours? I'll message you the address."

"It's the same."

"You never changed it?" She dropped her arms to her sides, and her body swayed like she wanted to step toward me too.

I just shook my head.

"Why?"

I didn't give her a reply to that one. I couldn't. I just let my eyes fall over her, taking her in. Real and healthy and right in front of me. Gut-wrenchingly fucking perfect. With a last nod goodbye, I turned to leave her café.

"I didn't give you the address."

Her voice sounded closer to me, like she did take that step.

"I remember the way," I mumbled, not bothering to turn around.

I was so fucked, but I knew this was nothing compared to what would happen when she realized why now, after all this time, I'd finally found my way back to Darling.

# 4

# Calista

**After**

I stared right at the spot Fane had been occupying only seconds before for an unhealthy amount of time.

I stared so long that by the time I locked up to head home, I was certain he was a mirage that I'd hallucinated on the grounds of smelling too many coffee beans.

The drive home was done on one hundred percent instinct. I couldn't even recall the turns I'd made or the signs I stopped at, but pulling onto my gravel drive, the sight of the little cottage was like a balm to my always-aching heart.

My house was perfect. So, so perfect.

I mean, sure, it was falling apart, and I didn't *actually* own it, and I was also pretty sure I was paying way too much for it. Mrs. Antinello was my landlord, and she was (respectfully) so old I'm certain no one had actively celebrated a number for her birthday since I was in single digits.

She also lived directly across the street and loved to swat literally everyone on the ankles with her cane.

To put it plainly, she frightened me. When she told me the rent, I smiled super wide to make sure I didn't cry and shook her hand, which felt like if I gripped it too firmly, it might detach from her body.

In saying all of that, she *did* allow dogs. And that was really all that mattered.

Most people might've had someone on speed dial to call and immediately talk to about hallucinating their ex. Not me.

I hadn't had a real conversation with my sister in years. When Mom got sick, I ran home, and she ran for the hills, which just about sums up the pair of us.

Delilah might have been my person once, but that was before I came back a stranger—to myself and everyone else.

Not anymore, though, and that was all on me.

My reality was that I lost every single person that I relied on all in the same night. All for different reasons, but I lost them, nonetheless.

But then there was Jerry. My big, beautiful, pony-sized Great Dane.

"Oh, Jerry!" It would be a cold day in hell when he peeled himself off his couch and met me at the front door like any other regular dog.

Yes, Jerry had his own couch. Mainly because he was too damn big to share one with me, and after the third time he launched me onto the floor with a firm kick to the spine, I decided enough was enough.

His groan of delight reverberated through the house, along with the solid thumping of his tail. In what I was sure was every dog trainer's nightmare, I answered the call of his unspoken demand to come hither and practically threw myself onto him.

With his big head between both my hands, I smothered him with kisses, his tail picking up speed with each forceful smooch.

Jerry was supposed to be a gift for Fane.

I know. *I know.* But we were a few weeks past our two-year anniversary, and Fane had always wanted a dog. More specifically, he wanted a Great Dane named Jerry. I searched high and low for this incredibly large canine, and the moment I saw his little gangly frame at a gentle and pure two months old staring at me from the other side of a plexiglass wall, I knew.

He was the one.

That was the night my dad called me.

*"Invasive ductal carcinoma." My dad's exhausted voice cracked through my*

*phone like the words weighed a thousand tons. "She's got breast cancer, darlin'."*

*That was the first and last time I ever heard Dallas Grey cry, and I hadn't even been there to hold him. To be someone who could carry that weight with him, so he knew he wasn't alone in the fear that he could lose the love of his life.*

*I stormed into the apartment Fane and I shared in a panic. Tears blurred my vision with nothing on my mind but this painful, aching need to get home. Every tether I had to sanity slowly snapping at the idea that I was losing hours, minutes, seconds with my mom.*

*"Calista." Fane's voice had been strong, just like the hands that held my face. That clutched me to a hard, familiar chest that continued to resound with the steady thumps of his heartbeat.*

*I'd never given much thought to heartbeats before, but right then, I was terrified that I hadn't been paying close enough attention to his. That I hadn't been marking them down and remembering them in case one day I ever had to live without them.*

*"Baby, you've got to tell me what's wrong or else I can't fix it." Fane had always been calm in situations where I'd only ever been able to feel panic. He was well-balanced. Thoughtful. He was unwavering. A lighthouse amid a raging storm.*

*"My mom," I croaked out, unable to see him clearly through the heavy onslaught of tears. "She's sick. We have to go home. Fane, my dad—" My voice broke, and he held me while the sobs racked my body. I didn't even try to pull it together. I knew that this would be my one and only chance to break down because I would do everything I could to do for my dad what Fane did for me.*

*Keep steady.*

*And that's when my whole world shattered. All it took was a single second and one word.*

*"No. Cali...I can't."*

I almost missed them. I think I wanted to miss them, but I'd heard those words leave his mouth and had enough respect for myself that I didn't ask him to repeat them. I remembered stepping out of his hold, turning around, and closing the door to our room.

Something snapped inside me. I didn't understand the how or why or what. I didn't even remember packing. I refused to look at him when I walked out on silent feet, setting my key to our first and only apartment on the kitchen island as I left.

I picked up Jerry on my way back to Darling, and he didn't make a peep for the whole five-hour drive. Not even when my hand held onto his fur with maybe a little too much force.

He just looked at me, and I looked at him, and we both knew that it could take some time, but we were going to save one another.

I groaned into the fur of his stomach. "I hallucinated a man today. The *worst* man." Jerry's tail stopped wagging, and he eyed me with the perfect amount of wariness. The look was made entirely more dramatic on account of his face being held down by gravity and the whites of his eyes on full display.

"Oh, don't you worry. You won't ever have to meet him," I patted his stomach. "But I think it might be karma for accidentally crushing Mrs. Antinello's tulips when I tripped over them yesterday." I looked up to gauge my dog's silent opinion, mostly because he had been the one to nudge me directly into the flower bed.

Jerry had fallen back asleep at some point between his concerned stare and my admission of unintentional vandalism.

"Holy shit, I need to stop waiting for him to reply," I mumbled to myself. Doing my best to get up without jostling the couch too much and waking him up.

It was five forty-five p.m., and hallucinations or not, I wasn't going to have my ass handed to me by the infamous Isla Grey for being late to a dinner date.

Now that she was better, she was even more passionate about being on time.

Mom's treatment had been brutal and fast-paced. From the moment she was given her diagnosis to her tests and biopsies, through to her treatment plan, and then to the decision she made to get a double mastectomy.

She'd faced it all with this unfaltering determination and grace that I was so in awe of. I didn't know how she did it, but I'd never been so proud to be her daughter as I was watching her go through one of the most harrowing things I think you can watch someone you love endure.

She did six months of chemo, and in April of last year, she was officially declared to be in remission. Though the road was long and so much of her life still revolved around hospital visits and medication, I'd seen so much of the woman she'd been before come back to life in the last twelve months that it was hard not to cry every time I saw her.

That included her fiery disposition regarding tardiness.

My parents lived in the same house that I'd grown up in. A beautiful, older-style farmhouse that had been renovated slowly and consistently over a couple of decades so that nothing was ever new at the same time. It had baby-blue shutters and a porch that wrapped all around the outside.

The moment you looked at it, it made you feel like you could take a deep breath.

At least, it used to.

I couldn't look at this house without my chest tightening. Without being gripped by the looming presence of a grief that hadn't descended but lingered on the outskirts of my sanity, ready to consume me at any moment.

"Mom! Dad!" I called before I even closed the car door behind me. It was exactly twelve minutes past six and I would be damned if I was clocking in a moment later.

"Cali girl!" I could hear my mom's sing-song voice trickle out of the kitchen through the open front door. The house already smelled amazing, and my stomach chose that moment to rumble, reminding me that I hadn't remembered to eat lunch…*again*.

Being wrapped in a hug from my mother turned me into a little girl again. She was warm and soft, and everything that haunted me outside of her embrace had no standing whatsoever when she slowly rocked me from side to side. I was enveloped in notes of bergamot and lemon, of jasmine and lilies.

"My big girl," she whispered into my hair, placing a kiss on my temple.

"Hi, Momma," I whispered back before she let me go and headed back to the kitchen.

"Your father is washing up, but you can set the table. He won't tell me why I'm cooking for four."

The way my asshole clenched was actually comical. It was also probably a health hazard. My only conclusion was that the universe was playing a joke on me because, right at that moment, a knock came from behind me. I didn't need to look to know who's hulking figure now encompassed the entire doorframe.

"Oh no," I gasped, squeezing my eyes shut like I'd hopefully disappear if I did it hard enough.

"Oh my *god*. Tell me I'm not seeing things!" The only way I knew she'd rushed past me was because I was encompassed with a fresh wave of her scent and not so subtly shoved out of the way so she could get to the not-hallucination and very much real man who had just knocked on her open front door.

"I wish I could," I thought I murmured too low for anyone to hear, but by the grunt behind me, I was pretty sure Fane had caught it.

"Mrs. Grey." Fane's voice moved through me like it was inspecting every cell in my body. I felt it behind my eyes, the way it made my skin prickle and heat and feel too tight for my body.

"Don't you start that." She gripped his arms and took a small step back as if she could both inspect him in his entirety and keep a hand on him at the same time. You couldn't, but she gave it a wonderful attempt.

"I can't believe it. How did you get away from the mines?"

Fane's eyes snapped to mine, and I took that as my cue to turn swiftly on my heels and head for the kitchen to find a job that I could do that didn't involve being anywhere near him.

"Right," I heard him say, not trying to hide the grin of satisfaction at the no doubt uncomfortable situation he was now in, even as I felt the hole that he was burning into the back of my head. "Yes, the mines."

# 5

# Calista

**After**

I wouldn't call myself the type to necessarily 'throw hands', but I was pretty sure I'd be good at it. The thought of taking a swing at Fane was the only thing keeping my rage in check as I stared at him across my parents' dining table. I'd never known what it felt like to truly loathe someone—until that moment.

I wanted to take a hardy scoop of the mashed potatoes off my plate and flick it at him.

Fane's charm was infuriating. There was something particularly brutal hearing him tell my mom she looked beautiful and apologizing for not being here sooner.

"Oh honey, you've done enough." She patted his cheek with the same affection she showed me and Abbey before she headed back into the kitchen.

He had certainly done enough, of that I was sure. But I'd have to find a way of figuring out what exactly that meant to my mom. I was sure we had very different opinions of what 'enough' was.

My parents hadn't been able to stop gushing over him. My mom hadn't stopped smiling once, and I was honestly impressed with how she still managed to chew her food. My dad was too busy to eat, considering that his eyes had turned into big hearts.

Turns out, Fane had, in fact, done some Googling. He'd actually done a *heavy* amount of Googling because, with every question my parents asked him, he had an answer. I'd be lying if I didn't admit that a small part of my soul shriveled even further at being robbed of seeing him fumble his way through that shitstorm.

I wanted to scream until my throat burned raw. Until all the rage and confusion clawing at my insides finally snuffed out. Because I wasn't supposed to see this man ever again.

In my head, the moment he said no to coming home, our relationship had ended. It was like a switch flipped. That one word shattered something inside me, and I hadn't stopped feeling the cracks since.

Everything I thought I knew—everything I'd seen in my parents, in how they loved each other, how they loved me and my sister—he'd destroyed it all in seconds.

And now he was here.

With no other options, my brain latched onto the one thing it could handle: anger.

Hot, steaming, fire-engine-fucking-red anger.

"What are you doing for work now you're back?" My dad asked him around a mouthful of steak, and I zoned in on their conversation for the first time because I was also incredibly curious about the answer to that question.

Two years, and he suddenly decided to show up and disorganize my life? In the very town he refused to grace with his presence? I don't think so.

"I'm working for my dad."

My fork clanged to my plate, and all three pairs of eyes were on me.

Fane held my gaze with an unflinching intensity that made my stomach coil. My entire body chilled. Ice formed in places that had just moments before been the consistency of molten lava. "You're working for your dad?"

"Yes," he said, and I know that my parents wouldn't have noticed, but I saw the way his jaw clenched. I saw the way the muscle twitched and how his hand tightened around the fork in his hand.

I remembered the night he told me about him. If there was one thing I knew wouldn't have changed about the man in front of me, it was the hate he held like an oath for his father.

It hit me then with startling clarity that I actually *didn't* know anything. I had no idea who the man across from me now was. Not anymore.

I let my disgust at the idea of it all color my face. Didn't even attempt to hide it.

"He's in development," Fane went on. "Recently, there's been a few investment opportunities in Darling. I just moved into a project manager role, so I've got a team of contractors here to scout the area."

"Scout the area?" I frowned at him. "Scout it for what?"

"Development." He didn't even look at me as he took a bite of his food.

My hand itched to fling up from under the table and flip him off, but as it stood, the tension between us was so taut any unknowing civilian could clothesline themselves on it and do some serious damage.

Subtlety had never been my strong suit, and I knew I was doing a very poor job of it right now because of the two alarmed looks from my parents. I should have received a medal of some kind for the effort it took to smoosh my face into something pleasant.

I fluttered my eyelashes at him so aggressively that I hoped it made him nauseous. He looked up at me from under his full lashes and heavy brows with an expression that made my stomach twist painfully.

I didn't recognize it. I didn't recognize *him*.

"He's been keeping tabs on a lot of small towns that are a relatively easy drive from major cities that could be done up as weekend getaways for city folks to get their small-town fix. His main focus has been Blazewood, Banks City, and Sterling."

"Those are all West Coast cities."

"Yep."

"But Darling is nowhere near those cities."

"He's monitoring hundreds of small towns and their potential for growth."

"That sounds stupid. You can't just turn a small town into a city getaway," I scoffed, pushing my plate away from me now that my appetite had left the building, much like I wish I had.

"They can, and they do." Fane took another bite of his steak and chewed it slowly.  It pissed me off.  "It's already been done to a dozen small towns. The desk work starts in Artington—analyzing the town's economy, businesses, and potential." His eyes flicked to mine for a split second then away, like he couldn't stand to even look at me while he did more damage than he'd already done. "Then we move on-site. Main streets, key real estate, infrastructure. Figure out what can be improved, and see what's missing.  Create investment opportunities, introduce accommodations, spas, seasonal activities. Everything people could want when they're playing at living the small-town dream."

Not only was it the most words I'd probably ever heard him say in one sitting, but my brain just wasn't working. He was churning out these words like they were a script, and for a second, it felt like he hated the way they sounded coming out of his mouth.

"We? Who the fuck is we?" My chest was rising too fast for anything casual, and my finger slid up the bridge of my nose rather aggressively.

"Calista!" my mom shouted at the same time as my dad said, "You're not too old for a time out in this house, missy!" But I was still looking at Fane.

"'We' is the business," he replied so calmly it actually gave me a heart palpitation.

"*Mackenzie Co.?*"

He just nodded like everything we were talking about exhausted him.

"You can't just go in and *change* towns that don't need changing. Those are people's homes. People's livelihoods. People's history."

I was seething. He *knew* what this town meant to me. It wasn't enough that he didn't want to live here. He had his heart set on bulldozing the whole thing.

"We don't ruin anything. A lot of what we do improves the things that already exist. We inject a bit of money into the small-town economy and bring in tourism. Expand the population. It keeps the towns alive."

"Oh my god," I breathed. "You actually believe the words that are coming out of your mouth, don't you?"

He didn't reply. He just kept eating. It was at that moment I caught sight of my parents. They were staring at us like two people who were absolutely not in love.

So, I did what any sane person would do, I laughed. I did this weird, forced chortle that had my dad half out of his seat prepared to do the Heimlich.

"Well…" I swallowed a lump in my throat that refused to dissipate. "Clearly, the day has gotten to me." The forced chortle continued, and it didn't stop until both my parents visibly relaxed.

"Hey, kid." My dad reached over and squeezed my hand. "I know you love this town. We all love this town. Think about it this way, you'll be able to be his guide on why he shouldn't meddle. You'll have plenty of time once Fane gets settled in at home."

Home.

*My* home.

I'd probably be clawing out my eyeballs if it wasn't for the horrified look on Fane's face. Because, *of course,* we would be living together. Why, on God's green earth, would my long-distance-turned-short-distance boyfriend live anywhere but with me? At home. In my *house.*

Oh my god. *With Jerry!*

"And I don't like you doing all those improvements on your own."

"Improvements?" Fane asked, his voice half amused and half uncertain if he even wanted to know the answer.

"She's refused to let me help her fix parts of that house that are falling apart. I hate to say it, but it's a bit of a shit box."

"Dad!" This wasn't the first time he'd called my little cottage a shit box.

"I'm sorry, darlin'. It has character, but I've gotta call a spade a spade, and you refused to let me help you fix it up. It wouldn't be a shit box if I had my way with it for a weekend."

"I'm handling it. It's a homeowner's rite of passage," I grumbled, knowing the argument was weak, but I wouldn't put more on his plate. All he needed to do was keep himself healthy.

When Mom got sick, he sort of fell off the wagon. It wasn't until I could actually smell him from across the house that I realized he hadn't showered for a whole week.

That's when I knew how bad things had gotten for him, so anything that wasn't focused on him just trying to be okay, to live and breathe and operate, became so incredibly unimportant.

Dad focused on Mom, and I focused on Dad. That's how it had been for the last two years.

"You don't own that damn house," Dad grumbled back.

"You—" Fane started to say something that I was certain I didn't want to hear.

"Well, it's getting late." I cut him off with a beaming smile and narrowed eyes that said *your opinions, thoughts, and feelings are unwanted here.*

"Look at that," my mom said, peering into the kitchen at the clock that read half past nine. "Honey, you haven't eaten much. Let me pack it up for you."

I placed a soft kiss on her cheek before we started to move around the table in a practiced pack-up routine that I'd been doing since I was a kid. I would do the plates, Dad would do the dishes in the middle of the table, Mom would do the cutlery, and Abbey usually did the glasses. Fane took it upon himself to take over that part despite the neon sign on my forehead that expressed how unwanted he was here.

Then we were out front on the gravel drive staring at each other, and I was still pretty confident that I could throw a mean punch.

"I have somewhere to stay," Fane said. His voice was rough and low, and I hated that it was the equivalent of honey running down the back of my throat.

"Too bad," I said, loathing what was about to happen but knowing that it needed to. "This is a small town, and that"—I pointed at his truck—"is a very big, very noticeable truck. If it's not parked at my house, then they"—I pointed at my parents' house—"will know before we've even woken up in the morning."

I didn't wait for him. I just turned and walked toward the cars and tried to ignore how much my car looked like roadkill next to his brand-spankin' new wheels. It didn't take long for his strides to overtake mine.

"You're going to have to follow me," I bit out between clenched teeth.

"I'm sure I can find my way," he mumbled over his shoulder, grinding out the words with the same restraint I was exercising. Which made no sense to me because of the two of us here, he was the asshat.

"You don't know the address." I stopped, looking at the back of his head incredulously.

"I'll just look for the shit box," he said before jumping into the cab of his truck and driving off before the echo of his words had even dissipated.

It was settled. I officially hated Fane Mackenzie.

# 6

# Fane

**After**

I had intended on driving right to her house, but I also knew that I'd have to explain how I knew her address, and that would open up a whole can of fucking worms I wasn't at all equipped at handling right now.

I parked my truck on the shoulder of the road just up from her parents' place and waited for her to drive by me in her car, which looked like it could be dismantled by a stiff wind. I kept the glare firmly on my face when she stopped and motioned for me to roll my window down.

This wasn't going to amount to anything good, that much I knew.

Despite the very high possibility that she was going to rip me yet another asshole, I rolled down the damn window.

She didn't say anything at first. She just started rummaging around in her car for a second before her face lit up with a manic sort of grin. It looked like she was reaching for something in the footwell of the passenger side, and when she pulled back to show me, it was in fact her middle finger.

"Have you gotten less mature in the last two years?"

"Yep!" She beamed at me. "Feel free to get lost and never come back!" she yelled before zooming off. I was only glad that it was dark because I knew she wouldn't be able to see me in her rearview mirror, and it was really fucking hard not to laugh.

I hadn't laughed much in the last two years. I had a plan—one goal that ruled my life. The same goal that had destroyed it. Whether the woman in the car ahead of me ever found out or not, I knew she'd never forgive me.

So, I let myself laugh, just for a second, because as much as I wanted to throw her over my knee and see the imprint of my hand glowing red on her ass, I'd missed the challenge that was Calista Rose Grey.

Never one to take anything lying down, even when it was in her best interest.

Cali pulled into the gravel drive of a small house that suited her down to the ground. It was bordered with hedges that went as high as the sagging eaves that surrounded the exterior, with flowers planted out front and along a walkway that led right to the sidewalk. A small gate sat on an angle at the end of the footpath, even though there was no fence on either side of it. It held a sign that looked handwritten on cardboard, wrapped aggressively in tape, and severely water-damaged, but the words were still legible. It said, "Jerry is large but full of love. Don't be frightened."

The slam of her car door yanked me from a dumbfounded spiral about her sign, who Jerry was, and why that name pinched something deep inside me. It also gave me just enough time to smooth the contorted look off my face and reset my glare before she saw.

Everything Cali did, from the moment she stepped out of her car, was accentuated by the anger rolling off her in waves.

Look, I wasn't an idiot.

Okay, maybe that wasn't completely true, but I wasn't *too* much of an idiot to where I thought continuing to rile up a woman who was clearly channeling the fear of God into everything she was doing was smart.

Then again, I wasn't too smart either.

Calista didn't even look back at me when I jumped out of my truck and walked up the path. It was then I realized I didn't even think of going and getting my stuff.

"Not bad for a shit box!" I called after her.

I'd dumped my duffel bag under the desk meant to be mine at the office we were renting on Main Street. A group of strangers swooping into a tight-knit community with promises of *improvements*?

Yeah, that never went over well.

The central, accessible location was supposed to help. Spoiler: it didn't.

It rarely ever did, and I couldn't blame them. It was just one of the many reasons I told my father to go fuck himself every chance I got. I didn't agree with a damn thing he was doing.

That look of disgust that colored Cali's features over dinner was the same look I had on my own face when I looked in the mirror at the end of each and every day.

It was a certain type of torture in working for the man who beat my mother in front of me from the time I could remember.

My earliest memories are of fear, anger, and hatred. Shaped by the lessons my father thought he was teaching me as I huddled in the corner, forced to watch.

Forced to witness it.

I hadn't been a very big kid. Scrawny at first, then long and gangly. My body had filled out without me noticing, without anyone noticing. Especially when I started to go to the gym purely so that I didn't have to go home. I would run for miles and miles, hoping that whatever road I was on would lead me far away from the life I had and the people in it.

I'd been sitting at the dining room table doing my homework, and he walked in, didn't even say a single word before he swung an open palm at my mother's face.

The roar of fury just erupted from me, born of every single moment that had come before that I'd shoved deep down.

It was fucked up.

It had all been festering and rotting and changing that part of your soul that is born pure and light into something dark and heavy. I didn't think about anything other than my want for my father to endure every ounce of pain he had dished out.

At seventeen, I remembered standing over him, knuckles split and heart hammering, while my mother held tight to one of my arms, trying to pull me away while also keeping herself close. Sobbing and broken and fucking terrified.

*"You will never touch her again," I spat at him. His face was covered in blood. His eyes wide with shock. "You will leave this fucking house, and you will never touch her again." My throat burned from the way I screamed those words at him. "Or so help me God, I will kill you. I will fucking kill you. Do you understand me?"*

*He stared at me for a long time before he gave a single nod.*

*"Get your shit and leave." I pulled back, one hand on my mom's shoulder, steering her back toward the dining table where I just sat back down after getting her an ice pack wrapped in a dishcloth, and kept doing my homework. She sat with me, and I could feel her eyes on my face the whole time. Like she'd never seen me before. Like she was deciding if I would become someone that scared her too.*

When I turned eighteen, that was when he reached out for me to come work for him. He probably thought it was some way to atone for what he'd done. I didn't really know, and I didn't fucking care.

"Are you coming in or not?" Cali's voice sliced through the stillness, breaking the grip of my past like it always did.

I stayed at the end of the pathway, staring up at the home she'd built without me. She'd been watching me for a while. I could see it in the softness creeping into her face, a softness I didn't deserve.

I reminded myself I was pissed at her too—for leaving in the dead of night with nothing but her key on the kitchen counter.

I schooled my face into the glare I'd made my trademark. She just rolled her eyes and unlocked the door.

"Now," she said, with her hand on the door handle the other clutching her leftovers, "Jerry's pretty docile at night, so you don't have to worry, but you'll see him in the morning, and he's never had anyone over, so—"

Cali didn't get to say anything else, because the moment she opened the front door, the galloping steps of what looked like a fucking *bear* was heading straight for me.

The next thing I knew I was airborne, then the wind was knocked out of me so violently I was half sure I'd cracked a rib.

It wasn't what I was expecting to look up into, but low and behold, the exceptionally moist jowls that were hanging very close to my open mouth belonged to what had to be an almost two-hundred-pound dog.

"Jerry!" Calista yelled in the sort of way you might imagine a mother would when fretting about the welfare of their baby.

Jerry—clearly *never* the size of a baby—loomed over me, unmoving despite my coughs and Cali's vain attempts at dislodging him.

"What are you doing? You've never run out that door in your whole life!"

All I knew at that moment, aside from the fact that she was clearly not speaking to me, was that I was looking up into the face of the sort of dog that I had dedicated a whole fucking Pinterest board to that Calista helped me put together.

I had *dreamed* of this dog.

I had dreamed of this exact dog, and I'd been determined to call him Jerry.

"Is that a dog? *My* dog?" I croaked out while she continued to tug back a dog that had a good fifty pounds on her. "Jerry?"

"No, he's a rare breed of guinea pig," she grunted out, trying her best to get him inside. "And Jerry is not your dog. He's *my* dog."

The best way to describe it was like watching someone pushing against a wall and expecting it to move.

"So glad you found another of your own species," I grunted back, getting to my feet. "I'm fine, by the way."

"Of course you're fine," she snapped. "Jerry couldn't hurt a fly."

"Oh sure," I groaned. "He'd just squish it to death."

She was putting her whole soul into trying to move that dog, and he wasn't budging. "I very much doubt it. He's terrified of them. Are you just going to stand there, or are you going to help me?" She huffed, pausing only to run her finger up the bridge of her nose.

"I'm just going to stand here." I crossed my arms, watching her try to move her dog.

"You're such a jackass," Calista mumbled, moving to lower herself eye to eye with Jerry. "Jerry, please. We have to go inside."

Jerry was clearly aware of what the words that were coming out of her mouth meant, but while her eyes were on him, his were on me, and his tail was thumping like mad on the ground.

"You know," I said, knowing the words would piss her off and letting them fly out of my mouth anyway, "I think he likes me."

"He does *not* like you."

"Oh, I think he does."

"He also likes to eat cat shit from Mrs. Antinello's yard, so I wouldn't be raving at his exceptional judgment skills."

"Well, whatever helps you sleep at night." I dropped my arms and walked toward them. "When you're done wrestling with your small horse, I'll be inside the house."

I strolled by casually. The moment I passed a groaning Calista, Jerry trotted inside beside me, and she landed right on her fine ass, right on the gently packed up leftovers from her mom.

"You haven't been invited in!" She sounded defeated and angry all at once that the laugh I barked was entirely unintentional.

"Rosie, I forgot how great you are at hosting. Feels like home already," I said from the top of the steps, looking down at her. Cali just lifted her middle finger up and didn't even bother meeting my gaze.

# 7

# Calista

**After**

Fane stood across from me in the small entry room.

The cottage was way too small to have an entry room, but it had one.

So, we stood in the world's most useless room. This weirdly passive-aggressive stare-off between me and…

What was I supposed to refer to him as now? My new-old-fake-ex-boyfriend?

Whatever he was, he was now in my house, and whatever I did to deserve this, I was very, *very* sorry.

Fane just stood there, tattooed arms crossed and scowl in place. His chestnut-colored hair was styled differently than I thought it was before. Longer on the top and back and a bit shorter on the sides. Messy and unruly like it had always been, the longer pieces tucked behind his ears.

"I won't let you ruin this town." I crossed my arms across my chest, mimicking his position and doing what I thought was one heck of a job making my five foot six inches look somewhat respectable against his admittedly imposing six foot five.

"I know." His jaw was so stiff it didn't even look like it moved despite having heard his words clear as a bell.

"I don't want you here," I tacked on for good measure.

"Shocker." His eyes stayed on me. They didn't drift for even a second. They'd always been intense in every sense of the word. I don't think there was a way for his violet eyes *not* to be intense. No matter what he was feeling, they were clear tells to the extent of his emotions.

Joy, sadness, excitement, nervousness.

Want.

"You could have had any town." I threw my arms out to either side of me. "Do you *know* how many small towns there are in this country? Probably a billion, and you picked *mine*"—I ignored the way my voice broke—"to come and ruin. Like you haven't done enough."

My chest was heaving. I was on the verge of imploding, and he stood there, stoic. Giving me *nothing.*

"You really don't have anything to say?"

"What do you want me to say?" The timbre of his voice made the room too full. Every moment in his presence made it harder and harder to breathe.

"I want you to say you'll pack up and leave."

"I can't do that."

"Can't or won't?"

"Both." His controlled and calm stance used to be something I relied on. It was the very thing that pulled me back from whatever panicked edge I was standing on time and time again. Now, it just made me want to pull him up on the ledge with me and shove him off.

"You don't know anything about Darling."

"So you keep saying." His broad shoulders lifted on a big inhale before they dropped back down, drawing my attention to the tattoos on his neck that hadn't been there the last time I'd seen him. They spanned up the sides and wrapped around to the back, disappearing under the waves of his hair.

I refused to let myself fall back into the habit of taking stock of every piece of art that covered his body. I didn't care how he decorated it anymore or the reasons why.

"—around?" His voice trickled into my head like I was coming out of water.

"Around what?" *Crap.*

"Darling?" He lifted one full eyebrow at me, and when I stayed silent, his eyes took on that mischievous shine I remembered when he was particularly entertained...or turned on.

God. *What* was I doing? No. *No.* I hadn't entertained any thoughts of him in the last two years, and I wasn't going to start now. I knew where that led, and I knew how it ended.

"I said," he went on, taking obvious pleasure in having to repeat himself for me, "Are you going to show me around?"

I didn't want to. I didn't actually want to spend *any* time with Fane. I didn't want to see him in a crowd, and I definitely didn't want to see him one on one.

So, when I opened my mouth to release the screaming *"Nope!"* that was floating around my brain, I physically jolted when I said, "Yep."

Even when my brain was still screaming, *"No, you dumbass! You meant to say NO!"* nothing else came out. Not a freaking *peep*.

He nodded like it was no big deal. Like none of this was a big deal. "When?"

"After work." The words were delivered with the sort of calm that didn't align with the alarm I was feeling at volunteering some of the only time I had to myself. "And weekends," I added on because, apparently, I needed to torture myself further. "Not both, obviously. Or maybe, I don't know I—"

"Need to make a list?" Fane pressed his lips together like he was trying not to laugh.

"Are you *laughing* at me? *Again?*" I was having déjà vu. This wasn't my life. At least it hadn't been my life this morning. It wasn't even my life this afternoon.

"No ma'am." He just shook his head, that glint in his eyes telling me he absolutely was.

"Stop calling me ma'am," I huffed, doing my best to scowl at him and not just flip him off again. After the second time I did it, I realized it was actually very therapeutic.

"I have some rules." I crossed my arms tighter and popped my hip out further.

"Okay." He nodded, brow furrowed and arms crossed.

I held up my hand and unfurled one finger. "I am the guide. You're the guidee."

"That's not a word."

"Next rule, I'm right, *all* the time."

"No, you're not."

"Next rule, you're not allowed to interrupt me."

"I didn't." His shock was almost convincing.

"Next rule,"—I was trying very hard not to yell—"you're not allowed to speak. At all." I watched him, my chest rising and falling like I was on the verge of running away or maybe charging right at him. I hadn't decided yet.

The decision was made for me when Fane raised his hand in the air, and the smile on his face finally cracked through the glare he'd had fitted like a tailored suit.

It was my turn to take a big breath, releasing it slowly through my nose. "Yes?"

"What if I have a question?"

"Then…then you can raise your hand."

"Like I'm at school?"

"Well, you *are* acting like an overgrown toddler, so if the shoe fits."

"Okay." He dropped his hand but didn't drop the smile, and the fact he didn't bite at my dig made me infinitely madder at him.

"Can I call you Rosie?"

"No."

"Baby?"

"*No,*" I gritted out through clenched teeth.

"Late for dinner?" His smile spoke volumes on how funny he thought he was.

Charge at him. I definitely wanted to charge at him.

The tension between us was so thick it felt seconds away from becoming a tangible thing. Heat flushed my cheeks, like I'd been sitting under the summer sun for way too long.

He hadn't lifted his gaze from me once. The weight of it made me shift. Made me aware of the sound of my own breath moving in and out of my mouth, of the dampness growing between my legs for reasons so far beyond my own comprehension. The heaviness that had settled just below my belly button.

I needed water. I needed something to hold onto.

*Get a fucking grip, Calista. You're a grown-ass woman who has control over her body.*

The moment his eyes left mine, I was released from whatever hold he had on me. It gave me enough mental clarity to notice how rigid he'd become. How tightly coiled he'd become.

So much of Fane was corded muscle. He'd always been solid, with rigid lines and valleys that created the map of his body.

Look, I don't have anything positive to say about the way all that driving, flaming heat consuming me settled into a heavy, thrumming pulse that radiated through my entire body. It spread through me until I was painfully aware of every sensation—the drag of my clothes against my skin, the way it was almost too much to bear. I couldn't decide if I wanted to bury myself in every sweater I owned or rip off every piece of clothing I had on.

It had been so long since I'd remotely felt an inkling of need for any other human that it slammed into me the way you might walk directly into a sliding glass door.

My day had been bizarre, and I gave myself full permission to blame it on that.

No, not just bizarre, but soul drainingly exhausting.

I could feel myself starting to droop under the weight of the last two years, never more crushing than here, in the small, useless room that held a single ottoman I never used and the one person I hated most in the world.

"I don't have a guest room." I kept as much space between us as I could, walking around Fane and into the living room. "You can take the couch."

"No." His voice came from so close behind me that I swear I felt his breath on the back of my neck. The hairs on every part of my body stood up.

"What do you mean, 'no'?" I asked the question while still looking away from him, wondering if this might be the moment that the slipping grip I had on my sanity finally gave way.

"I'm not sleeping on the couch," he said again, enunciating each and every word as clear as day.

I gave myself three seconds to take a deep breath before I turned to face him. He was so close to me that I could feel the heat radiating off his body.

The step I took back was more of a reflex from having someone so far into my personal space bubble it should have been classified as a felony.

"Where do you plan on sleeping then?" The question was supposed to be rhetorical. It was *supposed* to point out that there were no other options for him besides the couch or the floor.

Fane obviously didn't gather that because he pointed at the only closed door in the house that clearly led to my bedroom. "There."

"Ha!" The sound just burst out of me, shocking Jerry awake from where he'd situated himself back on his own couch. "No." I shook my head with vigor. "You're not sleeping in my bed."

"Why not?" His head tilted to the side, and for reasons completely out of my control, I took another step back.

"Because it's *my* bed, Fane," I seethed. "I don't share beds with people I don't know."

He took another step toward me, then another. Making me retreat with every thump of his boots on the creaking hardwood floors.

He wasn't just walking toward me; he was *stalking* me.

"Oh, I think you know me quite well, Calista."

It was messed up the way my body shivered from head to toe after watching his mouth say my name. The way I watched every syllable roll off his tongue and imagined the way it would feel on other parts of my body.

I was too busy trying to figure out a way to speak that didn't involve the use of my tongue, too busy trying to forget how familiar being surrounded by the smell of him was, that it didn't register the way it should have that he was still taking those measured steps toward me.

My back hit something solid, and I decided to add my yelp of surprise to the list of things I didn't have any super positive things to say about.

We could have stayed like that for hours, as far as I was concerned. Could have gone back in time, jumped dimensions, won the lottery.

Who the fuck knows.

It could have all happened, and I would have still been rooted to the spot I was currently in, looking into empty violet eyes, doing my best to block out every other memory I had of them except for the one that mattered.

Fane's hand around the doorknob wasn't what snapped me from whatever was happening to my brain.

A stroke, probably.

It was the fact that he let go of said handle. I stumbled back into the room, unable to get my footing until I landed right on the bed, right on my ass for the second time tonight.

I gave my head a little shake to clear the fog that wasn't lifting half as fast as I needed it to, and by then, it was already too late.

"No!" I yelled at the spot where he'd been standing. My head whipped around to find him undoing the button of his jeans.

"Oh…oh my god. Have you lost your *mind?* What are you doing?!" My hand flew up to cover my eyes.

"Getting ready for bed." His voice was low and rough. It had always been like that, like he never really used it much. It made my own throat ache.

"Why are you taking off your *pants?*" I was still yelling.

"You've seen me in a lot less than this, Rose." And that was the moment I knew he was enjoying this.

"You do *not* get to call me that." I seethed. "And we're not sharing a bed."

"The couch is free."

"*Fane,*" I seethed again, dropping my hand at the same time I got to my feet and turned to face him. "This is *my bed.*" It took everything in me not to stomp my foot like a child.

"I know." He started to pull the covers back, and I wanted to scream. He was so fucking calm.

"Hey," I said, trying to get his attention while he took his phone out of his pocket and set it next to the bed. He just ignored me, clearly done with whatever was going on between us. "*Hey!*" I said again, louder this time.

"That's my side."

Those empty eyes looked from the covers he held in a fist to my face, shadowed by the furrow of his brow that came out of nowhere.

Ah, this expression I knew.

He was confused. Not just regular confused but freaking perplexed.

His hand stayed curled around the duvet for a second longer before he released it one finger at a time and walked around to the other side of the bed. Strides stiff and body rigid and only in his black briefs and a shirt.

I threw my hands up, stomping out of the room and grinding my back teeth together.  My heart was beating so fast, pumping what had to be gallons of desperately frustrated, fiery anger all over my body.  He made me want to break all the plates in my kitchen, and I really loved my plates.

Instead, I grabbed a spare toothbrush from the cupboard in the hall and stomped back into my room, thrusting it at him without a word.

*Bad hostess, my ass.*

If he had to be here, that was fine.

I mean, it wasn't, but whatever.

I would eventually make my peace with that. Maybe. After all, this was a hole I had dug for myself a long while ago. I had no one else to blame.

Sure, my level of forethought on all potential ways it could play out started and ended with telling everyone I knew he was on the other side of the world, like somehow my passionate will alone would make it happen.

Instead, he showed up like he hadn't decimated my heart, saw the hole I'd dug, and just dove right in, taking me with him via a running tackle.

He was here, but that didn't mean I had to acknowledge him.

I wouldn't see him, speak to him, or notice him.

Within the walls of this house, Fane Mackenzie ceased to exist to me.

8

# Fane

**Before**

"I knew you were too good to be true," Cali said, hopping out of the truck and rounding the front.

"What do you mean?"

"I'm here to meet my fatal end." She shrugged one shoulder and looked around.

I rolled my eyes at her. "No, you're not."

"That's exactly what the person leading me to my doom would say!" She heaved a sigh. "At least I get a good view as I'm going out."

"Thanks."

"Oh." She wrinkled her nose, looking back at me. "No, I meant this pleasant junkyard you've brought us to."

I'd known Cali for four months. It had been four months of feeling like I'd known her my whole life. Of getting up and moving through each moment, each shift, each mundane task only because I knew that doing all those things brought me closer to seeing her again.

She was so completely *different* from anything I'd ever had in my life before that the way she made me laugh stopped shocking me a long time ago. I tipped my head back and released the bubbling, foreign feeling that started in the very center of my chest and pushed out of me with

47

determination.

I shook my head and walked to the back of the truck to set up all the blankets and pillows I'd thrown back there. I looked back at her, her face soft with this sort of starstruck expression that she made every time I laughed. Like she was constantly in awe that I found her funny.

"You coming, Rose?"

It only took us minutes to turn the back of my old, beaten-up truck into one of the pictures Cali had pinned to her Pinterest board about date ideas she thought would be cool. She didn't know this was what we were doing until she saw the blankets I'd hidden under a tarp at the back, and it was worth spending the money I didn't really have on blankets I'd probably never use again just to see that look on her face.

We were quiet for a long time, shoulder to shoulder, looking up at the clear, black sky above us. We were a little ways outside of Artington, but my best friend Ash's cousin owned this junkyard, and it had always been the perfect place to see the stars.

"Tell me what you were like growing up?" She asked it so innocently.

And why wouldn't she? Cali had no idea how fucked up my upbringing was. It felt almost criminal to put the weight of those memories on her. This woman who was light and bright and warm.

"It's not a nice story," I warned her, my voice catching at the memories.

"Okay," she said. Quiet but strong. Giving me the choice to share my past with her or not and no judgment regardless of whether I did or didn't.

So, I told her.

It had been awkward at first, piecing together words to depict the memories I had worked hard to forget. To expose her to the monster I had worked tirelessly to be nothing like in every capacity. To admit that I had been too young and too weak to do anything for my mother until she had endured her own hell for seventeen years. To confess that, as much as I wished it didn't, growing up like that had fucked me up more than I'd ever admitted before. Both out loud and to myself.

"Never felt like there was a safe place to land, to fall into," I said, eyes back on the sky above. "That sucked."

I think one of the best things about Cali was that she'd taken the time to learn how to be around me without working to change me. Without asking me all the time if I was okay, if something was wrong, if I was mad. She just realized that this was the way I was, and she wanted me anyway.

Keeping quiet was a habit I formed when I was a kid, and the only thing I wanted was to be invisible. When it was safest to simply disappear.

The older I got, the less it became about that and more about just not having all too much to say. I spoke when it was important, when it was necessary. When it was needed.

With her, it had been enough to let someone else hear the worst parts of me—the poison in my blood that felt like a ticking time bomb. This unavoidable clear view of my future. That something would happen, and I'd snap.

Cali wasn't like me. She told me about her family, her childhood, and what her town had meant to her. She shared all her light with me and didn't so much as flinch when all I had to give her was shadows.

It was enough that she heard it all and still held my hand as if the weight of me didn't scare her away. She didn't see me as tainted. When she spoke, I hadn't expected it—that she would think she needed to give me anything more than what she already had.

"You can fall into me," Cali whispered, her eyes glued to the stars above us.

I turned onto my side to look at her. Watching her eyes flicker rapidly, determined to find a shooting star. To cast one of the wishes she kept in the Notes app of her phone up and into the universe. I let my eyes run over the slope of her nose and watched how it crinkled every so often in concentration. Felt her hand twitch in mine every time it did.

I knew it before, but I was certain then. I could look at this woman every day for the rest of my life and never tire of the view.

It's a surreal feeling, knowing that you're looking at your whole fucking world. That for some reason, when millions of people never got answers to even their smallest, most mundane wishes, I got an answer to my biggest and wildest one.

"I mean it." Her voice was soft. Desperate not to disturb the world.

I felt my throat tighten because, fuck, I believed her.

"And what about you?" I asked instead.

"What about me?"

A small smile tugged at the corner of her mouth, lighting up those hazel eyes of hers—eyes I already knew somehow, even before I'd had the privilege of meeting them.

It was like Cali's soul sat so close to the surface, and for some reason, it had looked at me and said, *That one. I'll have that one*.

"Who will you fall into?"

"You," she said, turning onto her side fully.

"And you're sure I'll catch you?"

There it was. Right there for her to see. One of my biggest fears. That I wasn't enough for her. That I hadn't been ready for her when she found me, and I still walked right up to her anyway, desperate to know what it would feel like to have her palm slide into mine.

"I am." She was so sure. Her free hand pressed against my cheek, moving to the back of my head to sink her fingers into my hair.

"How?" I whispered and closed my eyes.

"Because," she whispered back just before I felt the air shift between us, and I could feel her moving closer to me. Freeing both her hands, she pushed me gently onto my back and climbed on top of me. Straddling me while my hands found their home on her hips.

Hips I loved. Hips I dreamed about.

"You already have."

And then she kissed me, and I knew I would never belong to anyone ever again, the way I belonged to her.

# 9

# Fane

**After**

We slept with a wall of pillows between us so high there was a serious concern about the potential to be smothered while I slept. Either by Cali holding a pillow over my face or by the tower doing it all on its own.

If I hadn't been so deliriously tired, I would have stayed up the entire night, all too aware of the fact it was her on the other side of the wall.

It had been pointless, her attempt at putting distance between us. I knew it, she probably knew it. Jerry probably knew it too.

I woke up at least thirty minutes before her. Jerry's soft snores trickled in from the living room, pulling me from what had to have been the best sleep I'd had in longer than I cared to admit.

At some point in the night, the pillows between us had disappeared, and Cali had ended up exactly where I knew I'd find her. For the two years she'd been mine, I woke up to her draped across my body like a ragdoll. Legs entwined with mine and one dainty hand splayed across my stomach.

I hadn't felt her move over to me in the night. I wasn't sure if she reached for me or if I reached for her.

The only thing I was sure of was how her leg was pressing against my achingly hard cock, and every small movement she made was making the ache in my balls worse and my length thicken.

51

There would be no mistaking it. The flimsy fabric of my briefs wasn't hiding a single fucking thing, and I knew this was probably karma for taking off my pants in the first place.

Cali shifted again, and I couldn't stop the grunt it pulled from me or the way I shifted beneath her, my hands fisting the bed sheets beneath us.

I was *not* going to thrust against the leg of my ex-girlfriend, who hates me. *I was not going to thrust against the leg of my ex-girlfriend, who hates me.*

Because—why the fuck wouldn't it happen—that was the moment her eyes fluttered open. It took her a full three seconds to realize what she was doing before a bloodcurdling scream shot out of her throat, and she launched herself off the bed.

Her abrupt departure gave me enough time to swing my legs off the side of the bed and reach for my jeans. I tried to cover the bulge in my briefs with one hand, squeezing to relieve the building pressure, but all it did was make my eyes roll back. At this moment, there was no escaping her. Not like I'd been able to before with distance and pathetic distractions.

I was *covered* in her smell, and just the thought sent another painful ache up from the base of my spine.

A handful of seconds after that, a loud thump sounded on the other side of her bedroom door that sounded a lot like Jerry's head making pretty solid contact.

There was really no other option; I ran from her room. Reaching her door in three long strides, I stepped over Jerry where he'd flopped down outside Cali's bedroom door.

Her bathroom was…tiny. It was so fucking tiny. The shower stall was barely big enough for me to fit into, my shoulders almost touching either wall. I didn't care that the water was still cold or that the door didn't have a lock. I stepped in and released a shuddering breath as I fisted my cock.

There wasn't even time to think of anything but how warm she'd been pressed against me. The scent of the same milk-and-honey body wash that I remembered but nothing like what I'd conjured up in my imagination. The way it was so completely intertwined with the essence of *her*. Her delicate hand up my shirt, pressing against my stomach. Her squirming, sleepy movements rubbing against me.

My cock thickened, impossibly so. My slow measured pumps weren't nearly enough to feed the need that consumed me, taking over every part of my brain, directing all the blood in my body to one very specific area.

I squeezed the base of my shaft, swiping the leaking pre-cum at the tip before it could be washed away by the warming water.

That's when Cali's voice trickled through the too-thin walls. She was talking to her dog, I knew that. Somehow, that knowledge didn't help in the slightest.

"Are you coming?" she murmured, probably leading her pony-sized dog outside, but all I heard was the gentle lilt of her voice. The memory of her lips moving along my jaw, the bite of her teeth on the lobe of my ear, and I was fucking done.

A choked *"Yes"* made its way out of my mouth, half stuck in my throat. I caught myself with one hand slapping onto the wet tiles next to my head, my orgasm erupting from me like it had a fucking vendetta. My legs shook with the force of it, and all I could do was watch as thick ropes of cum shot out to cover the shower wall, my jaw lax and eyelids half closed. My hand was still moving in lazy strokes until my cock started to soften.

I dropped my head to the cool tiles, breathing hard and wondering what the fuck just happened to me.

"Who's a good boy?" I heard Cali's muffled coos that were definitely not for me and couldn't stop my cringe.

"You're so fucked, Fane," I mumbled to myself before starting to clean up the mess I'd made. I'd arrived here with a half-formed plan, and none of it had involved fisting my dick while pretending the praise the woman who hated me was giving to her dog was for me.

My plan was so shit I wasn't sure I could even consider it a plan.

Images of her mouth at my ear, asking me if I was going to come, asking if I was a good boy, were all I thought of when I made a beeline for her front door, my hair still dripping wet. I didn't want to face her because, for some reason, I was sure she'd know what I'd just done. I also didn't fully trust myself to hear her voice or, fuck, even see her scowl at me. Those red heart-shaped lips of hers turning into a pout, and not be able to imagine them wrapped around my cock.

I drove to work with a semi-hard-on, recalling, again and again, the feeling of her pressed against me and put my behavior down to the last two years of celibacy.

It hadn't even been hard to endure. Nothing and no one had made me *want*. The very thought of touching anyone but Cali had made me physically sick.

"C'mon, *boss*!" Declan called out from the back of the room while he balanced on the back two legs of a plastic chair, effectively snapping me out of my thoughts of Calista and deflating the hard-on I was sure I'd be sporting all day.

At least he was finally good for something.

The chair looked like it had been plucked out of the trash, and I waited with bated breath for the thing to collapse beneath him.

"What's going on?" Ashton decided that was a good time to walk in.

I met Ash when I was eighteen and hadn't been able to shake the asshole since. When I told him I was going to work for my dad, he hadn't so much as breathed differently. All he'd done was be dressed the next morning, waiting by our front door, ready to come with me.

"Can't let you face off with the devil on your own, can I?" Nothing more, nothing less. Two years later, we were still in it together. He was the only real family I had left.

"Boss isn't staying at the accommodation with us." Declan wagged his eyebrows, and I immediately wanted to punch him.

"Anyone ever mentioned you're not welcome here at all, Dec?" Ash said around a mouth full of the massive bite of apple he'd just taken.

"Sure, why?" Dec had already moved back to his phone, completely unfazed.

I was pretty sure Declan was a psychopath. I'd caught him once at a job site outside Banks City trying to drown a bird in a birdbath. His hand shot out so fast, grabbing the bird, and before I could react, he'd shoved it under the water.

It took me a heartbeat to move, ask him what the fuck he was doing. When he let it go, he turned to look at me with this expression that I'd taken something vital from him. It was there and gone in a second, but I knew then that there was something broken about him, and not something that could be fixed.

"I was just trying to save it." He shrugged before picking back up his tools and getting on with what he was doing before, flashing me a megawatt smile.

I dragged my hand down my face to shake the memory, nodding my head in greeting as little by little the rest of the crew started to show up for work.

"So?" Ash sat down on the corner of my desk. "Care to share?"

"No," I bit out.

Ash knew why we were in Darling. He was fully aware of who Cali was. He'd been there the night we met.

I chose to plead the Fifth and keep my mouth shut. It wasn't going to keep him from finding out, but I wasn't going to help him.

"Oh!" His face was almost split in two at the sheer giddiness he was trying to keep contained. "Goody!" He rubbed his hands together. "Is—"

"All right." I stood up, effectively cutting him off but doing nothing to dampen the challenge he'd set for himself to figure out where I'd been. The moment he found out, I'd never hear the end of it.

"Everyone's been broken up into groups. The goal this week is to understand what it is we're working with throughout the four central zones we've outlined on the map of the town. Zones five through twelve are of no real consequence to us at this stage while we evaluate the viability of the town center."

Cali had been wrong when she said that I believed what I was saying about what Mackenzie Co. was doing to small towns. I hated every word coming out of my mouth, but I was here for a reason, and so right now, the end justified the means. It was what I repeated to myself day in and day out.

"I emailed everyone their lists this morning," I said, letting my gaze sweep over the room. "If you finish ahead of schedule, come find me. Otherwise,

I don't want to hear from you until your tasks are done. Clear?"

Chairs scraped as the crew half-rose from their seats, but before anyone could make it to the door, Declan's voice cut through the room like a cold draft.

"What about what people are saying?"

Groans rippled through the group as everyone sank back into their chairs, clearly resigned to whatever bullshit was about to spill out of his mouth.

"About what?" I leaned back, aiming for calm even as my patience thinned.

"About the development," he said, lounging in his chair like he had all the time in the world. "People aren't happy. Heard a rumor the mayor's pushing for it because he's up to his ears in gambling debt."

My jaw tightened as the room shifted. Everyone was glancing at each other now, the kind of curiosity that wasn't harmless. Rumors like this one made people panic.

"And who did you hear that from?" I asked, keeping my tone even.

Declan shrugged, a lazy hand fluttering in front of him. "Oh, you know… around." A deliberate smirk tugged at his lips, slow and smug. "But I'm sure it'll blow over. Wouldn't want anything to rattle this perfect little project, now would we?"

"If you've got something to say, Declan," I said, my voice dropping, "Say it now."

His smirk spread like he'd won some private victory. "Nothing at all. Just thrilled to be a part of your first project as a big boy in the family company, boss. Would be something awful for there to be any ulterior motives on it. That's all."

I leaned forward, elbows on the table, my eyes locked on his. "Because it seems like this needs saying, I don't care how things have been done before. Here, we're doing things right. No cutting corners. We're assessing the town, plain and simple. I don't care if a report has been done recently, or what the company's standard procedure is. I want things done by the book. I want every figure and fact checked twice. Am I clear?"

A halfhearted chorus of yeses mumbled their way across the room as chairs scraped and the crew finally shuffled out. Declan lingered. He winked, slow and deliberate, his face blank for just a second too long before his usual shit-eating grin slid into place.

Then he strode out, walking like his dick was too long for his pants.

"I hate that fucking guy," I said, dropping my head back into my hand.

"You've got to be fucking kidding me!" Ash pointed, gaping at me. "We haven't even been in town for twenty-four hours!"

I leaned back in my chair and looked up at him, lifting an eyebrow. "I'm actually pretty curious about your methods."

"I retraced your steps, and then I remembered the café you went into before you came out looking like a ghost."

"That's what you were thinking of this whole time while I was talking?"

"Yup," he said, popping the p on the end for emphasis.

"Good to know you're so committed to the job."

Ash was a tall guy. I had an inch or so on him, but if he could have, I imagine that he would have been swinging his legs back and forth from his spot sitting on my desk like a fucking school kid.

"Plus, I don't know what you're talking about." I started to rifle through paperwork on my desk that I wasn't sure even belonged to the project we were here to do.

"So, you don't know anything about visiting a café yesterday called Sunshine?"

"No."

"Are you sure?" He tilted his head to the side. "Because I could have *sworn* when you were dating Carly—"

"You're such a dick." I glared at him. The thing was, he wasn't wrong. I'd seen the name of that café, and my heart just about flew up and out of my mouth before I forced the useless organ back down.

Ash and Cali had always referred to each other by the wrong names. When I'd introduced them, the music had been so loud that neither of them had actually heard one another's names. The next time they met, Cali had called him Antwon and he'd laughed so hard he had one hand holding onto his junk for dear life while he rolled on the ground and tried not to piss himself.

"So?" He wasn't going to let it go.

I let out a long exhale. "I saw her."

"Okay." He nodded, "And?"

"I had dinner with her and her parents."

I waited for him to say something back, but after about a minute, I chanced a look and found his eyes the size of saucers.

"Are you clinically *insane?*"

I rolled my eyes at his dramatics. "Her dad came in while I was there, and apparently, they think that we never broke up."

He gasped. "Carly, you sneaky bitch." Ash's giddy smile was back in place.

"Watch your mouth." I stood up, covering his whole face with the palm of my hand and giving him a small shove. I doubled over in a wheeze after he stood up faster than I could compute and delivered a jab to my kidney. Ashton might have been leaner than I was, but that was only because where I favored cardio and weights, all he did was box.

"You're so fucked. This is awesome!" He loitered behind me as we headed out of the room. He was always careful not to make contact with anyone if he could help it, and over the years it was something I'd adapted to, always making sure he had plenty of space. We were the last two, and he was my only other group member, namely because he was also the deputy manager of this project.

"Great, hold on to that feeling when I tell you what I need from you," I said.

"I'm all ears."

"I need you to do the scouting yourself this week."

That stopped him in his tracks. "This week?"

"Yep."

"What about the other weeks?"

"Probably. But I'll do all the reporting. I just need your notes."

"We're here for like a month? Maybe longer?"

"Yep."

Ash started at me, so I stared back. And then the jackass broke out into that same stupid smile. "You can tell me all about it after you buy me a coffee from our new favorite café."

10

# Fane

**After**

The plan had not been to include Ash in the plan.

"You're not part of the plan." I leveled him with my signature glare just outside of Sunshine Café.

"Sure I am." He crossed his arms and widened his stance.

"No. You're not." I mimicked his stance.

He nodded like this was a normal conversation that two people had. "Okay, we'll put a pin in this for later. Just clarify something for me. You're being shown around Darling by a local?"

"Mm-hmm."

"And that local is Candy?"

I didn't dignify that question with a response because, no, it wasn't fucking Candy.

"And she's showing you around so we don't fuck with the town."

"Yep."

"But we're not fucking with the town anyway?"

"That's right."

"But you haven't told her that."

I didn't dignify that with a response either.

"Have you told her *anything* that you rehearsed in the mirror over the

60

last two years?"

"I didn't rehearse anything in the fucking mirror." I had, but that wasn't the point.

"Man, your balls are going to be *so* toast when she finds out!" He reached out and shoved me in the chest before he turned on his heels and headed straight into Cali's café.

The moment I noticed that the town of Darling had gone up for active evaluation and scouting, I went straight into my father's office and told him I wanted to take the lead on it. I couldn't stand being in the same room as him. Aside from the day I told him I'd take his offer on the job he'd extended my way for the last eight years, I hadn't gone in again until that moment.

I always knew it was a possibility that his sights would be set on Cali's town. I saw it on the list of prospects a year ago, and I knew what they'd do to it.

It was fucked up that I'd helped tear apart other towns. Fundamentally changed them from the inside out. I knew it made me a bad person, not caring in the slightest that I did because this had never been about them. It had always been about *her*.

In my desperate attempt to be as unsuccessful as possible, in some fucked-up attempt at proving that I was nothing like my father, I had been twenty-six, and the only qualification I had was working at a shitty bar.

After Cali left, I applied for at least forty jobs. Every day for a month, I applied. I went for interviews and handed out résumés, and every time, it was the same. A dubious look and the same fucking question: *Is this all the experience you have?*

I'd started working at Heavenly Horns as soon as I left home, and I never stopped. Every time I had the opportunity to move up, to manage the bar, I always said no. I didn't *want* to be successful.

It set me apart from the monster who made me.

It also meant I had nothing to show for myself. No savings, no retirement, nothing.

You can't give someone everything when you have nothing. I'd backed myself so thoroughly into a corner that the only option I had was to walk into Mackenzie Co. and take the job he was offering.

And then all I had to do was walk in and tell him I wanted Darling, and it was mine.

My father had stood up and walked over to me, placing a hand on my shoulder while he looked up at me and told me he was proud of me. I just stared at him and imagined all the different ways I might be able to kill him.

The little bell above the door tinkled, letting everyone know that we were entering.

It was early in the morning, and there was an older lady sitting right in the middle of the café, paper in hand, who turned to eye us with equal amounts of curiosity and apprehension.

"I heard the coffee here is shit," Ash called out just in time for Cali to round the corner, a tray of cookies in her mitten-covered hands.

To her credit, she only *almost* lost the tray. Fumbling it in tandem with the cascade of emotions that blurred across her face, and then she was jumping.

Honest to God, like a five-year-old at a birthday party *jumping*.

"*ALBERT!*" She screamed the name, and the lady who was still watching us sloshed her coffee in a jolt of surprise. Cali pretty much threw the cookies onto the counter next to her and ran for Ash. He caught her running jump, arms banding around her back, and a face-crinkling grin split his features.

I would be fucking damned if it didn't hurt.

I think it might have been the first time I'd ever seen Ash touch anybody voluntarily, but the shock of it was short-lived compared to how it felt seeing him get the greeting I wish I could have had from her. Even though I knew we'd both gotten the greeting we deserved from her.

It felt wrong to watch their reunion. Ash and Cali had fallen into the sibling sort of friendship that you only find once or twice in a lifetime, with friends who feel more like family. It occurred to me only then, selfishly, that Ash had lost her too, and Cali had lost him.

Cali's delighted laughter dissolved into small, shaking sobs. I watched one tear fall from her closed eyes and run down her cheek and decided I had punished myself enough for now and moved past them to the counter.

The rustle of fabric was the only telling sign that their embrace had come to an end. Even the somewhat nosy patron had turned her attention away.

"Hey, Allen." Cali's voice was hushed, and I closed my eyes against the pain that rang clear through her words. "Missed you."

"Hey, Chloe" Ash's voice was reserved too, quiet. "Missed you too."

It wasn't justified in the slightest, but their whole interaction pissed me off. I knew going from feeling guilty about the cause of their distance to being aggravated about how long they hugged was not a regular reaction to have.

I didn't fucking care.

"Great, so should I just make the coffee myself?" I turned to face them, glare in place and arms crossed. Cali spun to set her shining hazel eyes on me, and Ash tilted his head to the side with an amused look on his face that told me everything I needed to know about what he thought of my plan.

He thought it was shit.

"I thought you left." Cali's shoulder checked me as she walked back around to the other side of the counter, and she stumbled to the side. It was a reflex to reach out for her, my hand sliding around her upper arm to steady her.

We both looked at the point where my hand met the bare skin of her arm. Her small intake of breath echoed around the café, even with the trickle of country music playing softly in the background. The moment my fingers flexed, the spell was broken, and she yanked her arm free of my hold.

"For work, yes."

"I was hoping more for town limits." She grabbed the sheet of cooled-down cookies and shimmied them off the tray and into a lidless bowl.

"But you're so pleasant to be around, Calista."

"So…" Ash strolled up to stand beside me, stopping whatever was about to fly out of Cali's mouth. Her face changed immediately, and I refrained from elbowing my best friend in the ribs. "Mr. Soft and Approachable over here tells me you're taking him around town."

Cali's head snapped in my direction so fast I heard it crack.

"You are," I said.

"Why are you sharing the news like the town crier?" She was glowering at me, like anyone knowing she was spending time with me was preposterous.

"It's not weird for you to be spending time with your *boyfriend*, Calista." I lifted an eyebrow at her.

"You're *not—*" The clink of a cup settling onto a saucer cut her off immediately. We'd all forgotten about the random old lady. Well, Cali had.

"You're *not* wrong!" She plastered a smile so forced on her own face that I clamped my lips tight and settled into my own scowl deeper to keep myself in check. "I just know how busy you are with all your…stuff."

"Oh, you don't have to worry about that!" Ash chimed in helpfully. "I'll be doing all the scouting for both Fane and me. He's free and clear!"

"Free?" Cali looked distraught.

"And clear!" Ash added on. "Getting to know the nitty gritty from a town local is a huge benefit to the entire assessment," he said, sending her a wink that made her flush a bright cherry red.

"*Nitty gritty?*" she squeaked, almost going cross-eyed.

"Cali?" We all turned to look at the woman still sitting in the middle of the café.

"Yeah, Mags?" She tried to smile at Mags, but she looked more terrified than anything else.

"Aren't you going to introduce me to your fella?"

"*Fella!*" Ash mouthed to me, and I gave in to my inner temptation and sent an elbow into his ribs. He sent one back into the same spot he'd gotten me before, and the grunt didn't go unnoticed.

"Right." Cali walked as slowly as possible around the counter and stood a foot away from me.

That wouldn't do.

Her squeak of surprise shot straight to my dick. She was wearing a light-yellow sundress, and the warmth of her body seeped through the fabric where my hand curled around her ribs.

I shouldn't be touching her.

She wasn't mine to touch.

Even knowing those two things, I did it anyway.

"Mags." Cali sounded out of breath. "This is Fane."

"Pleasure to meet you, ma'am." I stepped forward and extended my hand to the older woman, who shook it back with a gentle grip.

"I think I've heard a thing or two about you," Mags said, leaning back into her chair.

"I'm sure it's all true."

"What if what I've heard is bad, young man?"

"Then it's definitely true."

"Oh, Calista. I like him," she said to Cali, who was rigid as a plank of wood tucked into my side.

"Yay." She couldn't have sounded less enthusiastic, her finger reaching up to push up her nose. "Mags owns the bar down the street. It's, uh, it's called Mags'," she added.

"We'll definitely be seeing you then," I told her with a smile. Ash nodded his head in agreement. "And this is Ash." I gestured to him.

"Cali, dear," Mags said, looking at her with a frown. "I don't think you know this young man's name. You called him Albert before."

She said 'Albert' by overexaggerating the shape of every letter with her mouth like Cali was hard of hearing.

"Okay." Cali pulled out of my grip. I'd pulled her closer to me without noticing, and the side of my body she'd been tucked into was left blistering cold and smelling of her cherry blossom shampoo.

Her fingers curled around the milk jug, and I couldn't stop staring. The way she moved, like every small motion was a part of something bigger, had me rooted to the floor. My throat went dry when she tucked a strand of hair behind her ear, her brow furrowed in concentration. I'd been obsessed with her then, and now? I was fucking hopeless.

"Fane," Mags called from behind. "What are you doing in town?"

"Development review, ma'am."

She frowned, and I was sure I'd just lost whatever growing acquaintance was between us. "Developing what?"

"That's yet to be decided. We're evaluating the town for possible growth and investment opportunities."

"Oh. That's…new," she said, not sounding surprised at all. Her eyes darted in Cali's direction. Her flowing movements had turned rigid and loud. Her eyes now steely and zoned entirely in on me.

"I'm taking into consideration the wants and opinions of the locals. Calista will be spending the next month showing me the roots of the town so that we can review reasons to leave Darling as is too."

"Oh!" Mags lit up at that. "That's good."

"Here's your coffee. Fane?"

"Hmm?"

"Can I talk to you out back?" She didn't even wait for me to answer before storming into the kitchen and out the back door that released an echoing slam into the café.

"Oh, your balls are most definitely toast." Ash didn't even try to whisper.

"I'll remove your balls if you don't shut up," I said through gritted teeth.

He grabbed his coffee and three cookies from the jar. Hands raised in feigned innocence. "Sorry, big man," he said around a mouthful. "Got to get to work."

I watched him leave, wishing I could leave with him, but not only was that not an option, Cali hadn't even made me a coffee.

"Excuse me." I nodded at Mags and headed out through the kitchen, my mood infinitely more sour than it had been when I'd walked here. I didn't even have time to breathe before Cali whirled on me.

"You're a lying liar. You…you *liar!*"

"Might want to tone down the profanity there, sailor." I had no idea what she was talking about.

She thrust one pointed finger in the direction of the café. "You can't just lie to old women."

"Okay." I was still confused, but I'm sure she thought I was just lying about that too, if the look on her face was anything to go by.

"You are going to tear up the town, and you just gave her false hope that you wouldn't!"

"No, I didn't." I crossed my arms.

"Yes, you *did!*" She was whisper-shouting now. "You told her you were taking into consideration the opinions of locals!"

"I am."

"Oh, *please*."

"So, you think I'm just here, mind already made up. Pretending to be your boyfriend, willingly spending time around you when you would clearly love to push me into oncoming traffic just so you can show me a bunch of things that won't even contribute to whatever decision I make?"

That's actually exactly what I was doing.

Cali could show me a fuck ton of reasons why I should approve the job to go ahead. She could show me everything and nothing, and it would have no sway on the decision I'd already made.

She jolted back a little, surprise clear on her face. "Well, I—"

"And you want to talk about liars?" I took a step toward her. "This whole town thinks we've been in a long-distance relationship for *two whole years.*"

"Yeah, well, upon deep reflection, the fact that I ever entertained this charade"—she gestured between us with an edge of hysteria—"was a stupid idea. I'm telling my parents the truth." She spun toward the door, taking the same angry steps she took last night.

"Oh, no, you don't." I reached for her arm, gripping it the way I had inside. This time, I didn't let go. Even when that spark from the contact of our skin raced down my spine or when her intake of breath shot straight to my cock, which was still fucking semi-hard from the last time she let out that noise.

"I spoke to them for fucking *hours* last night about a mine in Australia I don't even know anything about," I said, far too close to her. The thought of giving up this lie now that it was in motion made my gut churn.

It was fucked up and stupid and probably making everything worse, but it kept her close to me—and there wasn't a single version of this world where I'd willingly spend another second away from her. I shouldn't want this. I shouldn't be leaning into it just to hold onto her, but I was. Because the truth was, I'd take whatever scraps of her I could get.

"That's your problem," she said back, eyes narrowed and mouth pinched.

"No, it's not. It's *your* problem that you roped me into. So, this is how it's going to go." I let go of her arm to wrap my hand around the back of her neck, tracing my thumb along her jaw to angle her face up to mine. Forcing her to give me those hazel eyes of hers.

"I've got some rules of my own, Calista." I gave her the sort of smile that wasn't particularly pretty and felt a shiver rack her body. All it took was one step to remove the space between us, to feel her pressed up against me, and to force myself not to imagine how easy it would be to turn her around, flip up the flimsy material of her dress, and see if she was still averse to panties.

My guess was yes.

I could feel the flutter of her pulse against my palm, how rapid it was. If I needed any more proof, the hard point of her nipples that were visible against the material of her dress was the cherry on top, and I couldn't stop the smile of satisfaction that lit up my face.

Calista might hate me, but she still wanted me.

I flicked my eyes back up to hers. "In public, we're the perfect, madly-in-love couple you've sold to everyone."

"No."

I tutted. "Oh, you already made this bed. Now it's time to lie in it with me, baby."

# 11

## Calista

**After**

He was too close to me.

The scrape of his rough and calloused palm as he slid it around my neck like there hadn't been a whole two years between now and when he did it last made my stomach flip.

Flip and roll. Revel and relish. My body was having a celebration, like the way he held me was a victory.

It wasn't.

It was the opposite. It was something I had made myself learn how to live without, and he waltzed right into my life like it hadn't been one of the hardest things I'd ever had to do.

"Get your hands off me." My jaw was clenched so tight it was painful. I focused on that as much as I could instead of how the woodsy scent that had always belonged to Fane still clung to him.

Subtle but all-consuming.

Like he'd walked by something, and it clung to his shirt. His skin and hair. It was mixed so perfectly with something else that I had only ever been able to identify as purely Fane.

"Not until you sit your ass down and listen to what I have to say."

I widened my eyes as if to say, *The floor is yours, buddy.*

With his face set into a scowl that was anything but inviting, he walked me back three steps until the back of my legs hit an empty milk crate, and I was forced to sit.

"When we're in public, there will be no chance anyone will be able to question that you're mine."

I crossed my arms and gave him a withering look of my own.

If I didn't latch onto something to mix in with that thread of anger I was holding onto for dear life since he'd appeared out of the blue, I might start thinking about how I'd woken up with the smell of him lingering on my clothes and that it took everything in me not to let my hands dip in between my legs when I showered.

Which had also been wet. *Because of him.*

"That means," he continued, "we're going to act like a couple."

I rolled my eyes. "Thanks, Captain Obvious." He honestly looked like he wanted to bend me over his knee and teach me a lesson and, *oh my god*, I was *not* going to think about that.

Ew. *Ew.*

"I'm going to touch you, Calista."

I literally *jumped* from hearing his words that my ass came off the milk carton. "I beg your pardon?"

"When we're in public." He let out an aggravated sigh through his nose.

I rolled my eyes. "God, Fane. I know what it's like to be in a relationship with someone and what that entails." I threw my hands up and resisted the urge to stand up.

Fane's eyes seemed to darken a little at that, and he looked so imposing from where he stood above me. He crossed his arms and took a small step back from me, and it was like visibly seeing him change right before my eyes and morph into another version I didn't recognize of the man I used to know better than myself.

"Then you'll know that means you can't look at me like you wish I wasn't there. You can't freeze up like a fucking corpse when you stand next to me. When I kiss you–"

*"Kiss me?"* My legs catapulted me up from my sitting position so fast I was

certain I got at least a foot of air before I came crashing right back down to the ground. "You *won't* be kissing me."

"Yes, I will."

"*Why?*" My hands balled into fists.

*You're an adult, don't punch him. You're an adult, do* not *punch him.*

"Because, Calista." He took another deep breath, and I saw the way his head twitched like he wanted to crack it. When he spoke again, it was slow, deliberately sounding out every word. "Boyfriends," he gestured to himself, "do that with their girlfriends." He gestured to me.

*Girlfriends.* Plural.

I don't know why it didn't occur to me that Fane would have been dating in the last two years. In my effort to eradicate him completely from every part of my life, I had also decided to completely refuse to think about what his being with someone else would look like. Feel like.

Instead, it was perfect fodder for why losing him was perhaps the best thing that ever happened to me. He and his *girlfriends* could all be very happy somewhere far away from my town.

"*Fake* girlfriend," I hissed, ignoring all the things hearing him say those words did to my heart and hating him all the more for making me feel them all over again when he was the reason that nothing about it worked right anymore. "And only until I figure out a way to end it that won't make my parents suspicious."

This time, Fane rolled his eyes. It sucked that he knew them as well as he did because we both knew that any reason I gave them wouldn't be enough.

"I hate you," I told him.

"So you've said," he grumbled, running a hand through his hair and tugging on the strands.

"Would hate for you to forget it," I said back.

"How considerate of you."

God, he was infuriating. Just like a jack-in-the-box, my right hand flung up between us with my middle finger already extended. I hadn't consciously intended to do it, but it happened all the same, and I can't say I was mad about it.

Yep. Still very, *very* therapeutic.

We both looked at my hand. His face registered a very small amount of amused shock, and then his own hand was raised between us, mirroring the same gesture.

Fane was flipping me off.

He added one of those smirks that teenage girls deliver that could raise anyone's blood pressure so high they would fear for the health of their heart.

"Gah! Why are you even *here?* It could have been anyone else! Why *you?*" I yelled, all pretense of trying to manage my own sound levels out the window.

That was the precise moment that I heard Mags call out from the back door of the café, which Fane had left wide freaking open.

"Everything okay out here?" She sounded…not worried but hesitant.

Everything flashed before my eyes.

The look on my dad's face when small-town gossip got back to him about how I'd fabricated an entire relationship. I could see the confusion on my mom's face. They'd both look at me like they had no idea who I was. Like someone who could lie to them for two whole years during the hardest part of their lives without a second thought. Causing them to worry even more when my exact mission had been to remove it entirely.

I'd even gone on a fake holiday to the next town over for a whole week and ordered an *I Heart Australia* shirt and one of those hats with corks hanging around the brim from Amazon to bring back for them.

My dad wore that hat for a *month.* A month!

So, I did the only thing that made sense at that moment. I launched myself at Fane. My arms wound around his neck, my feet no longer touched the ground, and my eyes were already closed by the time I pressed my lips to his.

Fane didn't even stumble at the way I threw myself at him.

It didn't even take him a second to react before his arms were wrapped around my back, pressing me closer into him.

The way he kissed me was zero to a hundred. Like nothing had changed. Every single thing about him like this was achingly familiar.

He pulled back just for a second, eyes darting to the open door where Mags stood, then back to me. The smallest hint of a smile pulled up one side of his mouth.

"Is she still there?" I was breathless and wholly focused on the shape of his lips, determined to avoid his eyes. At seeing them this close. The flecks of green and warm, honey brown that would greet me like old friends I had cut off with an Irish goodbye.

Fane's only response was pulling one of his arms from around my back and sinking his fingers into my hair. Fisting the loose black strands, tilting my head back, and kissing me again.

There was no rush in the way his lips moved against mine. In the way his tongue pushed into my mouth and seized every last bit of control that I had. I got lost in it. In him.

In the bite of pain on my scalp from his grip. In the way I could feel the rapid beating of his heart pressed against my chest, joined in perfect synchronization with the beat of my own.

Every swipe of his tongue unleashed a memory I had carved out and locked away.

The memory of his stubble against my cheek, the sound of his husky groan as his fingers dug into the side of my ribs. The feeling of his erection, rock-hard and straining against his jeans between us. I couldn't have even pretended not to feel the length of him through my flimsy sundress, even if I wanted to.

Which I did. I wanted to ignore it, ignore *him*.

I remembered *everything* about him, and it reminded me with a jolt that though he may want me like *this*, that had never been the problem.

My hands reached between us, pushing on his chest. I still kept my eyes on his mouth, red and swollen and parted like what had just happened had somehow caught him off guard even though his hand was still fisted in my hair.

"Is she gone?" I didn't even recognize my voice. It sounded too broken for anything I'd ever let him see, and I pushed at his chest again.

"She left a while ago," he murmured. His voice was rough and full of the sort of need that I knew led to clothes coming off. To dirty, filthy things coming out of his mouth. To me turning into someone else completely.

Wait.

"She left a *while* ago?" I repeated the words back like they'd make more sense that way. I squirmed in his hold, which earned another groan from Fane.

"Keep squirming, and you'll make me come in my pants," he warned, his grip tightening.

"Then put me *down,* you caveman," I snapped, doubling my efforts and resisting the urge to knee him in the nuts. I felt the deep breath he took before setting me on my feet.

As soon as he stepped away, he shoved his hand down the front of his pants to adjust what, admittedly, looked like an incredibly uncomfortable situation.

I swiped a hand over my mouth. "Gross, Fane." I scowled at him, and his eyebrows became one with his hairline.

"*Gross?*"

"Yes," I mimicked, doing my best impression of his voice. It turns out *this* version of Fane did, in fact, lower my maturity levels to an all-time low.

"Kissing me is *gross?*" He was doing that thing with his mouth that made it clear he was trying not to smile. I'd ask him again if he was laughing at me, but he'd probably call me ma'am, and I would definitely punch him this time.

"Do you no longer speak English? Yes, that's what I said. Don't do it again."

"*You* kissed *me.*" He pointed one tattooed hand in my direction and I smacked it away from where it hovered too close to my face.

"The first time! And because we had an audience. You're the one that gripped my hair like…like some hair pervert!"

"Hair pervert?" He was actually laughing now. Shoulders shaking and eyes dancing.

"Don't kiss me again."

"But you're my girlfriend."

"I'll bite your tongue."

"Cali, I'm trying to get rid of my raging hard-on, and that is not helping." He was glaring at me again, but it looked more forced than anything after his laughter had died off. I could feel the way the aftermath of the sound settled around me, the way it threatened to chip at my armor.

"You need to leave." I pointed at the door that led back into the café. "And learn how to close doors. This"—I waved between us—"will not happen again."

"The you kissing me part? Or the boner?"

I could do nothing but gape at him. He winked at me, and my fists balled again at my sides. "Anyway, I have a bit of work I need to do in the next couple of days, and then we can start with the tours. I'm thinking I should also try and be your shadow? Get an understanding of what life here is like."

I opened my mouth to tell him he could do his own tours and that he could go fuck himself on all the rest of what he'd said, but it was also the reminder I needed that Fane wasn't here just to ruin my life, despite that being a clear motive for him for some ungodly reason.

He was here to ruin my town, and I could put my desperate want for his disappearance on the back burner while I saved Darling.

"See you at home!" he called over his shoulder just as he disappeared through the door that led into the kitchen.

I gave myself ten seconds to breathe. To talk myself down from the idea that going into his office after hours and TP-ing his desk was a good idea.

I'd be no good to Jerry if I was behind bars.

I lifted my chin and dropped my shoulders. Smoothing my hands down my dress, I decided that I would redirect all the energy being used toward hating Fane into my plan on how to convince him that he needed to leave

Darling alone.

Yes! *Yes.* Perfect.

I would make a list, because lists *always* helped. I wouldn't let this town become some overpopulated, overpriced, perfect-on-the-surface and rotten-in-the-middle idyllic getaway.

This place was the only thing I had left that was truly mine.

It took five seconds for my resolve to set in and only one for it to be shaken when I got behind the counter, ready to serve the small line of patrons who were waiting for their coffee and noticed that my jar of cookies—the *whole jar*—was missing.

Steam must have been pouring out of my ears because the guy in front of me, who was clearly part of the contractor team Fane was managing, took a small step back and raised his hands.

"It wasn't me." He looked like he wanted to turn around and haul ass out of Sunshine.

I plastered on my best smile, which made the guy's face crinkle in worry. "What can I get for you?" I asked instead, pulling a pen and notepad out from under the counter.

"Just a flat white, please."

"Sure thing." I got to work, quickly going through the motions of making his coffee. Losing myself in the familiarity of it.

"So," the guy said just as I finished steaming his milk. "You're the boss's girl?"

I heard him but chose to ignore him for a second while I composed myself and tried not to look like I should be sedated.

There was a decent-sized line now, at least nine people waiting to place an order. That's when Sammy walked in, her eyes wide at how many people were in the café as well as how another three people had just followed her in.

I was grateful she'd gotten my message this morning after I had a hunch that there would be too many customers for one person to handle for a weekday.

"Hey, Cal." She smiled before reaching under the counter for an apron, reminding me that I hadn't even put one on yet.

"Thanks for coming, Sammy."

"Oh, don't mention it." Her smile was warm and kind, the way it always was.

With no way to dodge the question from a man I didn't even know, I slapped on my cheeriest, most unsettling smile and handed him his coffee. "That's me!"

12

## Fane

**Before**

"I can't believe you've never played cards. Everyone plays cards," Cali said. Her bottom lip jutted out, and her eyes went round with concern.

I just watched her. Enchanted.

"Go Fish?" she asked, eyes both wide with disbelief and utterly horrified behind the dainty gold rim of her glasses. I had to press my lips together to stop the laughter.

"No." I shook my head.

"Fane, this is awful. I feel like you missed out on something important here. Something, I don't know, *integral* to every childhood."

Cali knew all about my upbringing. We'd talked about it more since that first night in my truck. More than I thought I'd ever talk about that time in my life, and not in a way that made it hurt more. We talked about it in a way that made it hurt less.

Made it lighter somehow.

Sometimes, the conversations were serious. Words we exchanged in the darkness of my bedroom where we'd hand over one another's stories. Where she'd tell me about how her dad used to push her on the swings as a kid, and that was when she learned all her multiplication.

And I would tell her about the time my dad hit my mom so hard I had sat

78

in the corner of our living room for two hours, my eyes unblinking while I stared at her, terrified that she'd never wake up.

She never gave me pity when my past was so completely the opposite of hers. She just held me closer. Made sure I knew that even if I couldn't see her, she was right there with me in the dark.

When she shared her stories, it wasn't like she was only relaying them, but like she was *giving* them to me. Freely, with no strings attached. Letting them become mine as much as they were hers. Stories that gave me something I never had—a past that didn't hurt to remember.

Other times, *these* were the sorts of conversations we had.

"Are you laughing at me?" Her hand flew up to her chest. "These are serious questions!"

"No, ma'am." I kept my expression as subdued as possible. "Very serious."

"What about Shithead?"

"There's a card game called Shithead?"

"Bullshit?"

"What do you mean? You're the one that just said it?"

Cali's face was blank for a split second before she threw her head back, and body-shaking laughter erupted from her. Long black hair was splayed over the armrest of the chair she had draped herself over across from where I sat on the couch.

There was something about the way laughter looked on her that made her infinitely sexier. Cali didn't laugh politely. She didn't tame it down or try to change the way it sounded for anyone's benefit.

Her laughter was loud. It took over every part of her.

Her face, her body, her hands.

She balled them into fists, and her toes curled in while she clutched at her stomach. It wasn't just something that she did, it was something that actively happened to her.

"Fane!" she wheezed my name a second before she landed on the floor with an unceremonious thump, her glasses falling off the moment she hit the ground. That just made her laugh even more. *"I'm going to pee my pants!"* she yelled, voice muffled from the way her face was pushed into the carpet.

The huge, stupid-looking grin on my own face was only something I became aware of after it had already happened.

That's what it was like to be around Calista Grey.

It was to suddenly be aware of the fact that you were happy for the first time in your life and have no recollection of when the process had even started, only that it had. That little by little, she'd taken the parts of you that were bruised and broken and helped you heal and put yourself back together with gentle hands and wide-trusting eyes.

"I can't believe you've never played any of these card games. They're life staples," she said, still giggling. "I know!" She pushed herself up from where she'd been pancaked on the floor. "We'll have a card game night! Ash can invite what's-her-face, and Abbey can come too!"

And just like that, she'd started to heal another part of me without even trying.

"What's that look mean?" she asked, the smile on her face so damn beautiful. She'd recovered, sitting back on her knees with her feet tucked under her. All she wore was one of my shirts, leaving her bronzed legs on full display. The waist-length waves of her hair were mussed and wild like they carried the chaos of everything she made me feel.

"What look?"

She pointed at my face. "That one."

I dragged my eyes back up to meet hers. "Just thinking."

"Oh yeah?" She stood, crossing the small space between us to settle on my lap. Her thighs slid around me, warm and familiar, her chest pressed to mine. "Care to share?"

My hands found her back, palms trailing upward, reveling in how every inch of her fit so perfectly against me.

"I was thinking about how I read somewhere," I murmured, my thumb brushing over the soft curve of her cheek, "How you can tell when you're in love."

Her breath hitched, her body stilling in my arms like she was bracing for the weight of my words. Her eyes widened, shining like I was handing her the answer to a question she'd been too scared to ask.

"They say," I went on, watching her pulse flutter on the side of her neck. It was wild, frantic, the opposite of my own steady beat. Because for the second time in my life, I was absolutely sure of what I was about to do. Second only to the moment I stood up from the bar where I sat with Ash, walked over to the beautiful girl with long black hair and asked her to dance. "You just know when you know," I said, my voice quieter now, like it was something sacred. Something only for her. I leaned in, close enough to feel the warmth of her breath against my skin. Close enough to let her see how deep it went, how unshakable it was. "And I know."

Her breathing hitched again. "You do?"

"I do."

"You're sure?"

She pulled a laugh from me, soft and unrestrained and only in existence because of her. How she didn't already know that she was everything I'd ever wanted and needed and dreamed of was still beyond me.

"I'm sure, baby."

"Okay, good." She looked down, her fingers fiddling with the hem of my shirt before she looked back up, letting me get lost in those eyes that looked more honey in the golden glow of the light pouring through the window of my living room. "Because me too. I know too."

I kissed her. I'd been kissing her for the last eight months, and it hadn't been enough.

"I love you," I whispered against her lips, wanting the words to embed themselves there, to find their home there, so that there wouldn't be a day in her life she didn't know what she was to me. *Who* she was to me.

"I love you," she said back, eyes holding that determined, steely glint they did when she was on a mission. When she needed to do something, and no one was going to stand in her way.

Both her hands settled on the sides of my face. "I am so in love with you, Fane Mackenzie. Do you hear me?"

I did. I heard her, and all I could do was pull her back to me. To kiss her again. *Taste* her again.

Cali's arms went up, and I pulled the shirt up and over her head. A routine we'd practiced over and over. I could predict everything down to the second.

The blush that bloomed on her chest and moved up her neck, turning the apples of her cheeks the most delicious shade of peach when it mixed with the honey tones of her skin. How her dusky nipples tightened into peaks, making my mouth water. The way her breathing hitched the moment I closed my mouth around one. The shiver that racked her body when I used my teeth, biting hard enough to sting.

I knew that it drove her crazy because, every time, without fail, she started to circle her hips. Grinding herself against the hard length of my cock until I slowly started to lose my mind.

"Rose," I gritted out. Pulling back to watch the way her hips moved over me.

"I want—" she started but cut herself off. Sometimes, she surprised me and said exactly what she wanted. What she wanted to do to me. What she wanted me to do to her.

"What, baby?" I was literally panting at the sight of her, still watching the way she moved and doing my fucking hardest not to blow in my pants. "Tell me."

"I want you inside of me." Her voice was a hushed whisper, a tangle of nerves. Just hearing them come out of her mouth caused an involuntary thrust of my hips.

"*Fucking Christ.*" It came out a choked sort of cry. She was in control, and I fucking loved it.

"*Fane.*" She moaned my name like it was the most delicious thing in the world. Cali stilled her hips, and a grunt of frustration tore from my chest. My eyes shot up to hers, and I could see the way her chest was heaving just as fast as mine. "I want to fuck you."

Her eyes were hooded. Molten pools of all of my dirtiest fantasies wound into one single look, and she didn't take them off me for a second. Not when her hand dipped below the waistband of my sweatpants and she wrapped her slender fingers around my cock, pulling me out and running the swollen head along the seam of her pussy.

It might've been the most erotic fucking thing I'd ever seen in my life.

Holding her panties to the side, Cali fed my cock inside of her. Eyes closed and head tipped back, taking every single inch of me so slowly that all I could do was grip her hips. I knew that my hold on her was probably too hard, that she'd have shadows of my fingerprints dotting the skin of one of my favorite parts of her body, but the thought of there being evidence of *this* long after it was over only made it better.

Made me need her more.

"Holy…holy fucking shit." I was breathless, my eyes looking from where I was still slowly disappearing inside of her. Cali had leaned back, and it gave me the perfect view of her pussy. Flushed and pink and swollen with her arousal glistening over both of us. "Shit, *fuck,* you have no idea…Cali, you're going to make me come."

"Not yet." Cali's voice glided over every nerve in my body, and if she thought that her request *not* to come was going to do anything but make the tightening at the base of my spine worse, she was dead wrong.

"Are you okay?" I grunted, knowing she always needed a second to adjust.

In answer, she rose onto her knees and plunged down on me in one fluid motion, making me cry out.

Making *her* cry out.

My grip on her tightened further, and my eyes rolled back. She did it over and over, her nails digging into the muscles on my chest, my shoulders, my back. Over and over again, she took every inch of me into her, like if I didn't reach as deep inside of her as I could, then we'd both fucking die.

"*Calista.*" Her name was a mindless growl. She was going to kill me. I was going to die the happiest man who ever lived.

"Not. Yet." She punctuated each word with the rise and fall of her body, leaving me staring at the way I disappeared inside her tight, wet heat. At how wet she was, how it coated the inside of her thighs. How it made me want to pull her off me just so I could drag my tongue over her perfect cunt and taste her while she fell apart.

"You always feel so good. So. *Fucking.* Good," she moaned, and I pulled her back to me, taking one of her full, heavy breasts in one hand and grazing her other nipple with my teeth.

"Are you going to come for me, baby?" I rasped against her skin, pulling my hand from where it had been locked onto her hip and swiping my thumb over her swollen clit. Dipping down to gather her arousal before moving it back up.

"Am I going to feel the way you fall apart just for me? The way your cunt grips me? Greedy and perfect and so fucking wet."

Cali's nails dug in harder, and I didn't even know what the fuck I was saying, only that seeing her come apart—*feeling* her come apart—seemed like the only reason I was put on this earth. To make her feel like *this*.

"Do you know how wet you are, my love? The mess you've made?" I bit and nipped my way up to her neck, sucking hard and reveling in the way she whimpered. How I knew how close she was to coming completely undone.

I pulled her flush to me, both arms wrapping behind her. One hand gripping her shoulder, the other sinking in the hair at the nape of her neck, wrapping the strands around my fingers and pulling tight, exposing her neck to me. Trailing my teeth up the curve of her throat, I left tender kisses where I could see her pulse fluttering, a shiver racking my body at the sounds that she was making.

"Pl-plea," she stuttered.

"Yes?" I murmured, still dragging my mouth against her skin, tasting her. Cali's control came to an absolute end when she let me wrap my arms around her, and I knew the slow and measured thrusts of my hips were driving her insane.

"*Please*," she whimpered.

"Please what, baby?"

"I—" A half-frustrated mewl, half-pleading cry tumbled out of her, and I knew she could feel my smile grow from where my face was tucked into the crook of her neck before I moved my mouth to the shell of her ear.

"Tell me you want to come on my cock, Calista," I breathed. "Tell me that this is *my* pussy, and you want me to spill myself so deep inside it you'll be feeling me for fucking days."

*"Jesus,"* she sobbed. "I—"

I stopped thrusting completely, and a growl ripped from her throat. The grip I had on her was absolute, and the only movement she could make was the rise and fall of her chest.

I ran the tip of my tongue along the shell of her ear and felt her shiver.

"I—" She tried again. "I want to come…on your cock. I—"

"Tell me, baby." I started to thrust again, slowly, just the way I knew she loved. "Whose pussy is this?"

"Yours," she moaned. "I want to feel you come inside me, Fane. *Please—*"

That was about all the willpower I had.

I pulled her down onto me, hard and fast. My hips pistoning into her with a ferocity that emptied every thought from my head but one. To feel her clench around me, to hear her call my name, to bring us both to the very edge of sanity that the thought of going over didn't seem like such a bad thing.

Cali came so violently that she went limp in my arms, my name nothing more than a raspy moan trickling from her mouth in slurred sounds, and with a final thrust, I emptied myself inside of her, my hands still locked around her. Unwilling and unable to let her go.

We stayed like that for a long time, until the sweat on our skin cooled and our breathing returned to normal.

"Mmm." Cali's small and gentle hum made me open my eyes. She was already looking at me, one hand over my heart.

"What?" I reached out to tuck one of her unruly strands of hair behind her ear.

"Feel," she murmured, pulling one of my own hands from where it sat on her waist and placing it over her heart. "We're in sync."

It took me a second to figure out what she was saying, but then the steady thrum of her heart pounded beneath my palm, and I got it. Our hearts were beating at the same time.

"You know," she said, a small smile playing at the corner of her mouth. "They say that when your heart starts to beat in sync with someone else's, it will stay that way forever."

"Forever?"

"Mmm," she hummed again before settling into my chest and tucking her head into the side of my neck.

"What did I do to deserve you?" I whispered. It was the same question I asked myself every single day.

"Everything," she whispered back, and even though I didn't believe her, I made a vow that I'd do everything I could to make damn sure one day I did.

# 13

## Calista

**After**

I'd ignored Fane for the entire week. Sort of.

I didn't speak to him. I didn't really look at him. Not even when he wedged himself between me and the stove while I stirred a sad can of pumpkin soup.

I just continued to stir and look right through him, which was, frankly, very difficult to do.

Fane wasn't a small man, and I may have willed myself into feeling nothing but disdain for him, but I challenge any living, breathing human to have someone who smelled the way he did and *looked* the way he did quite literally rub himself up and down the front of your body and remain statuesque.

I didn't so much as make a peep when he left the toilet seat up—something I knew he did just to see if I'd crack. Instead, I continued to funnel that energy into crafting the perfect plan to get through to him.

List after list, detail after detail, I worked like a woman possessed. Perfecting, revising, obsessing. My game plan was going to be bulletproof.

It would've been flawless, too—if only it didn't require me to spend time in the vicinity of the man in question.

Okay. Look, I noticed him once.

*Crap.* Twice.

He'd tailed me like some speed racer when I caught wind of the meeting that had been unofficially pulled together at town hall on Wednesday afternoon.

"I object!" I yelled the moment I pushed the doors open.

"That's not a thing here," Fane whispered next to my ear, so close I could feel his breath on my skin.

I turned, smacking my hands against his chest, ready to…I don't know. Kick his ass? Sure, let's go with that.

"Trouble in paradise?"

The voice made me freeze. I looked to my right just as Fane did, catching only a split second of the man's face—dark eyes, dark hair—before Fane's broad chest shifted into my line of sight, blocking him completely.

The split second I'd seen him, the man's smirk looked both sharp and lazy. He tutted before crooning, "Come now, Fane. Introduce me to the woman who's captured your heart. I won't bite."

Fane's grip on my arm tightened almost painfully. When I tried to look around him, he shifted us further down the middle aisle of seats. The man's laughter followed us like oily tendrils that were fighting to grab onto me. Goose bumps rose on my skin, and immediately, I wanted to step into the searing spray of a too-hot shower and remove the residue of it from my skin.

I didn't fight Fane as he dragged me toward the front of the room, but as soon as the haze of wrongness loosened its grip on me, I smacked his hands away and straightened my shirt.

"I want to speak to the mayor," I said to…I had no idea. I'd never been to a town meeting before.

"That would be me."

My head snapped to the front of the room, where a fairly young-looking guy with dull brown eyes and equally dull brown hair sat next to a woman who could have been his sister.

"You're Mayor Brown?" I deadpanned. I'd never met anyone who embodied their name so thoroughly. The literal poster child for beige.

"I am."

"Right." I cleared my throat, trying to step back but immediately bumped into Fane, forcing me to step forward. "I would like to object to the developmental work being considered."

"That's—"

"It's all right, Matilde." He put his hand on the lady's arm to settle her, and though her body relaxed, she didn't remove her glare. "I'll hear her out. Go on..."

"Calista."

"Go on, Calista." He nodded, and it was hard to take him seriously because, honestly, he looked about seventeen.

"Changing anything about this town will ruin the very things that make it so great."

A small chorus of agreement hummed from behind me, making me stand up taller.

"This town has a history. Generationally owned businesses. Character. It's the way it is because the people here care for it. If you make it into some money grab, that will all change." I was trying not to sound desperate. But I was.

"And that's why there is an assessment period," the mayor said smoothly, his gaze darting to Fane. "As Mr. Mackenzie behind you can attest."

I whirled on Fane. "You've met this cheese ball already?" I hissed, attempting discretion but very clearly failing based on the gasps that rippled around the room.

Fane just stared down at me, arms crossed, his expression unreadable. "Briefly."

"When?"

"When I got into town."

"That's right," Mayor Brown interjected, his tone now noticeably frostier. "And as a town, we've agreed to entertain the proposal."

"Who's 'we'?" I shot back. "Because I live in this town, and I didn't agree?"

The mayor ignored me. "In any case," he continued, "the only person at this point who can decide whether or not the project will move forward— something that would be very good for this town, mind you—is your husband."

I scoffed. "He is *not* my husband."

God. Fucking. Dammit.

You could've heard a pin drop.

"Yet!" I blurted, my voice way too loud. Mayor Beige jolted in surprise. "He's not my husband...*yet*."

Well, this was fucking awkward. "Congratulations...in advance."

"So, that's it?" I turned, scanning the room. Familiar faces stared back at me—neighbors, regulars at Sunshine Café, people I'd shared countless conversations with. Yet now, they avoided my gaze, their attention fixed on their hands or the scuffed floorboards.

The mayor cleared his throat, slipping back into his polished, dismissive tone. "If you don't have a productive comment to contribute, I suggest you take a seat."

"Mr. Mackenzie," the mayor added, "Perhaps you can encourage your wife to—"

The most aggressive snort I'd ever heard flew out of Fane's mouth and cut him off.

Fane's posture shifted, his presence radiating something sharp and dangerous. "What, exactly, do you think I should encourage her to do?" His tone was cold and razor-edged, making the room fall silent.

I glanced back, catching sight of the dark-haired man again. His hand lifted in a mocking wave, his smirk slipping into something darker. The ease with which he reeled it back sent an unwelcome chill down my spine. Like by his will alone, he could make Fane snap.

This was going nowhere.

"Whatever," I muttered, grabbing Fane's arm. When he didn't budge, I yanked harder. He leveled the mayor with one last scalding look before following me toward the exit.

As we passed the dark-haired man, he crooned, "See you soon, boss."

Fane's jaw twitched, his entire body coiled tight. For a second, I thought he might stop, turn back, and say something. Instead, he glanced down at me, his gaze still unreadable, then all but lifted me off my feet and hauled me out the door.

Once outside, because I was ignoring him—*of course*—all I could do was scream silently in my head, slap his hands away and flip him a double dose of the bird.

# 14

## Calista

**After**

Fane followed me all the way home like a lost puppy I didn't want to keep.

No matter where I went, no matter how much distance I tried to put between us, I'd turn around, and *bam!* There he was.

He didn't even try to hide it, either. Every time I caught him lurking, he'd flash me a smug little grin, gesture between us and say, "I'm shadowing you. This is work," before whipping out that stupid notebook he kept tucked in his back pocket like a prop.

'Shadowing' apparently included loitering in Sunshine, hovering near aisle six at the grocery store, adding snacks to my basket I did not pick out, and watching me pump gas like some overqualified attendant.

And I knew I was going insane because his constant hovering was making me paranoid.

The unease started small. A prickle at the back of my neck. The sensation of being watched—not the casual kind of attention, but the kind that worms its way under your skin, twisting and festering until it feels like your every move is being cataloged.

Half the time, I was convinced it was just Fane. But some moments, even when I knew exactly where he was—leaning against the counter in the café or flipping through some useless magazine in the grocery store, pretending not to notice the way I was glaring at him—it didn't go away.

It wasn't constant, either. That was the worst part. The bit that had me convinced I was losing my mind. I'd feel it, sharp and suffocating, and then I'd spin around to find Fane, arms crossed and infuriatingly calm, and for a while, it would vanish. Like spotting him was all it took to remind my brain to get a grip.

But it always came back, and I was convinced this lie I'd dropped us into was going to do way more damage than I initially thought.

I had a sweet reprieve from Fane's hovering after work on Thursday afternoon. It was glorious. I was going to take a shower, leave him no hot water again as my only means of retribution, and then settle in for a movie with Jerry.

All those plans fell to absolute shit when I got home to find Jerry had not only nudged the basket of clean laundry I'd left on the couch to fold, but I found him happily gnawing on a pair of my underwear.

Jerry was an angel. I'll never say a word otherwise, but he had a real penchant for eating my panties which, I know, was gross. But it didn't matter if they were fresh from the wash or brand new from the store, he had zero preference.

"Jerry." I set my stuff down by the door, observing him as if he was a live explosive. "Jerry, we've talked about this."

We had talked about it a total of five times.

Clearly, none of those conversations had made any impact.

The next twenty minutes consisted of me screaming, "Drop those panties!" while running around the house. For all his laziness, Jerry had the spirit of a whippet when he needed it. He jumped over the couch and ran under the dining table, upending it gloriously as he tore into my bedroom and collided with the bed so forcefully it shifted to the other side of the room.

Jerry bounded through the living room, my underwear flapping in his mouth like a victorious flag. "Jerry, drop it!" I hissed, tripping over the overturned laundry basket.

That was when Fane arrived home.

I turned toward the front door just as Fane opened it from the outside, stepping in like he owned the place.

His eyes swept over the chaos—me, mid-pounce; Jerry, panting triumphantly; my lace underwear dangling from his teeth—and his mouth twitched. "Am I interrupting something?"

He looked from me to Jerry to the laundry basket sprawled on the floor and then finally to the mangled pile of cotton that Jerry had dropped at his feet. A gift just for him after a long day.

Fane reached down to pick it up, and it might have been one of the less spectacular moments of my life when I caught his eye *through* the hole in the crotch.

"Are these yours?" Fane's eyes danced with something akin to victory. I crossed my arms and jutted a hip out, refusing to speak to him even though I had been forced to acknowledge his presence within the very walls I'd vowed not to.

"Rosie Posie, have you been ignoring me all week?" The answer to the question was obviously yes, and when I didn't answer him, his head tilted to the side in that predatory way of his. And Rosie Posie? He *knew* I hated that nickname. I was as confused as everyone else on why then, exactly, his words were like phantom hands ghosting down my body, stopping just beyond the juncture of my thighs where my pulse point was wreaking havoc.

"Jerry," he said, looking down at my dog, who was sitting at his feet like the proudest gift-giver that had ever lived. "Did you know your mom's been ignoring me?"

Jerry made a huffing grunt in confirmation. I guess I knew where his loyalties lay now.

"Are you allowed to eat panties, Jerry?"

He made another huffing sound identical to the first, and it took everything in me not to yell that, no, he was *not* allowed to eat panties.

But I was ignoring Fane. That was the goal here.

"Oh." Fane dropped his keys on the side table near the door and walked toward the laundry still on the floor. "Well then, your mom won't mind if we find you a few more pairs, will she?"

I swear to God, Jerry's grunt sounded exactly like the word "great," and he watched on, tail thumping, as Fane crouched down to the laundry pile and started to rifle through it.

My index finger started to tap on my arm, and I decided to try box breathing for the first time in my life. It did sweet fuck all, but I didn't crack.

"Calista, there's only one other pair of panties here." Fane lifted the scrap of purple lace up, standing back to his full height. "And this looks like a week's worth of washing."

I wanted to swat the smile right off his stupidly pretty face.

"Still not a fan of panties?" Slowly, he moved the garment over toward where Jerry waited with bated breath like it was his birthday and Christmas all at the same time.

"Well, bud," he said, finally looking at Jerry. "If your mom has no objections, I'd say this pair is up for grabs too. Unless, of course, you have anything you'd like to say, Cali?"

Oh, I had plenty to say, believe me, but not a peep came out of my mouth when he handed Jerry the pair of underwear. I stormed into the bathroom and did the only thing I could do. I had a very long, very hot shower until the water ran cold and grinned in delight when I heard Fane jump in after I was done and yelp after stepping directly under what had to be a blisteringly cold spray.

When being in the same house as him got to be too much, which it constantly was, I had the option of either smothering him with a pillow or going to see my dad.

So, I drove out to my parents' place and found him exactly where I knew he'd be, sitting on his chair, looking out at the mountains in the distance.

When my mom got sick, he decided to finally retire, though I use that term lightly. He still got up at the ass crack of dawn and busied himself around the property before he drove into the station. Officially, he'd taken on an administrative volunteer role, but everyone there was relieved he kept coming around. The man was a living encyclopedia of firefighting knowledge, and they all knew it.

Of course, I saw my mom, and sometimes she sat with us too, but our relationships had all changed in the last two years. A big part of me mourned the dynamic our family used to have, of the relationship that Abbey and I used to have.

People cope with sickness differently, and my mom responded a lot like Abbey. She'd closed her circle and tightened it to the point where only one person was allowed inside, pushing everyone else just far enough out of reach.

I'd made my peace with it. I understood that was how she coped, how she got through it. That's why Abbey's reaction hadn't shocked me as much as it might've once.

They were cut from the same cloth.

But so were me and my dad.

Our weekly sit-downs outside the family dinners were *our* thing. Sometimes, we talked; sometimes, we didn't. The moment I sat down in the porch chair, his hand would find mine, wrapping around it tightly like I was his tether.

He didn't hold it loosely. He held it like it meant something.

I'd sit down, and he'd kiss my cheek, greet me with one of his classic "Hey, kiddo!" lines, and take this deep breath like it was the first time he'd managed it all day.

The first time I showed up, it had been nothing different—same hello, same hand grip, same deep breath.

The second time in the same week his face lit up like a Christmas tree. "I'm a lucky man, Calista Grey!" he'd said, beaming.

But the third time, there was no hand holding, no kiss hello. My stomach churned at the thought that I'd worried him, that my visits had become more about my own need for clarity than being the thing that grounded him. I was supposed to be his first, easy, deep breath—not the furrow in his brows.

He didn't say a single thing. He knew me too well for that. He knew I'd talk when I was ready—or at least I would've before everything changed. Now? I was a vault.

Every word, every want, every wish hammered at the walls of my mind, but I refused to weigh him down with it.

When I sat down that third time he stood up straight away. My heart hammered the whole two minutes he was gone, and came back with a beer for each of us. I willed the pressure behind my eyes to settle, not to tip over the edge, not to be a reason those laugh lines around his eyes smoothed out again.

He handed me one, took my hand again, and together, we both took a deep breath.

It was different.

Everything was different. But it was enough.

When I got home after those visits, I felt a little more grounded—until I walked through the front door and found Fane still in my house.

All that is to say, I had almost completely ignored Fane. Almost.

I had also dutifully ignored the word of the day that pinged on the lock screen of my phone.

Maybe it was a convenient excuse to avoid trying to figure out what the words meant and how to include them in my day somehow. It felt a little like karma for ignoring that stupid app when it pinged on my bedside table, waking me up and telling me my new word of the day had been delivered.

Waiting for me to fail at expanding my vocabulary.

As I slowly came to on Saturday morning, I internally groaned at the way my cheek was pressed firmly to Fane's chest.

I liked to believe that the reason I was constantly in this situation since Fane decided it would be fine to invade my bed was that *he* was the one pulling me to him while we were both asleep. That was a big fat lie, and I was surprised he hadn't used it as ammunition in our verbal sparring wars.

We both knew it was me.

Fane was still firmly on his side of the bed. The wall of pillows had somehow been scattered around haphazardly, and my side of the bed was gloriously empty. The sheets were cold, cementing what I already knew: I had been here for a long while.

His breathing was steady, his chest rising and falling beneath my cheek.

His heartbeat thumping steadily beneath my ear.

I slowly let my head move back to take him in. Lips parted, and long, thick lashes fanned out on his cheeks. The scowling glare he had on consistently since arriving in town was smoothed out.

He looked peaceful, like *my* Fane. The one I had learned with painstaking detail over two years.

I swallowed, knowing I should move. This was so far over the line of inappropriate that it was unrecoverable if he opened his eyes and found me ogling him. Instead, I let myself take a second to look at him. To let my heart pang painfully at the fact that I'd never been this close to him before without him being mine.

Without being *his*.

I'd made a point of not looking at the tattoos he'd added to his body in the last two years. Fane had already had two full sleeves when I met him. A tapestry of things that he liked for no reason, things he liked for serious reasons, things that had resonated with him in some way or another.

He had tattoos all over his chest, legs, and arms. They had always fascinated me because so many of them were opposites to one another. There was a grim reaper on his back. It was this huge, shadowed depiction of it, and then he also had the phases of the moon going up his side and over his ribs. A skull with a snake coming out of its mouth and wrapping down his arm, and then a bunch of butterflies on his torso. A wolf, also on his back, howling in sorrow, and then a rubber ducky on his thigh.

I loved it because it explained him perfectly. He wasn't just one version of himself. He was so many different parts pulled together, and I loved every aspect of him without any hesitation.

The new tattoos on his neck were things I had no idea the meanings behind, but I wanted to. It was almost hard to sit still; how much I wished I knew. It was a mismatch of things. A rose, a timepiece, a mandala design that went up the column of his throat.

It made him look even more imposing than he did before. Like maybe he'd done it just so people would leave him more alone than they already did.

The hand he had resting on his stomach used to be unmarked on the top. Now it held what looked like a constellation. I had no idea which one it could have been.

That thought brought me back to reality.

Of course, I didn't know. Why would I? I had no right to know. It wasn't my business, and letting myself get soft wasn't going to help me when he left. The only thing I could do was make sure the only thing that was caught in the crossfire was me, not Darling.

I managed to extract myself from the firm hold he had around my waist, determined not to wake him. Desperate to have a second where I didn't need to be on guard. Where I could let my walls down and admit that this was getting harder, not easier.

I was not an angry person. Being constantly angry at Fane was already taking a toll on me, but it was the only way I knew how to keep my guard up—to keep myself from unraveling completely.

I just needed to endure it.

Grabbing my phone on my way out of the bedroom, I tiptoed to avoid the floorboards I knew would creak. My gaze flickered briefly to the dark lump of his belongings piled in the corner, an unwelcome reminder of how much my house had changed in just one week. Even the air felt different, saturated with the woodsy, warm scent that clung to the man in my bed like a freaking pheromone.

He smelled like a mix of hot showers and wilderness: fresh pine and clean soap. It was the kind of scent that made you lean in without realizing it—intoxicating.

I would *not* think about it. Starting now.

Before grabbing Jerry's lead to take him on his walk around the block, I checked my word of the day.

*Beleaguered.*

"Oh, perfect," I muttered. Apparently, the universe had jokes.

Jerry was sprawled belly-up on the couch, his legs sticking straight into the air. One eye cracked open as I approached, and his tail thumped a lazy rhythm against the cushions.

"Good morning, sweet boy." I dropped to my knees beside him, burying my face into his side.  His fur smelled faintly of Fane too, which was a betrayal I chose to ignore. "Time for a walk with your beleaguered mom." I kissed his nose and scratched under his chin, letting his soft grunts of contentment soothe the part of me that was still silently screaming.

# 15

## Calista

**After**

I'd managed to get up, get dressed purely from the clothes that were still sitting in the dryer, walk Jerry, get my ass out of the house, disconnect the battery of Fane's car as payback for the panties, and be on my merry way to work all before he'd even started to stir.

It felt like an incredible omen to head into what had turned out to be one of the busiest Saturdays we'd ever had.

I was in a good mood. A *great* mood. When Gus walked in this morning as soon as the door was unlocked, I hugged him. The poor man didn't know what to do with himself and somehow settled for patting me on the top of my head until I let him go.

He promptly followed it with a bristled, "I've been seeing Lorna for about a year now, but I'm flattered."

What I'm saying is that even being rejected by Gus for a come-on that didn't exist wasn't able to sour my mood.

Should I be hugging my customers? Probably not. I hugged Sammy too, and thankfully she didn't also try to let me down softly. She just hugged me back and gave me one of those soft smiles she wore like a badge of honor. Like she knew she was gentle and continued to be so despite how she grew up.

Sammy had witnessed things no one should ever see or witness, especially as a little girl, and had refused to let it change her. I was in awe of her for that.

We settled into a routine so familiar to us that the morning had turned to afternoon by the time I realized what the actual time was, and then there was a firm knock on the glass of the café.

Mags was sitting in the middle of the café, a little later than her usual weekday routine, reading her paper. That woman deserved an Oscar for the way she meddled and then pretended to know nothing about what she set into motion.

"Oh, look!" She yelled, startling everyone in Sunshine, which was full to the brim. "It's Calista's hunky boyfriend!"

My heart rate skyrocketed so fast I had to grip the counter with one hand while I kept steaming milk with my other.

Somewhere along the line I'd convinced myself that watching Fane feed my Great Dane a pair of my panties was a fever dream as penance for not being able to stop Jerry from obtaining a flyaway soccer ball from the under 6's match we had walked by during our walk this morning.

I apologized profusely and gave them everything I had in my pockets. It seemed that a hair tie, half a stick of chewing gum, and a quarter did not actually help.

"Oh, look." I plastered the biggest and brightest smile I always used when the alternative was merely bursting into tears and lifted my head. "There he is."

I started to wave at him, and as soon as all eyes were on him, I presented him with my middle finger. Grin still in place.

Fane was waving back. As soon as everyone looked back to me, he lifted his own middle finger up, and damn him, he looked edible.

I wasn't proud of that thought, but I was alive, wasn't I? I had eyes and functioning lady parts. There was no criticism you could hurl at me that I hadn't already whispered to myself.

His hair was still a little damp from a shower, and he wore a plain black shirt with those same dark blue jeans that fit him like a glove. All worn in and used up and glorious.

What? No, I meant gross. *Gross.* His jeans were eugh, yuck. Gross.

He had his black work boots on, and right next to him, looking proud as all hell to have Fane's hand gently scratching the top of his head, was Jerry.

He looked so insanely happy I couldn't stop the feeling that bloomed in my chest.

Warm and overflowing.

Thinking of how that puppy had looked up at me with lost eyes in the back room of a shelter and this feeling of absolute certainty that he and Fane were meant for one another. Looking at them now, I knew that they would have been as inseparable as they seemed to be right now.

That all came to a crashing halt when I noticed what Jerry had in his mouth. The light-blue cotton pair of panties that I knew had been tucked safely in a drawer in my room was hanging out the side of his mouth.

*That's* why he looked so damn happy. And that was also likely why Fane looked like he'd been shitting gold all morning.

"You little—" The ding of the bell above the café door cut me off when the man in question stuck his head just in the door.

"Morning, snookums!"

*Sweet lord.*

Wide eyes moved from Fane's jovial expression to my horrified one with coffee cups frozen in midair.

"Sorry I wasn't here sooner. I had a bit of car trouble. Strangest thing!" he said casually, leaning just far enough into the door to make sure everyone heard him.

"Oh, that's no worry, honey muffin. My day's been so busy I didn't even notice!" I matched his tone and then some. For a solid minute, we just stared at each other across the café, smiling so wide it felt like a contest to see who could look more unhinged.

"Well, pumpkin, when you have a second, I'd love a cappuccino."

"It would be my pleasure." It would absolutely *not* be my pleasure.

"Thanks, pookie bear!" Fane disappeared back outside just as someone in the back corner proceeded to spray their coffee right into the face of the person across from them. I'd never seen either of them before, so I assumed they worked for Fane.

"Dude!" The man now wearing his friend's coffee looked horrified.

"*He said 'pookie bear'!*" the guy still holding his coffee cup whispered back.

My face burned, the smile frozen in place. If I dropped the expression, I would probably storm right outside, and…I don't know. Take my dog back for starters.

I could feel Fane's eyes on me the whole time I made his coffee. Could feel his grin of satisfaction at thinking he'd gotten the upper hand.

"Hey, Sammy, can you take this out to Fane?" I asked sweetly, keeping my sights set on the man in question, who was looking right back, arms crossed and legs wide, with my dog still by his side. *Still* wagging his tail. Still with my panties in his mouth.

Sammy handed the cup to Fane, and the smile on my face was borderline insane as I watched him take a big sip of his drink and the moment that followed where he realized I made him a chai latte.

For those unaware, Fane did the cinnamon challenge after he lost a bet to Ash and has never been able to stomach cinnamon since. Just the look on his face as he sprayed the entire mouthful on the window of my café was worth it.

I was glad for the distraction of work today because it was also the first day of Fane's Darling tours, and my stomach had been twisted in knots since I woke up.

I had a list, of course, which removed about forty percent of my nerves, but the other sixty were all thanks to being near the man himself and the reality that this plan of mine could flop and I'd fail.

The café closed at two thirty p.m. on Saturdays, which was perfect, and with both me and Sammy cleaning up, I managed to get home not thirty minutes later.

The seven-minute drive home was all the time I had to let myself deflate. To relax enough that I could finally take a deep breath without feeling the weight of an elephant sitting on my chest. The moment I turned onto my street and saw Fane's truck parked in the driveway, I hoisted all my walls back up and prepared myself for battle.

The soft conversation of a show on TV trickled out onto the front porch, and I stepped inside to find Fane sitting on the couch with my dog's big head on his lap and one of his broad, tattooed hands absentmindedly scratching Jerry's stomach.

"Traitor," I murmured, keeping my eyes strictly on my dog and strictly *off* Fane. My plan was about to begin, and I wanted to throw up.

But, like any battle-seasoned soldier, I didn't let it show. Instead, I walked out of my bedroom in yet another flowy sundress—it was still too hot to wear anything else comfortably—and finally met Fane's eyes.

I'd felt them on me from the moment I walked into the house. Even through the wall that separated the living room and the bedroom, I felt his eyes on me.

"All right." I stood before him, hands on my hips and my glare of protection in place. "Are you ready?"

"Yes, ma'am." He stood up after carefully lifting Jerry's head off his lap. I hadn't really told Fane we'd be doing this today. Somehow the idea of catching him unaware seemed to translate to, *Wow, I hadn't been expecting this incredible tour. I love your town so much. Allow me to pack up and leave forever.*

"You're not busy?"

"Nope, we have a tour."

I frowned and crossed my arms, unjustifiably annoyed at him. "How did you even know that?"

"Your list is on the fridge."

Fuck. My list was on the stupid fridge.

I didn't realize how close I'd planted myself. Originally, I felt like being toe to toe with him would make me more intimidating. It didn't take a genius to figure out that was a stupid thing to assume, but I couldn't very well step back now.

I wasn't going to retreat, no matter how uncomfortable things got.

I cleared my throat. "Whatever, and don't call me ma'am." I turned my glare up to him, craning my neck as far back as I could go, just to see Fane staring down at me with a small smirk already in place. "And you're driving."

I turned on my heels and stalked to the front door, urging myself not to react outwardly in the slightest at his reply. Even when the hairs on the back of my neck stood on end and I could feel my heart galloping in my chest like a wild horse.

"Yes, ma'am."

This was my last chance. I knew I was entirely on my own. The mayor was a dick that looked like he'd barely graduated from high school, and if what he said was true, then Fane was the be all and end all.

My one and only shot.

# 16

## Calista

**After**

"What do you see?" I instructed Fane to park his truck right next to the park in the center of town, and I was sure we looked a little peculiar standing in the middle of it staring at the children's playground.

This was very much a *trust the process* tour.

Fane's hand shot up, and a very satisfied grin graced his face. I *knew* this was going to come back and bite me in the ass.

"Yes?" I sighed.

"Am I allowed to answer without raising my hand every time?"

"God, I just want to—" I cut myself off, opting to take a deep breath instead.

"Spank me?" He waggled his eyebrows at me, and my hand twitched at my side.

"Was that twitch because you *do* want to spank me? Or you just really want to exercise your right to use your middle finger?"

"I'm sure you can figure it out." I leveled him with my most unimpressed look.

"It's both, isn't it?"

I opted to say nothing because if I moved even a single muscle on my face, he'd know what I was thinking.

He was being too familiar. Too much like that person I'd binded myself to. I didn't want to laugh or smile and joke. I didn't want to *play* with this version of him that was cheeky and lighthearted and often made it a point to end every interaction with me out of my clothes and moaning his name.

"What do I see?" His features relaxed into something that resembled some type of seriousness when he realized he was going to get nothing more from me.

I watched him stand across from me, the bluebird day balancing him out. All bright and light where he was dark and mysterious. I have no idea how he did it, but he looked both out of place and like he grew right where he stood.

"Yes." I could feel his surprise without needing to look at his face. In the last week, if Fane so much as blinked funny, I would have probably bitten his head off. When I wasn't ignoring his existence, of course.

But not here. Not when this wasn't about him and me, not when something so much more important hung in the balance.

"Grass?"

"Are you *asking* me if you see grass?" I glanced at him from the corner of my eye and found him genuinely looking around the park with a crinkle between his brows. I couldn't see his eyes hidden behind the darkened lenses of his sunglasses, but I could imagine the way they'd be tracking over every inch of the space around us like I'd walked him right into an active minefield and provided him instructions on getting safely out in the form of a silent, interpretive dance.

"Grass." It was a statement that time, and I couldn't stop the roll of my eyes or the smile that wanted to crack through without permission. If I thought he'd miss it, I was sorely mistaken.

"Is that a *smile?*"

"And you've ruined it," I huffed and started to walk to the center of the grassy expanse. "I want you to look around and tell me what you see," I said again when Fane finally joined me.

"Families," he said thoughtfully, like he really was taking this seriously and not just placating me. "I see a playground with kids on it." He gestured toward the weathered and worn swing set in the corner. A little boy swinging his legs with all his might to get higher. A little girl's squeal as she made her way down the slide. "And trees." He looked at me, his brow no longer crinkled.

"And what do you hear?" I asked him. "You can close your eyes and focus on it. I

promise I won't do anything to you."

"Wonderful, that's reassured me a whole zero percent."

"Fane." His name was nothing more than an exasperated sigh, and I made sure I had a good clamp on my features when he took one step away from me for good measure before lifting his sunglasses onto the top of his head and closing his eyes.

"I hear the kids playing," he murmured. Thoughtful. "Birds, the wind…"

"Anything else?"

"Yes."

I glanced at him quickly before looking away again. "Are you going to share?"

Fane took a deep breath before he started to speak. "I can hear the way your dress sounds when your arm moves against it. The small humming sounds you make when you're watching something that makes you happy. The deep breaths you're taking, like you're so aware of how your lungs are expanding. Like you're grateful for it."

That…Well, that I hadn't been expecting.

I also hadn't been expecting for his eyes to be open and on me, or for the expression on his face to look quite as vulnerable as it did.

What was I even supposed to *do* with that?

There once was a time I would've looked at his face, seen the expression on it the same way I did now, and know for certain what he was feeling.

Not only did I not trust *him*, but I didn't trust myself. Not around him.

When Fane took a tentative step toward me, I pretended I didn't see it. Pretended I hadn't heard a word he'd said.

"There's a reason why I brought you here as the first stop on our tour." My voice sounded brittle and worn, and that just wouldn't do.

I pointed at the park that had started to fill with more children while we'd been standing here. "Some of my favorite memories were made right there."

"I remember you telling me." He sounded closer, like if I leaned back, I'd feel the hard planes of his chest against the curve of my back, and it would feel like *finally* I wouldn't have to be the only thing keeping myself upright.

The thought made my nose sting, and I stepped away to escape it.

"It looks the same." I pointed at the old swing set, its weathered frame holding strong. "My dad used to push me on that. And now those kids are making their own memories. One day, they'll grow up, leave, and maybe never come back. Or maybe they'll stay. But this swing set will still be here, looking just like this. Steady. Unchanged."

I turned around to face him, settling my eyes on the base of his throat. I traced the details of the tattoos I had promised myself I wouldn't catalog but already had instead of meeting his stare.

"They might fall in love, maybe lose their way, but this park will still be here. Dependable. Something they can count on. Do you know why?"

I didn't really expect him to reply, but his silence did make me finally lift my eyes to his. They had always been brilliant in the sunlight. Flickering between the hues of violet they usually favored and shades of the lightest blue. The copper flecks picked up the sunlight that always reminded me so much of him and reflected it back out, making them almost luminescent.

"Because it's been cared for. Looked after by people who love it. That's why it's lasted. That's what this town is, Fane. It's not a pit stop; it's a place people invest in. Not just with money but with years of their lives. If you change that, you lose everything that makes it special."

I'd been talking about a park for way too long, but it wasn't just about the park. The park was a symbol.

I willed him to see that, to understand it.

"Okay," he said, and I didn't even flinch when he reached to catch a flyaway tendril of hair between his fingers. I didn't miss the way he rubbed the strands between his fingers before tucking it behind my ear.

I studied him, and he let me. His expression was still open, and maybe for the first time since he got to town, he was hiding nothing. So, for right now, I decided to believe him. Even though almost every part of me was screaming at how reckless that was, how I knew what happened when I fell into him.

I knew it all, and I still believed him anyway. "Okay."

It was like he knew that this moment was too much. That we were both missing whatever walls we'd built. If anything, I was grateful to see his cocky little smirk slip back into place.

"So, are you going to take us to the local make-out spot next?"

Gratefulness over.

"*And* you've ruined it," I muttered, turning from him and walking back to his truck.

It was a very nice truck. I'd never known Fane Mackenzie to have such luxurious things, but I could admit that it was nice to see him doing well for himself despite it all.

"I might even let you kiss me again."

I lifted my middle finger high over my head, keeping my back to him, glad he couldn't see the way his laughter hit me. Like a punch to the sternum, sharp and unsteady. It was the painful stretch of a muscle unused for far too long. And yet, I leaned into it, because there was relief in knowing it hadn't just been in my mind. It was as beautiful as I remembered. When it faded, I sank into the peace that it left behind, grateful that *that* too was just like I remembered.

Fane ran ahead of me to open my door before we got back into his truck instead of making a comment (again) about how it must be weird for me to get into a car with real, working safety features. And I just said thank you instead of telling him to go sit on a cactus.

It was…nice.

It felt dangerous.

It *was* dangerous to be anything but completely uncivil toward him because if I wasn't being an asshole, I was going to be myself. That version of me didn't hate Fane as much as the other version claimed to.

That tentative peace followed us all the way home. It made the silence that had settled around us not as heavy as it felt at the start of the day.

I stayed in the shower until my fingers pruned, desperate for the hot water to knead my muscles, to dissolve the knots that never loosened. But today? They felt worse. The day had left me wrung out, left with the realization that I was getting too comfortable with having him around. I expected him to fight me with reasons why changing the park would be better for everyone. Instead, I was met with an alarmingly understanding "okay," and my door opened for me.

I was exhausted.

When I emerged, the smell of Fane's Chili had taken over the house, weaving its way under the bathroom door and right into my stomach. By the time I joined him on the couch, my defenses had already begun to crack. A bowl of food already waited, being eyed with a severe sort of want by Jerry, whose tail started to wag guiltily when he spotted me.

I didn't even care about the full-body shiver of delight that moved through me at the literal orgasm my taste buds were having.

"God, you suck," I mumbled.

"Oh, yeah?" He sounded amused. He sounded *warm*. Like I could slip right under his arm and close my eyes. He sounded safe.

I hid the way my stomach dropped and my chest squeezed with a feeling I could only describe as dread.

"Yes." I nodded into my bowl, pushing past the discomfort of it.

"The insult doesn't surprise me, but more context would be great so I can make sure I do it again."

I shot him a halfhearted glare and shoveled another spoonful into my mouth. "You're still such a good cook. It's not fair."

"Should I have lost that skill for some reason?" He pointed his sauce-covered spoon at me, right in front of Jerry, and didn't even flinch as he started to lick it. "Did you do one of those witchy spells to make my dick fall off?"

I looked over at him with eyes wide and really did try to hide my smile. "You're telling me it *worked?!*"

Fane laughed, unrestrained, and it hit me right where it hurt. It wasn't just the sound—it was the way it tugged at memories better left untouched. The image of him dropping a kiss on my head, whispering something in that same warm, easy voice.

We both knew his dick had absolutely not fallen off. Lest we forget the way I'd all but dry-humped him out the back of Sunshine.

"Oh, you're thinking of something dirty." Fane narrowed his eyes on me.

"No, I'm not." My reply came all too quickly.

"Yes, you are. Your face has gone all peachy." He pointed a tattooed hand in my face, and I swatted it out of the way, desperate to change the topic.

"You have more tattoos." *Ah, yes. Way to ease into it, Calista.*

"I do." His expression had turned thoughtful, the tilt to his head not as predatory as usual but more curious. Like he was daring me to ask him about them because he knew I wanted to know. A part of me wanted to give in to him, but the other part, a very large part, didn't want to give him the satisfaction.

I was grappling for that anger. The knot of which was tied around my heart had loosened through the afternoon. I needed it back.

"They're nice." My voice was flat. I regretted even bringing it up and hoped he'd just drop it when I directed all my attention back to the television.

"You want to know what they mean?" His tone lost its teasing edge, and for a moment, I wasn't sure which answer would hurt more—asking or pretending I didn't care.

"I don't." The lie sat heavy between us, but it was enough to sever whatever tentative thread had been pulling us closer.

"Thanks for dinner." I pushed away the half-eaten bowl and stood, not waiting for a reply.

I was kidding myself, thinking that retreating to the bedroom would give me a reprieve from Fane. He'd already sunken into every nook and cranny of this house.

"Good night, Rose." His voice was dark, husky, and it took everything in me not to turn around. To not to ask him one of the thousands of questions I had for him in the same breath that I demanded he leave.

Instead, I reached for that knot of anger, tightening it until it felt like I was choking, and slipped into the darkness of the bedroom.

I imagined he'd come after me, that he'd give me what I wanted: the perfect excuse to yell at him. To pick a fight. To fuel my anger.

When I heard the front door open and close, for one paralyzing moment, I wondered if he had been awake when I left him, slipping out the front door without a sound, if he would have felt anywhere near as broken as I felt right then.

17

# Fane

**After**

I knew I'd lost her the moment the words left my mouth.

Softness didn't work with this version of Cali. It wasn't what she needed.

At the time, calling Ashton and telling him I needed a beer seemed like the right thing to do.

That was not a good idea.

"Let me get this straight," Ash said, taking another deep swig of his beer before turning his glacial blue eyes back to me. "You've decided that being a dick to her is the best way to earn her trust?"

"I didn't decide to be a dick," I snapped.

"But that's what you just said."

"No." I exhaled sharply through my nose. "It's a fucked up knee-jerk reaction to, I don't know, rile her up."

"Right."

"I'm angry at her too," I admitted, though that didn't even scratch the surface. I was furious. Two years of this pent-up shit, and the only person I wanted to talk it out with, scream it out with, fuck it out with, was dead set on keeping me at arm's length. Not that I could blame her. I wasn't completely blind to her side of things. It just didn't make dealing with my side any easier.

115

We'd never fought like this before. When we argued, we did it together—no slammed doors, no cold shoulders.

"I know," Ash said, not dismissing me. He'd been there when I was at my lowest, peeling me off the mattress when I disappeared for a week. "But I don't see how being a dick is going to win her back."

"I'm not being a dick. And you're supposed to be helping me." I glared at him. "This isn't helping."

"Because as it stands," he said, ignoring me, "You've arrived in town,"—he held up a finger—"let her think you're going to tear it all apart for your sperm donor,"—he raised another finger—"and fed her underwear to her dog." A third finger joined the others.

Yes, okay, I fed her underwear to her dog. But she'd done nothing but ignore me and disconnected my car battery.

Fine, you know what? Yes. I was being a dick.

I groaned, dragging a hand down my face. "It's like this reflex, okay? She pushes, and I push back. It's the only time I get anything fucking *real* from her."

"Mmm." Ash nodded, taking another sip of beer. "Your plan sucks."

"Gee, thanks." I took a sip of my own beer, my head dropping to hang between my shoulders.

"And you won't tell her why you're really here?"

"She won't believe me."

"You won't even entertain the idea of explaining why the last two years happened?"

Before I could answer, Dallas Grey walked right up to our table.

"Fancy seein' you here!"

"Mr. Grey," I said, standing to shake his hand. "Nice to see you. This is my friend Ashton." I gestured to Ash before sitting back down.

Dallas Grey walked into the room like he owned it, radiating warmth with a sun-kissed smile that seemed to light up the whole bar. But behind the easy charm, there was a ruggedness that demanded respect. He was proof that a man could be hard without being cruel, a lesson I didn't learn growing up.

Before I met him, I would've associated that kind of hardness with brutality. But Dallas proved otherwise. The crinkle at the corners of his eyes when he smiled, the lightness in his hazel gaze—so much like his daughter's—made it clear: being hard didn't mean being heartless.

The differences between this man and my own father, the foundation of what I had grown up believing, were black and white. It made that pulsing flare of rage that flickered in and out of existence in the center of my chest flair, just for a second.

*The house had been quiet for so long that I'd started to find comfort in it. It was probably close to one in the morning now. I'd heard my mom walk up the stairs and gently close the door to her bedroom an hour ago.*

*Every single creak of the house made my eyes fly open.*

*Sometimes it was only minutes, sometimes seconds. The fleeting moments of sleep between each and every noise were things I wished I could have more of and less of all at once.*

*My eyes had started to droop just as the front door slammed shut. I didn't even remember moving, only staring wide-eyed at the door to my bedroom and keeping as quiet as possible, huddled against the headboard of my bed. I wished it was the wind, wished it was a car outside.*

*Wished this was anybody else's life but mine.*

*The way my father's footfalls sounded on the stairs had always terrified me. He was so much bigger than me, and I swore sometimes I could hear them even when they weren't there. They followed me around in the silent and empty house.*

*I clutched at the front of my shirt with small, white-knuckled fists. Hating, not for the first time, that I was so pathetically small. By far the smallest boy in the seventh grade. If I had a single wish, it would be that I could be so much bigger than him. That I could be strong enough to protect my mom from him.*

*I wanted him to look at me with the same fear that he loved seeing in our faces. That thought scared me most of the time because it made me feel like I was one decision away from becoming just like him.*

*My mom's panicked pleading seeped in under the door of my room, sending my heart thrashing in my chest. I used to run out to her. To call out to her. But it had only taken the back of his hand connecting with the side of my face once to know that doing that only made things worse for her.*

*"Do you see what you made me do?" He'd seethed from above me, a hand knotted in her long, chestnut hair. A hold she'd fought against valiantly in an attempt to get to me. I'd felt the blood dribbling out the corner of my mouth, felt the tears that leaked from my eyes, but I stayed silent.*

*Silence was safe. Even when it wasn't, it was still safer than making any noise at all.*

*The door to my room burst open, and the very center of all my nightmares filled the doorframe. Eyes red-rimmed. The buttons on his shirt missing like they'd been ripped off.*

*He stalked toward me, grabbed a fist full of the back of my shirt, and dragged me out of my room.*

*I saw her there, lying at the bottom of the stairs. The silent, racking sobs that made her body shiver. The only indication she was alive. He dragged me down the steps that were littered with the missing buttons of his shirt and stepped over my mother like she wasn't even there.*

*Like this person, who he was supposed to love and care for and protect at all costs, didn't mean a fucking thing to him.*

*He threw me into the corner of the living room, right where he loved to make sure I sat for each and every single 'lesson.' I collided with the wall, my shoulder making contact at a weird angle that made a sharp pain shoot up and into my neck. I didn't do anything but slump to the ground and track my eyes back to my mom, desperate to see her move. When she did, I clung to it like a lifeline.*

*"When people don't hear you, you make them listen, son," he said. His face was so close to mine I couldn't see him properly. "This is what it is to be a man."*

"Ash is fine," Ash said, leaning across the table to shake his hand too, snapping me from the clutches of that memory. Ash flicked his eyes to me, a crinkle of concern marring the spot between his brows like he could also see the weight of it all still pressed against my ribs. See the oily residue of the things my father had left me with linger like a shadow in the corner of the bar.

"Pleasure's mine, Ash. Though I'm pretty sure Cali told me your name was Aleron."

Ash closed his eyes and chuckled softly, the kind of laugh that came with being in on a joke no one else understood.

"I'm not even going to ask about that," Dallas said, crossing his arms. A broad, unrestrained grin plastered across his face.

"Would you like to sit?" I made a move to slide over in the booth.

"Oh, no. Isla's expectin' me back soon. Just out grabbin' a few things she needed for some cookin'."

"I've heard a lot of good things about your wife's cooking, sir." Ash piped up.

"That doesn't surprise me." Dallas nodded, clearly full of pride.

"No one's ever made a lasagna like Isla," I said, patting my stomach.

"Not even Cali?" Dallas quirked a knowing brow.

I answered without thinking. "Sir, I love your daughter, but she can't cook."

Ash looked horrified, his face screaming, *This is part of your plan? Your plan really fucking sucks.* But Dallas just threw his head back, laughing so hard he had to lean on the table.

"Oh, I know you love her, but she'll have your balls for that one."

"Don't worry about his balls, sir. They're already toa—*ow!*" Ash whipped his head toward me, offended like I'd committed a mortal sin.

"Anyway," I said, glaring at him, "I'll tell Cali you said hi. I, uh…" I reached up and scratched the back of my neck. "Are we still having dinner on Monday?"

Dallas placed a hand on my shoulder. "Every Thursday, son." His face softened. "We're real glad to have you at our table again, especially after all you've done. I hope you know it." He squeezed my shoulder, and it was like the rage ceased to exist entirely.

"It's the least I could do." I cleared my throat, avoiding Ashton's eyes and the way I could feel them boring into me.

"Plus, since gettin' better, there's no stoppin' that woman from cookin' up a storm. Aleron, you're more than welcome." Dallas tipped his hat our way before proceeding to also say goodbye to everyone in the entire bar, stopping only to hug Mags who was sitting at a table near the door.

Before I could look away, she caught my eye and gave me a wink.

There were moments like this. With Dallas and Mags—a woman who really didn't know me—where I thought if there was something inherently wrong with me, they'd see it. That Cali would've seen it and run.

She did run, though. I'd given her a reason. I wasn't debating that. But she'd still run. The thing was, I always knew I'd chase her, and it made me wonder if that rotten part of me had more control than I thought.

A better man would have let her heal. Would have let her be.

I was not a better man.

Ash kicked me under the table. "You're staring."

"This is so fucked," I muttered, dragging a hand down my face.

"What did he mean?"

"What?"

"Fane—"

"If I knew you'd be this unhelpful, I would have left you at home."

Ash sighed but let it go, taking a long drink.

"You're just going to keep being a dick and trusting it'll work?"

"Yep."

"Trusting who?" The voice was low and smooth. Declan stood at the edge of our table, his eyes already much too sharp like he was dissecting us where we sat.

"Oh, that's funny," Ash said, his tone shifting to something darker. Harder. "Because you're not in this conversation."

"What can I do for you, Declan?" I asked, keeping my tone neutral.

"Just overheard. Thought I could help."

"No thanks. We're leaving." Ash dismissed him without looking, but I was watching.

Declan's expression flickered, The tic in his jaw, the way his eye twitched just once, before his gaze swung back to me. His smile spread slowly, wrong in every way. "Back to that girl of yours, huh?"

The air around us shifted. His words hung heavy, but it wasn't just what he said—it was the way he looked at me. Like he was peeling me apart, stripping me down. I'd felt that kind of scrutiny before, but from Declan the intensity of it was new. At least, the intensity of it directed right at me was new. I couldn't exactly place why it felt so familiar.

"Careful," I said, my voice level and controlled despite every muscle in my body being wound tight. The instincts I'd spent years suppressing clawed at the surface, whispering how easily I could wipe that smile off his face.

Since arriving in Darling, Declan had made it abundantly clear exactly *what* he was. I hadn't given him more than a second thought before, but now he was intentionally placing himself right in my way.

I wasn't stupid, there was no possibility that it was anything but intentional.

I *knew* men like Declan, someone who thrived on provocation, who saw every reaction as a victory. The kind of man who would burn the chessboard just to win the fucking game.

He leaned in slightly, his gaze flicking briefly to Ash before landing back on me. His smile didn't reach his eyes, and whatever calming presence Dallas had instilled before he left corroded away. I didn't succumb to violence, but where Cali was concerned, there was a part of me that I knew wouldn't mind knowing what it felt like to have his blood coat my hands.

Then again, that wasn't overly appealing to me either. Maybe something different. A way to render him a prisoner in his own body. A quieter sort of violence.

"I'm just saying, some things are better left in the past. But the past has a way of catching up, doesn't it?" he said.

My hands flexed against the table, fingers curling into fists beneath it. For years, I'd suppressed this part of me—the part that craved to break something to stop it from breaking me first. Violence had always been a temptation. I'd slipped just once when I was seventeen, and since that moment I'd built my life around walking away from it. But where Cali was concerned? There was no line I wouldn't cross.

"I wouldn't know," I said. But I could feel the shift under my skin, and I wondered if he could see it. If he'd been taking these jabs at me just to prove to himself that there was something wrong inside of me.

It had terrified me that there was, but when I felt it stir now, thinking of Cali, I couldn't find it in myself to care that there was a part of me that would burn the whole fucking world down to keep her whole. Healthy. Safe.

"Good night, Declan," I said, keeping my voice neutral, though my jaw ached from how hard I was clenching it.

"Sweet dreams, boss," he replied, his tone light, but the words felt like a threat.

The fascination he had with calling me boss made Ash talk about how he was pretty sure Declan had some workplace romance kink. I definitely hit him in the balls for that one.

"You good?" Ash asked.

I just nodded. "Watch yourself around him." I frowned at the door he left out of.

I didn't have to be looking at my best friend to hear the eye roll in his words. "Yes, Mom."

"And thanks for tonight."

"Yep." He nodded at me once before walking out in the same direction that Declan did. I had to bite my tongue to make sure that Ash wouldn't go looking for trouble.

I drove home, replaying every moment between Cali and me since I'd gotten to town. It sure as shit hadn't gone to plan, but it was either the path I was on now or being shut out completely.

And she'd do it too. She'd ice me out.

There was this hardness to her that hadn't existed before. Something that developed in a person when they had only themselves to rely on. I knew it because I'd been fucking covered in it when I'd met her. This lack of trust in the world, in people. It was something I'd been intimately familiar with.

When I met her, she still believed in softness, in patience, in the idea that broken things could be fixed. Now, she moved through life like someone who knew the world would never meet her halfway.

She was soft with me then. Patient.

If Cali was angry, she could be angry. If she wanted to fight with me, I'd fight with her.

Those words were on repeat in my head when I got home. When I toed off my boots and left them by the door and stepped over Jerry to find Cali asleep on my side of the bed.

The sheets were rumpled, and I could tell where she'd started. My pillow was clutched tight in one fist, her face half buried in it.

I managed to slip into bed on her side without making her stir one bit. When I woke up hours later, when it was still dark and quiet, it was to her head on my chest and her heart beating right against mine.

Still in sync.

# 18

## Calista

**Before**

Fane told me to meet him in front of an apartment building that was about a fifteen-minute walk from the on-campus dorm I still shared with Jelly.

I couldn't believe it myself that I had finished my second year of studying and still had the wherewithal to share a room with her.

Since the first time I asked her to keep her clothesless shenanigans to an all-time quiet, I'd found a random naked stranger in my bed exactly three times and had also once been woken up by what had to be the most hard-core sex I ever had the displeasure of involuntarily witnessing.

I mean that I woke up in the middle of the night because they *fell on top of me*.

That was three days ago.

I called Fane to come and get me, and I'd been staying with him and Ash ever since. I *refused* to go home, which sucked because Fane didn't live anywhere near campus.

**Me: Hey, I'm here.**
**Fane: Floor 3, Apartment 26.**

I could feel the confused scrunch of my brows settle into a semi-permanent state from the moment I entered the building till the moment the elevator doors opened.

This building was nice. The part of Artington we were in was definitely classified as the nice part. It made sense, considering the University of Artinginton was just up the street, but we were nowhere near Fane's, and we didn't know anyone who lived here.

We'd been together for just over a year, so all our friends were pretty much the same. Unless he'd branched out unknowingly, I was pretty sure we had no friends in this building.

The door to Apartment 26 was wide open, and there was Fane, standing in the middle of an open-plan apartment. The floorboards were ashen-color wood with white walls and modern light fixtures. The kitchen drew my focus straight away with its midnight-blue cabinets and marble countertops.

It was *huge,* and it made me think of Fane. He loved to cook. More specifically, he loved to cook for *me,* and boy did I love to let him.

There was one long hallway that disappeared off the living space that had huge, half-mooned windows that let in all the sunlight of the day. The space immediately felt warm and homey even as it sat empty.

"Are we breaking and entering?" I said, after taking a minute to appreciate the way this man looked in a pair of black fitted jeans. I'd never really been one to keep my compliments to myself. "Your ass looks really good in those jeans too."

"Funny," Fane said, turning to face me. "I was told that exact same thing this morning."

"By who?"

"My girlfriend."

"You have a *girlfriend?*"

"Mmm," he hummed, walked up to me, and let his hands wander from my ribs down my back, letting them rest just above the curve of my ass. "I do."

"Well, she sounds great." I placed a hand on each of his cheeks and gave them a little smoosh.

"She is." He nodded, his words coming out wonky.

"A real giver."

Fane's smile couldn't be contained by the light hold I had on his cheeks. I'd come to realize that there were fewer things in life that gave me this feeling of intense, overwhelming gratitude as being someone who got to see the way he smiled. Second only to getting to hear him laugh.

He didn't give them out freely, and usually the ones he did give out were restrained. Kind but subdued.

Not with me. I had his all-in smiles. When Fane smiled at me, he did it with his soul, and my God, he was beautiful.

"She certainly gave this morning." He gave me a quick wink and a kiss to the corner of my mouth before he straightened up and stepped back.

My face was immediately flaming red because now I was thinking about this morning. Him, naked and warm and solid. The way his stomach muscles contracted with every rapid breath, his hands white-knuckled as they gripped the iron frame of his bed, the sounds that poured out of his mouth as I eased him into mine.

Great. Now, I was actively having a hot flash, which just made him grin even wider because, damn him, he *knew* where my mind had gone. If the look on his face said anything, he was pretty happy with himself about it.

"So." I cleared my throat and rolled my eyes at him. "If you've already robbed this apartment, I don't know what else I could help you with."

"The next part is where you come in." He trailed behind me, keeping just enough distance between us.

"And what's that?"

"Getting all our stuff in here."

That stopped me in my tracks.

"But this isn't your apartment."

Fane looked at me with equal parts excitement and vulnerability. "No, it's not."

"Okay." I nodded, not at all following him, but from the tone of his voice, my stomach had begun doing flips.

"However," he went on, and I just stood there, heart lodged in my esophagus, waiting for whatever he was about to say. He cleared his throat, keeping his eyes on mine. "It is *our* apartment."

There was the right amount of blood in every part of my body until he said those words, and then suddenly there wasn't. It was rushing around in a panic, trying to figure out where to go.

Fane's face went from unsure to worried in a split second, and then he was there, arms wrapped around me. Always keeping me steady.

"Baby," he murmured, ducking down to get me to look at him. "Baby, look at me."

I shook my head, too busy trying to look around him.

"I—" I had no words. I had nothing to say. What *was* there to say when you were in the midst of living out something you had actively wished for your entire life?

"You don't like it," he said like it was a fact. A reprimand he was giving himself.

"Fane." I shook my head again and tried to step away from him so that I could see him without craning my neck.

"I'm going to kick Ash's ass. I asked him if this was too soon. He said it was too *late*. What does that even mean?" Fane dropped his arms from where they were wound around me and turned away from me, running a hand through his long, shoulder-length hair. He usually kept it up, but today he'd left it down, and it was doing incredibly sinister things to me.

*"Fane!"* I wasn't the sort of person who raised their voice, but every now and then when he got in his own head, it was like he couldn't hear me and it was all I could do to snap him out of it.

The look he gave me was heartbreaking. It was every ounce of the vulnerability I saw from before but without any of the shy hopefulness that had accompanied it.

"Fane," I croaked out, knowing it was only a second before my eyes were too misty to see him properly. "I *love* it."

"Yeah?"

He was so damn oblivious sometimes.

"Are you kidding me?" I laughed, swiping at my eyes, watching as another of those rare and beautiful soul smiles split across his face again. "You're telling me I get to live with the love of my life for the *rest* of my life?" I spluttered.

"Are you sure it's not because you just don't like living with Jelly?"

"That's definitely why. I'll never recover from seeing Bernard Evans from that angle."

"You said his leg was *hoisted*?"

I nodded rapidly, my tears starting to fall, "Hoisted on my headboard."

He tipped his head back, filling what had just become our first home with one of my favorite sounds in the world—his laughter. Like a tether to my soul, that sound tugged me right toward him until I was wrapping my arms around him and tucking my head under his chin. The perfect fit.

I hiccuped into his jacket, unabashedly wiping my nose on him before meeting his gaze. "You're just making all my dreams come true without even trying."

His smile melted into something small and tender, like he didn't believe my words but was certainly trying to. "I'm actually trying very hard."

"You're doing a super job," I said, stretching on the tips of my toes, my mouth hovering just an inch from his.

"Thank you."

He closed the distance between us, molding his mouth against mine. My body sagged at the relief of it, a groan of satisfaction poured out of me at the same time as one rumbled from deep in his chest.

That was all it took—just that one moment—and I needed him.

With one arm around me, Fane picked me up, still pressing me firmly against him and brought his mouth back to mine. I had no idea how he did it, but he managed to carry me across the apartment, close the door, *and* leave me breathless with the sort of searing kiss that no one in their right mind could ever forget.

Fane kissed me as if it were the last time, and wanted to regret nothing.

The brush of his stubble, the swipe of his tongue, the nip of his teeth on my lower lip. It was an overwhelming amount of sensations for one person to feel all on their own.

"Calista," Fane rasped, his eyes rolling at the scrape of my nails against his scalp. Sinking my fingers into his hair had become an obsession of mine from the first moment I'd done it. "I need you now," he ground out, his mouth claiming mine in another all-consuming kiss. One that made me acutely aware of how wet I was, how desperate I was to feel him again, even though I'd had him inside me just hours before.

He walked us over to the kitchen counter and the moment he set me down, my hands dropped straight to his jeans. "I really love these, but they need to come off. Now."

The small smile of satisfaction on Fane's face sent another pulse of desire through me that made me almost positive I could have come without him even touching me. I was pushed even closer to the edge when he shrugged off his jacket and reached back to pull off his shirt with one hand.

"Jesus Christ," I breathed, my hands shaking. The button on his jeans finally gave, and I wasted exactly zero seconds reaching into his black briefs.

Everything about Fane was the perfect mixture of hard and soft. That was also the case for his cock. I watched him, enraptured, when I wrapped my hand around his steely length, so thick that my fingers didn't touch, and marveled at being the person who got to see him come undone.

I moved my hand in slow, sure strokes, captivated by the way his breathing hitched. The way his fingers flexed from where they were splayed along my rib cage over my dress. A small gasp floated out of my parted lips, and Fane's violet eyes snapped open, focusing right on me. They took stock of my hooded eyes, my shallow breathing, the way my throat worked on an impossible swallow.

"Tell me, Rose," he rasped, letting his eyes fall from my face down to my tits, which were full and heavy. My nipples pebbled and were far too sensitive to be scraping against the fabric of my dress. "You're desperate to feel me fill that tight little cunt of yours, aren't you?"

I nodded my head probably a little too enthusiastically.

"I want your words, baby. I want to hear you say it."

"Yes," I breathed. "I am."

"If I pull up your dress, will I find your pussy bare, Calista?"

"Y-yes," I stuttered, trying to keep my focus on his eyes, to keep from being transfixed at the way my hand still glided up and down his cock.

Fane's eyes dragged down my body again, and I felt the path of his gaze as if it were the pads of his fingers. The flat expanse of his tongue. A shiver racked through me.

"Fane." A plea, a prayer, a question all in one.

I finally dropped my eyes, enthralled with the way my hand looked wrapped around him. Entirely enamored by the way his stomach muscles were shifting. Clenching and unclenching, like the restraint he was showing didn't come as easily as he was putting on. Like I was driving him as insane as he was driving me.

Fane reached for the hem of my dress where it settled just above my knees. His eyes locked at the juncture of my thighs as he slowly, *torturously,* lifted up the material inch by inch until I was exposed to him fully.

The sound that escaped him was a mixture of pain and pleasure. I was too focused on the way he looked to be concerned about anything else. The flush in his cheeks, the swipe of his tongue along his bottom lip.

The trail of his fingers along my inner thigh sent a jolt through me, making my pussy clench around nothing at all, making my legs spread wider on reflex.

Fane's eyes darted to my face. "Dirty girl," he breathed before sinking two fingers deep into me.

The intrusion had been so unexpected I released my hold on his cock, my hands fumbling for the edge of the counter with a white-knuckled grip. A yelp of surprise echoed around the empty apartment, ringing in my ears while he pumped two long fingers in and out of me, using the same torturous pace I'd been using on him.

The moment his thumb brushed over my swollen clit I was already toppling over the edge. Wave after wave of pleasure pulsed through me, Fane's fingers never changing their steady pace, drawing out my orgasm until it was too much. Until my hand wrapped around his wrist to stop him.

"Fane." I was pretty sure I slurred his name. *"Please."*

"Please, what?" Through the haze of my fading release, I could see how clear his eyes looked. The violet in them looked electric. Enraptured. He looked spellbound.

"Fuck me." I wasn't remotely self-conscious of the neediness of my own voice. The strength of it. The moment Fane Mackenzie touched me, I didn't even know myself. Someone strong-willed, steady in her own right. The only thing I *did* know was that if he didn't keep touching me, if I didn't feel him the way I needed to, then I would absolutely die.

The smile he gave me was knowing because he was all too aware of what he did to me, and he loved it.

I watched him wrap his large hand around his cock, pumping it twice before squeezing the base. "Are you going to watch, Rose?" he asked at the very same moment he ran the head of his cock along the seam of my pussy.

He stopped abruptly and my eyes shot open. "Lift your arms up, baby," he said, his voice gentle and warm. It had surprised me at first the way he could be soft and rough with me, all at once.

I lifted my arms, and Fane lifted my dress up and over my head so that I was completely naked before him. Lowering his head, he took one peaked nipple between his teeth, biting with just enough pressure to make me groan before tracing the tip of his tongue up the valley of my breasts all the way back to my mouth. He gripped my throat with his free hand, kissing me brutally, all tongue and teeth.

"Perfect," he said against my lips before pulling back and notching the head of his cock at my entrance.

"Watch, Calista," he said between gritted teeth, pushing into me slowly. And because I couldn't resist him, I looked down.

"Oh, *fuck*," I choked out. It didn't matter how many times I'd done exactly this, it never got *less* hot.

"Do you see how fucking perfect you are for me?" he rasped. I chanced a quick look at his face, but he was solely focused on the way he was pushing into me. "Fucking *Christ*."

"F-Fane." I could have thought his name or said it out loud, I really had no idea.

"You're so beautiful," he murmured, mesmerized. "Mine. How the fuck are you *mine?*"

Fane pushed right into the hilt, pausing the way he always did while I adjusted to the size of him. I watched him lift one hand from my thigh, dragging it up my stomach and across my heaving chest and up to my throat until the two fingers he'd had inside me were pushing at the seam of my mouth.

"Open your mouth, baby."

And I did. Fane pushed his fingers flat against my tongue, so far back I gagged. The sound pulled at the corner of his mouth a little, and with a wicked glint in his eyes, he started to move.

There was no slow and soft. Only his digits in my mouth kept me steady while I watched him push into me again and again. The slapping of his body meeting mine filled the apartment around us in a cacophony of overlapping noises that made me really hope that the walls between us and our new neighbors were thick enough for them not to have this moment be their introduction to us.

Fane pulled his fingers from my mouth while his hand left a trail of my own saliva down my neck to where he pushed softly on my chest, urging me to lie back on the counter.

There was nothing but the sound of us coming together. Over and over, mixed with the sound of my arousal.

"You're so fucking wet for me, Rose," Fane said, his hand dragging from the center of my chest down, putting pressure just below my belly button. "So perfectly tight."

I whimpered his name, my eyes starting to roll at the budding pressure of another orgasm that pulsed at the bottom of my spine. "Fane, I—"

"I know, baby." His voice was rough, his grip on my hip tightened, and the pressure on my stomach increased. "I want to feel you come, Calista. I want to feel the way you squeeze my cock. Let me feel it. *Please.*" The hand on my stomach moved to my clit, where he rubbed hard, fast circles.

My back arched off the kitchen counter, and stars took over my vision. I might have even passed out.

It was small, delicate kisses up my stomach and a teasing lick over my nipple that settled me back into my body. My heart was still thrumming, and for all the pleasure he'd just injected into my body, one look at Fane had me ready to jump his bones again.

He was so classically handsome with this rugged edge. He would look exquisite in a suit in a boardroom or on the back of a horse in a pair of faded blue jeans and a cowboy hat.

"We're going to need to sanitize this counter," I murmured, reveling in the way it felt to have him laugh into the skin of my neck.

He pulled back and stunned me stupid with the look on his face, like even though I told him he was actively making my dreams come true, I *was* his dream come true.

That's how Fane looked at me.

"Welcome home, baby," he murmured.

I blinked rapidly, trying to swallow back the emotion clogging in my throat. Of being able to sit in the knowledge that this was the first home of many we might have, and I would get to keep Fane Mackenzie for the rest of my life.

# 19

# Fane

**After**

"I don't understand your obsession with that stupid town." A voice that sounded a lot like Cali's sister crackled under the door, waking me up.

"You don't need to understand it." There was a lack of bite in Cali's voice that told me everything I needed to know about how many versions of this conversation there had been before this particular rendition.

"I don't know why you called me about it then."

"I called you." Cali released a grunting noise that made me rub my eyes in an effort to really wake up and focus on what the fuck was happening. "Because you're my sister, and I thought maybe I could...talk to you."

"You talk to me all the time, Calista."

"We hardly talk anymore. But you are right, when we do, *I* talk to *you*." Another grunt. "And you usually say nothing at all and then hang up because something comes up."

It was silent for a beat. "I just don't understand your fixation with Darling."

"It's our home, Abbey." There was no hiding the hurt in Cali's voice that time, and I had the sudden urge to scream at her sister. The entire interaction didn't make any sense to me. Cali had always been close with her sister. More than close. They were practically inseparable.

"No, it's not. It's where we grew up, but it's not my home. What I have here, in Artington—this is my home. The job I have here, my friends, my hobbies, my apartment. I have more than just Darling." Abbey sounded defensive, like she was trying to prove a point from a completely different argument.

I realized I was doing my best not to breathe after Abbey's voice cut off. Realized my chest was aching for an entirely different reason than lack of air when Cali did.

"Well," she said, voice breaking. "*All* I have is Darling."

"Look, I've got to go. I'll call you later, okay?" Abbey didn't even wait for Cali to reply before the line cut out, and the entire house plummeted into silence.

I swung my legs off the bed and reached for my pants before walking out of Cali's bedroom to find her…well, she was standing on the kitchen counter.

It probably wasn't the best idea to silently walk up behind her, but I did it anyway.

"What are you doing?" My voice was still thick with sleep.

Any trace amounts of wanting to go back to bed were immediately eradicated from my system at the ear-piercing scream Cali vaulted into the air a second before she lost her footing and went flying backward.

I caught her with an arm around her back and under her legs. Still completely clueless as to why she was standing on the counter of her kitchen to begin with.

"God, you're *everywhere*." She looked as pissed off as she sounded.

"You were standing on the counter." I met her pissed-off expression with my confused one.

"I…that's none of your business. Put me down." She started to wiggle in my hold. It just made me hold her tighter.

"Not until you tell me why."

"Fane," she huffed, swatting at flyaway strands of her unbound hair that had fallen across her face.

"Are you really so stubborn you can't answer a single damn question?"

Well, that sure as fuck was not the right thing to say.

I could practically *hear* Ashton whispering in my ear that my balls were so far past being toast I should invest in a new pair altogether.

"I can't reach the cupboards." She ground the words out like they had personally offended her. "Now, *put me down.*"

Her hand was clenched into a fist, and the look on her face was one she'd given me more times than I could count since I'd gotten to town. It was a look that said she wanted to absolutely punch me in the face.

That was the first time I noticed that her cabinets were all the way to the fucking ceiling and half the size of regular cabinets. I mean, I'd been in this kitchen, actively fucking using it, and it just…didn't register.

I frowned at them. "What's wrong with your cabinets?"

She whirled on me. "There's nothing wrong with my cabinets, *Fane.*" She said my name like it was an insult. I was glad she'd turned her head a fraction to gesture at them because I knew I couldn't hide the way the corner of my mouth twitched that time.

This feistiness was definitely new, but fuck me if I didn't like it.

"Why are they so high?"

"You really have to stick your nose into everything. The fact that you're… you're…" Her hands started to flail. "*Defecating* all over my town isn't enough?"

My body literally *seized* at the effort of holding in my laugh.

"Are you fucking *laughing* at me right now?"

"No—"

"If you call me ma'am, it will be the last thing you say with teeth that you grew yourself."

"Noted." I cleared my throat and composed my face. "Cali, why are your cabinets to the ceiling?"

"I installed them myself." She lifted her chin and squared her shoulders, daring me to say anything other than that she did a great job.

"They've been installed correctly. It's just they're—"

"They're what?" She was trying to hold on to the fury for dear life. I could see it. But I could also see the faint purple marks under her eyes that were new, right along with this need to kick me in the balls almost every second of every day. It was that, along with the conversation I heard between her and her sister, that made me shut my mouth.

I'd find another way to get under her skin, if only to find the *real* version of the woman in front of me. Changed or not, I was determined to see her without any walls. Only then would we be able to lay all our cards on the table. To finally have the argument that was two years in the making.

"They're straight. You did good."

"I—" Cali cut herself off. "What?"

"They look level." I gestured to the cabinets that, now that I noticed, were *comically* high. "Did you lift them yourself while fitting them to the wall?"

From the corner of my eye, I watched her cross her arms and jut her hip out. "Yes."

Well, that explained the size choice. Anything else would have been too heavy for her to lift on her own.

"Nice." I nodded, turning back toward the bathroom.

"*Nice?* What do you mean, *nice?*"

"It's a compliment, Calista. Take it." I closed the door between us, cutting off anything she was going to say. I could also hear Ash in that moment saying, "*Oh, yeah, way to not be a dick, you asshole.*"

The hot pelting water on my back didn't do a whole lot to ease any of the tension I felt. It was twisted the way my body reacted to anything she did. Her smell, her sounds, even her fucking insults sent the blood rushing directly out of my head and into my cock.

I wrapped my hand around the base, squeezing tight, my eyes falling closed at the single pump I gave myself before releasing my hold.

I'd been semi-hard from the moment I laid my eyes on her. Except for that one morning when I hadn't been prepared to wake up to the feel of her warm and soft and fucking *on* me, I hadn't touched myself.

Fuck me, did I want to, but not like this.

That interaction had set the tone for the rest of the weekend.

After that Cali had disappeared for most of the day. It could have been her plan all along, given the café was closed, but I was sure it had something to do with what happened the day before. With her needing space.

I decided it was a good opportunity to introduce myself to her neighbors. They already knew who I was, which I should've guessed. Both the house to the right of Cali's and the one across the street greeted me with that small-town distrust of city construction companies intending to ruin their town. So, they were polite as fuck if not a little standoffish.

I recognized one woman who'd been in the town meeting that I'd followed Cali to. Even though she only dared to speak to me through a small crack in the door, the more I answered her questions, the wider that gap got.

What business did I have coming around and sticking my nose where it didn't belong? The same sentiment that Cali had but delivered with a lot fewer expletives and middle fingers.

I told them the truth.

I definitely shouldn't have done that knowing I hadn't even mentioned it to Cali, but she wouldn't believe me even if I did. Maybe a little more selfishly, what reason would I have to stay if she knew?

By the end of my conversations with them, which had taken well over two hours a piece, I was on great terms with both households.

When Cali had finally arrived home, I'd just finished speaking with Mrs. Antinello, who I'd learned was her landlord. The older woman had somehow roped me into vacuuming her driveway.

*Vacuuming her driveway.*

I mostly just nodded my head because I was too shocked at her request.

"See, I knew not all bad boys were idiots," she said, patting my cheek and bustling inside with her cane to retrieve her vacuum.

The thing was ancient, with a cord so small I had to use four different extension cords I'd hunted for around Cali's house just to get it to reach outside. I was halfway through vacuuming when Cali marched up to me and poked me so aggressively in my side that I pretty much screamed.

"What the fuck!"

"You're *vacuuming her driveway?*" She looked incredulous. Her aggressively whispered reprimand doing nothing to dampen how upset she clearly was.

"I mean, yes? She asked me to." Then the other thing she said popped into my head. "She also called me a bad boy."

"And you said *yes?*" Her arms flew out to either side.

Oh. *Oh.* "She asked you to do this, didn't she?" I was fucking beaming now. "And you said no."

"*Of course I said no!*" Cali practically screamed without any sounds, and I was in fucking heaven.

"And that's why she hates you?" I guessed.

If looks could kill, I'd be dead as fuck right now. "You...*you...*"

"Me...*me?*" I was digging my own grave for sure, but she'd been gone all day, and I missed her. What better way to let her know than driving her to the very brink of sanity?

"You make me *sick.*" She did not whisper that time. She just turned on her heels and marched right back to her house, but not before grabbing a handful of leaves from the garden and sprinkling them across Mrs. Antinello's driveway and flipping me off.

I was still so in love with this woman, it was fucking criminal.

Cali had descended into mostly ignoring me again for the week that followed. With the exception of her telling me to fuck off when she turned around and jumped out of her skin after finding me shadowing her for work purposes (obviously).

Today was the first time I was breaking that habit.

I had to make it to the office next door for a few things. Now that all the evaluations of the central part of town were down, I'd been slowly getting reports from all the different groups on what they found, what looked promising, and what could pose an issue.

There was really nothing negative about what came back. Darling was just big enough that the small-town economy here was actually thriving. There was enough opportunity that people didn't go looking elsewhere to find it, and if I'd been here doing the job my father thought I was doing, there would be no questioning whether or not we'd move forward with this project.

If I showed this to the mayor, the man would probably shit his pants with excitement.

I picked up my phone to call Ash.

"Big man."

"Just finishing up these review reports."

"How's it looking?"

"I need everyone to revisit their evaluations," I murmured, rereading one of the decks that were handed in for the fifth time. "I need the guys to highlight, for every area in every zone, which parts are privately owned and which are owned by the town—not just the overarching percentages." I leaned back, rubbing my eyes. "I also need a detailed outline of upkeep responsibilities for each area, including who's actually maintaining them. The budget records show no funds allocated for the maintenance of these zones, even though the majority are marked as town-owned."

"You think the cheese ball is playing dirty?"

Looks like Cali's little performance had reached everybody's ears. "I do. I'm guessing these evaluations wouldn't hold up long term if that's the case."

"You're so smart, pookie bear," Ash cooed through the phone, and I heard the laughter of the guys on the other end.

As soon as I ended the call, I locked up the office and walked back into Sunshine, that's where I found Declan planted at the counter, looking like he owned the place. His hands were pressed flat, his shoulders rolled forward just enough to make it clear he wasn't there for a casual chat.

Cali's gaze flicked to mine. For a fleeting second—so brief I might've imagined it—I thought I saw relief in her eyes.

"Fane," she breathed, my name soft but heavy. Like she'd been holding her breath.

"All good, baby?" I asked, but my focus was on Declan. On the way he hung his head just slightly, like I'd interrupted something important. Like I wasn't supposed to be here.

Cali didn't say anything, just gave me a short nod and slid a coffee across the counter toward him before stepping back.

"You're never far, are you, boss?" Declan's tone was light, but the way he said it—full of dark amusement—set my teeth on edge.

"Don't you have a job to be doing?" I shot back, keeping my voice calm, even. My hands hung casually at my sides, all while I pictured the different things I could slip into his morning coffee that would make his brain melt out his nose.

"Sure do." His smile widened, slow and deliberate, like he wanted to see if I'd bite.

"Then go do it."

Declan didn't move right away, didn't break eye contact. He wasn't done yet—not really. His gaze slid back to Cali, lingering, calculating in a way that made something inside me twist.

I fucking *knew* that look.

I'd seen it in my father's eyes right before he lashed out. I'd seen the aftermath of it in the emptiness of my mother's gaze after he was done. When she thought no one was watching, but I was still there in that fucking corner of that fucking room.

It was getting louder—the part of me that whispered all the ways I could make the world a better place by removing people in it like *that*. Clawing at the surface, demanding I do something. Because I knew what happened when no one stepped in. I'd fucking *lived* it.

He would die, slowly, *painfully,* before he laid a hand on Cali.

Declan's smirk deepened, like he knew he'd gotten under my skin. Like he could sense exactly what I was holding back. It was as if he was somehow privy to the darkest parts of my soul and reveled in making me relive everything that it housed.

I made to follow him, driven by the sharp edge of memory and instinct, every muscle coiled tight. I was so honed in on him that I hadn't even noticed Mags halfway in the café, her arm wrapped protectively around Gus, until I turned.

"Gus!" Cali exclaimed. "Are you okay? You weren't here this morning."

"Oh, I'm fine." The older man's cheeks were a bright red.

"You're not fine." Mags frowned at him. "Someone broke into his shop."

"What?" Cali's face fell, and she walked around the counter. "I'm so sorry, Gus." She wrapped herself around the older man, his round belly between them stopping her from getting any closer.

"Gus owns the mechanics shop a couple streets back," Mags explained, a grim look on her face.

"I promise I'm not hitting on you." Cali gave him a wink, and Gus rolled his eyes.

"Lorna hasn't let me hear the end of that one," he huffed.

Cali's laugh was light and happy, and it made me realize that it was the second time since I'd been here that I heard a genuine laugh from her, and the only time that it hadn't ended in tears.

I fucking hated it. The idea that this woman didn't laugh the way she used to.

"You take a seat, and I'll bring you your coffee."

"And cookies," he mumbled.

"Yes, Gus, and your cookies." Her smile dropped when she turned back and found me standing closer to her than I'd been before.

"You okay?" I asked quietly.

She nodded, a small crease between her brows. Her eyes darted around my face like even though I'd been right in front of her, she hadn't really seen me until right then. "Yeah."

I searched her face for a second longer before I nodded my head and stepped to the side, letting her by. I didn't believe her, and everything in me wanted to demand she tell me what Declan had done to make her look at me, of all people, with relief.

"Any idea who might have done something like that?" Mags was rubbing Gus's back in gentle circles.

"Nope." He shook his head, face jiggling at the jerkiness of his actions. "Side door lock was snapped clean off, and the place was a mess."

"Do you know what they took?" I asked before I thought better of it.

"No, sir." Gus frowned. "Won't be able to tell 'till I clean it up. Don't move like I used to, so might take me a while."

"I'll have some of the guys come and help you," I offered, already reaching into my pocket to flick Ash a message.

"Oh, I can't ask you to do that." The red that had slowly been dissipating flooded back into his face.

"You didn't. I'll come by with some guys now to help." My phone dinged with a reply from Ash as soon as the offer was out of my mouth.

"I've got four guys free, plus me makes five." I stood up, and Gus followed suit, gruff and holding tight to the shoulder straps of his overalls.

"Cali, could—" Cali handed Gus a to-go cup, cutting him off mid-sentence.

"Got you covered," she said, handing him a bag full to bursting with cookies. "But don't tell Lorna about the extra cookies. She already gives me grief for the second one I let you have."

Gus didn't say anything more to her, just delivered another gruff nod, his face so red I feared for the man's health.

"After you." I indicated to the door, nodding at Mags as I passed by her.

"Fane," Cali called after me, stopping me with my hand on the door. By the time I'd turned around, she was standing there, a to-go cup in one hand and a paper bag in the other. She held them both out to me, her face completely blank.

I took them, an eyebrow raised in silent question. She rolled her eyes, and my chest fucking squeezed at the faint twitch of her lips. Not a laugh or a smile, but it was something. A crack in her armor.

"It's coffee," she said. "I promise."

"No cinnamon?"

"Scout's honor." She held up two fingers in a salute.

I nodded at her and started to turn, but she spoke again. "And thank you. For helping Gus."

"No problem." I gave her another nod and one more to Mags before I walked out, finding Gus waiting on the sidewalk, half the bag of cookies already gone, and the feel of Cali's eyes on my back the entire time I walked away.

# 20

# Calista

**After**

I had run like it was my religion every single day except Sundays from the moment I moved back to this town, and today marked the eleventh day of me breaking that streak.

It had been the perfect way to balance out what I was sure was the worst diet known to humankind. I was incredible at putting together Kraft Mac and Cheese and ensuring my ramen noodles were cooked perfectly. It took a long time to convince myself that it was better than getting takeout all the time, but if I were honest, I'd probably get takeout if I could afford it.

I could not afford it.

It wasn't like I was rationing toilet paper, but there was no extra money laying around.

After about a week of Fane living in my house, he'd clearly gotten fed up with the less than impressive stocking standard of my fridge and had taken over the cooking and grocery shopping like it was his personal mission. I hadn't lifted a finger, let alone exercised, but I was eating better than I had in years.

I figured it was also the least he could do, considering the whole arriving-unannounced-and-being-a-pain-in-my-ass thing.

When my mom got sick, I *may* have told a little white lie that I'd gotten a post-degree scholarship that cleared my student debt. While I'd made it up when I told my dad, I did learn that they were things that actually existed. They just didn't exist for me.

What *did* exist for me, was a fairly hefty personal debt that I'd taken out to pay back my parents every cent they'd poured into my unfinished business degree. I'd been funneling as much money as possible into paying that back.

My parents had spent their whole lives saving up for my education with no thought for themselves. It was a no-brainer that the money needed to go toward my mom's treatment, and between that and the money they had from Abbey not going to college, they'd assured me that they had everything handled.

I wasn't sure I believed them, and I wasn't sure they totally believed me, but there was an unspoken agreement not to push one another on it.

I still put whatever I could spare into their bank account every month through a direct deposit. It wasn't enough for them to really even notice, but it was better than feeling like I was doing nothing.

Between all of that constantly swirling around in my brain, there was also the fact that my word of the day over the last four days hadn't been something I could use in a sentence. Two of those words I had to Google, and all in all, the experience felt like it was kicking me while I was already down.

I was on the cusp of being broke and was reminded daily about my limited vocabulary by an app that I still couldn't afford, but continued to voluntarily pay for.

It painted a really sad picture, if I was being honest.

I'd started to close down the cafe and Fane was still nowhere to be found. He'd left this morning with Gus, and apart from a message to say he'd be there the rest of the day, I'd been on my own.

I was used to being on my own. Sure it'd been weird at first, going from a lifetime of having people around me–a group of other humans you could rely on for anything, no matter the place or time–to being completely and totally on your own.

I mean, except for Jerry.

Hence, it shouldn't have felt like *this*, like it was something I wasn't used to. The day moved on like it always had, if not a bit busier with the added clientele. I still saw my dad. Still made him his coffee, handed him his cookies, and promised I wouldn't be late to dinner.

The only thing that was different was the fact that I was exceptionally aware of Fane's absence, and that was just so fucking stupid of me.

The moment my feet hit the pavement, it was bliss. When I could get Jerry off his couch, I brought him with me, and today just happened to be one of those exception-to-the-rule sort of days. Honestly, I was like eighty percent sure that the only reason he was so eager was because he thought Fane was outside.

I didn't try to run for any specific duration of time. There was no real distance I wanted to eat up. I just let myself run. Let my mind be empty for a while.

My arm nearly dislocated when Jerry skidded to a halt, barking with a ferocity I rarely heard. Not his usual, *Don't make me touch wet grass,* grumble, but the deep, guttural growl that screamed, *Come closer, and I'll relieve you of all your favorite parts.*

Running in Darling wasn't like running in the city. I didn't have to have an earbud out. I didn't have to message someone else my route or when I was leaving the apartment and when I got home. I didn't have to constantly be aware of my surroundings.

I'd been so in my own head that it didn't really hit me that I'd run all the way back into town or that I was standing right across the street from the same man who'd come into Sunshine this morning.

Declan.

*"It's all right, you can let me in on the secret." He'd spoken to me like we were friends in on an inside joke. Like he was more than a stranger who'd walked into my café and placed an order.*

*"What are you doing with Fane? I know you're not together anymore, but I've always been a fan of games. I could play along."*

The guy was a fucking creep, and it didn't take much for me to put together that whatever was going on between him and Fane wasn't good.

The moment the door opened and those familiar violet eyes set on me, they swept down my body in a move so completely *known* to me that I wasn't even sure Fane realized he did it. The quick calculation of whether I was in one piece. Then there was the way his brow had dipped ever so slightly, and his jaw clenched.

I could have told him what the guy said, but what if that led him to do something stupid? What if he did something that made him leave town? What if someone else, someone I didn't know well enough to confront and try to change their mind to leave Darling alone, replaced him?

Everything that could have happened rushed through my mind. Despite it all, the thing that scared me the most was the dead look in Declan's eyes and the idea that even though Fane was bigger, there was this niggling in the back of my head that he could get hurt. If I told him and that did happen? It would've been my fault and I didn't want or need that on my conscience.

If there was one thing I'd learned to do over the last two years, it was deal with shit on my own. So I kept my mouth shut, and by the weird as fuck look on the guy's face where he stared right back at me from the other side of the street, I could wager a guess that he took it as a sign we were on the same side.

Same side of what? Who the fuck knows, but whatever sixth sense I had that told me when I was definitely in the wrong place at the wrong time kicked in. I didn't think twice when I turned where I stood and bolted.

I knew Jerry felt it too, the way the street felt colder. How the very air around the guy seemed to want to exist anywhere but near him. Jerry didn't drag behind like he did when I tried to get him to run faster than his usual trot. He didn't pull against his leash.

He just ran.

He pulled ahead of me, forcing me to run faster than I would have been able to on my own.

For one fleeting second, I thought I imagined it. Seeing this stranger I didn't know in literally any capacity except for one single interaction. That my mind had finally teetered beyond the fine line that I had been walking between sane and absolutely unhinged.

It was the wrong thing to do in my situation. Everyone and their mother always said, *Don't look behind you.* I shouldn't have done it, but I chanced a single look.

I'd never known fear like I had in that moment when I turned to find Declan running behind me and gaining. A scream lodged itself in my throat, trying to claw past the deep, gasping breaths I was pushing out.

My legs were burning, and my heart was thrashing. My house was roughly five miles from the center of town, but cutting through parks and people's yards took it down to maybe three. That's all I kept telling myself.

Three miles.

Three miles, and then I was home. Where I could hide behind a locked door and call Fane.

My mind had reached for his name and clutched onto it. Held it like a lifeline.

There was music still blasting in my ears. I hadn't had time to take out my earbuds or pause it, and even though it was loud, I could swear I heard the way his shoes were connecting with the pavement.

Two miles.

My vision started to blur. The terror that was coursing through me was overflowing and pouring out my fucking eyes. Even though a sob managed to make its way out somehow between my gasping breaths and the scream that I barely held back, I didn't stop.

Jerry didn't falter once. His long legs propelled us forward.

One mile.

I waited as long as I could before I turned around again, and there was no time to stop the scream that tore from my throat. I swear my heart stopped beating entirely, just for a second.

Declan was so close to me now that if I faltered for even a second, he would've been able to reach out and grab me.

It felt like this was something from a fucking horror movie, not my life.

For two years I'd gone every day with not so much as an unexpected sneeze, and in less than two weeks my entire life had been turned upside down. I was lying to my *entire* town, and now I was being chased by a psychopath.

I rounded the last corner to my house, so sure that I could feel the tips of his fingers skimming the back of my shirt. The ends of my hair.

I could see my house, and I let myself look one more time. The moment I turned my head to look behind me, I smacked right into something solid. My scream was so visceral I felt the way it ripped at my vocal cords.

In my head, I always imagined I would immediately take a fighting stance.

I would do whatever I saw on TV and fight until I couldn't fight any more. The reality was my eyes clamped so tight I thought they'd never open again, and my hands came up protectively on either side of my head.

My entire body was aching. I'd never run that far for that long at a sprint before. My knees were aching, my head was pounding, and I couldn't breathe.

Someone was gripping my upper arms, and all I could think was that Declan had beat me home. He'd taken a shortcut, and I'd be late to dinner. My mom would be so pissed, my dad would be concerned about her blood pressure, and Fane would come back and find me missing or dead, and Jerry—

Rough, strong hands wrapped around my arms and hauled me up. It was a single second between thinking I was going to die and knowing I'd never been safer in my life the moment Fane pulled me to him, that clean woodsy scent I would know anywhere washing over me.

"Fucking hell, Calista—" He sounded mad and scared and worried all at the same time, which didn't reconcile with the new version of him I knew. Right then I didn't care, not as I gripped his shirt in both my fists and whipped my head around. To warn him that there was...no one there.

There was no one there, and I wondered for one terrifying moment if I'd made the entire thing up. There wasn't a trace of him. Not one.

My house was halfway down the street, which was empty, quiet, and peaceful in the dim light of the early evening.

"He's...he's..." I wanted to stand on my own two legs, but they weren't working.

"He? He who?"

"He's…" My brain was broken. Well, it wasn't connecting to my mouth, but as small tremors started to turn into violent shaking, I was almost certain I was going into shock.

"Fuck," Fane grunted and lifted me up into his arms. I didn't take my eyes off the corner I'd flown around like a bat out of hell until we were in the house and the door was closed behind us.

I was both aware and completely lost in time while Fane worked, acting like he'd done this thousands of times before. My hands were still clamped on his shirt, and when he pulled the covers back on the bed and set me down, he tried to lift himself up to leave, but my hands wouldn't fucking work.

"S-s-so—" My voice cracked.

"Jesus Christ." The look on his face was the same as it had been outside, but there was a wildness to his eyes I didn't think I'd ever seen before.

I knew he was being as gentle as possible trying to remove my hands from his shirt, but there was just no moving them.

"Fine. Keep the shirt." If I hadn't been sure my heart was about to explode and questioning the state of my own sanity, it might have been the sexiest thing I'd ever seen the way Fane reached for the back of his shirt and pulled it over his head. He turned so fast I didn't see any of his decorated golden skin except for his back, where the same tattoos I'd always known stared back at me.

It didn't make any sense, but it reassured me. The reaper, a hand of bone extended out from its heavy cloak. Beckoning.

To most it was probably ominous. You wouldn't voluntarily take that hand unless you had a death wish.

Whenever I looked at it though, I'd always thought that if I did take it, how safe and sheltered I would be in the shadowed folds of his robes. Just before he reached for his bag that still sat in the corner of the room, I finally took a breath that felt like it filled my lungs.

Fane was back in an instant, grabbing pillows and putting them under my legs before heading back into the living room and coming back with an extra blanket that he layered on top of me.

"Jer-Jerry." Panic laced my voice.

"He's fine, baby." He sounded far away, focused on what he was doing. And then he started to take off his shoes…and then his pants.

This man and his obsession with taking off his damn pants.

"N-no. I don't w-want—"

"I'm going to look after you, and you're going to let me." His voice was calm and gentle, but the way his chest was rising and falling betrayed that facade. "I know you don't want me here, but I *am* here. So, please. *Please*, let me. Tomorrow you can remember that you hate me, and I'll remember everything I did to deserve it, but for right now, let me."

I was shivering so much my teeth were vibrating against each other, and I decided to give into him, just this once. As soon as I nodded my head, he spurred into action.

"You're in shock, Calista. I need to calm you down and keep you warm." He spoke the words like he was reading them right from a pamphlet. He shucked his pants all the way off and got into bed beside me, pulling me against him. My hands discarded the shirt I hadn't been able to let go of in favor of the one he had replaced it with. I didn't reprimand myself either when I pressed my cheek over the warm cotton just above his heart and counted every heartbeat. That's when he started to speak.

"I managed to hide my country mix playlist from Ashton until three months ago. The one that Spotify made for you when you were using my account? I listen to it all the time, and I picked him up from the gym and didn't change it fast enough. He bought me a cowboy hat for my birthday last month."

A laugh bubbled out of me, surprising us both. It was shaky, but it was real.

"I got drunk and finally tried asparagus," he murmured, lips pressed to my hair.

"A-a-and?" I stammered, fingers trying to grip him to me tighter.

"Super gross. You were right."

A second bubble of laughter trickled up and out of my throat and I felt Fane chuckle in response. He kept talking. Random, stupid things until, eventually, the tremors in my body began to subside, the adrenaline draining away and leaving behind a bone-deep exhaustion. I didn't want to move. I didn't want to think. All I wanted was to stay here, held in the safety of his arms, with his thumb tracing lazy patterns along my skin.

Fane started to hum. The deep and soothing rumble of his chest made my eyes fall shut the second I heard the start to his favorite song.

His thumb was still moving along the skin of my hip bone. I must've fallen asleep because when I woke up, I was pretty much lying on top of him, and the room was completely dark around us. If I thought I could get away with it, I was sorely mistaken.

He was already looking down at me when I tried to peek up at him through my lashes.

"Hey," he whispered.

"Crap," I mumbled, pushing up and away from him. His hands tightened on me for a second before he let me go. "Sorry."

Fane pushed himself up to sit on the bed, leaned over to turn on the lamp on the bedside table. The warm glow that lit the room made the purple hue of his eyes look like they were housing a hale storm, the weight of his gaze was heavy when he settled it on me.

"We're talking about it, Cali."

"I know this all seems a bit wild, but it was nothing."

"Nothing?" His eyebrows hit his hairline.

"Nothing." I nodded, impressed with how I managed to even look him in the eyes.

"You were running like your life depended on it, slammed right into me, and then went into shock. The way you screamed..." He spoke slowly like he thought just talking about it would send me back into a catatonic state.

"Well, yes. I..." I scratched the back of my head and cleared my throat. "Thought I saw something."

"You're lying to me. You said, 'He.'"

I wanted to tell him.

But every reason why I shouldn't was right there at the forefront of my mind. "I don't remember saying that."

"You're still lying." It wasn't said like an accusation but a fact. Like he knew me so well he could tell, just like that.

The fucked-up thing was I was sure he could. "I'm not."

"You're lying to me because you don't trust me, and that's fine. You don't *need* to trust me to tell me what had you white as a fucking ghost and terrified."

Well, there was no debating that. Fane was many things, but he wasn't an idiot.

The thing was, I wasn't either, and everything that ran through my head this morning still rang true. I was terrified. Of course, I was terrified, I wasn't made of stone. Despite my willingness to 'throw hands' during dinner at my parents house, I was deeply aware that all anyone would need is to land one, mildly offensive hit and I'd be a goner.

But I was even *more* terrified of what would happen to him if he got involved.

In the calmest voice I could manage, I said, "I scared myself. I overreacted."

"Calista—" My name was a growl coming out of his mouth.

"Drop it, Fane. I was…being *dramatic*." Ugh. I wanted to tit-punch myself for that one.

"You're joking." He scoffed, looking so unimpressed I wanted to laugh, as inappropriate as it would have been right then. That's when I noticed the time.

"Oh my god." I'd never scrambled off my bed so fast in my life. "Oh my god, they're going to kill me."

It was half past seven. As in, an entire hour after we should have been at dinner.

"Fucking *shit*." I pulled off my workout clothes without even remotely caring that I was pretty much completely naked in front of Fane. I'd die a little bit over that later, along with the fact that I had been pressed against him while there were actual rivulets of sweat dripping off my body.

"Rose." Fane continued to sit on my bed, arms crossed and an amused look on his face. I wanted to flick it right off, even though the rigidness of his entire body told me that, more than anything, he wanted to figure out what the fuck happened.

I was hopping on one leg, trying to shimmy on my jeans with one hand while looking for literally anything to cover my top half with the other. "Fane, get up. We're late for dinner. My mom's going to hand me my ass."

I was still hopping and pretty confident I was trying to get my head through the armhole of a sweatshirt when Fane spoke again.

"As much as I'm enjoying this, which I am, *thoroughly*, I already called Ash. He's taking one for the team, let your folks know that I wasn't feeling well, and you stayed home to look after me."

A light breeze could have knocked me over.

"This conversation isn't over, Calista." I heard him get up and walk toward me.

"Oh, yes, it is." I will admit that I wish I'd been a little more composed physically so my delivery of that line was taken with the seriousness I said it with.

I didn't let myself think about the fact that my head was stuck in the sleeve of my sweatshirt and my pants were halfway on. Instead, I held my breath and pretended that just like I couldn't see him, and he couldn't see me.

"You might hate the fact that I know you, but I do. Whatever it is you don't want to tell me, I'll figure it out, and then I'll help you whether you and your stubborn, perfect ass wants me to or not. Oh, and you're welcome."

I flipped him off.

# 21

## Calista

**After**

I slept like shit.

Like actual shit.

The entire night was filled with screams that fell short, turning into pathetic, useless gasps that jolted me awake. With running in my head and twitching myself awake. With sweating until I was soaked through and waking up thinking the doors were unlocked and the windows were open.

Every time without fail, my hand reached out for Fane the second I woke up. Given that most times I was lying on or near him, it didn't take long to find him. The moment I did, I pushed myself away from him, relieved that regardless of my restlessness, he stayed sound asleep.

He'd always been a light sleeper. He'd told me once that when he was growing up, he was scared that if he slept too deeply, he wouldn't wake up in time to reach his mom. A pin drop could've stirred him awake.

Of everything that had changed between us, that might be the only real thing that made me happy. That maybe someone, at some point, had managed to feel safe enough to sleep through the night.

With that thought in tow I gave up entirely the moment it started to lighten outside, creeping out of bed with a lead weight in my stomach, a pounding heart and throbbing headache. It felt like I was severely hungover

155

but didn't get to experience any of the fun parts that usually led to this sort of dreary end.

The second I was out of my bedroom and the door closed behind me, Jerry's massive head was nudging into me. His nose was working overtime, sniffing and huffing as he checked me over. Making sure I was still whole.

I sank to the floor outside my room, resting my head against him. He didn't move, his steady presence grounding me in a way I desperately needed. Jerry had been my constant when everything else spun out of control from the moment we settled into our new life in Darling. I'd been adrift, and he had been my anchor in a way.

I stayed like that for a while, lost in thought, replaying everything from yesterday. Every misstep. Every choice. The moment I ran straight into Fane and thought it was over—that *I* was over.

It made me realize that I'd gone my whole life without feeling the way I did yesterday. Scared and entirely willing to give up something I loved because of that feeling, just to make it stop.

The thought of never running again had crossed my mind. It lingered, sharp and heavy, because giving up running felt safer. But something about that thought—it didn't *fit* right. Like I was giving in to something far bigger than fear. Like I'd be letting down more than just myself.

And maybe it wasn't just running. Maybe it was about the way I'd always reached for someone else when I needed to feel steady. First Dad, then Fane, then Jerry. Every time life knocked me off balance, I looked outward instead of inward.

I'd never realized that in such stark clarity before.

And there was still a very big part of me that wanted to throw in the towel, to go back to leaning on someone else, but I didn't want it to be because I *had* to. I wanted it because I didn't but I chose to anyway. I knew how much life had already taken from me. Knew how hard I'd worked to bring myself back from nothing, even if my soul was still rough and cracked. If so much of it still felt tender.

I got as far as standing in front of the front door. It felt like I'd only been standing there for a second, ignoring Jerry's nudges and insistence to take him with me.

If I could just make it around the block, that would be enough. If I could just *step outside*, that would be enough.

My hand twitched for the doorknob three times but never made contact. On the fourth and final attempt, I heard him walk up behind me. Felt the way he stood just close enough for his chest to touch my back on his inhales.

"You have no concept of personal space." My voice was rough, like all those screams hadn't been just in my dreams. There was no bite to my words at all, but it was easier to be like this with him than to be any other way.

"I love to run."

His statement caught me so off guard that I snorted so violently I started to cough. "I remember you lying on the floor of the gym crying 'Take me now!' after a five-mile jog on the treadmill."

"I wasn't crying, and that *wasn't* jogging. I'm good at jogging, *that* was attempting an olympic record."

"You were definitely crying."

"Hold on—"

I turned around, a big, bright grin on my face that Fane instantly narrowed his eyes at. "Like a big baby."

"That's—"

"A big, buff, gym baby." My smile was so huge that my eyes were crinkling. The look on Fane's face was so priceless that I couldn't help but laugh. My head tipped back, and my arms wrapped tight around my stomach, unable to do anything but hold on.

"Okay, laughy pants, are we going for a run or not?"

"*Laughy pants?*" That just made me laugh even harder, especially with his dry delivery of the words. "Good one, Mr. Soft and Approachable."

Fane reached around me and snapped the lock on the front door, pulling it open and grumbling about how he was going to toast Ashton's balls. Despite the last twenty-four hours—despite the last two years—the smile on my face felt genuine for the first time in a long time.

"What the fu—" My arms fumbled for the doorframe, and it was only because of Fane's arm miraculously appearing and banding around my waist that I didn't trip over what had to be twenty pounds of lasagna.

He pulled me back into him, crushing me against his chest and what I was going to assume was just some morning wood that hadn't gotten the hint or the benefit of being tucked away in something sturdier than running shorts.

The tips of Fane's fingers flexed, and I felt the pad of each individual digit press against my skin. The way my back arched wasn't on purpose. Both my hands moved to his arm before I did the exact opposite of what I commanded my brain to do. I moved my hips, grinding my ass on the growing thickness I felt behind me.

It was the single, gasping exhale that Fane released that made my eyes fly open. Eyes that I hadn't even known were closed, and I used my hold on his arm to fling it off me like he had fucking cooties and hurdled over the stack of lasagnas on my doorstep.

"That was—Sorry, uh, your…your parts…are awake."

Your *parts are awake?* Sweet Lord, kill me now.

I was definitely aware of the silent, shaking laughter racking through Fane's body. I decided to rise above it and focus instead on the pile of family dinners on my porch, like any very normal, very *not* horny, morning runner would.

There was no mistaking the beautiful, precise, scrawling letters on the sticky note stuck to the top container.

*For sweet Fane, I hope you feel better.*
  *Love, Isla.*

And then there was another note just under it in a scrawl that very much belonged to my father and done in something resembling a poorly sharpened pencil.

*Fane, I had a bite. Sorry.*

Fane's pointer finger shot across the space I'd hurdled, pushing up on my chin to close my mouth. I swatted his hand away and glowered at him.

"You see that? Your mom thinks I'm sweet."

I huffed, running my finger up the bridge of my nose. "Well, my mom clearly doesn't know you that well."

"Are you jealous, Rosie girl?"

"You...*you...*" I was pointing right at him like lightning might spontaneously fly out the tip of my finger and smite him.

"No, wait. I can guess. I make you sick?" He ran a hand through his hair before crossing his arms in this smug, cocky stance.

"Among many other things," I muttered, spinning on my heels to avoid looking at him.

Fane grabbed the food and darted back inside before reemerging and locking the door, his shoes laced. "I could probably guess those things too," he continued, that infuriating beam still plastered across his face as he started to stretch.

I should have been stretching too, but instead I crossed my arms and gave him my most unimpressed expression. "I highly doubt it."

"I make you nervous?"

I scoffed. "Try annoyed."

"I make you all gooey on the inside?"

"Sure, in a *my organs are failing* sort of way."

"I think I turn you on, Calista." He was still stretching, but the smile had dropped off his face. Replaced with a look that translated roughly to *I could rip off all your clothes without damaging the buttons.*

"You actually remove all the moisture from my body." I was eighty percent sure I held my composure...until he opened his mouth to reply.

"Yeah, from too many orga—"

I slid my earbuds into place, giving him my best *suck it* smile and cutting off whatever he was going to say. I had a pretty good idea, and if the way my entire body was humming was any indication, I was firmly in the danger zone of volunteering to experience the sort of dehydration he was describing. Which I didn't want to do.

Right? Yes. *Yes.*

Even with my music blaring, it didn't stop his laughter from trickling in and evaporating almost every single one of the clouds that had turned my life into one overcast, gray, and dreary twilight.

I looked over my shoulder once, not fully able to evade the small amount of lingering terror from the day before, to find Fane running right behind me.

It didn't even occur to me that the smile that still lingered on my face was something I should have hidden away. Not when the one he was giving me now sent the remainder of those heavy rain clouds that followed me around running for the hills, leaving me to bask, just for a bit, in nothing but never-ending sunshine.

# 22

## Fane

**Before**

"I can't do anymore." I was holding onto the sides of the treadmill with a death grip, my words made infinitely more dramatic by Cali's playlist blasting from the gym speakers with "Mess It Up" by Gracie Abrams on repeat.

I might never admit it, but her playlists had grown on me. Her taste in music had infiltrated my Spotify so thoroughly that I hadn't really had a choice at the start, but I could admit to belting out a country song or two in the shower now.

"We've been running for twenty minutes." Cali guffawed from her spot beside me, hardly breaking a sweat. "And you've run longer than this."

"Run, yes," I panted, "You've been sprinting."

"This is not a sprint." She waved one slender hand in my direction.

I glared at her. "It really fucking is." I smacked the emergency stop button on the treadmill, and just before it stopped, I let it take me, depositing me in a sad pile of fucking *sadness* on the gym floor.

"Oh my fuck." I think there were actual tears pouring out of my eyes. "Just take me now," I whimpered.

"Fane Mackenzie, are you crying?"

I cracked an eye open to find Cali leaning over me.

"No." I was definitely crying.

"You said you could outrun me." She jutted a hip out and raised one dark brow.

"*Run*," I emphasized. "Not sprint like we're being chased by the walking dead."

"For such a big, scary-looking guy, you're a bit of a softie."

"There's nothing soft about me." I frowned at her, doing my best to flex my arms even though I was about to fucking die.

"Oh yeah?" A little grin started to spread on her face. I was intimately familiar with that look. I reached up and gripped her hips, pulling her down onto me with a squeal.

"Fane!" She slapped two hands onto my chest. "This is a public gym." She looked around, her brows furrowed.

"And it's close to midnight. No one is here."

"That doesn't mean we should—"

"I'm not going to fuck you at the gym, Rose." I kept my hands gripped on her hips, bringing my chest flush with hers. "I just wanted to prove to you how incredibly not *soft* I am." I kept my hold on her firm, grinding her down along the hard length of my cock.

"This is…inappropriate."

"You gave me your *fuck me* eyes first."

"I did not—"

"Liars get punished, baby."

"Well," she swallowed, chest rising faster with each passing second. "In that case, I *definitely* didn't."

I started to lean up, intent on stealing a kiss before I left her to her running to finish up with my weights while I thought about all the ways I would, in fact, punish her so deliciously when we got home when she leaned back a little. A look of complete and total seriousness on her face.

"Are we going to talk about it?" she murmured, eyes softening, fingers twining together around the back of my neck.

"About what?"

"Stupid doesn't suit you, Fane." She gave me an eyeroll and hopped off me.

"I just don't think going to see her is a good idea." I scratched at my eyebrow before getting to my feet. It was my mom's birthday on Sunday, and though I tried to make it home to visit her for that day every year, I wasn't sure I should anymore.

"You're her son," Cali said softly, like it was the simplest thing in the world. Like it should be enough.

But it wasn't. Not for her. Not for me.

"I know I remind her of him," I muttered, my voice rougher than I intended and she flinched at the bitterness, and guilt twisted low in my gut.

"I didn't mean—"

"No." I cut her off, forcing a long breath. "You're right."

Cali didn't look away, her steady gaze digging into the parts of me I kept locked down. "When you picture a future where you don't see her anymore, what do you feel?"

Relief.

The word sat heavy on my tongue. Shame curdled in my chest because what kind of son feels *relief* at the thought of losing his mother?

Cali walked over to me, winding her arms around my waist and resting her chin on my chest. "You've decided already."

"I have." I tucked a piece of hair behind her ear. Grounding myself in her softness. Her *goodness*.

"Don't you think she deserves a real goodbye?" She pressed her cheek to my chest, and I rested my head on top of hers.

"She does," I murmured, dropping a kiss onto the top of her head.

The next morning, I parked right outside my childhood home. I could never understand why she didn't just leave. Sell it, and find something else. Move on. But then I thought that maybe it gave her a sense of strength, taking back her life in the house that almost took it from her.

To me, it remained like a ghost, tethered to the spot in which it stood, unable to move on from the horrors it witnessed.

"Want me to wait here?" Cali asked, hand squeezing mine where I held it in her lap.

"No, I want her to meet you." I didn't let go of her hand when we walked up the path to the house, my grip on her fingers tightening with the anxiety that built with every step I took. I wasn't overly surprised that my mom opened the door before I even had the chance to knock.

She looked good. Healthy. Happy.

I think that should have eased something inside me, but it didn't. I didn't know anything about her life. I didn't do a whole lot of reaching out, and neither did she, but when she looked at me, the traces of happiness I did see flickered.

"Fane." Her voice was soft and sweet, and even though I looked just like her—same dark brown hair, same violet eyes—I knew I was a reminder of everything that had been her hellish reality for seventeen years.

"Hey, Mom." I stopped just short of the front door, my heart in my throat. Clearing it didn't help. It just emphasized the strain of being there. "Happy birthday." I handed her the flowers we'd picked up on the way here.

"Thank you, sweetie." She took them and held them close to her chest like a shield. A much needed defense. I don't think it escaped Cali that she wasn't inviting us in.

"Mom, this is Cali." I gestured, watching her eyes move from me to her. Watching them soften ever so slightly.

"It's lovely to meet you, Cali. I'm Georgia." She stuck her hand out, but Cali being Cali, she just went for it. Arms stretched out, she pulled my mom into one of her milk and honey scented hugs. She was rigid at first, but slowly she softened into Cali's hold. Arms coming up and around her.

"I can't tell you how nice it is to meet you," Cali said, her voice thick with the emotion she always wore on her sleeve.

"I didn't know Fane had a girlfriend." Her eyes flicked to mine, and I saw the guilt there at how nonexistent our relationship was.

"Not much of a talker, this guy." Cali pointed her thumb at me before rolling her eyes. "Dancing though, he excels at."

My mom barked a laugh before a hand flew up to cover her mouth, her eyes widening like she couldn't believe she'd just done that. "Really?"

"Scouts honor, Georgia." Cali's smile was stunning.

We stood there for probably twenty minutes talking.

Well, I didn't say a word. I only watched the easy conversation they had fallen into, the way Cali could do with anyone. When it was all said and done, my mother clutched the flowers a little closer to her chest, her eyes flicking to me for a second before they settled on Cali.

"I…I hope he treats you well, Cali."

Her words hit harder than I expected, confirmation that she worried I was just like him. That I could ever be anything like him. My jaw tightened, but before I could say anything, I felt Cali's arms wrap around my waist. Her gaze found mine, steady and sure.

"Your son is the best man I've ever met," she whispered, giving her answer to me instead of my mom, like she knew I needed it more. "Of the two of us, I'm the lucky one, and I'll never let him forget it."

Her eyes swam with tears before she reached up on her toes to press a kiss to my jaw before turning back to my mom. "It was nice to meet you." With that, she turned and headed back for the car, giving me the moment she knew I needed.

"Fane—"

"I get it," I said, cutting her off gently. "You don't really know me." My smile was sad, but genuine.

"I'm sorry," she whispered, her grip tightening on the flowers until they began to bend. It was clear to me she was apologising for more than the exchange she just had with Cali.

A frown settled into the divet of my brow, my eyes locked to the toes of my boots while snippets of our life together flickered through my mind. It took a minute, but eventually I looked back at my mother and I nodded, "Me too."

"So—

"I'm not going to come back after this." There was no better way to do it than just rip off the band-aid. She didn't say anything, and I knew I didn't imagine the way her shoulders lowered a little, like she was relieved too.

"I'll always love you, but…" I turned around, catching Cali's eyes through the window of the car. "But I don't think either of us can do more than what we've already done."

"I don't know what to say." Her body swayed like she wanted to step forward or maybe retreat back.

"That's okay." I gave her another smile before I took my own step back. There wasn't really anything else *to* say. Sometimes this is what it looked like to put the people you loved first, to put *yourself* first.

It looked like letting go and walking away.

I hadn't expected her to rush for me, to wrap her hands around me. It shocked me so much that my arms were frozen in the air, and I twisted my head around to look at Cali with what I knew was overwhelming panic in my eyes. She mimed wrapping her arms around someone before pointing at my mom, so I did.

I wrapped my arms around her, holding her tight while I felt her small, silent shakes. When she pulled back, she nodded at me, the violet eyes she'd given to me looking clearer. Focused.

"A clean break." She nodded.

I didn't say anything, this was her moment to work through what I already had.

"You'll be okay." It was a statement because we both knew I'd learned the consequences of what needing her looked like. Not for me, but for her. I hadn't made that mistake again.

"So will you." It had been a long time since she needed me too.

With that, she watched me for a second longer before gently picking up her flowers and walking back into her house, not looking back as she shut the door behind her.

Cali had tears running down her face when I got back into the car. She dove across the console, her face crushed to the crook of my neck. "Are you okay?" I could feel her tears seeping into the cotton of my shirt.

"Look at me." I waited for her to pull back, my hand still running up and down the length of her spine.

"I have my whole world right here in this car."

"But she's your *mom*."

"And we'll be better apart." I swiped a tear off her cheek, my chest tightening at the heart of this woman, and how I was lucky enough to be one of the people she handed a piece of it to.

"Are you sure?" she whispered, the confusion on her brow a dead giveaway that what I'd just done wasn't something she might ever be able to comprehend.

"It starts and ends with you, and I've never needed anything more than that. You're it."

That look didn't disappear, but it was joined with another. One I was familiar with. That same one she wore when she told me that after a lifetime of never having a safe place to land, she'd be that for me. Cali nodded, wiping her eyes. "Okay."

"Okay," I repeated, kissing her temple before she settled back into her seat and threaded her fingers through mine, not letting go the entire way home.

For the first time in my life, I felt free.

# 23

# Calista

**After**

"This is ridiculous," I mumbled.

Every time I looked in my rearview mirror, Fane started waving like a maniac, or blowing kisses, or holding up his hand in half of a heart.

Naturally, I just held up my middle finger back, but the gesture just seemed to spur him on. Like in his head, that was the equivalent of me holding half a hand-heart up back.

Two minutes into the seven-minute drive to the café, I caved and called him.

"Hey, baby."

Fane's rough voice wrapped around me. It was the equivalent of a soft landing, of hands moving through your hair. Of fingertips gliding up and down the bare skin of your back.

He'd answered the phone just like that—every single phone call for two years—and for a second I was thrust back to right then. Submerged completely in everything else that came with it.

"Cali?"

"Don't call me baby." My heart was thundering in my chest, and I hated he knew what he'd done to me, purely by the sharpness of my voice.

"You called?"

I flicked my eyes up to the rearview to find him right as rain, completely unrattled.

"This isn't necessary."

"What isn't?"

"You're tailing me like private security."

"I'm going to take that as a compliment." I looked up to see him holding up the half of a heart with one hand again and sporting a lopsided grin.

"What are you doing?" I snapped.

"It's half a heart." He sounded genuinely concerned that I didn't know that.

"I know what it is, Fane. I mean, *why* are you doing it?"

"Are you going to tell me what happened yesterday?"

"No."

"Well, then I won't tell you why I'm doing half a heart."

"You're acting like a child."

"Ah, yes. A big, buff, gym baby. How could I forget?"

"You're just proving my point."

"You can flip me off again if you want. It's kind of a turn-on."

"There's something wrong with you."

"Yeah, all the blood in my body has rushed straight to my d—"

I hung up the phone call and lifted up my middle finger until I saw Fane run his tongue along his top teeth and mouth, "Give it to me," with way too much enthusiasm.

The only benefit of being the car in front was that he couldn't see me smiling like an idiot and swallowing down random little chortles of laughter that kept trying to escape my body. The force of withholding them making my eyes water.

The truth was, I was glad he was following me in. I also didn't hate that he ran with me yesterday.

Yes, I knew that feeling anything remotely positive about being near or around him was actively working against my pledge to loathe him with the fire of a thousand suns, but Fane had always been the embodiment of feeling like you were home. Safe and warm and *right*. No matter what my brain knew, my body hadn't quite been able to forget that.

I parked my car down the alley next to the café and around back where I always did. The space spanned behind all the businesses and shops along the main street.

Fane was idling right outside the alley when I walked back onto the street.

"I've got some work stuff to do today. I'll be back at closing."

"You're not staying?" I sounded disappointed, and I wanted to disappear entirely when I tacked on a little "Yay!" at the end to try and cover that fact.

"I'd tell you to keep your panties on, but we both know you're not wearing any." He winked at me. It wasn't just a regular wink. It was the wink of all winks. This sexy, smooth, and effortless-looking thing that would have absolutely ruined my panties..if I had any on.

I did my best to get through the day, like I couldn't feel the response my body had to Fane making a mess of my thighs.

When Gus walked in, it was the perfect opportunity to take back control of my day by using my word of the day.

Okay, yes, I had to Google it, but I had no issue using it in a sentence, and that felt like a win I really needed.

The moment Gus placed his regular order, I pounced. "Gus, you've made a felicitous choice!"

He proceeded to look from me down to his already stained shirt and then asked, "Is it on me?"

"What? No. It's my word of the day."

"Is this like when you were phlegmy a couple weeks ago?"

I handed Gus his coffee and cookies with a tight-lipped smile. "Yes, Gus."

"Right." He picked up his order before giving me a serious look and said, "Well, I'm glad it cleared up."

The rest of the day was just like that; the embodiment of climbing a flight of stairs and taking an extra step when you'd already gotten to the top.

My dad arrived in his usual time slot as second customer and asked about Fane. Asked if we got the lasagnas he'd dropped off, and said that Ashton—who he was still calling Aleron much to my delight—was an "outstanding kid" who was now expected at all future family dinners.

I was typing out a message to Fane to ask for Ash's number just as Mags walked in, right on time, but looking like someone had rained all over her parade.

"Mags?" I tucked my phone away and rounded the counter. "Are you all right?"

She sat down and let out the most exaggerated sigh I'd ever heard. It was hard to tell whether she was up to her old tricks or if she was in a real state of panic, which forced you to take her seriously one hundred percent of the time.

"The stall for Mags' is all set to go at the fair like every year."

"That's awesome!" I smiled at her, taking the seat across from her.

"Except my bartenders pulled out."

"All of them?" She had like five of them.

"Every single one."

"I'm so sorry, Mags. Could Delilah fill in? Or you said Dylan is staying with her, maybe him?" I hadn't seen Dylan since we were in high school, and Delilah had never poured a beer in her life that was drinkable.

She waved me away. "She can't pour a beer to save her life." It turned out this was one of those times when Mags was actually not in a state of panic, but rather in the midst of yet another diabolical plan. "Say, what about that guy of yours?"

"My...Fane?"

"I remember you saying he used to be a bartender."

"I don't think I—"

"Perfect, it's settled. You two will man the tent! You won't need to do a thing. It will be there and set up, ready for you to go. Just pour the beers and collect the cash."

"Wait, Mags—"

"Oh, I do appreciate it, sweetheart." She leaned over the table and patted my cheek in the same tender way she'd done my whole life.

"You're not staying?"

"I'll be back later! Have an appointment for my hair."

And then she was gone and I'd been once again delicately manipulated into doing her bidding. The rest of the day was more navigating the new normal of a busier day while simultaneously getting more and more excited about the prospect of telling Fane that he would be tending a bar tent at the Darling Autumn Fair in just over a week.

It felt like getting a universe version of Fane's panty-melting winks.

I finished cleaning with a little grin on my face, officially excited about being roped into Mags's shenanigans after having the day to strew on it and think about how I could both gently torture Fane and also use the experience to my advantage.

After locking up I looked around, but I didn't see him out front. It was only once I walked back down the alley beside the café did his truck roll into view, right on time.

My heart tripped over itself, stuttering in a way that felt sharp and heavy. The sight of Fane—right there, so real, so grounded—did something to me that I couldn't name, and it frustrated me that I didn't hate it as much as I should've. He wagged his fingers at me, that ever-infuriating smirk tugging at his lips, and I responded with a dramatic roll of my eyes. Too easy. Too natural.

Then I saw it.

I was three steps away from my car when I saw it—a piece of paper tucked under the windshield wiper. My heart lurched, slamming into my ribs with a force that left me breathless.

I knew Fane was watching me. I could feel his eyes on my back. Knew he'd see even the smallest way I tensed up.

I knew what it was before I even picked it up, but I forced myself to unfold the paper and read the crudely written words.

***That was fun, wasn't it? I told you I love to play.***

I felt his words like a noose tightening around my throat. My resolve, the very same I'd demanded of myself the morning after he'd chased me, felt brittle. Made even more so by the trembling in my hands.

I folded the note back up, stuffed it in my back pocket, and whipped my head around to see what I already knew would be happening.

Fane. Door open. Half out of his truck, and a storm brewing behind those wild violet eyes.

That look. I knew it. Controlled fury, tempered by something more dangerous. Something I refused to acknowledge.

Quickly unlocking the car, I jumped in and shoved the key in the ignition. I pulled the note out of my pocket where I knew he saw me put it and shoved it to the back of the glove compartment like the thing was made of hot coals. I didn't glance back. I didn't let my eyes so much as flick to the rearview mirror.

The car jolted into drive, and I pulled out without looking back. I couldn't.

Even as my hands shook and my body tingled with the sensation of a thousand tiny ants crawling just under my skin. Even as the irrational thought struck me that there was someone in my back seat, breathing down my neck.

I knew there was no possible way for him to be hunting me while I was in my car, but still, I swear I could hear the way his shoes slapped on the road behind me, gaining on me no matter how fast I drove.

Fane couldn't know. Couldn't think it was his responsibility to step in. Not because he wasn't capable, but because I wouldn't let him. Whatever guilt he felt for the past, whatever silent penance he thought he owed, it didn't give him the right to become entangled in this.

Declan wanted a reaction, but I wouldn't give it to him—not through Fane, not through anyone.

I forced my lungs to pull in air and lifted my chin. Rolled back my shoulders and kept my eyes on the road in front of me. My fingers were still trembling, but I tightened them on the wheel, forcing that steadiness into my grip.

The weight of it made me want to crumble, but I had carried much worse.

24

## Fane

**After**

Cali flew out of her parking spot like she was fleeing a goddamn crime scene.

"Fuck," I muttered, getting back into my truck and slamming the door. It took two seconds to catch up with her.

I should've known better than to think her stubbornness would have dulled in any capacity in our time apart. It hadn't stayed the same, though. It was sharper now, more desperate in the way she clung to it.

Calista was always the perfect blend of being independent and handling shit on her own, but also self-aware enough to step back and ask for help when she needed it. I knew she thought that needing to ask for help made her incapable in some way, but I'd always been in awe of her ability to do it. To know her limit.

The thing was, even after all the days that had separated me from her, I knew her better than I knew myself.

And the things I didn't know? Well, I'd always been an exceptionally fast learner when it came to anything to do with that woman.

The fact that something was going on frustrated me like nothing else because it felt like it was right under my fucking nose, and I couldn't pick it.

174

I pulled into her driveway seconds after she did, slamming the gearshift into park. Before she'd even gotten the door unlocked, I was right behind her.

"Calista, for fuck's sake," I bit out, the frustration I was feeling clear in every word I spoke as I followed her inside. I swiped my hands down my face in an effort to compose myself even a tiny fucking bit. To not wrap my hand around her throat and glide my other one up the soft skin of the inside of her thigh, to coax it out of her, so I could just fucking *fix* it.

I thought she was going straight for the bedroom, but instead she'd obviously stopped right in the middle of the living room, where there was a clear view of the kitchen, and I ran straight into her.

My arm wrapped around her on instinct in an effort to steady myself and not take her down while I found my balance again. It meant I ended up pulling her flush to me in an almost exact replica of what had happened this morning.

"Whoa—"

"What in the *fuck*"—Cali's hand gripped my arm, nails digging in to the point that I cringed—"is *that?*" She whirled out of my hold and flung an arm behind her, waving it in a way that just screamed *internal panic.*

"Can you be more specific?" I gave her a crooked grin because I knew what she was referring to. She was talking about her—

"Cabinets, Fane." Her hand was still panic waving in the direction of the kitchen.

I crossed my arms. "Yes, okay. I see them."

"You *see* them?" When Cali got flustered, she talked with her hands in a big way. This meant she literally used her fingers to widen her eyes, and I only just managed to cover my laugh with a cough.

"Yes."

"Okay, well, do you *see* how they're now at…at *regular* person height?"

I made a show of flicking my eyes behind her, then back. "I do."

"That's not where I installed them."

"No, it's not."

"You…you moved my cabinets?" She literally mimed opening cabinet doors and taking something out of them.

"Yep."

"Why would you do that, *Fane*?" She put extra emphasis on my name, and despite it not being the time for it, coupling her voice, my name, and the fact that she'd just been pressed against me for the second time in one day, it shot straight to my dick.

"Because, *Calista,* you had to stand on your kitchen counter to get a mug. Let's not also forget that you literally *fell off it* this morning, and I had to catch you."

"I wouldn't have fallen if you hadn't snuck up on me." She took a step closer and jabbed me in the chest with one accusatory finger.

I grabbed her wrist and held it between us. "So you're saying you've *never* fallen off the counter before?"

"Whatever you're doing here that's making you feel like you need to, I don't know, *help*…it's not needed. I don't *need* you to do any of this."

"You didn't answer my question."

"No, Fane. I haven't fallen off the damn counter."

"Have you fallen off *anything* in your attempt to do everything yourself?"

"I have…*not.*" Her eyes flickered away for a split second.

"You *liar.*" I wrapped another hand around her waist. "You're so fucking stubborn, do you know that?"

"And you clearly still have no concept of personal space," she breathed back, her nose brushing mine.

"You didn't seem to mind this morning," I taunted her, grinning at that peachy blush that crept onto her face. "Not that I'm complaining."

"You're insufferable." Her hand that was caught between us pushed on my chest, but it was half-hearted, like it was something she thought she *should* do, not something she actually *wanted* to do.

"Let me kiss you."

The words were out of my mouth before I realized I'd even spoken them. For a moment, I couldn't breathe. I couldn't take my eyes off her lips, how they parted in surprise. Her sharp intake of breath. That was definitely a thought that should have stayed inside my head, but I'd always been all in where Calista Grey was concerned.

My tongue dragged along my bottom lip as I tried to remember—really remember—what it felt like to kiss her. To have her kiss me back the way she used to.

Like I was hers.

I was seconds from crossing a line, I knew that, but my grip around her waist tightened. That milk-and-honey scent of hers was everywhere, pulling me in deeper.

"No one's here to see it," she murmured.

Her eyes were on my mouth, and I saw a flicker of those walls around her shudder in the rapid rise and fall of her chest and the twitch of her fingers that were splayed on my chest. In my head, I was charging at those walls. Clawing at them, roaring at them in fury. Roaring at her to let me in.

"Doesn't matter," I rasped. So insanely desperate for her I didn't care how clearly she could see it.

I moved closer to her, my mouth watering at the idea of tasting her. Of how it would feel to take that full bottom lip of hers between my teeth. The sound I knew she'd make the moment I did.

"That's not the rule."

"Rose—"

"I—you need to let me go, Fane."

Her voice was weak, and I knew if I pushed a little harder, she would relent.

I closed my eyes and released the breath I'd been holding. Letting her go was something I tried to do many times over.

I uncurled my arm from her and stepped away because I didn't want her to *relent*. I didn't want her to give in, like it was crossing a line she had drawn in the ground for herself. I wanted her to choose me. To pick me because she wanted to, not because I pushed her.

So, I forced a smirk, pulling on the mask we'd both been wearing since I got here. This place of trading jabs and barbed words felt safer than the raw, open wounds underneath.

"I also fixed all the sagging eaves around the house and cleared out your gutters. You had a *lot* of shit in your gutters."

"Hey!"

She was *not* happy at that one.

"Whoever does them doesn't do a good job." I crossed my arms, knowing the dig would hit because I had a pretty good idea of who did them.

"I do a perfectly fine job." She scowled at me, and I'd take that look any day over the broken one that had taken over her face when she told me to let her go.

"Well, your 'perfectly fine' job sucks." I was being a dick, and I'd expected her to push back, but I hadn't expected what actually came out of her mouth.

"You try falling off a ladder from way up there, and then try to get back up." Her mouth snapped shut, her teeth making an audible click from the ferocity of it. It could have been heard from space.

"You…" I sucked in a deep breath to collect myself. It didn't fucking work. "You *fell* off a fucking ladder?"

"No." Her answer came too quick, not to mention she'd literally just it.

"Calista, you—are you—what?" My brain short-circuited, filling with image after image of her crumpled on the ground, hurt and alone, because she was too damn stubborn to ask for help. My stomach churned, the guilt a heavy, nauseating weight, because I knew.

I was the reason she'd been alone in the first place. Despite every decision I made being so that she wasn't. So that she didn't have to worry about shit like this. She was supposed to be home with her parents, with her sister.

Not here. Not like this.

"Were you hurt?" The question came out rough and heavy, my voice betraying every ounce of the fear crawling up my throat. I couldn't look her in the eye because I knew—*I knew*—the answer was going to rip me apart.

She was silent for too long before she answered my question. "I—"

"Stop *lying* to me." My hands balled into fists at my sides, and I didn't care that my words were abrupt. Didn't care that it might send us five steps back in whatever tolerance she was forming for me.

"I fractured two ribs and got a mild concussion," she admitted, her voice so quiet.

The sound I made was almost inhuman. A broken growl, a groan, something that clawed its way out of my chest. I hated myself more in that moment than I had in every other moment of my life combined.

I dragged a hand down my face and tried not to fucking fall apart. "Look, I know you don't need my help. That you don't want it, that you want me to leave. I get it, Calista. But I *am* here. Let me help. Please."

"Fane—"

"*Please.*"

She had no reason to. I knew she didn't trust me, knew what she thought of me. I asked anyway. Begged.

"Okay," she said quietly. "While you're here, if I need help, I'll ask."

We stayed quiet, standing across from one another for as long as it took for my pulse to slow down. I was at a loss of what to do, what to say. Just being around her now felt stupid. Fucking pointless. Utterly undeserved. My eyes didn't shift from the spot on the floor I'd zoned in on, as if it would be able to give me a way to go back and fix what I'd done, until I heard her move away.

"You're *kidding* me."

I looked up and found her standing just inside her bedroom, hip cocked and arms crossed. When I didn't say anything, she pointed to the floorboards beneath her feet and made a show of dramatically stomping on one.

"*Where* is the creak?"

"I fixed it."

"You went *under* the house?" She sounded genuinely appalled, and the look on her face tugged at the corner of my mouth. I ran my hand over my face to try to stop it, but I was too late.

"Are you *laughing* at me, Fane Mackenzie?"

I knew what she was doing. Even though she wanted me gone, she was still doing what she'd always done—fixing the parts of me that she didn't even break, and she did it without blinking. Without breaking a sweat. Without even fucking realizing it half the time, and if I hadn't been so fucking in love with her from the moment I saw her, I'd have fallen right then and there.

"No, ma'am."

She threw her hands out dramatically, like what I said and what I did were lining up, and it wasn't what she expected. "What are you *doing?*" she whined, the question seemingly more for herself than for me.

"I'm fixing your shit box," I deadpanned.

Her gasp was comical. So was the way she clutched at imaginary pearls. "Houses have feelings!"

I rolled my eyes. "So you've said."

Cali used to yell, "Hello!" into our empty apartment when we were gone all day because she *knew the house had been lonely*.

"Don't roll your eyes at me." She hadn't even been looking at me when I did it.

"Sorry, Mom." I trailed behind her into the kitchen.

She snorted. "You've been spending too much time around Ashton."

"I'm going to tell him you called him by his real name."

She waved me off. "Antonio will never believe it."

Cali reached up to the cupboard to grab herself a glass–easily, might I add.

I knew she felt my eyes on her while she took her time filling it with water and drinking it down slowly.

She turned to face me, her eyes already narrowed, but the honey in their hazel depths stood out more. Sparkling. They were fucking *twinkling* when she raised her hand up between us, middle finger already extended.

"Every time you do that, you know it just turns me on."

She rolled her eyes. "Consider it fodder for your spank bank the next time you decide to touch yourself."

"Rest assured, whenever I touch myself, you're the only thing I think about."

"Fane!" Her hair twirled behind her when she spun back toward me. "You—that's not—you aren't allowed to say that sort of stuff out loud."

"Does it make you uncomfortable?" I pushed off the counter and walked toward her.

She crossed her arms and arched a perfectly sculpted eyebrow at me. "What would all your *girlfriends* think?"

That took me so off guard that my head flew back without permission from the force of my laughing scoff. "Please, Calista."

"You said you had girlfriends. Plural." She backed up a step.

"Are you jealous?" I tilted my head to the side and reveled in the way her throat worked, trying to swallow. Once, twice, before her finger reached up and slid up her nose.

"I heard you say 'girlfriends.'" She ignored me completely. Crossing her arms, the pillowy tops of her tits pushing up, even more visible. I didn't bother hiding the way my eyes lingered on them.

"Eyes are up here, buddy." She gestured to her face with the same panicked, flappy hand from before.

"You heard wrong." I took another step forward, then another, until she was backed up against the sink, and I had one hand on either side of her.

"I have to be honest, I'm having a lot of fun with all of these verbal sparring matches we're having, but that mouth of yours might need to be filled with something else to put an end to all those snarky quips you seem to have become so fond of."

"Fane, this isn't a game." She pushed at my chest, but I didn't budge. Instead, I grabbed her and pulled her to me. Being around her and not being able to touch her was a very specific brand of torture. The way her breath caught in her throat when I reached down, letting a hand slide along the back of her leg until I got to her knee and hoisted it up to sit at my hip.

Cali's hands gripped tight onto two fistfuls of my shirt.

"Fane, what—"

"Tell me to stop right now and I will." Her mouth stayed open, but the words promptly stopped flowing. I could feel the way she wavered between pushing me away and pulling me closer with the grip she had on my shirt.

I could feel the molten heat of her pussy through the barrier of my jeans between us, and one hard grind of my painfully hard cock against her sent her eyes fluttering. It would be so easy to unbutton my jeans and sink right into her. Right here, right now. I could fucking imagine it—the way her nails would dig into me, how her breathing would turn shallow, how her pussy would grip onto me. Pull me in until the only thing I knew was her.

The image in my head almost sent my eyes rolling back in their sockets.

"I know you don't trust a thing that comes out of my mouth, but believe me when I tell you that you were the last woman I touched and the *only* woman I will ever touch for the rest of my life. There's been no one but you. There will *never* be anyone but you."

Cali let out a little whimper that sent a zap down my spine, and my grip on her tightened.

What I wanted was to drop to my knees right in front of her. To make my way under the hem of what was yet another one of her pretty little sundresses that were getting too flimsy for the colder weather that was rolling in and spread her wide. To drag my tongue along the seam of her perfect cunt that I knew was soaking wet for me. Feel her hand in my hair and the way she would grind herself against my mouth. The way she'd say my name, begging me to let her come.

Instead, I dropped her leg and stepped back. Watching the way her eyes dropped to the bulge in my jeans and the very noticeable wet spot she left behind, just like I knew there would be.

"I'm going to put a lasagna in the oven."

She started nodding. "Yep. I'll...I'll..." She cleared her throat. "Turn on that home improvement show."

"Great." I leaned down to press a kiss to her cheek, and that snapped her out of her trance. Her face went from golden, sun-kissed skin to bright cherry red in a matter of seconds.

"Ew," she said, wiping at her cheek and pushing me away from her. "Just for that, I've decided to put you up for managing a booth at the Autumn Fair next weekend."

"Perfect." I sent her a wink just before pulling the frozen dish out of the freezer.

"And you'll have to meet everyone from town and be nice to them and serve them beer."

"That sounds awesome."

"And you'll have to face everyone as the person who's going to ruin their town."

"That's not what I'm doing."

"Oh, and you're a liar too, so you should probably be upfront about that."

"I'll take that under advisement." I put the lasagna in the oven, closed the door, and turned to face Cali, who still had her attention on my still very hard cock.

Her eyes flicked up to mine, and she let out an honest to God growl. Like a little lion cub. "You make me—"

"Sick," I finished for her with a grin. "I know."

# 25

# Fane

**After**

"Put me *down!*" Cali whisper-yelled while simultaneously squealing. I was pretty sure there was a giggle in there somewhere that she tried to disguise with a pretty burly-sounding "*Grr.*"

"Nope." I reached up and slapped her ass lightly.

"Fane!" She really did yell that time. "You did not just do that!"

"Do what? This?" I slapped her ass again, and this time the giggle was definitely there before yet another grizzly harrumphing sound.

"Fane!" Cali's squealing laugh was worth every second of all the middle fingers and cuss words I was sure were in my future. I set her down right next to my car.

"Motherfucking *fucking*...fuck!" Cali stomped her foot, and the move was so unexpected my eyebrows shot up to my hairline. "You...you're not allowed to do any of that ever again." She held her hands up in a big X in front of her.

"Sorry." I wasn't sorry at all.

"I can drive myself." She crossed her arms. "And you touched my ass. Twice."

"I know you can, but I'm going to help and do it for you. And it's a nice ass, but you're right. I should've asked first."

"I—" Her blush was fluorescent. "Thank you," she mumbled before she frowned at herself and mouthed the word, *What?*

"Get in, we're going to be late." I jerked my head toward the open passenger side door.

"I'm not—"

"Cali, I swear to God, I will physically put you in that seat."

Her face had gone slack, and her mouth hung open, but she did it, grumbling all about how she'd see how I'd like it if she slapped *my* ass and then something else that sounded a lot like, "What? No. Why would I touch his ass?"

Needless to say, she sulked the whole drive into Sunshine, arms crossed and whole body angled away from me. My attention was half on her, half on the road, and just like every other time her café came into question, the need as to why she picked that name wanted to be screamed in her general vicinity.

It sat like a lead weight at the bottom of my stomach. Like that same pathetic bit of hope that had been doused the moment I got into town suddenly started to show signs of a pulse.

But I held back. Even though my plan sucked, things were…I don't know what they were. But they were changing, and I was approaching her like I would a scared little kitten. With caution and patience and protective gear.

"People are going to think I'm your hostage," she said, jumping out of the truck and heading off down the alley to the café.

"People are going to think we're in *love*," I corrected her, following just behind.

She snorted, tossing her words at me over her shoulder. "What a rude shock that will be for them."

Oh, well. That wouldn't do.

"Cali," I said, voice sharp and urgent, stopping her mid-step. She turned in an instant, eyes raking over me with a furrow between her brows. Assessing.

She stepped toward me, and whether she knew she was doing it or not, her hands gripped fistfuls of my shirt, pressing her body against mine and then her head started to turn over her shoulder.

"There's a crowd," I murmured, my hand sliding to the nape of her neck, fingers threading into the silky strands of her hair. "And we do have appearances to keep." My thumb brushed against her skin, tilting her head back ever so slightly.

"If they don't think we're in love," I rasped, my lips hovering just over hers, "Then we'll just have to rectify that immediately."

I didn't let her think about it. I didn't give her time to argue. I kissed her.

Maybe what was happening hadn't actually hit her, or maybe she was a stellar actress because she kissed me right back. It was like stepping directly into a moment in time I had fucking dreamed of, day after day.

Her body melted into me, lips soft and eager. This kiss was nothing like the one I had stolen from her weeks ago.

Yes, there was a crowd across the street, but it was more of a group of older women who were promptly bustling into what looked like a fabric store from the glance that I gave them.

I was expecting Cali to give me a tight-lipped nothing before dragging her hand across her mouth and saying I had cooties or something equally as ridiculous.

I hadn't expected *this*.

She met my hesitance with an arm sneaking around my neck to pull me closer to her. I whimpered—fucking *whimpered*—at the way she let me pull her close. At the way that I got to feel her, feel the way *she* wanted me close, the way she kept me there.

Leaning down, I wrapped an arm around her and backed us into the alley before she wrapped her legs around my waist, and I pressed her against the wall.

Cali's hands were in my hair, gripping the strands in tight fists, tugging until the bite of pain made me grunt, going straight to my cock.

Gone was the fight she carried in every interaction since I'd arrived. Kissing her now felt like returning home after war—raw, tender, and too overwhelming to fully process.

She didn't fight me and if she had drawn a line in the sand for herself, she stepped over it willingly.

The way her mouth moved with mine wasn't angry. It was desperate. It was *starved*. It was like she missed me in the same way I had missed her, even though the very sentiment of that seemed impossible.

She tasted perfect. With every swipe of my tongue into her mouth, she pulled me tighter into her, her hands tugging harder. Her moaning pleas turned even more urgent.

My hand snaked between us, brushing the button of her jeans.

My fucking luck, this was the first time she'd worn pants to work in two whole fucking weeks. That was when we pulled apart, when those wide, trusting eyes I remembered but hadn't seen once since I got here settled onto me. Open and guardless and wanting.

Just when she pulled back to give me room, a delicate throat clearing came from the mouth of the alley.

"I…am so sorry to interrupt this." Sammy had her eyes right on the ground beneath her feet. "But we have a bit of a line and…" She gestured toward the front of the café.

Cali's eyes were on me, widening with each passing second as she realized that we'd been practically dry-humping on a wall next to her place of work, and not silently.

I slowly dropped a frozen Cali to her feet, unable to stop the full-body shiver at the feel of her pressed against me. It was a fucking mission to drag my eyes from hers, lids still heavy with the need that made my balls ache so damn bad the need to reach into my pants and squeeze them was almost overwhelming.

I leaned around the corner just to come face-to-face with what was, just as Sammy said, a very big line of people waiting to get the best coffee in town. The first person I saw was Ashton, who was smiling at me like he should be committed.

"Hey, Fane!" he yelled, or more accurately screamed, drawing every single pair of eyes. He then proceeded to point at my crotch. "Is that a portafilter in your pants, or are you just happy to see me?"

I ducked back behind the wall, cussing out my best friend while I shoved my hand into my jeans to readjust my now painfully hard cock. Cali's hand flew up to cover her mouth, a second too late in stopping the chortle that erupted from her. Her wide eyes met mine before she threw her head back and let loose the loudest cackling laugh I'd heard in years.

Her eyes were squeezed tight, but still a tear escaped and fell down her cheek. She was powerless to stop it all the while she clutched at her stomach, letting wave after wave of laughter just pour out of her.

I stood there, stunned stupid for a second. Watching her. Listening to her. Fucking bewitched by her.

I snatched the keys from her hand and threw her over my shoulder again, giving her ass another smack and marching her around the corner.

Ash's grin was maniacal and spent the entire time I was unlocking the café poking Cali in the ribs.

To her credit, she managed to both fight him off and punch him definitely close enough to the dick region that he relented.

By the time she was back on her feet, her face was beet red, her hair was disheveled, and I had settled into my usual corner of Sunshine.

Without a word, I got into work, shielded in part by all the caffeine deprived patrons that had bustled in after us.

All the presentations Ash had gotten everyone to refine showed me exactly what I thought it would. The best part was that, essentially, I now had enough to put together a case for no one to touch this town with a ten-foot pole.

Normally, if the project was viable, this would mean moving on to budgeting and project projections—allocating funds, estimating returns, and putting together a plan to present to the board. But none of that mattered anymore. Darling wasn't just resistant to development; the data painted a clear picture of how spectacularly it would fail.

The numbers didn't lie. Any attempt to develop the town in the way the original plans suggested would result in a tanked investment and a PR nightmare for Mackenzie Co.

In plain words, I didn't need to be here anymore.

All the work that needed to be done, to finalize and then present it to the board, didn't need to be done here, but no one needed to know that.

At least, not yet. Leaving wasn't an option. The very idea of it made my organs twist uncomfortably.

Darling had never been the whole goal, and that was selfish, I know. It had been the excuse to finally make my way back to Calista Grey. To face the possibility that I might not be able to fix what I'd broken, but that I'd be damned if I didn't fucking try.

There were ways to delay. A few tweaks to the timeline, some loose ends that needed 'tidying up'. The first step was giving the crew a few days off, which conveniently gave me the breathing room I needed.

That was the last email I sent before Cali stopped in front of me, her hip jutted out and those heart-shaped lips of hers pursed to the side in that way that always made me want to bite them.

She didn't say a word. She didn't have to. Her narrowed eyes did all the talking as she turned on her heel and headed for the door to lock up.

And just like I always would, I followed her.

# 26

# Calista

**After**

"Are you going to tell me where we're going?" Fane asked, turning out of the gravel drive of the cottage he'd so lovingly now dubbed the "Shit Box," thanks to my dad.

"Nope. Turn left here." I clasped my hands together and placed them in my lap, to which Fane snorted a laugh at.

"You're ridiculous."

"Your face is ridiculous." My comebacks had a lot to be desired, but it was the first thing that came out of my mouth. Fane just lifted his middle finger up between us, and I did my best to scowl at him. It didn't stick, and I quickly looked out the window before he saw my smile.

"Saw that," he quipped.

Remember when I said this was entering into dangerous territory? Well, we were so far into dangerous territory I was quickly losing sight of the way out.

I didn't know what happened.

Mentally, I was still rationalizing the fact that I was one hundred percent going to let him stick his hand down my pants for the good of the town. I was letting him hoist my leg up to drag what had to be an incredibly painful situation–that he was clearly doing his darndest to hide away–along the length of my pussy. My very wet and aching pussy, because that was the only way to get him to leave Darling alone.

I was so deeply full of shit it was unhealthy. More than unhealthy. It was a real, honest to God issue.

Because physically? Physically, when Fane touched me, the last two years didn't exist. I hadn't been alone. I hadn't been a fractured version of myself.

When he touched me, I believed every single word that came out of his mouth. I was someone who saw his actions lining up with his words and felt like if I toed the edge of this abyss I was perilously walking along, it wouldn't be so bad if I fell.

"Do I need to do anything?"

"To me?" Why that was the response my head churned up and spat out, I had no fucking idea. Fane's eyebrow raised tentatively, and his eyes tracked over my features curiously.

"My ears are always open to your needs and how I can be of assistance, baby." Fane's voice rumbled through the car, and I felt them settle in the pit of my stomach. "But I meant for the drive."

"The drive!" Was I yelling?

"You're yelling." The way the sun hit his eyes made the copper flecks reflective. Like tiny gems in pools of violet.

I cleared my throat. "Straight here and then get on the highway."

"Oh, a little out of town adventure? I thought this was a Darling tour."

"It is. Number two, and probably the most important."

"Will you tell me why?"

"Not yet."

"Cali—"

"Once you get on the highway, take the first exit."

Fane did everything I instructed without complaint. And me? Well, I did my absolute darndest not to look at his forearms while he drove and continued to refuse to admit to myself that I think I had a real thing for neck tattoos.

I was sure he could feel my eyes on him, but the way he sat didn't change. His posture was relaxed, with one hand on the wheel and the other resting on the door, his hand in his hair. If you didn't know him, you wouldn't know the word "soft" could apply to him. And maybe it didn't.

Fane was imposing.

The sharp line of his jaw that held a faint shadow, burnished-brown hair that I was sure never existed without his hand running through it at least once. Arms, thick and corded with muscle, decorated in tattoos that were now down to his hands, where he had a constellation on it that I still hadn't had the nerve to ask him about. The other had a compass in the same design as the pocket watch on his neck. Beautiful and shadowed and dark.

"Take a right here," I murmured, still lost in him.

Fane's hand twitched a couple of times like he wanted to reach across and place it on my knee. To grab my hand and lift my knuckles to his mouth.

I knew we both remembered the way he used to do just that before. Now, he just sat there, letting me look.

My chest ached and my stomach dropped. This tangled mess of disappointment in myself, anger at him, and anger at the whole freaking world, just swirling around.

I cleared my throat and noticed only then that the truck had stopped. It was too late now to pretend he hadn't seen everything I'd been thinking.

Too late to hide the brutal pain that lingered in the tissue of every part of my body as if what my life had turned into in the last two years wasn't something that hurt me constantly.

That the life before it wasn't something I mourned all the time.

"Cali." Fane's voice broke. He reached out, taking my hand and entwining his fingers with mine. "I need to talk to you."

I watched our hands in my lap and felt my body slump in exhaustion. I knew he had things he wanted to say, and I'd been so adamant that he didn't deserve to have his words heard. I didn't owe him anything, even though the wondering at what he had to say ate away at me like an itch I couldn't scratch.

I nodded. "I know. But, not yet."

"Cali." That was his *I'm building up to fight you on this* voice, and it tugged at the corner of my mouth.

Closing my eyes, I pulled in a deep breath before pulling my hand from his and remembered the 'why' that started this all in the first place.

"We're here," I said, jumping out of the truck, the gavel shoulder Fane had pulled off onto the exact place we actually needed to be. The moment I heard the telling click of the car lock, I found the hidden path with ease, listening to his footsteps behind me as we disappeared into the trees.

"I'm just shocked," he said.

I kept my eyes laser-focused on the relatively overgrown path in front of me. "I don't see why."

"You don't see *why*?" Even though Fane was behind me, I had no issue imagining the incredulous look on his face. "We went hiking a total of three times together over two years, and I had to carry you on my back for most of each of those experiences."

"One word." I held up a single digit over my shoulder. "Leeches."

"Oh, please," he scoffed, his heavy footfalls sure and steady where I had just tripped for the fourth time. "They were tiny!"

I spun to face him, *my* face now incredulous. "*Tiny?*" I wasn't proud of my screech, but just talking about the leeches made it feel like I had a billion on me. "You took me to the same place three different times, and each time you said 'No, Cali baby. There are no leeches on this trail.'" I did my best impression of his voice to drive the point home.

Fane's laughter was rebounding off the trees around us. Hands braced on his knees. He'd reached that point of laughter where no sound came out at all, only wheezing air followed by a hiccup.

"Real mature, Fane." I cocked a hip out and crossed my arms, holding in my own stupid giggles that were trying to claw their way out. Fane's laughter had always been contagious, especially when he was like this.

"You sounded like Elvis!*" he wheezed, trying to stand up but folding over again.

"Shut up!" I whined, my smile finally breaking through. "Stop laughing! This is important."

"Okay. *Okay.*" He cleared his throat, trying to stand up, but one look at my face and he absolutely lost it. "I can't look at your face!"

"Fane!" I walked back over to him and tried to hoist him up to standing. His hand reached out and wound around me, his forehead pressing against my collarbone. I could feel the vibrations of his laughter shaking my body and spent the next five minutes trying to peel him off me, repeating the words, "I'm so serious right now!" and "You better stop, or else!"

Apparently he found that to be equally as entertaining, until finally I got out of his hold, and he managed to stand up straight, fighting the last lingering bubbles of laughter that were still climbing to the surface.

"We're here because this is another important part of why you need to leave Darling alone."

"Yep." He was pressing his lips together and nodding his head.

"And don't hug me."

"No hugs, got it." Fane gave me a double thumbs-up that said, "Fat chance."

"Fane, we're not friends." I crossed my arms and gave him my fiercest expression.

"No, we're not."

I jolted back at his agreement because I hadn't expected—

"We're *lovers.*"

"What? No."

"Way to lean into the role, Cali baby." Fane did his own Elvis impression before hitting me with double finger guns and pushing past me.

It was only another few minutes of walking, of his laughter trickling back to where I was still tripping behind him, until we got to our destination. I knew he'd reached it because he went completely silent.

I walked up and stopped right next to him.

"Darling was originally called Darling Falls." You could just barely hear me over the rushing sound of the waterfall right before us, held perfectly within its own secret little alcove that you couldn't hear until you were right in front of it.

It was the most beautiful cascade of water you'd ever seen, so perfectly picturesque in the way it flowed over the cliff's edge and down into the pool of water below.

The water was so clear it looked like rippling glass. Like something this untouched shouldn't still exist in the world we lived in.

"Holy fuck." Fane's voice was almost entirely drowned out by the noise.

"When my dad's dad was a kid, everyone was getting sick of families coming and using The Falls. The trail that led here was getting overworn. There was garbage everywhere, and everything was just being…used up. The people who came to visit didn't care about how they left it, so everyone started to drop the 'Falls' off the end of the name of the town. Signs were cut down, and eventually the old name was phased out completely. They changed the names of the schools, businesses, everything."

I knew this was a risky move to bring him here. If anything, this could be just the thing to convince him that Darling was even more appealing than it had been before, but I took a risk on knowing how he felt about being outside. How he always made sure to leave a place the way he'd found it.

"This could totally come back to bite me in the ass, but I don't think I need to say too much more to show you why this"—I pointed in front of us—"is the best reason of all to leave this town the way you found it."

Fane finally peeled his eyes off the water and looked down at me. "Not the best reason of all."

He let that sentence settle between us, and the first thing I wanted to do was roll my eyes. To let his words be more things I didn't believe. To see them for what they were; another thing to lure me in, promise to keep me safe, and then take it all back when I needed them most.

But I was so. fucking. tired.

I wasn't this angry, hateful person. And though I felt it, pulsing and alive, that wasn't all there was to it. To *me.* Beneath it, something softer pushed back. Hidden below the surface of that raging storm. Quiet, but full of yearning that was getting harder to ignore.

It spoke like a siren to those furious parts of me. It whispered stories and memories of how it once felt to be held by him. To trust him, even when I knew better now. It was terrifying and tempting all at once.

I hadn't forgiven him, and I don't think I'd ever forget what had happened, but like I gave myself the moment in the car, I'd give myself today. I'd let myself pretend everything was okay and that the man standing next to me hadn't eviscerated me without blinking.

"Two for two, Calista." Fane's sounded even huskier with the backing track of the rushing water. "Not bad for free, local tours."

I rolled my eyes, flipped him off, and tried not to break down completely when he grabbed my hand and placed a kiss to the back of it.

His entire face changed like he hadn't meant to do that. Like it was muscle memory. A reflex.

"Want to swim?" I asked.

"The whole *pack like you're going to be getting wet* thing makes a lot more sense. I thought we were heading to an orgy." I wasn't sure if he was being serious or not, but I'd never heard the word "orgy" so many times in one morning as I had today.

The sun was high, shining down on us through the gaps in the canopy. I nibbled on my bottom lip, standing just behind Fane as he pulled off his shirt and headed straight for the water. The moment his toes touched the water, his head whipped over his shoulder. "It's fucking toasty!"

My grin was unstoppable. "The waterfall comes directly from natural hot springs," I called back. "They're a little ways away, so by the time it gets here, it's more warm than hot, but you can swim here pretty much all year."

"Cali, this is insane." He looked starstruck.

"I knew you'd like it." My words were too soft for him to hear, and at any rate, he'd turned back around, and I watched as the lone, howling wolf on his back disappeared under the water.

He reemerged, flicking his hair up and out of the way and the most intoxicating look on his face. He was almost completely submerged, his eyes just above the water while he waited for me to make a decision.

*This is such dangerous territory.*

The words kept falling into my brain, and I was constantly slap-fighting them away, but never more so than right when I pulled my dress up and over my head and made my way into the water, aware of every single inch of the skin on my body while Fane drank me in like a man starved. Like he'd never been so close to everything he could ever want but was forced to keep his distance.

That's how Fane looked at me. Like I was his, and even though I knew I wasn't, I walked into the water and let myself pretend with that too.

27

# Calista

**After**

I knew what stepping into the water meant.

There had been a question in Fane's eyes while he watched me take step after step toward the water, the rest of his face lifting out of the clear pool, taking me in hungrily.

Where I knew he hadn't taken his eyes off me once, I hadn't been able to keep mine on him.

I suddenly felt so incredibly stupid. I'd just strutted my ass into the water with confidence coming out the wazoo, and now all I really wanted was to turn around and haul ass out of there.

Everything with Fane, like it had been from the moment I saw him standing in Sunshine, was too much and not enough. I wanted to be impossibly closer to him, and I wanted to be so far away that there would never be a chance of crossing paths with him again for the rest of my life.

Both of those options turned my stomach for different reasons.

I'd made it all the way into the water, the water meeting my waist in the center where he stood. I was honest to God, vibrating. Despite the temperature of the water, my teeth started to chatter. I sunk them into my bottom lip, pressing down and trying to keep my eyes on the way my hand was gliding along the surface and not at how I saw ripples coming from behind me.

Not at the body I felt rise from the water, the heat blazing off him that had nothing to do with the natural springs.

"Calista." I felt his voice everywhere. Just the idea of him made me clench my thighs together.

*God, this was fucking ridiculous.*

I cleared my throat. "So, there you have it. Waterfall, check!" I made a checkmark in the air, and the second I did it, I wanted to drown myself. "Great, okay. All done." I don't even know who I was talking to, but I did know my legs had decided that they would try and save me from myself and march me right out of the water.

I got one step before Fane's arm wrapped around me and pulled me back to him. I shivered at the press of his chest against my back. At feeling his skin on mine. Every point of contact felt tingly like tiny little chemical reactions were happening, and with every spark, my willpower to walk away from him was dwindling.

My eyes fluttered close when he dragged his nose up the back of my neck.

"This position seems to be a common theme with you," I gasped.

"Mmm," he hummed, his smile pressing against the sensitive skin where my neck met my shoulder. "You did always love this position."

"Fane, what are…" I grappled to keep hold of my train of thought. "What are you doing?"

"I've decided." He said the words with such finality. All the air escaped my lungs when both his hands gripped my waist and in one, swift motion he turned me to face him.

My mouth opened and closed a few times, desperate to say something along the lines of *"I'm so happy for you,"* or *"It must feel great to have made your first decisions at the age of twenty-eight,"* but any flimsy sarcastic quip died on my tongue when Fane's hands dragged up my body. They were so broad I could feel the way his fingertips almost touched at my back where he splayed them along my rib cage.

"When I got here and I said I'd go along with everything, I said I wanted something in return. This is what I want."

"Fane, I—"

"Mercy, Calista," he murmured, cutting me off. "Just for a while. I…" His eyelids were heavy, the pupils of his eyes so blown out all that was left was a thin ring of purple, with all his attention totally transfixed on my lips. He held me away from him, and I knew the moment I gave him my answer, the space between us would disappear. "Let me touch you. *Please.*" There was a desperation in his voice that didn't match up with all the things I had collected about him in the last few weeks.

Didn't match up with the person he had become in my mind over the last two years.

It reminded me of when he was mine, and I was his.

"Yes." The word was barely out of my mouth before he kissed me.

He kissed me in the sort of way that broke people down and then built them back up, piece by piece, leaving them forever changed.

One of Fane's hands moved from my waist and dragged over the top of my breasts before wrapping around my throat, pulling me closer to him until we were crushed together.

"I haven't been living without you." He pushed the words into the spot behind my ear before sucking hard. His mouth tracing and teeth nipping and tongue licking his way down my throat.

I was almost completely useless at that moment. My hands gripped his forearms, and I dug my nails in, determined to remind myself that this was real.

That this was *Fane.*

His other hand crept up from my waist, toying with the string of my bikini top. He pulled back for a moment, enough to ask me if he could with a single look.

I would do literally *anything* for him right now.

Tugging the tie that was secured around my neck, he watched as the flimsy fabric peeled off me. My chest was heaving, exposing my tits. Heavy and full and aching.

My nipples were hardened peaks, brushing against his chest with every breath I took. I looked down between us, seeing nothing but skin and water, fascinated by the way we looked together. The way I remembered it so vividly and still I couldn't remember it feeling like *this.*

I looked down, and that's when I saw it. The words so clearly tattooed on his chest, right over his heart, that I stopped breathing entirely.

My eyes shot up to meet his. I knew he was seeing so much right then, most of all confusion. So, *so* much confusion. Panic and uncertainty and more panic.

"Later," he murmured, shaking his head. "I promise, just let me touch you now." And then he kissed me again, and it was all over. Whatever fight I had left in me died before it even had the chance to take over.

Being with Fane had always felt so completely intoxicating that it was like it wasn't me. I wasn't capable of being able to feel the things he made me feel. Of being touched the way he touched me. I became someone so completely different from who I was that it was like some sort of contact high. I lost myself in him like nothing else I'd ever experienced before him or since.

I felt the way his hands roamed over my body now, how he skimmed the palm of one hand lightly over the sensitive peak of my nipple before massaging me roughly, all while he took the other in between his teeth, biting so hard I cried out. Head tipping back and legs coming up to circle around his hips, I knew I'd been wrong.

I'd never been lost.

It was clear to me now that the only time I truly knew exactly who I was had been in those moments. The only time when I'd had absolute clarity and confidence in answering the questions that had plagued me. Who am I? Who do I want to be? What do I want?

*"Fane,"* I gasped, my hand sinking into his hair and missing the length it used to be.

"You have the most perfect tits." He took a nipple into his mouth again before releasing it with a pop, lapping at my chest with his tongue and sending pulse after pulse of pleasure through me until it was becoming unbearable.

I couldn't help how I started to grind my hips against him. I could feel him. How hard he was, pressed against my stomach.

"Do you remember when you let me fuck them, Cali?" Fane dragged his teeth along my jaw before pulling my head back with the grip he had in my hair. "How you pushed them together for me and let me come all over your pretty little neck?"

I just nodded because fuck yes, I remembered. Who the hell would ever forget something like that?

"Do you remember what you did after that?" Fane captured my mouth in another bruising kiss. No soft or delicate touches, just a buildup of desire that hadn't been sated and had begun to overflow.

"Y-yes."

"Tell me." It was a rough command that made my pussy clench around nothing, and a moan tumbled from my lips.

My back was pressed against something cool, making me arch further into him. Fane just took it as an invitation to drop his mouth back to my tits, soft purple marks blooming all over them now.

"Fane," I breathed his name. My heart was pounding so fast I was sure he could hear it.

"Tell me, Calista."

"You…" Another whimper interrupted my words. He hadn't touched me anywhere else but playing with my nipples, and I was so insanely worked up that I could probably come just like this. "You asked me to sit on…"

"On my what, baby?"

"Your face," I gasped, just as the back of one finger dragged down the seam of my covered pussy. "What is *happening?*"

That was definitely an inside thought.

"What's happening is that I want you to remember the way you ground that perfect cunt of yours all over my face, and I got to watch you while I had my tongue in your tight, wet—"

"Jesus Christ, Fane." I finally opened my eyes and found his already on me. Bright and reflecting the water around us. Mesmerizing.

"You were being a little too considerate, trying to hold your weight." Fane took the lobe of my ear in his mouth while his hands found their way around my waist again. "You said you were worried you'd suffocate me. Do you remember what I said?"

I nodded, and he just tutted. "Don't take your words from me now, Rose. Not after I've waited so long to hear them again. What did I say?"

I was fucking panting. "You said, 'God, I hope so.'"

"Mmm," he hummed, dragging his tongue up the side of my throat and leaving a chaste kiss on the corner of my mouth before he hoisted me up and out of the water, setting me on top of the wide, flat rock that he'd backed us up against. I was almost entirely naked with my bikini bottom wedged up so high that there was nothing left to the imagination about the shape of me.

My whole body was aching, my legs twitching to open. My hands itched to reach up and squeeze my own tits, to play with my nipples the way he had, to give myself some relief.

"While we'll have to do our best to reenact that later, this will do for now."

With one splayed hand on the center of my chest, he gently pushed me back until I was lying flat on the rock. The cold, the wet, and even the possibility of fucking leeches right now couldn't have gotten me to move.

"Are you wet for me, Rose?" Fane's voice was low and gravelly, the words vibrating through me as he left open-mouthed kisses along the insides of my thighs. I couldn't take my eyes off him now, not as he got closer to where I was fucking desperate for him or when he elicited a surprised yelp from me when he wrapped his arms around my legs and gave me a little tug toward the edge of the rock and sank back down into the water.

"Yes," I breathed, voice trembling.

"I have thought of you—*just like this*—every fucking day." He freed one hand and brought it around to drag down the seam of my folds again, pushing the fabric of my swimsuit into my pussy lips. "The closest to heaven that I have ever been is right between your legs, baby. And I have been a man deprived of all that's good while I've dragged myself back to you."

Fane's lips latched onto my clit over the fabric, making me whimper at the relief of the contact, sucking hard before running his nose along the length of me, inhaling deeply. My hands gave up on trying to find something to hold on to around me and settled into his hair. If the grin on his face was anything to go by, I'd say that's what he was waiting for.

*"Please."*

"I do love it when you beg." He pulled the fabric of my swim bottoms to the side, exposing me to him completely. "But you don't need to beg me here, baby. I've been dreaming about this meal for years."

There was no other way to describe what Fane did except with one word. *Feast.*

I was writhing beneath him. He moved one hand to the flat plane of my stomach, holding me down while his tongue lapped over every inch of me. Delving in with no restraint before he moved his mouth from me too soon. I could feel his grin along the skin of my thighs while he played, leaving nips and bites.

I saw my life flash before my eyes when Fane started to fuck me with two thick fingers. I screamed that time, not used to being so full, and my *god,* was I full.

His name kept falling off my own tongue; a plea and a curse. His fingers continuing to pump into me. The pace they set was unforgiving and met with the rough way he sucked my clit, my head started to spin.

"You feel perfect. Your tight little cunt is gripping my fingers, baby. I can feel the way you're clenching. Are you going to come for me?"

Good Lord, this man's mouth.

If I wasn't so consumed with what he was doing to my body, I wouldn't be able to look him in the face. I'd probably still not be able to look him in the face after this.

"Come on my fingers, Calista. I want to taste every last bit of you." He added a third finger and latched his mouth back to the swollen, sensitive flesh of my clit. It took two more pumps, and I fell apart so thoroughly that my ears started to ring and stars took over my entire vision.

My legs collapsed on either side of me, exposing me even further while he kept moving his fingers in and out of me. When he finally pulled them away, my bleary eyes settled on him, and I watched him lick them clean before dragging his tongue up the length of my slit one final time.

I whimpered at the contact, my hands reaching down to push him away. He caught my wrists and pulled me back into the water, still limp and reeling. Kissing me so thoroughly that I could taste myself on his lips. Long, languid strokes of his tongue until I was grinding myself on him, already wanting more.

He slowed down our pace, leaving me only half coherent before pulling the loose ties of my swimming top back up, covering me and tenderly retying the knot at the back of my neck.

Pressed against him, I could feel every inch—hard and thick and impossibly heavy—and I wanted nothing more in that moment than to taste him too. To feel his hand in my hair while I licked him from base to tip. To run my tongue along the slit of the swollen head of his cock and savor him. To see the look on his face when I made him feel good.

My hand moved instinctively, sliding down the ridges of his stomach, the taut muscles trembling under my fingertips. I pushed at the band of his swim trunks and through the clear water, I watched his cock spring free. The soft gasp he released, filled with relief, sent a shiver straight down my spine. It made me *salivate*.

I wrapped my hand around the base of his cock, fingers barely touching, and gave him one hard stroke. He was soft and hard and hot in my hand all at once and with lips parted and his eyes closed, he looked perfect.

I wanted…*everything*. I wanted his hands back on me, his mouth back on me. To be under him, over him, completely and totally at his mercy.

I wanted to watch the way he looked while I felt him sink inside me.

"Cali," he croaked like he was in actual pain. His hand moved down my arm until it covered mine. I was absorbed by the sight of it. The strain of tendons in his forearm while he grappled with his restraint. The contracting of his stomach muscles when I gave his length another slow and languid pump, enthralled by the small jut his hips made.

What I hadn't expected was for him to slowly peel my hand off him. The weight of what he'd done grew heavier every passing second while he tucked himself away.

I felt the frown slowly take over my face. My eyes darted from the water to the words on his chest to the look on his face. Jaw set and eyes hard. Determined in his resolve, yet at the same time, he seemed to be *tormented* by it.

"You…" I shook my head. I didn't know what I was supposed to say.

"Believe me when I tell you, I want you to touch me," his tone was raw. Unflinching.

"I…don't understand."

"I want to feel your hands on me," he whispered. His eyes dropped to my mouth a second before his thumb traced my bottom lip. "Feel your mouth on me. To *watch* you…" Fane shook his head minutely like he needed to physically remove the image from his mind. "But I can't. Not like this."

"Like this?" I hated how vulnerable I sounded. The shock of what was happening was like a power outage on my defenses.

"There are too many walls between us, Cali."

If I thought he sounded like he was in pain before, it had nothing on the way he sounded now, the way he looked. "We need to talk first. I don't think it's smart for us to…" He took a deep, shaking breath.

I pushed at his chest. "Not like *this*? What does that mean?"

"It means that there's too much shit unsaid between us right now. That I need you to hear me out before we can—"

"And you don't think *I* have things that I want to say to *you?*" God, I was so fucking *stupid*.

"Cali—"

"No. Fuck you, Fane." I pushed away from him in earnest now, wading through the water to get out. My heart was thrashing, and I felt so incredibly foolish. "News flash, letting you stick your face between my legs doesn't eradicate anything that's happened between us. It doesn't mean that, all of a sudden, the way I feel about you is miraculously different."

"Cali, that's not what I fucking meant. If you just wait one—"

"You're not the only one here who has thought about what they'd say if we ever saw each other again. God, I fucking *hate*—"

Fane was right behind me while we moved out of the water. "If you say you hate me one more time, I swear to *fuck*—"

"You have no idea what I do or don't feel. No idea at all. And if you think that by somehow making me vulnerable and giving in, then hold back like some fucking noble jackass is going to make me, what? Soften up and want to hear anything you say more than I did before? Well, you're sorely mistaken."

"I wasn't trying to *soften you up*."

I didn't need to look at him to know he was tugging at his hair. He'd always struggled to find his words, the *right* words, and yes, there was a part of me that wanted to just fucking stop. To give him the patience and space to figure it out the way I used to. But also, I was well within my right to rip him a whole new asshole.

There was a crack behind us that made me turn around. Fane was there in an instant, an arm circling around my chest protectively, both of us barely breathing while we looked over the forest around us.

I had to double-take the arm slung across me before I realized what he was doing. "Get your hands off me!" I turned around and shoved him again, which did a whole lot of nothing. The man was fucking huge.

"And that"—I point at the words on his chest—"that's a sick fucking joke, you...you fucking sicko!"

"Stop yelling at me, and listen to me for *two seconds*."

"No." The word came out a deranged laugh and really said it all about my mental state. "I'm leaving, and if you're not at the truck when I get there, I'm leaving without you." I pulled my dress over my head and tugged my shoes back on. I knew he would catch up to me in less time than it would take to blink.

"Ask me when I got the tattoo." His footfalls were steady and sure behind me.

"I don't care," I said, tripping for the second time.

"Ask me, Calista."

"I don't fucking *care*, Fane."

"I got it the day you left."

"Stop it!"

"The day you left, I took one of the notes you always use to write for me. That you left around the house."

"*Stop!*" I was all but screaming at him now. Because I could see it, what he was describing. My linked letters on bright pink sticky notes on the fridge, the closet door, the bathroom mirror. Because I hadn't wanted him to ever forget how much I fucking *loved* him.

"And I got it tattooed, in your writing, right over my heart. So that I'd never fucking forget that for as long as I live, even if you're not next to me, it's beating the same as yours. Because I *can't*—" His voice broke, and he cut himself off.

I didn't want to listen to his words. They didn't *match up*.

"Do you remember writing that for me? What that meant?"

*Don't listen, don't listen.*

"Every fucking day, you wrote them for me. '*Forever synced.*'"

Nothing about him being here, showing up, made anything match up. *He* was the one who didn't want *me*. He said *no*.

I was so busy going through that moment over and over, and the way his presence now felt like an assault on everything I'd forced myself to believe.

Wiping furiously at the tears still falling, I stormed for the driver's side, hoping I'd somehow lost him on the way back. Hoping that he would just disappear from my life again.

*That*, I had learned to live with.

*This?* Whatever was happening now? I had no idea how to navigate it. How to survive it.

A rough hand wrapped around my arm, and I ignored the way my body sang at the contact. The way my heart tripped over itself. How the warmth of that single touch ignited my very fucking soul.

Instead, I ripped it from his grasp and whirled on it. The words died in my mouth. Shriveled up into nothing at the look on his face.

Defeated.

Like he'd been a man with one last thread of hope, and it had just snapped.

"I'll drive," he murmured, not even looking at me. All he did was walk around to the passenger side and open my door.

I was in a daze. He was going from hot to cold, and still, I felt like I knew *nothing*. That I was missing something, but I didn't know what. I didn't trust my judgment even if I wanted to, and that just made the tears fall harder.

I was out of the car before it had even stopped in the gravel drive of the cottage, desperate for some distance. To take a breath of air that didn't smell like him, but I felt him at my back immediately, looming and haunting.

The tension sitting between us like a steel pole, keeping us from coming any closer, but stopping us from moving away as we found ourselves once again in the useless front room of my house.

"Not a single thing I have said to you since I got here has been a lie." Fane's voice was both the balm that soothed me and the blade that sliced, and I couldn't make up my mind which was worse.

"I don't even know who you are, Fane." My voice held every ounce of the heaviness that had taken over my body. The weight of the words that I'd thought on, day after day, had become so much a part of me that I'd gotten used to the way they dragged me down.

It was a losing battle for me now. I could feel my knees threatening to buckle.

"Yes, you do." He took a tiny step toward me before stopping himself. His jaw twitched at the same time his hands clenched at his sides.

He closed his eyes for a breath before speaking again. "You know *exactly* who I am, and I know you. I know you so thoroughly I don't think I could even exist and not find my way back to you. Be *pulled* back to you. Every single thing I've done has been for you."

He paused at the scoff that flew out of my mouth, and all it did was serve to make his eyes darken. His face drew in, and it was like I was actively watching all the light leave his body like he was trying to show me that this was all he had been for the last two years.

His voice was gravelly when he spoke again. "I'll take everything you can throw at me. I want it. The anger, the pain, the fucking frustration. I will *happily* take it. I deserve it, I know I do." His laugh was sad and empty, and so not like the one that left me with nothing but open blue skies. The laughter that sent those heavy, unforgiving clouds so far I couldn't see them. This one drew them in, called out for them. Wanted to be suffocated by their darkness.

His eyes flicked up to meet mine, hard and unwavering. "Take your pound of flesh, Calista. Cut it from me any which way you like. I won't fight you. I would rather you fight with me than nothing at all."

I wanted to scream.

"Whatever you're doing right now, it's not going to last." I was shaking my head vehemently. I could feel myself slipping, nearing that edge I'd fallen over once before with such a solid sense of confidence that I would not meet my end at the bottom. "You're here because you're sad. Maybe you're lonely. Guilty? I don't know, but there is nothing left here, Fane." I waved a panicked hand between us. "Don't you understand that? It's all fucking *broken*, and I have cut myself *repeatedly* trying to clean up the mess that was left behind, and I couldn't. I...I *hate* you." Those last three words had been the same lie I told myself consistently. The blanket that shrouded me, kept me safe and protected.

"I don't believe you."

"That doesn't make it any less true," I whispered, my voice trembling under the weight of it all. The urge to yell at him was there, but the fight was draining from me, seeping out like a slow bleed. I felt like I was being crushed alive, suffocated by everything I'd been holding in. I needed to cut something loose, to let something go, or I wasn't sure I'd ever find the strength to stand back up.

"I have two whole fucking years of memories, right here." He pointed at his temple, taking another step closer to me. "That tells me hate isn't something that could *ever* exist between us." He dragged a hand down his face. "Rose, I need to tell you...just, five minutes. Hear me out for *five minutes.*"

I shook my head, turning away from him, desperate for space.

"Cali." He was right behind me, his voice as jagged and broken as mine.

"I do. I *hate* you," I sobbed, walking into different rooms of the house just to keep moving, past Jerry, who had never looked so lost in his life.

*"No!"* Fane yelled, voice cracking and splintering something inside of me. My anger didn't leave, but it bent, twisted, reshaped itself into something closer to sorrow. A hollow ache I couldn't hold back.

The weight of those years without him suddenly felt unbearable. The hold on the words I had wanted to scream at him, and also never wanted him to hear, shattering.

I whirled on him, chest heaving and vision blurred. Swallowing again and again to keep the sobs at bay. To make way for the words that were coming, whether I wanted them to or not.

Finally.

"Do you know what it's like to try and *want* somebody, when you're in love with someone else?"

"Cali—" Fane frowned, shaking his head at the whiplash he was no doubt feeling.

*"No!"* I choked, consumed by the dread of reliving that moment. Of feeling like I didn't just betray *him*, but I betrayed myself. "You might have been able to turn away from whatever you felt for me. Turn it off and walk away, but I *loved* you." My voice broke. "And not in the way you love sunsets, or you love your favorite fucking movie. I. *Loved*. You. And when I had to deal with that alone? It was like I was drowning. I…"

I took a deep breath, I needed to calm down. When I spoke again, my voice was quiet, and my tears had stopped, and all that was left were those bloody, weeping wounds that had never healed.

"I know that's not your problem. It's mine. I'm not trying to say it's your problem. But you want to know why I hate you so much? *That's* why," I said, rushing back to the living room to grab my bag, dropping a kiss onto Jerry's nose that he met with a cry of his own.

I needed to get out of this house that was too small for all the things that were just said within its walls. All the confessions it held.

I opened the front door, forcing myself to look back at him where he stood just behind me. "I hate you because you forced me to try to want someone else when all I have *ever* wanted was you."

I held his stare, giving him what he wanted—no walls between us.

He looked like all he wanted to do was pull me to him, to wrap me up in him and help me fix everything the way he always had been able to before. I wanted to let him. But more than that, I was desperate for the explanation he had for me—this big, imposing, fucking haunting *why* that would make it all make sense.

The answer to *why* we had ended up where we were instead of where we should have been. The truth was, I wasn't sure I was ready for the answer.

I'd thought about what it would be since the moment I left. Built it up and broke it down from something small and insignificant to something huge and life-changing, and I didn't know which would hurt less.

I didn't slam the door behind me. I just closed it quietly and didn't look back.

I had no idea where I was going or what I was doing. All I knew was that I was desperate for the first time in my life to be nowhere near Darling.

The real fucking kicker? I didn't hate Fane Mackenzie, and I never have. I never could. As much as I tried, as I desperately wanted to. It would have made everything so much easier, but no. There was no possibility of hate in my heart for him.

It was definitely not safe for me to be driving right now. What I really wanted was to drive to my parents' place, to run to my dad and feel him wrap me in his arms the way he used to. To hold me close and rock me from side to side. I discarded that thought immediately, knowing it would only make him worry because I couldn't even tell *him* the truth. I'd lied to him so completely since I'd arrived back in town, and if I came clean, all he would do is overthink everything I said, everything I did, and blame himself for the decisions that I'd made.

Two years worth of worry would flood him, and I'd never survive it, having to watch his heart break again.

I grabbed my phone and dialed the only other person I could think to go to.

"Cali?" Delilah's frown was audible and her hesitancy a palpable thing, like she thought this might have been a butt dial.

"I know we haven't talked properly in a really long time, and I haven't been a good friend, or even a friend at all, but I really need a drink, and I don't want to do it alone."

The last part came out a sob, turning into a cry of relief when she replied.

"I'll meet you at Mags's in ten."

# 28

# Fane

**After**

The moment I walked into the bar, Ashton waved at me like we were on opposite sides of a fun park, yelling something I couldn't hear over the music that was playing.

I was thankful that the corner he'd taken up residence in with a couple other guys from work seemed to be protected from the way the speakers were destroying people's eardrums.

"If I knew the way to get you to a bar was to tell you that the love of your life was guzzling down drinks like it was her divine given path in life, I would have saved myself a whole lot of trouble."

"And you're out, why?" I slid into the booth next to him, already wishing I could leave. After leaving my job at Heavenly Horns, the appeal of frequenting a bar just vanished from my mind. When Ash begged, I indulged him from time to time, but I was more than happy to down a few drinks at home.

"There's a bachelorette party going on." He gestured to the group of women standing by the bar, the one in white giving him particularly gooey eyes. When I looked back at him, he was giving her a little finger wave.

"Tell me you didn't seduce the bride-to-be."

"What? No! 'Course not. I went for the one in white." He was still waving at her when I punched him in the arm, and like it was an automated reply, his fist came flying back at me, which I dodged before flicking his ear.

"That's the fucking bride, you jackass."

"Hey! That fucking *hurt.*" He started poking at my side, which eventually morphed into this slapping fight until I had him in a headlock, and he was trying to slide under the table to evade it.

"I tap out!" he choked out after the two other guys from work had gotten up and left in a hurry.

"You let me have that one," I grumbled. As much as I could hold my own, I'd never been able to hold anything where Ash was concerned. The man was a different breed.

"Yeah, well, it seemed like bad karma to kick a man already down." Ashton sat back in the booth, sliding over so that our arms were no longer touching, and took a big gulp of his beer before passing it over to me with a firm clap on my back.

"She's—"

"I know." I'd known exactly where Cali was the second I walked in. She was pretty much directly diagonal to where we were sitting, with a girl with hair almost as black as hers, but the ends were a bright royal blue.

"I got here about an hour ago. They seemed to have been settled for a while."

I stared at her, watching the way she talked so animatedly with the woman across from her. Their hands were entangled in the middle of the table. Heads bowed together one moment and tipped back in big, face-splitting laughter the next.

"There's also that guy." Ashton pointed to the door I walked in and the guy sitting in a chair right beside it. He could've looked like someone who was part of the contractor team that had come to town with us, with his black jeans, cargo boots, and black hoodie, but I would've known if he was.

"Is he—"

"Sleeping? No. I thought that too, but if Blue over there so much as breathes in a way that doesn't seem remotely normal, dark and handsome over *there* gets this look in his eyes that I'm pretty sure translates directly into, *I'll rip your dick off.*"

"You need help."

"He's my eye twin." Ash gave this little one-shoulder shrug that made it seem like this should be a huge deal, and he was downplaying it.

"Am I supposed to be impressed?"

The punch he gave my arm hurt it so bad I felt it in my balls. "God, you're the fucking *worst.*"

"*Is it a big deal?*" He repeated the words with a look of utter betrayal on his face while he mimicked stabbing a knife into his heart and twisting it. "Is the Pope Catholic? Fucking *yes*, it's a big deal, you wiener. He's got icies too." He gestured to his icy-blue eyes. "Makes us look like yin and yang. Me with the blond hair. Him with the black hair." Ashton was staring at him with his chin propped in his hand and fucking hearts in his eyes. An exaggerated sigh deflated his body, and he slumped back in the booth, his head rolling to face me.

"So." He reached out to poke my cheek, and I slapped his hand. "Want to talk about it?"

I leaned back, slumping next to him and taking the beer glass he offered me for another drink. "She hates me."

"No, she doesn't." The thing about Ash was he could go from being all *eye twin* to the most dependable, unswayable guy.

"You didn't hear what she said. The look on her face." Everything I was telling him was broad, I knew that. But he knew I wasn't going to give him details, not where Cali was concerned. He knew us both well enough to not need more.

"She doesn't hate you, Fane. She probably wants to. What she likely hates more is that she doesn't hate you at all."

"You're so wise for someone who refers to his own eyes as 'icies.'"

"I appreciate that." He took back his beer glass. "How's your plan going?"

"You know, it was coming along."

"Yeah?"

"Yep." I held my hand out for his beer.

"And then you fucked it?"

"Big time."

Ash reached over to clap me on the shoulder again in what I was sure was his way of softening his impending *I told you so* when the girls stood up and our backs snapped to attention, eyes on them. With their hands clasped and faces completely determined, they made their way toward the dance floor.

"This is going to be amazing." Ash grinned, watching Cali wobble toward the group of writhing bodies.

"Is this…are they playing Bad Omens?"

"Mmm," Ash hummed around his mouth full of beer. "Mags said it was 'Youths' Music Night'. I told her she needed a new name, and she looked at me like I had a set of balls resting on my forehead."

The beer that had been in my mouth pretty much sprayed out my nose, and I started coughing. Ash just kept talking while simultaneously patting me on the back, which turned out to be not helpful at all.

"I also told her she needed a new DJ. Whoever it is played that new single from Lady Luck, which I approved of, but followed it up with some song about hills sung by what I'm pretty sure was a quartet."

I was still coughing, and Ash just shoved his mostly empty beer back at me to help, and that was when she saw me. I half expected a bloodcurdling scream to rip out of her. Instead, her head tipped to the side a little, and slowly she lifted her middle finger up at me.

I couldn't take my eyes off her. I settled back into the booth and tilted my head back, lifting my middle finger to her in return.

"Is this some weird foreplay thing you guys have started doing?" Ashton's warm breath was right at my ear, and I felt no remorse when my palm made firm, if not unintentional, contact to his face.

"Fucking *ow!*"

"Your moist breath in my ear is so fucking unwelcome, I can't even tell you." I flipped him off too before I looked back to Cali. Ashton was busy mumbling about how I should be so lucky when I noticed the guy he'd pointed out before.

I hadn't even seen him move, but he had. He was standing further along the wall with his eyes laser-focused on the girl Cali was with.

It was almost painful having to sit here. To watch Cali without any inhibitions, walls completely down, even if it was because of way too much liquor in her system, judging by the amount of shot glasses on the table they'd been sitting at.

I hated that she was right there, just within my reach, and yet I had no right to touch her.

"You're doing your whole sad boy smolder thing."

"My what?" I snapped.

"Your sad boy smolder." Ash leaned around so that he was putting his face in my line of sight. I pushed it away, covering said face with my entire hand.

"I don't smolder."

He barked a laugh. "Yes, you do. In a very sad boy way."

"Shut up." I tried to put my hand back on his face, which he evaded with the sort of skill that definitely reinforced that getting him in a headlock had been because he'd let me.

"Just go up there."

"No. She needs this. A night off with a friend."

I couldn't stop seeing the way she'd looked before she left. I knew that she was making a point. Making me regret my words when I told her in no uncertain terms that I didn't want any of these fucking walls between us.

I had dreamed, every damn day, about what it would be like to finally be close enough to her where I could count the freckles on her cheeks. See the way her pulse flickered in her throat, hear the way she breathed. Calm and steady while she lay with her head on my chest.

I savored every second that my eyes traced over her, watching the way she tipped her head back and threw her hands up above her head. Still in her sundress from earlier, she looked fucking beautiful.

"Is she *flossing?*" Ashton sounded like he was about to wet himself, and I delivered a solid punch to his shoulder. Cali had never been able to dance, but it didn't make me want to look away from her any less, even as she transitioned to that move where she was cleaning each ear with an imaginary Q-tip before throwing it away.

I turned to Ash then. "I'm going to get her back."

"I know," he said, eyes meeting mine. He'd always been so sure of me, even when I hadn't been sure of myself.

Ash rolled his head back toward the dance floor, mouth opening like he was about to ask me to move so he could go grab another beer when I felt his body still, and he breathed a curse. By the time I looked back to the dance floor, it was too late.

I'd had my eyes off her for one fucking second. That was all. Just one.

Dark and Handsome, as Ash dubbed him, had already made his way onto the dance floor. An arm wrapped around the waist of Cali's friend, mouth at her ear, while her eyes struggled to focus on literally anything.

My eyes snapped back to Cali, who'd turned away from us, away from her friend. She was still swaying among the packed dance floor, oblivious to everything but the music and the alcohol coursing through her. I saw the moment Declan's hands found her waist, fingers curling possessively as if claiming her, and slid down to her hips.

I watched as her head lolled back against his shoulder, tilting slightly as though to see who it was. There was a hint of a smile on her lips. My stomach dropped, a cold rush of dread sweeping through me.

It was like every fucked-up nightmare I'd ever had was unfolding in real-time.The kind where you know the ending is going to destroy you but you can't wake up. I was out of the booth in a heartbeat, Ash close on my heels. My blood boiled hotter with every step, my vision narrowing in on them until nothing else existed but her and the bastard touching her.

And then she saw him.

Her eyes widened, and the sound that tore out of her throat was something primal, raw, filled with pure terror. It froze the entire fucking dance floor.

Cali's elbow swung in a wide arc, catching Declan across the face just as her scream tore through the air. The sound echoed in my head, branding me with the realization that this wasn't fear of a stranger or some drunken overreaction. This was her body reacting on instinct, fighting for fucking survival.

I'd heard her scream like that once before.

"No!" Her voice cracked on the word as she stumbled back, crashing into me. Her back connected with my chest, but the impact didn't stop her from spinning around, swaying as her hands came up in front of her like she was prepared to strike me too.

Then, like a switch flipped, her body sagged. Recognition dawned in her hazy eyes, and relief washed over her features, slowly chipping away at the terror that had frozen her. She stumbled forward, her forehead coming to rest against my chest, her hands clutching at my shirt in tight, trembling fists.

"Do you see him too?" Her voice was barely a whisper, slurred and fragile as it filtered through the pounding music.

The question cut me deeper than anything she could've screamed. Her grip on me tightened, her fingers curling into the fabric like it was the only thing tethering her to the ground.

"I see him, baby," I murmured into the top of her head. I lifted my hand up, letting it sit on the back of her neck, but I didn't take my eyes off Declan.

He'd staggered back a few steps, one hand brushing his jaw where she'd hit him. The crowd around us had gone eerily still, people watching as his eyes slowly moved over them, meeting one pair after another. His face darkened with each connection, the flush of anger creeping up his neck until it was like his skin was about to burst. Then his gaze landed on her, and I wanted to pull the eyes from his head.

It was the flicker in his eyes that set my teeth on edge, a brief moment where they softened—possessive and twisted—like he thought she belonged to him. Then they found mine.

Everything about him changed. There was no hiding the hate that burned there, the sick delight curling his lips into a sneer that dared me to do something about it. He wanted me to snap, to lose control right here in front of everyone.

But my control was something I'd honed since I was a child and I had much more appealing ideas of how exactly he'd lose his life than the sort of violence his mind was no doubt conjuring up about how he might prefer I lost mine.

He'd looked at me like that before when I caught him drowning that bird. This time, he didn't bother hiding it. Not the smugness. Not the challenge. Not the promise.

Declan took a step back, the sneer still plastered on his face. My body felt calm though, with my hand resting on the back of Cali's neck. Her breath warming my chest. I didn't need to follow him to the dark alley beside the bar like a ravenous, vengeful child to let him know that his days were limited. He could see it clear enough for himself.

I had nothing to prove to him, but he'd die all the same.

That thought settled in me, like a balm on a burn.

Declan slowly backed out of the bar, his eyes never leaving Cali. They trailed over her like he was memorizing her, like this was only the first act in whatever fucked up play he'd written in his head.

The longer he was gone, the more the tension in the room eased. I could feel it in the way Cali's body relaxed against mine, the trembling subsiding little by little. It wasn't until her head tipped to the side, her glassy eyes blinking up at me, that I let myself take a breath.

"I'm still very sad at you." She frowned and held up a finger in thought, like nothing had happened. "Mad. I am mad at you, but please take me home."

"What about your friend?" I looked around but noticed she was gone and so was Dark and Handsome. Cali just waved. "Dylan was here with the eyes of a flock on her."

"Eyes of a flock?" I quirked an eyebrow.

"Yep. The whole flock." She lifted her hand in a halfhearted circle motion. "All the birds." Cali crooked her finger in my direction, and I leaned down. She didn't whisper though. In fact, I was sure a great number of people heard what came out of her mouth. "I told her about the whole hair pervert thing!"

"*Hair pervert?*" Ashton mouthed the words at me over Cali's head, and he looked like, for all the world, this might've been the best fucking day of his life.

"Hey, Cathy?" Ashton snapped his fingers in front of Cali's face, and she swatted him away before giving him the finger. It felt like all was right in the world, just for a moment, to see him on the other end of that gesture. "Between one and ten?"

Ash asked Cali a question I'd heard a thousand times. It was like an encrypted shorthand they used to get to the point quickly on important things. How drunk they were, how hungry, how likely they thought it would be for either of them to shave off just one eyebrow. That last one had been a ten and left both of them looking ridiculous for a month and a half.

He was still laughing when Cali said, "Thirteen."

"I'm never going to let you forget this."

"Go and hug a bunny, you big flapjack."

"This is *awesome.*" Ashton looked way too happy when he pulled out his phone and took a photo of Cali now inspecting her middle finger so close to her own face she was going cross-eyed.

"Okay, that's more than enough. Delete that." I pointed at his phone before I scooped her up into my arms. She let out a little yelp but quickly let her head fall to my shoulder.

"No chance, pookie bear."

"Don't go after him, Ashton." I looked him straight in the eyes, letting him know if anyone was going to keep Cali safe, it would be me.

"It's here if you need it." Ashton tapped the middle of his forehead, his signature gesture, a wordless promise that he was ready to step in if I asked.

I walked out of the bar with Cali in my arms, ignoring all the eyes that were on us, and got her situated in the front of my truck.

The drive home was quiet. The only sound was the tires on the road and Cali's mumbles about hair and birds. Every so often, she shifted, her hand reaching out like she was searching for something—maybe for someone. Each time, my knuckles whitened against the steering wheel.

Jerry met us at the front door with quiet whimpers, his wet nose touched all over Cali's legs. When she'd left, he'd been beside himself. Sat right at the front door and watched it. Ears pricked and on guard for her to come back.

I settled her into bed, leaving only to let Jerry out one last time and check the locks on the doors and windows.

It felt weird getting into bed with her now. It's not like we were on good terms before, but we'd moved past whatever had been going on before, when it was just verbal sparring matches and getting under each other's skin. When it was vacuuming her landlord's driveway just to get a rise out of her.

I should give her the space she needed and sleep on the couch with the dog, and I swear to God I was going to, but then her hand reached out across the mattress like she was looking for me, seeking me out and my heart fucking stuttered. When she didn't find me and managed to peel her head off the pillow and look around, she found me standing like an idiot at the end of the bed, staring at her.

"Well, that's not weird at all," she grumbled before flopping her head back down to the pillow. Even drunk and sad-mad at me, she still made me laugh.

"What are you doing? You're like a big, tattooed Edward Cullen. Come on," she grumbled again, voice muffled by the pillow, before patting the empty side of the bed.

I could have tried to fight her on it. I should have. We'd already established that I wasn't a good man, though.

I walked around and pulled the covers back, sliding in between the cool sheets, rolling on my side and staring right at her. Her hand flung right out, narrowly missing my face before she settled it on the top of my head, fingers entwined with my hair like she'd done a hundred times before.

"All right, who's first?" Her words were definitely less slurred than they'd been at the bar, but they had a sleepy edge to them now.

"First for what?" I murmured.

"Three for three."

I snorted. "I'm not drunk, Cali, it wouldn't be fair."

She snorted. "Things not being fair is my life memo."

"Your...you mean motto?"

"Sure." She shrugged and nuzzled into her pillow. "Three for three."

"Cali—" I started to fight her on it again. Three for Three was a game we'd made up when we were drunk. When we were both without inhibitions.

"Well, do you promise to just answer like you have none?"

"I mean—"

"Then it's subtle."

"*Settled.*" I laughed, grabbing a free pillow and throwing it at her face. When she pulled it away, she gave me this goofy smile that settled something in me. "Okay, fine," I murmured, "You go first."

"All right," she hummed, closing her eyes for a second before she opened them.

"What do your new tattoos mean?" She wasn't looking at me when she spoke, instead I could feel her focus on my neck.

"You won't believe anything I say."

"I will." Her hazel eyes snapped to mine. "I promise."

I waited a second, weighing her words, and in the end it didn't matter. "They're all about you," I whispered, but I think she knew that already.

Her fingers moved across the sheets, gently tracing over the timepiece that you couldn't really see on the left side of my neck.

"This one?" she breathed.

"A pocket watch." I swallowed, knowing there was no turning back once she heard it all. "That was the time I woke up and realized you were gone."

Her fingers froze, but she didn't look at me. I saw the way her lashes fluttered, a quiet shudder rolling through her as her hand moved to the rose inked on the opposite side of my neck.

Cali didn't look at me, but I saw her eyes, the way they got imperceptibly glassier.

"This one?" she rasped, hands dancing over to the other side of my neck, to the rose.

"I think you know that one."

She nodded, and one tear spilled over the edge of those wide, trusting eyes of hers. "Cali Rose," she said. "For me."

"For you." I reached out to swipe the tear she let run free, and her hand reached out for mine. Dainty fingers wrapped around mine, holding it to her chest like an anchor.

"This one." She asked about the design that climbed up the center of my throat.

"I thought it looked really cool," I admitted, a grin tugging at the corner of my mouth. She hiccupped a laugh, rolling her eyes.

She reached for the hand she wasn't holding. Fingers gliding over ink on my skin before locking her gaze with mine.

"Ursa Major. Your constellation."

She stared at it for so long I didn't dare interrupt, afraid to disrupt whatever was running through her mind. When she finally spoke, her voice was quiet. "And this one?" Her hand hovered over the compass inked on my other hand, forever pointing north.

"So I'd find my way back to you," I rasped, and the air between us grew impossibly still.

Cali closed her eyes, and I watched as she tried to hold it together. I knew that none of this made sense to her, that she still didn't want to hear what I had to say. I was half torn wanting to even tell her. It had been my cross to bear for so long that it would be easier to just not. I knew she wouldn't believe me, and I couldn't bring myself to tell her *why* when I knew she wouldn't listen.

But she heard everything I said just then, and when the silent tears started to rack her frame, I pulled her into me, humming into the hair on the top of her head. Breathing in her cherry blossom and milk-and-honey smell that soothed all my jagged edges. I held her long after she'd fallen asleep, like if I gripped her tight enough, *long* enough, I could fix everything I'd broken.

It didn't matter that we hadn't finished our game. That she'd only asked one of her three questions. That I hadn't asked any of mine.

I fell asleep wrapped around her, her legs intertwined with mine, feeling at peace despite it all for the first time in years. Like this was right where I was supposed to be.

When I woke up, I was still wrapped around Cali, and I opened my eyes to find hers already bright and clear. Looking at the tattoos on my neck, the tattoos on my hands, and then finally, to me.

"Was it true?" she whispered.

"Every word."

I saw how she was battling herself on it. Wanting to both believe me and not trusting herself to all at once. Her eyes drifted over me once more before she took a deep breath, and her body practically sagged into the bed. I saw the tension and apprehension and uncertainty ebb away.

The little smile that appeared on her face might have been the most beautiful thing I'd ever seen.

"Okay."

"I have one more thing to say," I murmured.

"You're going to ruin this moment, aren't you?" Her smile turned wry, but there was no malice in it.

"Yesterday—"

"Fane, no. It's—"

"Please, Cali. This is important."

If she said she didn't want to talk about it again, I'd respect it. Sometimes it felt like I was walking on eggshells around her. Terrified that I'd make the wrong move, and I'd lose her again. Sometimes it felt like the ground beneath my feet was steady enough for me to push a little harder.

When she didn't say anything, I kept going.

"I have thought about you every single day from the moment you left." Her eyes snapped to the clock on my neck. "I've thought of everything. Every single piece of you." I swallowed hard. "It probably won't help my cause to tell you I'm pissed at you too, but no matter the answers you have to my questions, I'm going to want you anyway. No matter what your 'why' is, it doesn't matter to me. It's never mattered."

"My 'why'?"

"Why you left." My chest was fucking aching.

Her brow furrowed deeper. "What's your 'why'?"

"Why I let you." I reached up and tucked a wayward strand of hair behind her ear. "That's why I said no. Because you might hear my answer and hate it, and if I let you…if you touched me and you still left? I wouldn't survive that. Not twice."

It was the most honest I'd been with myself since I could remember, the most open I think I'd ever been.

Her fingers stilled, gripping the hem of my shirt. She took a deep breath, letting it out slowly. "So, we need to talk."

"We do."

She peeked up at me, a ghost of her smile returning. "Can you make me breakfast first?"

"Yes, ma'am."

# 29

# Calista

**After**

I walked out of the bathroom Monday morning, still scrunching the ends of my hair with a towel, and rounded the corner into the kitchen.

"Hey, do you—" Fane turned, words freezing mid-sentence. His mouth opened and closed like he was malfunctioning. Those violet eyes of his—brighter than usual—didn't leave my face, locked onto me.

"What?" My face felt like it was on fire. Actual fire. I dragged a finger up my nose, pushing my glasses back up out of habit.

"You…you're wearing your glasses," he said, his frown pulling a giggle out of me. At the sound, his lips curved into an easy smile, his hand tugged at his hair in a way that felt far too casual for how hard my heart was beating.

"Yeah, it's been a while." I shrugged, trying to play it off, even though these glasses hadn't seen daylight since the day I moved back to Darling—desperate to come to terms with the fact that the person I had been was no longer the person I was.

I wanted something physical, something real to show how I'd irrevocably changed.

The glasses were the first thing that came to mind.

"You look…" he murmured, finding his words. "I think you look beautiful either way." The words settled in my chest like a warm blanket on a cold night. Like a fine thread and needle, slowly but surely closing me up.

For the first time in a long time, it felt like there were no walls between us. No rules or ribbons of tension strung so tight they threatened to snap. It was like taking that first clean breath after the smoke cleared.

Even during my weekly visit with Dad, where we sat hand in hand, staring out at the mountains that framed Darling, a part of me itched to get home. Back to Fane.

The conversation we both knew we needed to have hung between us like a storm cloud, but neither of us made much effort to break it open. It was a team effort, really. We took turns steering clear.

Whenever Fane tried to broach it, I suddenly had to let Jerry out to do his business. When I made the mistake of nudging toward it, he'd miraculously get the world's most important phone call.

I knew we were treading lightly in the in-between that we'd found ourselves in, but it was never more apparent that it couldn't be where we stayed forever. Not when we sat in the quiet of his truck before getting out, our eyes locking, and all I wanted was for him to reach out and touch me.

Or I walked by the bathroom just as he was getting out with nothing but a towel draped around his hips. I hadn't been able to tear my eyes off the water that still clung to his skin, or how he gripped his towel, knuckles going white. I'd been seconds away from ripping it out of his grasp and sinking to my knees in front of him.

And definitely not when he was cooking dinner for us again, and I planted myself on the counter just to talk to him. Just doing that felt so fucking easy. The way we could fill the air with everything and nothing. How the silence between us wasn't uncomfortable. It was peaceful.

I'd missed it. Been completely oblivious to the extent which I'd craved it.

We talked about everything except what we needed to talk about. Pretending like I didn't want to touch him. Like I didn't want him to touch me. Like this was enough and I was going to be okay no matter what his 'why' turned out to be.

Conveniently forgetting the entire reason he was here in the first place.

It didn't escape me that he'd come to Darling for a reason that wasn't me, and what was happening now was just a result of the lie I'd roped him into. The thing was, it didn't *feel* like that.

I felt like I'd gotten my best friend back. It was hard not to feel the way my heart started to reach out to him too, and how hard it was to pull it back.

*Not yet.* I had to tell myself over and over. *Not yet.*

Dinner at my parents' place had been hilarious, especially because Ashton had shown up for the second week in a row, charming my mom and antagonizing my dad with charm in equal measure. By the time Fane and I left, I felt light.

I felt *alive*, and I didn't know what to do with that. It felt fragile.

"Have a good one, lovebirds," Ashton called out to us before he got back into his car, and Fane and I both flipped him off. The grin he gave me was panty-melting, and I was suddenly, painfully aware of his hand in mine. The roughness of his skin against my palm. The way those hands had felt gliding up my inner thighs, spreading me open before his mouth—

"Home!" I yelled the word so loud that Fane jumped. "Let's go home." I trudged ahead of him. When I heard his husky laughter behind me, because I knew *he* knew what was going on in my head, I just lifted my middle finger over my shoulder.

"I told you, baby," Fane called out, his voice dripping with heat. "That just turns me on."

By the time I slammed the car door shut, the ghost of a smile had already broken through my forced scowl. He slid into the driver's seat, gave me one of his signature winks, and I rolled my eyes, praying he couldn't see the way my thighs pressed together.

I woke up early Friday morning, restless in a way that left my skin tight and my heart racing. My dreams had been vivid, filled with wandering hands and breathless cries, of being so impossibly full that I couldn't remember how to breathe. They'd been of Fane.

Above me. Behind me. *Inside* me.

I was pretty sure I had been grinding myself on his leg, and instead of having to explain that to him in a way that *wouldn't* end with me needing to hop back into the shower, throwing whatever mediocre attempt I made at being quiet to the wind, I got up and creeped out of the bedroom.

Since Declan walked out of Mags', there'd been no more notes on my car. No more prickling sensation on my runs. It was as if he'd vanished—not just his stalkerish tendencies, but from Darling entirely.

He hadn't shown up to work. I overheard Ashton talking to Fane about it on Tuesday when he was in his usual spot in the back corner of the café. Ash came in looking tense and drawn, his shoulders tight. Though their conversation was low and clipped, I caught enough to know Declan's absence was noted—and not in a good way.

Fane had dropped me off on Wednesday as usual before he spent that day doing something for Mackenzie Co. I wasn't sure what it was exactly, but I'd also not really asked any questions. I was still working on the assumption I was getting through to him on the 'against' side of developing Darling.

We had the Autumn Fair coming up on the weekend, and then I had one last ace up my sleeve. A final push to convince him. But with Declan gone, I felt more than fine heading into town on my own.

I also couldn't remember the last time I'd gone this long without driving my car, and since Ashton had driven it back for me the morning after Delilah and I tore up the dance floor at Mags', it just sat in the driveway.

I settled into the driver's seat, mumbling a little apology and hoping the car didn't feel like I'd moved on and forgotten her when I pulled my buzzing phone from my pocket to a message from Delilah.

The other thing that had shifted in my life was reconnecting with Delilah. We'd spoken every day since them, trading the messes of our lives as if no time had passed at all. Once that dam broke, our friendship flowed on like there hadn't been a two-year hiatus.

I flicked off my reply and drove into work with a smile on my face, feeling like my life had substance for the first time in a long time—even though my car was definitely throwing a hissy fit at a few different stop signs.

*See, I told you they had feelings.*

When Fane showed up an hour later, hair still damp from his shower, and flopped into his usual seat in the back corner, I couldn't help but add a little extra sway to my hips as I carried over his cappuccino. His first sip was cautious—like he was bracing himself for another chai latte prank—but his raised brow and satisfied hum filtered through the café after I'd already started heading back behind the counter, the sound mixed seamlessly with my stifled laughter.

He'd ducked outside just as I was closing. When I spotted him loitering outside talking to Ash, I felt immature amounts of giddiness when I snapped the lock on the door and slipped out the back, taking a small, wicked pleasure in evading him all day. Both for the sanity of my hormones but also, because playing with him like this was fucking *fun*. It was easy and natural and exciting.

Words that I wouldn't have described my life as if you'd asked me weeks ago.

The look on his face when I pulled out of the alley and onto the street was worth every second of my effort.

His eyes flared wide in surprise before his head whipped to the closed door of the café and then back to me. The biggest, brightest, shit-eating grin on my face was just for him, with my arm hanging out the window, flipping him the bird.

His laughter lit up my whole world at that moment. I felt it everywhere and not that I thought it was possible, but my smile stretched wider. So big that I was scared I wouldn't be able to see past the way my eyes crinkled at the delight of it all.

"This isn't over!" he called after me, delighted amusement all over his own face. I should've guessed my luck at being a step ahead of him all day had run dry when my drive-by fell flat on its face because one of the town's three traffic lights, conveniently located right outside my café, had just turned yellow.

I pulled my hand in and went to press on the brakes to slow down, sure that Fane would meander over the moment I was stopped and make some quick guess about me being a getaway driver in another life, but...nothing happened.

I frowned and pressed on the brake pedal again, but the car wasn't slowing down. There was no resistance, the pedal just smacked against the floor of the car, and when I looked up, all I could see was a silver truck picking up speed, Declan behind the wheel, and coming straight for me.

I feel like it's pretty common for people to say that in the moments when they think they're about to die, everything slows down. That time passes by so slowly that you have time to zone in on the details around you, like dust particles and the different layers of sound that surround you.

That didn't happen to me.

I had one second. That's what it felt like.

Declan was in stunning clarity, the way he was staring at me, picking up speed like he knew I couldn't slow down. Like he *knew* I couldn't stop.

I used my second to whip my head to the side, finding those brilliant violet eyes on me. Wide with fear, Fane's name ripped from my throat while I yanked the steering wheel as far as it would go to the right, and then there was nothing.

# 30

## Fane

**After**

The things running through my head felt like they were louder, more violent, surrounded by the white, stale hospital room we were in.

Cali's hand was warm and soft where I gripped it in mine.

She looked perfect right now. Utterly untouched.

You couldn't see the wound on her head they stitched closed or the bruising that had started to bloom around it. You couldn't tell that she had a concussion. Didn't know that she winced when she moved her head from the whiplash or the bruising across her chest from her seat belt.

But I knew it was there. I saw the blood trickling down the side of her head when her car had finally stopped, and she managed to unbuckle herself and open the door. I was right there the moment her legs gave out, and I gently lowered her to the ground.

"Rose," I murmured. My heart was going fucking wild. Torn between never wanting to take my eyes off her again and looking up to see where Declan was. I gave in, feeling his eyes boring into me from where he was sitting and staring at us from his truck. Our eyes met for a second before he turned the car back on and disappeared, like nothing had fucking happened.

"Fane," Cali said, her voice faint, her eyes fluttering half-closed. "Don't tell Fane, okay?"

"Baby, hey, look at me." I was terrified to touch her, certain that she shouldn't be fucking moving. I moved my hands up, trying to hold her head still when she winced after turning it, like she was looking for something. Her hand reached up to touch the side of her head, and when her fingers came away with blood on them, her eyes went wide with panic.

"Oh crap," she mumbled before looking at the bright red drips that had already descended onto her blue shirt. "This is never going to come out."

I choked a laugh, and she finally settled her eyes on me, the mossy green in them piercing. "I'll buy you a new damn shirt."

"Fane." Her body sagged in relief the moment she realized I was there before she made a sharp inhale. "Don't tell my dad. He'll worry."

I didn't tell her that he probably already knew, but I just nodded at her, keeping her head still and my eyes on hers.

"You saw him that time too?" she murmured, and before I could even reply, she kept going. "I thought I made it up the first time."

The first time what? That's what had been on the tip of my tongue when the ambulance pulled up, and I gave them a recount of what had happened. I rode with Cali all the way to the small hospital, and it was hard to even bring myself to blink. To miss out on having my eyes on her for even a second.

I stood and watched as they assessed her. When they told her dad, who had ended up beating us to the hospital, regardless of Cali's wish not to tell him. He hadn't faltered, just listened to everything they said with gruff determination.

I didn't even take my eyes off her when Dallas asked me to let him know if anything changed and if he needed to come back.

They stayed right on her when she reached her hand out to me, and I wrapped my hands around hers until she fell asleep.

The door to her room opened and closed.

"How is she?" Ash asked from the foot of her bed.

"She'll be okay," I murmured. That's what I kept repeating. *She'll be okay, she'll be okay, she'll be okay.* "What did you find?" I pulled my eyes away from Cali's sleeping form at last and leaned back in my chair, my body aching from being in one position for so long.

"His truck was ditched a couple miles outside of town, burned out. I put a call out, but I don't have a lot of people this…"

"Rural?"

Ash gave me one of his classic pretty boy smiles. "Yeah."

"Thanks for your help." I turned my attention back to Cali.

"There's one more thing." He walked around Cali's bed and handed me a crumpled note. "Found it in Cali's car."

I unfolded the note, the messy, unrefined scrawl glaring up at me like a taunt.

My eyes shot to Ash's, the words choking in my throat. I'd seen the look on her face when she picked that note off her dash. Like she'd seen a fucking ghost.

And I'd let it go.

Because I'd been too damn scared I'd push her away to push her at all.

"My guess is he messed with her brakes," Ashton said, his voice low. "She'd been leaking brake fluid for a while, but the hole was tiny—small enough that it would've taken days for her to notice anything. Probably couldn't make up his mind on what he was going to do, judging by the shitload of tools in the back of his truck. They matched the description of the missing gear from Gus's shop."

"She hasn't been using her car," I told him, still staring at the note in my hand.

"You think this is because of the bar thing?"

"He said something to her at Sunshine too," I muttered, "She never said anything more about it."

Another thing I hadn't wanted to push her on.

"The guy's a fucking psycho, Fane. It's not the first time I've seen someone like him lose his shit because he was turned down by a girl."

"And if it's more than that?"

Ashton's gaze hardened. The glint in his eyes spoke to the darkness he harbored like a secret beneath his humor and his wit. "Then we'll get to the bottom of it."

"Ashton—"

"For now," he interrupted, eyes piercing and focused on me. "She needs you not to lose your shit. Don't make this about you. The moment you start blaming yourself, it all falls apart."

"I'm the one who fucking *brought* us here," I seethed at him between gritted teeth, low and pained. Leave it to him to know exactly what I was thinking.

"Yep." He nodded, unflinching. "But news flash, Fane. They were coming here whether you stepped in or not. They would have sent a crew in with or without your permission, and where would we be then if not halfway through tearing apart this fucking town?" He lifted his eyebrows at me, daring me to argue with him.

I stayed silent, jaw clenched.

"That's what I thought." He crossed his arms. "The guys just got into town after their leave last week. I'm going to have them do evaluations of the outer zones for the next two days before sending them home to work on those presentations."

"We don't need anything else. It's done. We have everything we need to shoot down the project. You know that."

"Yep, but you need time." He looked pointedly at Cali before looking back to me. "I'll stay in town, message a few guys to come out to help for a while."

"Your dad won't miss them?" I asked, knowing that he'd put anything on the line to help someone he cared about, even if it meant causing problems for himself later on.

"Even if he did, he wouldn't say a thing about it." He turned to leave and stopped at the door to look back at me. "Get some rest. You look like you're about to fucking pass out."

I flipped him off just as he blew me a kiss before slipping out. When I turned my focus back on Cali, her eyes were open and on me.

"You're a terrible fake sleeper." I pulled her hand up to my lips, grazing them over the back of her knuckles. Her sleepy smile lasted only a second before it melted into a small frown that made her brows pinch together.

"I thought he cut off his family."

"Mmm," I hummed into her skin. "Just his mom."

Her eyebrows quirked for a second before her frown reappeared. "He's right, you know."

"About what?"

"You do look like you're about to pass out."

"I can't look away from you," I whispered, overwhelmed by the knowledge that I'd only just gotten her back and she could've been taken from me. That there was all this fucking *life* I was supposed to live with this woman, and every second of it had been put into jeopardy.

Her voice gripped onto me, pulling me back into the room. "Is Declan gone?"

"You said you thought you made him up the first time," I said instead, voice steady, but my body was so tense my bones were aching.

"I—"

"I almost watched you *die* today, Calista." Neither of us looked away. I told her I wanted no walls between us, but the truth was I'd kept mine up too.

So, I let her see it.

All the fucking fear that coursed through my body the moment my name had left her mouth. She was terrified, and she called for *me,* and I hadn't been able to do a damn thing. Again. "Please don't lie to me."

I watched her swallow three times before she spoke and felt her hand squeeze mine harder.

"He was the one who chased me." Her voice shook, and I ran one hand up her forearm. "That day in the café, he said he knew we weren't really together. He said he wanted to play too. I—honestly, I still don't even know what that means, but when I went for my run with Jerry, he was just standing in town, out in front of Sunshine, and Jerry went ballistic. I'd never seen him like that before, and I just ran. If…" Her voice broke. "Jerry was pulling me so much faster than I could run on my own. He was so close to grabbing me. I thought when I ran into you, that it was him, and I…"

"Why didn't you tell me?"

"Because he was doing it to get to you. If I told you…" She huffed a disbelieving laugh. "What if you *left?* What if you went after him, and he hurt you?" She tried to shake her head and let out a wince. "I could handle it."

I wasn't going to push her more on it. I could piece together the rest of it myself, and despite what Ash had said, I knew that the reason he went after her was because of me.

"Don't do that." She tugged on my hand, her tired eyes brightening and locking with mine.

"Do what?"

"Blame yourself. It's written all over your face." She pointed weakly at me, her IV tugging lightly at her wrist. "That look says you think you could have somehow stopped it. You couldn't."

"I'm not going to fight with you anymore." I shook my head, sitting taller, my voice resolute.

"Fane." She gave me her signature deadpan look. Challenging me already.

"I'm serious. I'm not going to waste any more time pretending like I'm mad at you. That I'm not so fucking in love with you. That I haven't been able to breathe for the last two years without you."

"You're—" She looked like I'd started speaking pig Latin.

"In love with you," I confirmed, leaning closer. "Since the first moment I saw you, and every day since then, I've been all yours, baby. My plan up until now has sucked, but—"

"Your plan?" Her brow lifted.

"I'm sure Ashton will fill you in at an incredibly inappropriate time."

She stared at me like she was seeing me a little more clearly. I hadn't expected her to say anything back to me, but the very idea that she might think that who she was to me had changed so completely and that I'd been too caught up in my own head–too choked up with my own words–to tell her. It made me sick.

That Calista Grey would think that she was anything other than the center of my entire fucking universe.

"When can we go home?"

"Tomorrow," I murmured. "They're keeping you for observation."

"What about Jerry?"

"Delilah went and got him for the night."

"What?" She would have looked less shocked if I'd turned into a leprechaun.

"She almost tore off my balls when she showed up. Her boyfriend held her back."

Cali's giggle washed over me, and the pressure in my chest eased. "What did you do?"

"You were sleeping, and she was crying like a hyena. I didn't want her to wake you up."

She hummed, looking at me with eyes narrowed and a little grin playing on the corners of her mouth. "I better rest up then, we have a big day tomorrow."

I lifted a brow in question, because she'd lost me entirely.

"The Autumn Fair," she said simply.

"You can't be serious." It was my turn to give her a deadpan look.

"Yes, I am absolutely serious. This is tour three. Meeting the people of the town, participating in something small-townish. Seeing the community here and how changing the town will change its people. You're so far removed from it that you and your contractors can't see that."

"Cali—" I knew even as I said her name I wasn't going to win the argument, even if it was to tell her that I already knew that. That neither this nor any of the tours had been important in the way she thought.

"What happened to no more fighting with me?" She quirked an eyebrow, and she knew she had me.

"Fine."

"Please, rein in your enthusiasm."

"Rein in *your* enthusiasm."

"Oh, good one, buddy." She did a tiny little huffing laugh that reminded me of Sheldon's character in *The Big Bang Theory*.

"Okay, *Sheldon*."

I snorted, and Cali pulled her hand from mine just to flip me off.

"Careful." I didn't even try to hide my grin. "You know what that does to me."

Cali rolled her eyes before sliding her hand back into mine. "Where's Declan?" She said it so casually as if she didn't want to seem like she cared, but the grip she had on my hand told an entirely different story.

"Skipped town," I told her, pulling her hand back to my lips. "Ash has some people coming in to double-check, but it's pretty clear he took off when…"

"When he hit my car and thought he'd killed me?" Her voice was sharp, but beneath it, I could hear the tremble.

What could I say to that? Nothing. Nothing would erase the image of her face, pale and panicked, or the sound of her screaming my name, a sound that had buried itself into my chest, rattling against my ribs like it would never leave.

Her fingers tightened again, her voice a whisper now. "So, we're safe?"

"You're safe, baby," I promised, my voice low and steady, the kind of promise that held weight. My free hand smoothed over hers as if I could physically press the truth into her skin.

Her eyes flickered to mine, uncertain but searching. "You're safe," I said again, willing her to believe it, because even if it wasn't true quite yet, it would be soon enough.

# 31

# Calista

**After**

"This is so depressing," I whimpered, standing next to Fane in my driveway, staring at my car. "She was still so young."

"Cali," he sounded so unimpressed. "This car is like, thirty years old."

"Thirty, flirty, and thriving," I whispered, sliding my hand along the side of it.

"The airbags didn't even deploy." His hands were on his hips, and he was facing me fully now. "Do you understand how *crucial* that is for a car to do?"

"If she had some, I'm sure they would have!" I grumbled and turned to head inside. Ideally, I would have had a little more flair, but the doctor said that it would take at least a week before I started feeling more like myself again.

"I'm sorry." Fane didn't sound sorry at all. "You mean you *knew* there were no airbags in it?"

"I paid three hundred dollars for this car, Fane," I sighed. "Of course I knew."

"I—" He did this tai chi-looking move like he was pushing down all the frustration in his body. "You are going to give me an aneurysm. This isn't something to joke about, Calista."

The words came out low, almost a growl, and his entire demeanor shifted. The air between us grew heavier, darker, like a storm had rolled in without warning. His body went rigid, tension coiling through him as his hands clenched at his sides until it all just disappeared.

Poof. Gone.

Like he was the eye of that storm now, at ease with the chaos it brought. That easy frustration he'd shown moments before was gone, replaced by something far more dangerous.

I swallowed hard, my earlier humor evaporating under the weight of his quiet anger. For a moment, I forgot to breathe, caught between the overwhelming intensity in his eyes and the way his chest rose and fell like he was fighting to hold himself back.

"I know," I said softly, my voice barely above a whisper. "I know it's not a joke."

The good news was that Ash managed to get a ping on one of Declan's cards a few hours away from Darling around midnight and then another back in Artington in the early hours of the morning.

"But he's not coming back, Fane," I added, my tone lighter, trying to ease the crackling tension still hanging in the air. "If we can't laugh about it, I'll have an aneurysm too."

He didn't say anything else, just closed the distance between us and wrapped me in a hug for the third time today. It felt like the most natural thing in the world, but also like these weren't things that were meant for me. Like they didn't belong to me. Not really.

He held me anyway, strong and steady, just like he'd done a thousand times before. Like he'd do a thousand times again if I let him.

Regardless, I was the sort of girl who kept her word. So, after a very hot shower, some painkillers for the bitch of a headache, and finally calling my dad back after we'd left the hospital before he managed to arrive, we were hauled up in Fane's truck heading for the park right in the middle of town.

I wasn't trying to avoid my dad. The opposite, in fact. I knew that if I did anything but play it off as a minor ding and nothing more, then he would try to tear himself in half to be at my door every morning instead of with my mom, where he was supposed to be.

"Dad, I promise. Keeping me overnight was overkill. Fane and I are almost at the Autumn Fair."

"You should be at home, Cali." He sounded gruff and like I was about to give *him* an aneurysm too.

"I made a promise to Mags. Fane has already made me swear that all I will do is sit down and take people's cash."

"She won't get up off her…back end." He gave me this look that said, *Is saying 'back end' to your dad any better than saying ass?* and I had to clamp a hand over my mouth to muffle the aggressive-sounding chortle trying to escape.

"I'm hoping she might even nap," he continued, voice dry as ever. "I bought a set of noise-canceling headphones and a pillow just in case."

"You didn't!" I turned my head slowly toward him.

"Sure did, baby."

"You're so dramatic," I mumbled, but honestly, the thought of a midday siesta kind of spoke to my soul right now.

With a final reassurance that I was okay and settling on Tuesday next week for our next dinner date on account of Mom's doctor's appointment, Fane pulled into the designated vendor parking.

"Now," I said, trying to slip back into my *Cali: Tour Guide of Darling* persona while swatting his hand away like the world's most annoying fly every time he tried to tuck some hair behind my ear. "I need you to focus."

"I am focusing."

"No, you're not." I swatted his hand away again. "The purpose of *this* tour is so that you can meet the people of the town, *not* as someone trying to infiltrate their sacred space."

"That sounds super sexual." He leaned in, his lips quirking into a mischievous grin. "Sacred space?"

"*Fane!*" I whined.

"*Cali!*" he whined back, his smile so stupidly handsome I had to hold my hand up in between us to stop my view. "You need to stop."

"Why?" He tried to look around my hand, and I just matched his movements.

"Because you're…making this hard. I can't focus when you're—"

"Smiling at you?"

"Yes."

"Being nice?"

"*Yes.*"

"Professing my love for you?"

I groaned and covered my face with my hands instead. "Stop saying that. It's—"

"Confusing?" His tone softened, a thread of seriousness weaving through his teasing.

"Fane, *please*—"

"Okay, fine." He lifted his hands in mock surrender. "But even though I am looking forward to our day, you should know I made up my mind about the fate of this town before I even arrived."

I literally felt my face fall. My heart skipped over itself, the feeling was like my chest caved in a little as the weight of his words settled over me. "W-what?"

"I was never going to let anything happen to your town, baby." His voice was steady, unshakable, as if the statement should have been the most obvious thing in the world.

Before I could find the words—or the breath—to respond, he was already out of the car. He circled around to my side, opening the door with a smile that should have eased the tightness in my chest but only made it worse. His hand was warm and firm as he helped me out, leading me into the swirl of townspeople and straight to Mags's tent.

I was *so fucking confused.*

It wasn't new—being at a loss when it came to Fane—but it didn't make it any easier. I tried to focus on the people at the festival, speaking with them and thanking them for their thoughts and that they were so glad I was okay when they heard about the accident.

Fane, on the other hand, slipped into the rhythm of the festival like he belonged there. He poured beers at Mags's tent with the kind of ease that made my stomach twist. It wasn't surprising. He may not have always loved working at Heavenly Horns, but he'd always been good at it. The sight of him laughing and chatting with the locals felt…wrong. Like he was seamlessly inserting himself into a place I wasn't sure he had the right to be.

The more the day ticked by, the more I couldn't shake that feeling, that sinking dread.

I'd come into this with a plan, a clear idea of how today would go. How I'd show him the heart of Darling, how I'd prove this town wasn't just a mark on a map but a living, breathing community worth preserving. That plan was in tatters now.

All the headway I'd made in seeing his actions and his words sync up felt like all half-truths I'd conjured up in my head. Like things I'd convinced myself of because I wanted to believe in him so badly.

How naïve I'd been.

He'd made me believe that he was here to ruin the only thing I had left that was *mine*.

Was it *fun* for him? To watch me scramble and figure out a way to convince him that this one, tiny slice of the world deserved to be left untouched?

Even if it had been a game at the start for him, what about after? What about now? He'd had his fun. He'd clearly had his answer on what he was going to do since well before he even showed up, and instead of making it quick and easy, he dragged it out.

Blew up my whole fucking life.

A life I had painstakingly put together with pieces that I knew didn't fit right, but they'd held nonetheless.

I felt his eyes on me the whole day. The further I sunk into myself, the harder he stared, and I felt like I was going to be sick.

"Cali, what's wrong?" His voice was gentle enough to make my eyes prick with the onslaught of tears of anger, tears of pain, tears of fucking frustration and humiliation. Of telling my stupid heart *not yet. Not fucking yet.* And having to face the truth that it went ahead and leaped for him anyway.

"I want to go home," I said, my voice trembling with the weight of everything.

"Cali—"

"Take me home, Fane."

The car ride home was silent, even though I could feel how desperate he was to break it. Jerry didn't even bother to get off the couch when we walked through the front door, a sure sign that he was getting as used to having Fane in his life as I was, and that alone felt like another twist of the knife.

"Are we going to talk about it?"

"I have nothing to say to you." I crossed my arms, standing across from him in the same pointless entry room that had witnessed all the different ways this man had torn apart my heart, and it still didn't make the room any more useful.

"I don't get it. What happened? Is this about what I said in the car?"

"Oh." I perked up, finger flying into the air like I'd never had an idea before in my life. "You mean when you said that you'd already decided that you weren't going to touch Darling for any sort of development?"

"Yes?"

"So, you thought it was a good idea to just roll into town anyway. To show up unannounced after two whole years like that would be a completely *fine* thing to do?"

"I—"

"That you thought it would be *fine* to dismantle the brand-new foundation I had created for myself. To move into my house. To *sleep* in my *fucking bed!*" All those tears from before started to run down my face, and I smacked them away furiously.

"I created a *life* here. A life without you. How dare you come here and ruin it all. I was fine, Fane. I had become *fine.*"

"The Calista I knew would have never settled for 'fine.'" He even did the air quotation marks, and I wanted to scream at him because he knew how much they infuriated me.

"The Calista you knew," I spat the words at him. "Had her heart shattered into a thousand pieces and had no one to help her pick any of it up. It might just be me, but that sort of thing tends to change a person."

He looked like I'd slapped him. Like maybe if I had, it would have been better than forcing him to hear the words.

"Cali." He took a step toward me, hands limp at his sides and face utterly devastated. He took a deep breath, and I realized whether I wanted it or not, whether I was prepared to hear it or not, I was about to get his 'why'.

"I was twenty-six," he began. His voice was raw and jagged and tortured. "And you scared the shit out of me."

I scoffed.

"You don't think I was scared too?" I threw the words back at him, uncaring that the neighbors were likely witnessing the way my heart was breaking all over again. "I was *terrified,* Fane. I barely even knew who *I* was when I met you, and all of a sudden, there you were. This person who had so fucking quickly become *everything*. Maybe it was wrong of me to put that pressure on you, I'll own that, but it doesn't change the fact that you *were*. And when my whole world started to crumble, you were the last fucking retaining wall, and you walked away from me."

"I didn't." The muscle in his jaw twitched, and I was positive I heard his bones creaking.

"You did," I shot back. "You—"

"I had nothing to offer you, Cali. *Nothing,*" he cut me off, taking another step toward me. "I was a kid with no sense of responsibility, no fucking idea of how to look after someone the way I wanted to look after you. And when I needed to, I *didn't know how.*"

"There was nothing for you to fix, Fane!" My throat hurt from the way the words tore at it. Slicing through the same way they'd ripped me apart just from sitting in my chest. "I just needed *you.*"

He shook his head vehemently, determined not to hear my words. Like he'd had this conversation in his own head a thousand times already.

"You know what ran through my head the moment you told me your mom was sick and you had to go? I thought, 'Where will we live?' I thought about how I was supposed to support us both so that you didn't have to worry about me, about anything. How I was supposed to make sure that you didn't have to think about a single thing so that you could be there for your family? And I came up with nothing. *Nothing.* Me being there only made everything heavier when I should have been able to take it all from you. That's what you *do* for the people you love. You share their burden, take it entirely if you can, fucking *fix* it! Not add to it."

A hand went through his hair, fingers unrelenting in the way they pulled at his chestnut strands while he kept talking. "Because I had more pride than any man ever should, and I was scared, and didn't take the opportunities being handed to me because of some stupid idea that being the opposite of my dad would be a sure way into making sure I never ended up anything like him, even though I *know* I'm nothing fucking like him. I know because you loved me. *You* loved *me.* This…this person who is *everything.* Fucking *more* than everything, and *you loved me.* That's all I needed, and instead, I didn't believe it was enough."

His chest was heaving now, and I was frozen, rooted to the spot as his words tore me apart.

"Without me, you would have been looked after. Cared for. Fucking *supported.*" He choked the words out because we both knew that's not what had happened. That I had been alone, left to drive myself to the emergency room when I fell off a ladder trying to clean my own gutters forty minutes to the next town over so my parents wouldn't find out. "That's why I let you go. Because every other scenario was better than anything I could have given you."

God, he was so *wrong.* So, devastatingly wrong.

"When I woke up and found you fucking *gone*—" His voice broke, and I covered my mouth to stifle the sob that it pulled from me. "I panicked. I called you over and over and over again. I messaged you, and then finally I messaged your sister, and she said you were home. That your dad had just called her. She asked when I was joining you."

He let out a choked laugh. "I told her soon. Then I hung up, got a tattoo, and went home to bed. I didn't get up until Ash banged down my door. I just kept thinking about how you were gone. How I let you leave."

Fane cleared his throat and then kept going. I'd never heard him talk so much before, but he always said he would speak when it was important.

"No one would give me work. I had no experience, no connections. My résumé was a joke—a bartending job I couldn't even get a solid reference for. So, I walked into Mackenzie Co. and asked for a job. The irony wasn't lost on me. I spent years trying to be the opposite of him, and the only thing it got me was losing you."

His jaw clenched, his voice growing rougher. "He was so fucking happy to hire me it made me sick. I worked every day, taking overtime, training—anything to climb my way up. I finally started making good money. Great money. And then he wanted Darling." His voice trailed off into a cracked sort of whisper, and it was like I was watching him rip his entire soul open for me, letting me see every part of him.

There was nothing I didn't want. No matter what came next, I didn't care. I wanted everything.

"And the first thing I thought was, *No*. Not Darling. *Your* Darling. I walked right into his office and told him I wanted it, and that's all I needed to do. The project was mine, and finally, I was going to see you." His hand dragged down his face, and he let out a choked laugh. "I refused to let myself see you again until I was sure I could be the sort of man that was worthy of at least a tiny chance at giving you the life you deserved."

Fane stood directly in front of me now, there was almost no space between us. Almost.

"And if I'd gotten married?" My voice was stronger than I felt.

"Then I would have made sure you were happy."

"You would have turned around and walked away?"

"If that's what you wanted."

I just stared at him, realizing that I was wrong before. That my heart wasn't breaking all over again. This was what it felt like to have someone help put it back together.

"Do you want me to walk away, Rose?"

He would, I realized. He'd grin and bear it. Turn on his heels and never come back if I asked him to.

"No," I said. The very word that had once broken me turned into the very thing that made me whole again. "No, I don't want you to walk away."

"So, you're saying—"

"I want you to kiss me, you infuriating man."

# 32

# Calista

**After**

Fane's hands were trembling when he raised them between us, his chest rising and falling rapidly. His eyes were frantic, roaming over my face. My body.

"I don't know where to touch you," he admitted, sounding so lost.

"I think that's the first time you've ever said that."

"Well, I've never tried to do it after you were in a car accident."

I reached up to grab his hands. The moment I covered them with my own, his shaking stopped. "I'm not going to shatter, and if something hurts, I will tell you. Now kiss me or I'll—"

I didn't get to finish that sentence, and I'd never been so glad to be interrupted.

Fane's hands slid around me, pulling me into him gently. His movements were slow, measured, and careful, but his grip on me was ironclad.

The way he kissed me was soft. The way his tongue dragged across my bottom lip was tentative while he explored the way I tasted all over again.

I wanted so much more from him than what he was giving me, but with every soft touch, every kiss he left on the corner of my mouth—my eyelids, my cheeks—I was losing myself.

No. *Finding* myself.

Fane dragged open-mouthed kisses along my jaw and down the column of my throat. The hand that had settled at the nape of my neck was strong, moving my head slowly to give himself better access while also making sure it was supported.

Every touch made me feel lighter than I had been the second before. Every swipe of his tongue against my heated skin was like a burst of light behind my closed eyes, littering my pitch-black sky with stars.

So many I was losing count.

So many that when they started to fall, I used every single one to attach a wish to until I had none left, and I was right back where I started, in the only place I wanted to be.

"God, I missed you." Fane pushed the words into the skin of my throat. Into the spot just behind my ear that made my entire body erupt into goose bumps. When his mouth finally kissed me again, every part of the remaining walls around us crumbled until it was just him and me.

My fingers pressed against the warm skin under his shirt, and my whole body shivered, like I was shaking off snow that had settled over me during the longest winter of my life.

It was intoxicating—the feel of his skin—but using my hands wasn't enough. I wanted him pressed against me, with nothing between us. No space, clothes, or fucking misunderstandings.

None of it.

"Fane," I rasped in the space between kisses, and just the sight of him made my knees shake. Eyes hooded, hair mussed, lips swollen. "I need more."

"You'll—"

"Tell you if anything is too much," I whispered against his lips and held his gaze when I slowly started to sink to my knees.

The way he looked at me made me feel beautiful. Adored. He told me once that his whole world started and ended with me and for the first time in a long time, I believed him.

"You don't—" he rasped, cutting himself off with a shake of his head.

"I can stop." I looked up at him, an eyebrow raised with my hand frozen on his zipper. That definitely shut him up.

The smirk on my face melted away the moment I reached a hand into his briefs and freed his cock.

A rush of air left Fane's lungs, and a large, broad hand settled on the back of my head. That single touch sent my pulse thrumming. Making the heartbeat that settled at the apex of my thighs throb and my pussy clench around nothing. Aching.

My mouth started to water the longer I looked at him. Long and thick and heavy. I wrapped my hand around his base, squeezing once before gliding my hand up and down.  Fane's hips shot forward, a string of expletives falling from his mouth, and I met his hooded, sparkling eyes with mine as I dragged my tongue up the underside of his cock until I reached the head, taking my time trailing my tongue through his slit and tasting the drop of pre-cum.

"Holy fuck, *Cali.*"

Slowly, I wrapped my lips around the head of his cock and sucked hard, hollowing my cheeks, before easing the rest of him past my lips. His eyes were transfixed on the way he disappeared into my mouth—inch by inch—until he hit the back of my throat, and I was breathing through my nose. I swallowed, desperate to take him even further, moaning at the sounds pouring out of him when I reached up and wrapped a hand around what wouldn't fit.

I took my time tasting him.

Until he couldn't help himself, and his hips started to move.

The grip he had on my hair tightened, the strands pulling with the perfect amount of pain and I released my hold on his cock, moving around to cup his balls, reveling at the choked inhale he made.

"Christ, Calista. You're doing so fucking good," he murmured, his other hand dragging a thumb lightly over my cheek in complete and total contrast to the way his hips were picking up speed, the way his hand shifted from my hair to the back of my neck, trying his best to be careful but unable to stop himself from sliding into my mouth. Down my throat.

Another moan vibrated in my chest, pulling him from the haze he'd been in. His movements slowed, his eyes widening with concern. I could see the unspoken question forming on his lips—if I was okay, if I wanted him to stop.

Before he could so much as pull out an inch, I was frantically unbuttoning my jeans. When I managed to slide a finger into my soaking wet folds—when the tip of my finger started to make short, restrained circles over my sensitive clit—my eyes rolled back, and I released another whimpering moan. The vibration of the sound made him thrust down my throat so far that my air supply was cut off completely.

I looked up at him only to be met with the devilish smile on his face. The sight of him like that, looming above me, made my core clench and body shake.

"I'll move when you come." His focus flickered between where my lips were wrapped around him and where my hand disappeared into my jeans.

My body racked with a sob that couldn't escape, with his tightening grip on my hair and that aching need to be filled, the building pressure in my chest making every sensation maddening.

It was seconds before I started to come. My body jolting, throat constricting. Fane hissed through his teeth before he released his hold on me and pulled out of my mouth entirely.

For a heartbeat all we could do was watch each other, chests heaving. With a ringing in my ears so intense, I was honestly impressed I hadn't just flopped into a pile of open nerve endings on the floor.

Fane's cock jerked between us, drawing my attention back to him, at the fact that he hadn't come yet. I reached for him, my own arousal still glistening on my outstretched fingers when he hauled me to my feet, his hand snapping out to encircle my wrist and I watched as he pulled my fingers to his mouth.

Holy fucking Hell.

His tongue swirled over my digits, my knees still way too unsteady for the way the sensation moved through my body. My nipples were budding to impossibly tight peaks, and the slickness between my thighs was so bad that I might never be able to wear these jeans again.

"You'll tell me if it's too much?" His voice was rough and commanding, but his arm around me was steady and sure as he lifted me off the ground and carried me across the house.

"Yes," I breathed, my whole body a pulsing live wire. "Are you going to fuck me now?"

That devilish grin came back in full force as soon as he set me on the bed. "I'm not going to fuck you, Cali," he murmured, reaching for the hem of my shirt. "I'm going to savor you."

I lifted my arms above my head, pushing through the pinching in my chest at the motion. Fane pulled the loose cotton off me, discarding it in a corner of the room and setting his gaze on me.

Every hair on my body seemed to stand on end. We were thunder clouds, electricity bouncing between our bodies, skirting across the surface of my skin. My lips were tingling, the tips of my fingers, my eyelids, my fucking *bones* were rattling at the way he looked at me.

Fane knelt before me, his hands steady as he spread my legs to make room for himself. Without warning, he took one sensitive nipple between his teeth, coaxing a shuddering gasp from me, before he released it with a soft pop.

"You're not wearing a bra, Calista."

"They're...they suck."

"If I pull these jeans down, are you going to have panties on?" He spoke softly, mouth dragging across my skin until he reached my other nipple, but not before placing one tender kiss on the deep purple bruising that had bloomed over my chest. His movements slowed down at that, his eyes lingering.

"Fane, it doesn't hurt," I whispered, and of course, that was a lie. My entire body was aching like I'd just been tossed to the side by a charging bull, but if he stopped now, I was going to lose my ever-loving mind. Every pinch, every ache, it was insignificant. Utterly unimportant in the light of what he was doing to me.

I saw the moment the decision was made in his mind, that he was going to trust me on this, that I'd tell him when it was too much.

It would be too much when I was dead, so there was no chance I was stopping a single thing, especially with the sort of words that were pouring out of his mouth.

"Your cunt, Calista. Is it soaked?"

I nodded my head lightly, and he tutted the way he always did when he was after my words.

"Yes," I rasped, my hand sinking into the longer hair at the back of his head. "It is."

"And the panties?" He trailed a finger down the center of my chest, down my stomach, which tensed and released at the light contact of his touch.

"No," I gasped. "No. None. I have none."

"Dirty girl," he chided, lips curving into a wicked grin.

His kiss was all teeth and tongue. So consuming my head was spinning until he released my bottom lip with a sharp nip. With one arm wrapped securely around my back, he hauled me further up the bed, his other splayed over my ribs.  The rough and worn pads of his fingers grounding me. Unraveling me.

Lifting off me, I watched him reach back to grab a fistful of his own shirt, pulling it off and throwing it in the same general direction he tossed my shirt.

He was a sight to behold. Just so blindingly beautiful.

Solid lines, valleys, and hills of sculpted muscles decorated with tattoos that made no sense and all the sense in the world. Those two words that I hadn't been able to stop thinking of tattooed over his heart. I couldn't help myself when I slowly sat up and reached my fingers out to glide over them.

He watched me do it, tracking every movement. Didn't rush me even though I could feel his heart hammering under the tips of my fingers.

There would be time for softness later, and I was glad for this moment of it now, but I tucked it away inside where it was safe before lying back down on the bed before him and building up to speak the sort of words I knew would snap any thread of restraint that remained.

That's what I wanted now. I wanted messy, unrestrained, maddening.

"I want you to take off my jeans," I breathed, "and taste me."

His eyebrows lifted ever so slightly, eyes sparkling and nostrils flaring imperceptibly. "Is that right?"

"Yes." My heart was thrashing while I pushed the words at him. Words that always sat on the tip of my tongue whenever he touched me but were hard for me to get out, no matter how much I wanted to.

Fane made quick work of my jeans until I was completely bare before him. He settled between my thighs, and as he spoke, he started to push my legs open wider, exposing me more.

"Taste you here?" He placed an open-mouthed kiss on my inner thigh.

I shook my head despite the pain, the edge of it dulled by the roaring in my ears. "No."

"What about here?" He kissed the other thigh.

"Fane," I whimpered, hands reaching for his hair, lifting my hips in desperation.

"You have the most perfect pussy, Calista." He spoke the words reverently. "Did you know that?" And then he dragged his lips across my folds, and I was pretty sure I passed out for a second.

"Th-thank you." I watched him staring right at my sex. Aching and wet and desperate for his touch.

"So polite," he murmured, flicking his tongue across my clit, making me cry out. "But I don't want polite. I want to hear you beg for exactly what you want."

"Please," I whispered. "*Please*, I…I want you to eat my pussy."

"Your *what* pussy?" He had his eyes on me, and my eyes almost rolled back into my skull when I felt his breath skitter across my sensitive flesh. "You're fucking leaking for me, baby. Tell me."

"My perfect pussy," I gasped just as Fane dragged his tongue up the length of my slit. The feeling of it was so intense after being spread wide for him, waiting and aching, that my legs tried to close. Even when I pulled his hair, wanting him closer, grinding on his mouth so desperately I wasn't sure he could even breathe.

When he pushed two fingers into me, hard and steadfast, there was no hope for me. I broke apart. Shattering repeatedly, my body shaking and my legs falling limp.

When Fane moved over top of me, I felt him settle his body against mine with just the right amount of pressure before he dropped the softest kiss to my hairline, right near where they had to stitch me closed.

When he started to push off, I clung to him, my fingers digging into the muscles on his shoulders and back, legs coming up to circle his waist.

"Condom," he panted, arms shaking where he held himself up.

"You don't need one," I said. I was desperate for there to be nothing between us. I wanted all of him. "There's been no one but you."

He frowned at me, confused.

"I said you made me *try* to want someone else. Not that I ever did. I've always been just yours, Fane." I tried to pull him closer to me with my legs, but there was no use in trying to overpower him.

Fane got off the bed, shucking off his jeans until he was standing completely naked.

His golden skin wrapped around defined muscles. A little grin on his mouth when he caught me staring at the ridiculous rubber duck on his thigh.

Instead of climbing back over me, Fane settled on his knees between my thighs and reached out to grip my hips. He hauled me onto his lap, my body still on the bed, until I could feel the head of his cock at my entrance.

He gripped himself in one hand, running his swollen tip along the seam of my pussy, coating himself in my arousal.

"So wet for me," he hummed quietly. "Always such a good girl, aren't you, Rosie?"

His eyes flicked to mine just as I started to feel him push into me, stretching me wide until I was sure I'd never been so full in my life. Until my fingers that were clawing at the sheets did nothing to keep me grounded, and I was having an out of fucking body experience.

"So fucking perfect," Fane gritted out between his clenched teeth. "Look at you. Taking me so well."

His words wrapped around me, soothing the slight sting of being stretched to accommodate him, helping my body start to relax. The moment my muscles softened, Fane gave my hips a firm pull, sheathing himself inside me fully, his body folding over mine and capturing my cry with his mouth.

When he started to move, it was safe to say I short circuited.

Everywhere he touched me was too much, too sensitive. The feel of his cock, sliding all the way out of me, slow and torturous, until he slammed back in, hitting so deep I felt it in my chest.

I felt incredible. The pain and tenderness of my body from before were completely gone, healed and whole after being covered in the blazing rays of sun that came directly from Fane.

"More," I gasped, my fingers digging into his biceps.

He shook his head. Face set with determination, one hand holding my hip so tight I knew there would be marks left behind.

"Please," I sobbed. "Give me more."

With a guttural growl of defeat, of finally giving in, Fane pulled out of me. He flipped me over and thrust back inside before I even had time to take a breath.

"Hold the headboard." He spoke next to my ear, voice rough and thick and sounding every bit as intoxicated as I felt. "And remember that you asked for this."

I did exactly what he asked. My yelp of surprise earned a throaty chuckle from him when the palm of his hand made contact with my ass.

The pace he set was hard and fast, and all I could do was focus on my grip on the frame of the bed, my knuckles turning white at the effort of holding on.

My head was spinning at the onslaught of pleasure I didn't even think I was capable of feeling, at withstanding. The smack of his body meeting mine was all that surrounded us, mixed in only with the mumbled praises he gave me.

"So fucking tight. You're perfect."

"You're dripping, baby. Down your thighs, I can see it."

"*Heaven.*"

He was everywhere. All around me. Fusing once again to those parts of me he'd settled in before. That he'd ripped away, leaving wounds that never healed.

"Fane, I'm…oh, god." I tried to turn to look at him, but his chest pressed against my back, and one of his hands dragged down my stomach, brushing over my clit.

His fingers started to move. Firm, sure strokes across the bundle of nerves. When my release barreled into me, I pulled a hand from the headboard, latching onto his forearm, my nails digging in as my mouth opened on a silent scream.

Then he was saying my name, repeating it like a prayer. Pumping into me slowly until he eventually stopped completely and withdrew inch by aching inch.

I was frozen in place, my muscles locked and my hand aching from the hold I still had on the bed frame.

I could feel Fane's cum leaking down my leg, the mental visual it gave me making my body shiver in delight, loosening my limbs enough that my hand finally dropped its hold and my face unceremoniously hit the pillow.

Fane still had a hold on my hip, keeping my ass in the air.

"You have no idea how fucking sexy you look right now," he hummed, placing a kiss over the stinging skin that he spanked before I felt two fingers drag up my inner thigh, collecting his release a moment before he pushed it back inside of me. I moaned, my pussy clenching around the intrusion of his fingers.

"Perfect," he murmured, the word flooded with satisfaction. He released his hold on me and gently lowered my body to the bed before curling himself behind me. He pulled a blanket up from the end of the bed to cover us, and settled an arm around my waist, shifting his other under my head.

My eyes were already closed, and I was sure I thanked him for absolutely wrecking me, in those exact words, if his hoarse laugh was anything to go by. I felt it move through me when he placed a kiss just behind my ear and again on my shoulder.

When I felt him take in a deep breath, he started to hum.

The song that we had danced to when I first met him. The same song that he would hold me close to while he moved us around the living room of our old apartment.

*Won't you fall for me?*
  *Won't you fall for me?*
  *With my love as your garden*
  *Won't you fall for me?*
  *Won't you fall for me*
  *From reality?*
  *I am yours in the end*
  *So won't you fall for me?*

# 33

## Calista

**After**

When I woke up in the middle of the night and tried to move, my whole body shuddered in pain. I dug my teeth into my bottom lip to try and stifle the whimper, but Fane woke up the moment the near silent squeak left my mouth.

"You slept through my nightmares at having to run for my life," I panted, the pain taking my breath away. "But you wake up from *that*."

"I was awake then too," he murmured, gently peeling himself away from me and getting up to leave the room. When he came back, he was holding a glass of water and a bottle of painkillers.

"You didn't say anything." I watched him set everything down on my bedside table and help me sit up.

"I thought you'd toast my balls if I asked you if you were okay." He said the words so seriously I couldn't stop my laugh, which promptly turned into a cry when my chest spasmed.

"No, no," I cried, squeezing my eyes tight. "No laughing."

"You told me you'd tell me if it was too much." He leveled me with the most disapproving look I'd ever seen on his face.

"It was practically a religious experience." I winced, taking the pills he held out. "I have no regrets."

A slow, self-satisfied smile crept onto his face, and he looked so goofy, especially when he started to wag his eyebrows and his hair was still disheveled from sleep.

"If you make me laugh again, I'll definitely toast your balls."

He clamped his lips together, mumbling a quiet, "Sorry, laughy pants," that he didn't mean in the slightest.

Fane helped me settle back into bed, wrapping himself around me where he'd been before. Sleep found me almost immediately, and by the time I woke up again, I was alone in the bed and there was music filtering in from under the closed bedroom door.

Peeling myself off the mattress hurt about as much as I thought it would, but not as much as the throbbing ache of my whole body last night. I was sore in places I hadn't been sore in for a very long time. Despite it all, despite knowing it was definitely not what we should have been doing after I'd almost been pancaked by Declan, I couldn't bring myself to regret a single second of it.

I was still sitting on the edge of the bed, a ghost of a smile lingering on my face as I replayed every detail of yesterday afternoon, of last night, in my head. I'd been content to go slowly. I *had* to go slowly, because honestly? Even breathing fucking hurt. But when my phone lit up from a message from my dad, I noticed the time and maybe threw up a little.

It was ten a.m.

As in, a whole three and half hours later than Sunshine was meant to be open.

I rushed around the room—which really meant shuffling about three percent faster than I had been just seconds before—grabbing a shirt and stumbling out of the bedroom.

I might have been crying, but whether it was from the overwhelming anxiety of being late for work for the first time since I'd opened Sunshine or from how stiff my entire body felt, I honestly couldn't say.

Fane was mid-pancake flip when he saw me, and for some reason that equated to *him* panicking and trying to catch the pancake midair.

"*Fucking balls!*" He dropped the pancake as quickly as he caught it, and before it even had a chance to hit the ground, Jerry snatched it up and made a beeline for his couch.

"What did I even just witness?" I mumbled, staring between Fane and Jerry and the now-empty pan he still had clutched in one hand.

"Why are you awake?" That same disapproving look from yesterday was back in full force.

"Because I'm alive," I grumbled, shuffling the rest of the way toward him before performing the world's smallest unannounced trust fall and dropping my forehead to his chest. "Everything hurts."

Fane's hand that wasn't holding the hot pan wrapped around me, sliding up and down my back in the most comforting rhythm that I may have dozed off for a second. "I'm sorry, baby."

I lifted my head slowly, looking up at him, and my heart sank when I saw the devastation in his eyes. "Don't do that." I reached up on my tiptoes to kiss the underside of his jaw.

"Do what?" If there was any doubt before, the delivery of that question confirmed it: Fane was absolutely moping.

"You know what." I quirked an eyebrow at him and slowly slid onto a stool at the kitchen counter. The kitchen was tiny so there was only one chair, but up until a month ago, I hadn't needed more than one chair. "I regret nothing."

"Calista, you—"

"Are a grown woman who knew what she was asking for. I wanted every part of what happened last night. Okay?"

The muscle in his jaw twitched once, twice, before he gave me a curt nod and, much opposed to the brooding demeanor he had going on, proceeded to pour another pancake while wearing my floral apron.

I didn't know exactly how to explain it, but despite the soreness of my body and—the soreness between my legs—I felt steady for the first time in a long time. I looked at Fane, and my head felt clear. My chest was free of the lingering heaviness that had become so much a part of me I didn't fully recognize myself without it.

All I knew was that being here, with Fane, it felt right. It felt *good*.

"If you keep looking at me like that, I'm going to have to remove myself from the room." Fane set down a heaping pile of pancakes in front of me, topped with the most mouthwatering caramelized banana you'd ever seen in your life. Right on cue, my stomach let out the loudest, grizzliest growl that ever existed.

"You made my pancakes." I stared at them in awe. "I think I missed these more than you."

"Really nice." Fane kissed the side of my head, and I could feel his grin. It sent a pang through my chest at the realization that we'd lost two years together.

One gentle finger pressed up under my chin, and I looked up into his eyes and felt my bottom lip quiver a fraction before I caught it between my teeth.

"Tell me so I can fix it," he murmured.

I closed my eyes at his words—words he'd said to me so many times before, pressed them into my soul, etched onto my bones. It terrified me how much hearing them now soothed my racing heart.

Instead of telling him all that, I blurted the second thing making my stomach churn.

"I'm late for work," I croaked, right before I shoveled an arguably too-large bite of pancake into my mouth, my eyes on him the whole time.

"That was sexy." He grinned, catching a runaway drop of syrup that was creeping down my chin with his thumb before licking it off.

I'm not proud of the way I froze mid-chew, my mouth hanging wide open. There would have been no doubt in anyone's mind what was going through my mind right then. I crossed my legs and focused all my attention on the plate of food in front of me.

"What—"

"You know what," I mumbled, hoping maybe he wouldn't understand a word I was saying and would just walk away.

"I'm not sure I do." I saw him cross his arms across his broad chest from my periphery.

I released the mother of all sighs. "If I look at you, I'm going to jump your bones, and I'm afraid that might kill me. So maybe you should just go have your shower and then you can drive me to work."

I didn't need to look at him to know he was grinning that stupid, beaming grin of his that wasn't actually stupid at all. It was totally not what I needed to see in order to maintain my morning of celibacy.

"I'll take you in to grab a coffee because I want one too, but you're not working today."

"That makes no sense." I was still refusing to look at him. "How are we getting coffee then?"

"Ash stopped by early this morning to grab the keys."

"Ash is running the café?" I yelled into an empty kitchen, unable to turn my head toward Fane's retreating body fast enough before the bathroom door clicked shut. I did manage to move my head in time to see Jerry silently stalking back into the kitchen for another pancake that I may or may not have dropped onto the floor from my overflowing plate.

As soon as Fane pulled into a spot out the back of the café, he turned the car off, hopped out, and walked around to open my door, but he didn't move back.

To be honest, I was surprised he'd held out as long as he had in asking me about the name of the café. If our roles were reversed, it might have been the first thing I did.

"Why Sunshine?" His question was tentative, and his eyes kept darting between our clasped hands and my face.

It was a relief to have nothing but the want to be truthful with him. *This* was how it was meant to be between us.

"Your laugh reminds me of sunshine." He already knew that, I must've told him a thousand times. "It always made me warm, happy. Peaceful." I closed my eyes, a little hum pulling from my chest at just the mere thought of it. "Before you, it was my parents and Abbey. It always came from someone else. I needed to create something like that of my own. I didn't want to rely on anyone for that sort of peace. I'd hoped this would do it."

"Did it?"

I nodded, slipping my fingers between his where they rested on my legs.

"In a way."

"Good." He nodded, a small, sad smile ghosting over his mouth.

When Ash led me into the back room of the café, there were stacks of home-cooked dishes, flowers, and cards from so many people—people whose coffee orders I knew by heart. I hadn't ever expected them to show up for me the way they had, steadfast in this belief I'd hammered into my mind that if I wanted warmth and happiness and peace, then I needed to make it for myself.

Seeing the way that I was proved so incredibly wrong loosened something in me.

The feel of Fane there—how solid he was beneath my touch—it made the entire concept of the café seem ridiculous. Yes, I was proud of it, insanely so, of what I'd managed to achieve all on my own. But it was never more clear to me now how short it had fallen in the space I had tried to fill with it.

This. *This* was peace.

All my life, I'd chased the vibrancy of laughter, yearning to be smothered in it. I always thought that's what I was after, never giving much thought to the quiet that came after—the kind of peace that lingered softly, like the calm after a storm.

It wasn't the laughter I'd been chasing. It was this. That steadiness I'd seen growing up, in my parents, in the spaces between their smiles.

In the end, I hadn't needed to search for it. Peace had found me—all on its own.

"The last tour is today." I reached out to drag a finger down the slope of Fane's nose, and it made me remember the sad little heap my glasses had ended up in after they flew off my face and out the open window when my car went spinning. I thought I'd be sadder about the loss of them—about that last, fragile part of the person I used to be.

But instead, it felt freeing, in a way.

"I told you—" he started to grumble, turning onto his side and tugging me into him gently.

"It's an important one, plus it's on my list." My words were mumbled from the way my face was tucked against his chest, and I felt his body start to shake with sleepy little hiccups of laughter.

"Well, if it's on the list..." he mumbled into my hair.

"Can you make us pancakes again?" I asked after a second of him not moving. I was pretty sure he was about to fall asleep again.

With a deep sigh, he rolled to the end of the bed, mumbling something about how being soft and approachable was ruining his sleep. He padded into the kitchen in nothing but his briefs, a hand shoved down them for some ungodly reason in a move I was pretty sure was repeated by all of the men on planet Earth.

"Please wash your hands before you cook!" I called out, starting to roll myself off the bed too.

"You've literally had your mouth wrapped around my co—" Fane's words got cut off with a very un-Fane-like squeak thanks to both my pointer fingers digging into his ribs.

He spun to face me, a frying pan held in one hand and the other hand flipping me off, like presenting an attacker with your middle finger mid-fight would be the best use of a free hand.

I held up my two pointer fingers, wiggling them in anticipation of another attack.

"I already washed them!" He grinned, but he didn't lower the frying pan or his middle finger.

I lowered my own 'weapons' and stepped forward with a sweet smile. I reached up on my tiptoes and pressed a kiss to his lips.

"You know," he started in between kisses, "Sometimes you can be a little scary."

"Guess you'll have to teach me a lesson or two," I whispered, matching his grin.

He groaned and dropped his head to my shoulder. "Eleven days."

Fane had refused to touch me until the two-week mark of me getting better had hit.

"Fane—"

"Nope." He pulled back, dropping a kiss to the corner of my mouth and a light smack on my ass. "Hop in the shower, and your pancakes will be ready when you're out."

"You don't want to join me?"

"I hardly fit in your shower alone, so as much as I'd love to see you wet and naked, I don't think we'd leave that scenario without further injury."

I gave him my best pout, and when he leaned down to whisper in my ear about the list of things he was keeping track of that he would be doing to me when the eleven days had passed, I made sure that he heard every moan and cry that left my lips as I sunk two fingers into my pussy, replaying his words in my head. Wishing it was his fingers, not mine.

As promised, there were pancakes waiting for me when I walked out of the bathroom. I only knew that because of the smell that had threaded through every room of the house. I didn't actually have a chance to see them because the moment the bathroom door opened, Fane was on me.

His kiss was desperate and possessive. His hand grabbed the towel and pulled it from me. I gasped at the way his hands roamed over my still wet body. His palms skated down, taking two handfuls of my ass before squeezing roughly.

My hands found his biceps, steadying myself, and that's when I realized he didn't have a stitch of clothing on either.

He wasted no time before a hand delved between my legs. Fane captured my cry with his mouth as he sunk one long digit into my still sensitive core before pulling it out, and with a final, claiming kiss, he stepped away from me.

It was like I'd been sucked into a hurricane and spat out the other end. I was having a hard time remembering my own freaking name, let alone understand what the fuck just happened.

He'd managed to turn us around, leaving me just outside of the bathroom while he stepped back into the still steam-filled room. I watched as he lifted the finger he'd just buried inside me up to his mouth, closing his lips over it, his eyes dragging down my naked form.

My chest was heaving, legs shaking like all the strength from my body had been siphoned out in the space of a heartbeat. I watched him with greedy eyes of my own, solid and beautiful. His cock jutted out, hard and thick. I watched it jerk the moment he tasted me off his finger, and the moment I stepped forward, a wicked smile took shape, and he tutted, gripping the door beside him.

"Eleven days."

I was still standing there, naked and stupefied, when the shower turned on and I heard his first groan filter from under the door.

The smile on his face was only half satisfied when he found me eating the pancakes after he'd stepped out of the bathroom, and that was the only thing that made me feel even remotely better. That and the middle finger I had already extended his way before I'd even heard the door handle rattle.

An hour later, we were on the highway heading just outside of Darling.

"This is the way back to Artington." Fane raised an eyebrow at me before snapping his eyes back to the road.

I hummed in acknowledgment but didn't say anything else until we got to the part of the highway I was waiting for. "Do you see that shoulder up there?"

"Mm-hmm."

"Pull in there and put the windows down."

The truck rolled to a stop and after shifting it into park Fane pulled the key from the ignition. He turned to look at me, his eyes filled with the kind of patient curiosity that made my heart ache. Like I had every answer he'd ever need. Like I was his true north.

I focused my attention first on his hand still resting on the steering wheel that had the compass, my whole body erupting into goose bumps while I recalled the words he'd said about the meanings of his tattoos.

Now, the compass wasn't pointing at me. It was pointing right at the very place we'd come here to see.

"Do you see that?" I pointed to the ranch house that was settled on the most beautiful property I'd ever seen.

"The house?"

"That's Primrose Ranch. It actually belonged to Sammy's grandfather. He died a few years ago. No one lives there now, but she still goes once a week to clean it up."

He didn't say anything, just waited for me to keep going.

"Dylan is Sammy's cousin. I don't know if you know that."

I saw him shake his head from the corner of my eye.

I nodded, still tracing the house with my eyes. "Growing up, I was always wherever Delilah was, and she was always wherever Dylan was. He was always here with his older brother, Jessie. Sammy too, with her older brother."

Fane looked from my face to the house like he was trying to picture a little version of me sitting on the steps of the big wrap-around porch.

"I loved it here," I said softly. "As a kid, I thought I'd never love another house more than the one I grew up in. But over the last couple of years, I'd come here, park in this exact spot, just to stare at it. I think I've realized I love it more. I didn't realize *why* until last night, though."

"Why?" Fane was still looking away from me, his eyes glued to the house too.

"Tell me what you see?"

He didn't hesitate this time. "I see space. A house. Mountains."

"What do you feel?"

"Your hand in mine. The sun on my face."

I hummed as I closed my own eyes and asked him my last question.

I closed my eyes, letting his words sink in. "What do you hear?"

After a second, he finally whispered his reply. "Nothing."

"How does it all make you feel?" I asked him before slowly opening my eyes to find his already on me, catching the sun the way they always did. Brilliant. Incandescent.

"Peaceful."

I smiled, a small exhale of relief slipping past my lips.

I'd always thought this was what reminded me of Darling the most—the perfect representation of the town I loved. But it was never more clear to me now that I'd always thought of Darling as loud, laughter-filled, and vibrant.

This place, though. This quiet, purple-hued corner of the world? It reminded me of Fane.

"Peace is hard to come by," I said. "Why would you ever want to disturb the pockets of it that exist?"

He leaned over the seat, his lips finding mine in a kiss that was slow and intentional. Then he placed another on my jaw, lingering just long enough for me to feel the weight of his understanding.

I knew he'd heard everything I'd said. Loud and clear.

# 34

# Calista

**After**

Ashton confessed that we were now completely out of ingredients for cookies.

After I chased him around, trying to pinch any part of his body I could grab onto, and he started crying like a little baby asking Fane for help, I was hauled out of my own café. My only consolation was a verbal promise that the cookie ingredients would be replaced before I was back to work the following Friday and that he had a good number for someone who could help me with my aggression.

"I love her aggression, you asshole. Replace the cookies!" Fane called out over his shoulder.

When he set me down out front, I was staring at him with nothing short of heart eyes. "You're my hero," I declared, pulling out my phone.

"What are you doing?"

He tried looking at my phone and the Notes app I'd pulled up before I pressed my phone to my chest.

"Just adding to my list."

"What kind of list?" He slung an arm over my shoulder while we walked.

"You'll see."

"Is it a sex list?"

"You think about sex way too much." (It was absolutely a sex list.)

One I did my best to keep from his prying eyes by trying to walk ahead of him.

"For calling Ashton an asshole?" He was grinning down at me now, eyebrows raised like he didn't quite believe me.

"You looked sexy while doing it." I shrugged. "Like a big, tattooed, sexy city cowboy."

Fane hummed, pretending to think about it. "I can work with this."

Pulling out his phone, he dialed Ashton, keeping his eyes on me while he spoke. "Hey Ash, if you don't replace those cookie ingredients by tomorrow, I'll toast your balls."

He winked at me, and I snorted so loudly it echoed.

"And you need to make it up to her...No, managing the café isn't enough, especially when you eat all her stock...If you bring a cake to dinner tonight that will count as making it up to her? Yes...No, you can't use her ingredients...Yes, you can ask Sammy for help." He pressed the phone against his shoulder, turning to me quickly. "Can Sammy come to dinner?"

I nodded my head enthusiastically, "Of course."

"Yes, Sammy can come to dinner."

When he hung up, he slid his phone into his pocket and watched as I pulled mine out, quickly adding something to the list before putting it away, and the look on his face was priceless.

When we got home, I found him behind the closed door of the bedroom, caught red-handed going through the sex list. He made it up to me by peeling off my jeans and dropping his head between my legs, apologizing profusely despite his no touch rule...*twice.*

Ashton and Sammy were already at my parents' house by the time we got there. I had no idea what in the world was going on, but whatever it was, it looked good on both of them.

There was something incredibly healing for my heart to see the way my mom lit up at having so many people sitting at her dinner table, even though there was a part that ached at Abbey's absence. Ashton's cake was right in the center with writing on the top that said *Sorry Carrie*, and Sammy spent a good portion of the evening explaining to my dad who Carrie was.

"Flavor?"

"Vanilla."

"How many attempts did it take you?"

"This was number two, and it's mostly burned. You just can't see it because of the icing."

"Did Sammy help?"

"With the icing."

"All right, apology accepted."

Ashton did that little fist shake that tennis players did when they were kicking ass, and Sammy snorted so loudly my dad got up thinking the sound came from someone knocking on the front door. I almost peed my pants.

Just when I thought I'd calmed down, I took a sip of water, and a second wave of giggles hit me, sending my water praying right over Ashton's piece of cake.

Fane ended up in the fetal position on the floor, wheezing until the entire table was red faced and teary eyed.

When the chaos settled, all that remained were the soft smiles that lingered on everyone's faces, shoulders loose and tension-free. Despite its slightly questionable taste, everyone had even gone back for seconds of Ashton's infamous Carrie cake.

When we left for the night, my mom held onto me a little longer. Squeezed a little tighter.

"All these people are here because of you, sweet girl," she said, tucking a black, wavy strand of hair behind my ear.

"No," I told her with a gentle shake of my head. "Just like me, they're here because of you."

And it was true. My parents had always been the warmest, most welcoming people. Arms open for anyone and everyone, and the better my mom got, the more willing she was to let her circle get wider again. To let people back in to sit in the glow of her laughter and warmth. Both her and my dad.

In the last couple of years, it felt like we'd reversed our roles as parent and child. I spent so much time making sure they were okay—cared for, looked after—and when things needed fixing, I fixed them.

I'd confirm appointments so my dad only needed to check the calendar on the fridge before taking her. Stock their fridge, clean their clothes, their house, their car.

When we left that evening, my mom tucked into my dad's side, I could see the life that had seeped from them slowly creeping back into their eyes. I felt the way they both watched me, like they were silently asking if it was okay. If I could see that they might be strong enough now to take back the role of parent they'd handed to me for so long.

I kept my beaming smile in place, my hand waving out the window until they were out of view, strong for them both until the last second—before it all came flooding out.

When Fane swore under his breath and started to pull the car over, this weird, honking noise flew out of my mouth. It was the culmination of trying to inhale, saying, "No, I'm fine!" and crying, all at once.

"I don't know what to do!" Fane's head swiveled between the windshield and me, where I was still trying to choke out the words, "I'm fine," without sounding like barnyard poultry.

In the end, my frantic waving, which felt very reminiscent of an uncoordinated aircraft marshaller, was enough to get us home. By the time we'd parked, my tears had dried up, and Fane looked no less terrified than he did before.

He didn't say a word, just sat with me in the silence of his truck, his thumb moving soothingly over the back of my hand.

"They seem…" There were so many versions of that sentence running through my head I didn't know which to go with.

""Okay?" Fane offered, his voice low and steady. I knew from my half-formed statement that he understood where my head was at. My heart too.

"Yeah," I whispered. "Okay."

The word felt so big, so loaded. I was trying to say a hundred things with just those two syllables. Fane nodded, understanding every unspoken word despite none of it making sense.

"You helped get them there," he said simply, turning his hand to thread his fingers through mine.

"I didn't—" It was a reflex to deny that I had done anything, but Fane's grip tightened just enough to stop me.

"You did." His tone was gentle but firm, cutting through every excuse I wanted to make. "I'm sorry you had to do it on your own."

My throat closed up, and the tears that I thought I'd run out of started welling up again.

All of my deepest, darkest secrets were held by Fane. The man was a vault. Anything that went in stayed there, locked tight, and kept safe. I'd never found anyone who I could confess my heaviest thoughts to like I could with him. Now it was like I'd finally managed to come out of the most harrowing storm of my life, and I could finally let them all out.

"I did my best," I admitted, my voice cracking as the words I'd been holding in for so long finally spilled out. "And now I'm just so tired."

"I know, baby," he said.

"I don't want to do it anymore. Be steady. I know that sounds selfish, but I'm not built for it, I have no idea how you do it." There were so many times in the last two years I needed Fane. Needed him to shoulder the weight from me, but I realized too that without being forced to stand on my own, I would have never believed I could've done it.

But I did do it, and I was damn proud of myself for it.

That's why when I thought of Fane and the decision he'd made for both of us, I couldn't be mad at him anymore.

"How about another compromise?" he asked.

"Okay."

He gave me a small, reassuring smile. "When you need to be steady again, you will be. But when you don't, when you're tired, you can pass it to me. I'll hold it until you're ready for it again."

I stared at him, his words sinking into me like sunlight on cold skin. "And when you're tired?"

"Then you'll be steady," he said, his voice so sure, like it was the simplest thing in the world. "We'll take turns, Cali. That's how this works."

The certainty in his voice settled something deep inside me, a part I didn't even realize was still restless.

"Okay," I said. A quiet promise. "Deal."

Fane smiled softly, brushing his thumb over my knuckles. "Good."

For a moment, the truck was quiet again, the weight of everything we'd just shared settling in. Then his lips twitched, that familiar mischievous grin sneaking in.

"What now?" I asked warily, narrowing my eyes at him.

"You've got cake on your face."

I blinked. "What?"

He nodded solemnly, reaching out to trace his thumb along my jawline. "Right…here."

"Fane, if you—" But before I could finish, his thumb swiped something sticky off my cheek, and he held it up triumphantly, speckled with frosting.

"It's cake," he said, grinning like a kid.

"Oh my god," I groaned, covering my face with my hands. "Why didn't you say anything earlier?"

He shrugged. "It was kind of cute."

"Cute?" I glared at him, swiping furiously at my face. "I had vanilla frosting on my face this whole time, and you didn't think to mention it?"

"You've been laughing and crying all night. Honestly, it just blended in."

"Fane!" I smacked his arm just as he opened his door and hopped out.

"Wait, wait," he called out, just as I rounded the front and found him leaning against the truck for support. "Don't worry, you're still super hot. Just…maybe a little sticky."

"Oh, you're dead," I growled, shoving past him toward the house.

He followed behind me, grinning from ear to ear. "So, does this mean you're not taking something off the sex list?"

"You know what?" I shot back without turning around. "Yes. Number three."

His groan echoed behind me as we entered the house. I headed straight for the bathroom, slamming the door in his face and muffling his dramatic pleas. But despite myself, I couldn't stop the smile tugging at my lips.

When I walked out wrapped in my towel, the house was quiet. Neither Fane nor Jerry were anywhere to be found.

Slipping on a pair of sweatpants and one of Fane's sweaters, I dried my hair just enough to head outside and went in search of them, only to find them right at the bottom of the stairs.

Picnic blankets were laid out over one another, all the pillows and blankets from our bed arranged into the coziest-looking spread I'd ever seen. Fane was on one side, and Jerry was right next to him sprawled on his back. Light snores puffed from him into the cool night air.

"Found you," I said from the top steps. Fane turned, a small, relaxed smile on his face, warm and sleepy and patted the blankets beside him.

As soon as I settled in, Fane slid his arm under me, dragged me against him, and placed a kiss on my temple while I tucked my feet between his legs.

The night was clear, and even though the last time we'd done this had been incredible for city limits, it had nothing on this moment, right here.

"Woah," I breathed, my hand finding its way under Fane's shirt to press against his stomach, and a little hum purred in my throat. There was something addictive about the very specific warmth that radiated off his skin.

The words were on my tongue. Three tiny words that had honestly always belonged to him, that he'd already given me. Freely. Many times over in so many different ways since he got here, and I'd been too scared to say for so many reasons.

There was a list of things I needed to give Fane. Things that had always been his, really. I might not have been able to give him everything—not yet—but I could start here.

I took a deep breath and said, "I have something to tell you."

"Hit me."

"I found Jerry at that shelter off Brumble Street."

"The one with the inflatable tube man out front?"

"Yeah. It was on my rotation. I went into that one and maybe five others every week for like two months, and then one day there he was. When I saw him, the first thing I thought was, 'Holy bananas, you belong to Fane.'"

"What?" He tried to shift his body, and I heard his heart start to pick up from where my ear was pressed to his chest, but I gripped him, holding him still.

"The night I left." Fane went so still beside me his chest was hardly moving. "I was confused and lost and…I wanted to come home to you, but I couldn't. So, I just drove around for hours. When the shelter opened, I went and picked him up, and then we headed straight to Darling. Then there I was, this single, super hot chick who now owned her ex-boyfriend's dream dog."

Fane's bark of laughter launched out of him, waking up Jerry again, who let us know his displeasure with an aggravated huff. "*Super* hot."

"I know, but quiet, please. This is my story."

"Sorry," he whispered, pulling me in closer.

"I guess what I'm saying is that he's really always been yours."

"You're not joking." He looked down at me, brows drawn in a tentative sort of hope that made me wish I'd told him this a long time ago.

"He's mine too," I said, smirking. "But he's always been half yours. Just so you know." After a beat, I added, "And I didn't take off number three from the sex list."

Fane groaned, rolling onto his side, pulling me back down into the blanket nest and peppering my face with kisses until I was a giggle, red faced mess and despite late hour, Fane pulled me close and yelled up into the sky, brimming full of stars of us, *"This is the best night of my whole fucking life!"*

# 35

## Calista

**After**

After our last tour to Primrose Ranch, it was like the two years between us didn't exist.

Those years didn't exist in the spaces of time where he held me close and we watched TV on the couch. When I sat on the kitchen counter and we talked while he made a meal for us to share. When we rocked side to side around the living room to his favorite song and he quietly sang along to the lyrics with our hands clutched to his chest.

But then they also very much existed.

They existed in the lines etched into his face that hadn't been there before. When he would work in the back corner of the café that I owned and built all on my own. In the way we'd both grown separately during our time apart, and with that came the realization that those parts of us had become strangers to one another. Different versions of who we'd been, learning one another all over again.

They existed in Jerry, who was between us at every possible moment, staring at Fane like he hung the moon. When he would look at me, his gray-blue eyes asking the question, *He's mine? I get to keep him, right?*

On the couch, during walks, outside in the backyard where we'd looked up at the sky almost every night since that first time Fane had done it with the pillows from our bed, Jerry was there. Proud as all hell to be the center of attention, his soft snores the backing track to our quiet murmured conversations.

It felt perfect, but there were times when that perfection carried a weight.

It was hard not to feel it.

All the what-ifs on how it could have been different.

"I'm sorry," I whispered to him in the darkness of our bedroom with my hands pressed against his warm skin, his mouth leaving soft, delicate kisses at the hollow of my throat.

"Me too," he whispered back, closing this chapter that we'd lingered at the end of, unsure if we were allowed to close it.

But we were, and as he sunk into me, the overwhelming pleasure he made me feel turned that heaviness into something else. Structures and monuments just for us. A tribute to what this path of ours looked like.

So different from what we had originally thought, but still perfect. With every thrust, every moment we lost ourselves in one another, it was *perfect*. The only thing that mattered anymore was the echo of Fane's words. His direction, his praise, his questions.

When he finally left to head back to Artington, it wasn't shocking. We'd talked about it over and over, and I was both a little startled and not at all when he told me he'd already planned on never going back for good.

"Whole lot of confidence you had there, buddy." I dug my pointer fingers into his sides when he told me that, even though the sentiment had made my insides tingle and my heart flutter. I'd somehow ended up beneath Fane with his hands finding every ticklish place on my body until I was crying, and Jerry jumped from his couch onto ours in a physical demand not to be left out of all the fun.

When we woke up Saturday morning, the tone of Fane's impending trip had changed.

Everything about him leaving seemed wrong. *Everything.*

It wasn't one specific thing. I couldn't place it, but my stomach filled with a lead weight that made it hard to roll out of bed, to help him pack.

To watch him go.

"Just a few days to close everything up and hand in my notice," he said. Eyes dark and heavy with the same emotion that hung thickly in the air around us where he stood at the front door, duffel bag slung over his shoulder.

"Yep!" I was doing the smile I called on only in cases of emergencies when the threat of tears and mental breakdowns was so likely I had no other choice but to bring out the big guns.

He didn't say anything in response to that. What he did do was drop his bag to the floor and walk right up to me and then his lips were on mine.

Moving. Tasting. Remembering. Making sure I didn't forget.

The moment he wrapped his arms around my waist and pulled me to him, mine slid around his neck, and he walked us the few steps needed to get us back to our bedroom.

I fumbled with his belt, tugging down his jeans and pulling out his cock within mere seconds of my back hitting the bed. When I pushed on his chest, he held tight to my legs that were wrapped around him and flipped us.

Our mouths were fused together, hands clutching tightly, fingertips bruising. Fane, still with his boots on, lifted up the shirt that I had on—his shirt—with nothing beneath and watched as I ran the head of his cock along the seam of my pussy before notching him at my entrance and dropping down on him, inch by inch, until my legs were shaking. With a tight grip on my hips, he thrust into the hilt, and the only sound was our ragged breathing while he waited for me to adjust to the way we fit together.

Fane captured every one of my cries when I started to roll my hips, when I picked up speed, lifting and lowering myself in a panicked rhythm.

Desperate and frenzied.

I held onto every grunt that purred from his chest. Relished the places on my body his hands lingered.

His name tumbled out of my mouth on a loop as I held him tighter like this was it. Like I was about to lose him for a second time, even though he'd told me more times than I could count that this was it for him. He was coming back.

Those three words were still right there. I'd tried to show him in other ways, I was desperate for him to know every thought in my head, but they remained where they were, unspoken.

"I know, baby," he grunted against my lips, and then he was standing up, pressing me against the wall, letting one of my legs fall from his waist while he hooked the other higher, filling me deeper, harder.

"*Fuck*," I whimpered, my hands gripping the strands of his hair that had slowly started to grow out since he'd been here. "I don't want you to go." I pressed the words into the skin of his neck before I latched my mouth there, sucking hard and feeling the way his cock jerked inside me.

"Two days," he panted. "I'm coming right back to you." One hand snaked up my torso, pulling up his shirt and exposing my breasts. I pulled a hand from his hair to pinch and tug on one nipple before dropping it down between my legs and rubbing quick, hard circles over my clit that Fane watched with his lips parted and eyelids hooded.

"Okay," I panted, nodding.

"My truth north. Right here." The hand gripping my shirt moved over my heart, and I looked down at his chest, where his shirt covered his toned, honeyed skin, and knew the words that were inked right there. The time on his neck, the rose—*my* rose—the hand covering my heart, and the compass on it that pointed right at me.

"Okay," I said again, meaning it.

Fane's mouth descended on mine, and when I came with his name on my lips, he tasted every syllable. With a final thrust, I felt him thicken inside of me before he stilled, my name falling from his mouth like the holy tongue.

I only let myself think about him coming home and how fucking incredible it would be when he did. That as soon as he was back, this niggling feeling in the pit of my gut would have been for nothing. I told myself it only existed because there was only one time before this that one of us left the other, and it hadn't been temporary.

It was all I knew, that's why this was so fucking scary.

I stayed on the porch until his car disappeared, and only when Jerry let out his own little whine long after the rumble of Fane's truck disappeared, did I look down at him, give him a little scratch under the chin and walk back into the house.

The whole place used to feel perfect for me and Jerry, now it felt too big, too empty. The way Jerry stared at the front door the entire morning while I made breakfast and showered to get ready for work, I could tell he felt it too.

By the time I'd gotten out, he'd somehow managed to grab one of Fane's shirts from the laundry hamper and take it to his couch, where he dropped his head right on top of it, looking so forlorn that I snapped a photo and sent it to the man in question.

**Calista:** [Photo]

**Calista: Just in case you were wondering who misses you more. It's Jerry…**

**Fane: Miss you too, buddy.**

**Fane: What about Jerry's mom?**

**Calista: Are you texting and driving?**

**Fane: Stopped for gas. Where's your photo of how much you miss me?**

**Calista: You saw me an hour ago, I think you're obsessed.**

**Fane: :(**

**Calista:** [Photo]

My phone started to ring on my way into work, pinging through the car thanks to the bluetooth system in Delilah's car that was so beyond advanced compared to what I'd been driving it felt closer to being an alien spacecraft than a vehicle intended for the roads.

When she had dropped off Jerry, she'd told me point blank it was mine to use until further notice. I tried to hand her keys back to her and so she proceeded to throw them onto the porch and run towards the idling car that housed Dylan, all ready to zoom away as her getaway driver.

"Hello?"

"Cali, you're naked in that photo."

"I am?" A hand flew to my chest, even though he couldn't see it.

I heard the door to his truck close through the phone. "How am I supposed to focus on saving Darling if I'm thinking about the way your tits look covered in water?"

"Just trying to be helpful."

"My dick is hard, and I can't remember where I'm supposed to be going."

"Oh no," I cooed. "That actually sounds really awful." I moved my hand from my chest to cover the laugh I couldn't hold back.

"You're such a brat."

"Maybe you should teach me a lesson with number three on the sex list."

Fane groaned so loudly that the smile on my face made my cheeks hurt.

"You're killing me," he whimpered just as I put the car into park out the back of Sunshine.

"I'm seeing Delilah tonight for dinner, and then maybe you can call me, and you can guess whether or not I've been wearing panties all day."

Fane was only sort of able to speak a few coherent words after that. One of them being "Rosie" and another being "filthy." Needless to say, the expression on my face was the perfect mix of flushed and happy.

The moment Gus strolled in for his coffee, then when my dad showed up a few minutes later, I knew that the churning in my gut from this morning had been stupid.

Sammy and I managed the Saturday shift with ease now that the contractors had left town. I had expected to see Ashton come in, but when I asked Sammy about him, she just frowned, lost somewhere in her own head, and walked off to clear the tables.

That was probably the weirdest thing that happened all day.

Fane had messaged when he got back to Artington with a photo of him on his hotel bed, face squished into a pillow, and another about how he was heading into a board meeting and that working on the weekends should be a crime. I sent him a picture response at that line, this time of me flipping him off while wearing an oven mitt…in the back kitchen of the café…working on the weekend.

The voice memo I got back consisted of a range of incredibly not safe for work language about what my aggression did to him, and Sammy was quick to remind me any chance she got about the blush that stained my cheeks for the rest of the day.

By the time I parked outside Delilah's and found myself sitting at her kitchen counter with a mega-pint of wine, my feet were sore, my hands were a little crampy, but my cup was so damn full I hardly knew myself. Or maybe I did, and it had just been a really fucking long time since I'd seen her.

Dylan was out when I arrived, but halfway through our pizza and movie date, he walked through the front door, dropped the largest carton of chocolate ice cream I'd maybe ever seen on the coffee table, and kissed the absolute shit out of Delilah before disappearing down the hall.

"Holy moly." I was fanning my face with one hand and stifling my laughter with the other while Delilah looked like she was about to spontaneously combust.

"He's…passionate," she mumbled, both hands pressed to her face.

"I'll say." That earned me a pillow to the face and Delilah turning an even brighter shade of red. An hour later, when Dylan came out, shoulder propped against the hallway entrance and eyes focused entirely on Delilah, I took my cue to leave.

"I should go. It's like a whole hour and a half past Jerry's dinnertime, and he always demands extra when I'm late with dishing it up. Plus, I feel like I should get out of the way of your…passion."

"Good idea," Dylan grumbled while Delilah just rolled her eyes, but I saw the little smile there. I couldn't help the way my heart dropped knowing that Fane wouldn't be there when I got home.

"Message me when you get home so I know you're safe," Delilah said, waving one last time from her front door before Dylan appeared behind her and closed it with a firm push. He really hadn't changed one bit since we were kids.

The house was dark and quiet when I pulled up out front, and the only real reason I was going inside was because Jerry had been home on his own all day, and I was desperate to hold his big head in my hands and deliver the loudest smooch of all smooches. To talk to him and see if I could persuade him to snuggle with me all night in Fane's absence.

I sent Delilah a message quickly before hopping out of the car and heading for the door. The moment Jerry was happy, fed, and sleeping back on his bed, all the things that might be waiting for me on the other side of a video call with Fane were sending waves of heat careening over me. Mind, body and freaking soul.

The second I tried to put the key into the lock of the house, I knew something was wrong. Namely, because the door was open. I couldn't tell because I'd stupidly forgotten to turn the porch light on before I left. I never forgot the porch light, but I'd been so focused on everything else that had been circulating in my head that I'd missed it.

My phone was clutched in my hand, but any part of my brain that was telling me I needed to call someone—the police, my dad, Fane, Ashton, Delilah, *anyone*—stopped working entirely when the door opened on silent hinges, another of the things Fane had fixed, and I saw Jerry lying in the entry room.

Still and unmoving.

The sound that I made wasn't something I could explain. It was a gasp, a cry, a plea. It was choking on air I couldn't breathe. Something that encompassed every single way my heart was trembling where it thrashed inside my chest, desperate to get out.

My phone, my keys, my bag—it all got left and forgotten at the front door. The pain that shot up through my knees barely registered when I landed next to Jerry and pressed my ear to his chest. The noise I made that time was nothing short of a cry of desperate relief. His heart was beating, maybe it was a little sluggish, but I couldn't really tell from the rushing that had started in my ears.

"Fuck, *fuck, fuck.* Jerry?" My voice wavered when I reached for his head and placed a trembling hand in front of his shiny black nose to feel his breath moving in and out. It was shallow and light, but with the absence of his usual deep and heavy breathing, the clear and hard-to-miss rise and fall of his body, it felt like nothing at all.

The moment I realized that he was alive, something clicked in my brain. Two years of needing to be steady for everyone else, myself included, kicked back in. I'd managed to let go of the tension in my body that was a result of living that way bit by bit since Fane had come to Darling, and it all rushed back into me like muscle memory.

Like armor slipping right into place.

My phone. I needed my phone.

When I turned around, an arm already extended for where I had dropped it just outside the door my hand crumpled in on itself, a sharp pain shooting up my arm from the impact of shoving it right into a door.

My front door. My now *closed* front door.

I hadn't closed it. I hadn't noticed it swing shut or click into place. I wasn't even sure how that could be possible when the lock had been broken. It *had* been broken, right?

With my hand clutched to my chest, I turned back to Jerry and found myself staring down the barrel of a gun.

Declan wore a cruel, disjointed grin. His eyes were black pits—black holes sucking all the air from the room—widened a fraction with excitement at whatever he saw on my face.

A scream rallied in my chest. My lungs expanded, ready to shred my throat apart a second before he lifted his other hand, and I saw the glint of a knife that he flipped, catching it again like it was a fun little part trick, and he wanted to show off.

"If you make a sound." He dropped the gun to his side and replaced it with his knife to the side of my neck, the metal cool as it accompanied a small sting when he pushed the point of it into my skin. "I will kill you."

# 36

## Calista

**After**

"Up we get." Declan used the knife at my throat to get me to rise from where I'd been crouched next to Jerry.

My body was on autopilot, which was working just fine for me right now because every signal I was demanding my brain to send out wasn't computing. My tongue refused to work, my arms refused to move. To lash out.

I was picturing it on repeat in my head—the different ways that I would be able to disarm him. None of the moves I'd done before, but that didn't matter. If I could just get myself to do *something,* it would be better than what was happening right now, which was me, alone in my house, and a psychopath holding a knife to my throat.

Jerry was lying still on the floor, the silence around him so deafening it was like the entire world had disappeared. I focused on his chest, trying to catch the faintest rise and fall. If I focused on that, I wouldn't crumble. Not yet.

"You're awfully quiet, Calista." Declan leaned into the space between us, his face morphing into a mocking pout. "From everything I've gathered, this house is usually quite loud." He leaned back, his smile turning feral as he used his gun to gesture to the bedroom. "Especially in there."

His insinuation made my stomach churn, the violation sharp and personal. Rage flared in me, hot and quick, but it didn't burn away the fear. He'd watched us. Fane and me. That realization made my blood boil, but the knife against my throat reminded me how easily he could cut me down. My weapon—the one that should have been at my side—lay unconscious at my feet.

"I thought you said not to make a sound."

Declan's smile faltered for a moment before twisting into something feral, dangerous. "No one likes a fucking smart ass, Calista," he hissed, and I swear to God, I saw his black eyes swirl like something foul lurked underneath.

I swallowed four times before I managed to open my mouth and push out any more words. Half because I was doing my best not to tell him to go and fuck himself and half because my anger was definitely a coping mechanism to mediate the tremor I felt starting in my hands at the very real fact that I was here, alone, and had for the first time in my entire life had a gun pointed to my head.

"You're supposed to be in Artington." My voice came out strong. Calm and steady, and I was so fucking impressed with myself, particularly when I caught the tiny blink of surprise from this asshole when I didn't start blubbering. Don't get me wrong, I was pretty sure if I could've, I would have already pissed myself, but it turned out I was made from a lot stronger stuff. I just really needed to catch up with the fact that maybe I wasn't innately soft.

*Maybe* I wouldn't go down without a fight.

The thought gave me something else to hold onto, something to focus on.

"Ah, right. Well, you see, I am *intimately* aware of Ashton and all his little connections, not to mention their lacking legality." He started to wave his gun around while he spoke. "I did go back, just for a few days. Just to set a few things into motion. Swapped my cards with a buddy of mine. He didn't even know!" Declan raised his eyebrows at me in some weird, silent way of letting me know he thought that would impress me. A brilliant move in...whatever this was.

A game. That's all this was to him, and he'd decided to make me an unwilling player.

"But, and this is where it gets really fun, I've been *right here!*" He whispered the last bit like a secret, and all the food I'd crammed down my throat with Delilah threatened to come back up. "Actually, that's not true. I've been out *there*"—Declan gestured his gun toward the front door—"while he was in *here*. With *you*." The barrel of his gun swung back to rest right in the middle of my forehead. It was no easier to live through it the second time, especially with a knife at my throat.

"Fane?" I just wanted to keep him talking. It was the only thing running through my mind. If he was talking to me, then I was alive. "Is this like some unrequited love thing?" I swallowed and tried not to wince at the way the knife shifted where he held it.

Declan's smile dropped instantly, and it was like looking at a completely different person. No less fucking rotten, but a different kind of rotten. It pulsed from him now, and it was very clear that I had not only missed the mark, but I'd sent my assumption out so wide that I felt the way his hand twitched at my throat. How easy it would be for him to flick his wrist all because I couldn't hold my tongue.

In my defense, I'd never been in this position before, so I had no idea that my defense mechanism was me turning into a fucking dumbass with zero concern for her own well-being.

"I watched you," he hissed. "Night after night. I was curious to see how broken you were after I hit you with my car. Did you like how I had a little fun with your brakes?"

"You tried to kill me."

He waved his gun, dismissing my statement before dropping it down to his side. "Don't be so dramatic, Rosie. Can I call you Rosie? I like it."

"No, you fucking ca—*ah,*" I gasped, grinding my teeth together when he pressed the knife further into the side of my throat. The sting of it made my jaw cramp, and I felt the tickle of something dripping down my neck, soaking my shirt.

"Shh, shh, shh." Declan tucked the gun into the back of his jeans with a casual ease that spoke to how comfortable he was in this moment. His free hand rose, fingers trailing along my cheek with a feather-light touch that felt grotesquely intimate. I forced myself to keep swallowing, my throat constricting against the rising bile.

I didn't see it coming.

One second, the knife was there, sharp and cold against my neck. The next, it was gone, his hand swinging back in a blur.

The slap landed with a crack so loud it reverberated in my skull. Pain didn't register at first—it was just sound and shock. And then it hit me. My skin ignited, a searing blaze consuming the entire left side of my face. It felt like a swarm of fire ants were crawling under my skin, biting and stinging as they spread across my cheek, my lips, beneath my eyelid.

My nose throbbed, sharp and hot, and the vision in my left eye blurred, leaving me momentarily disoriented.

I couldn't stop the yelp of surprise that escaped me—a small, involuntary sound that felt like a betrayal. I wished with every ounce of strength I had that I'd swallowed it down, buried it deep where he couldn't find it.

But the damage was done.

That horrifying giddiness flickered back into his expression, spreading like oil across an ocean, slick and sinister. His knife was back at my throat in an instant, the cold press of it rooting me to the spot. The quips I'd been clinging to—the fleeting scraps of defiance that had kept me upright—died in my throat, leaving only the sound of my shallow breaths to fill the silence.

I wasn't running outside.

I didn't have Jerry.

And there would be no Fane at the end of this to catch me.

There was only me and the terrifying likelihood that I might not be enough.

"Rosie suits you. So soft, delicate. I think I'll call you Rosie. I mean, of course, if that's okay with you?"

I nodded my head stiffly, my neck pinching a little at the way my head had so aggressively wrenched to the side.

Declan dragged the back of his knuckles across the cheek he'd just hit, his touch mockingly tender. I couldn't feel it, just the dull, stinging heat radiating from the skin that I knew was already swelling.

"So pretty, Rosie. How you're changing color right before my eyes." His voice was low and conversational, like we were discussing fucking paint samples. His smile twisted, warping into something manic. "I have to admit, I wasn't sure if this was going to be as fun as some of my other ideas, but...I really am having a great time. Are you?"

I opened my mouth to speak, but nothing came out. I watched, terror coursing through me, locking my bones and squeezing at my rib cage, while his face started to drop.

"Yes," I forced the word past my trembling lips.

Declan's smile returned, wide and gleeful. "Oh, good. *Good.*"

He nodded, leaning forward to press a kiss to the side of my face. Lingering in a way that felt suffocating. I was grateful—pathetically, desperately grateful—that I couldn't feel much. Just the small, sharp sting near my eyebrow and the growing pressure that made it clear it was puffing and swelling.

Before I had time to react, Declan's knife disappeared from my throat, his hand snapping out to grab my ponytail. The yank was so sudden, so violent, my head jerked back with a cry that broke free before I could stop it. My eyes watered from the strain, and the angle made swallowing nearly impossible. I couldn't see him anymore, but I *felt* him.

Felt the way he yanked me sideways so he could step around Jerry's still body before pressing himself against me. Fully. Completely. There wasn't an inch of space left between us, and the hard, horrifying evidence of what this was doing to him pressed against my stomach.

Bile rose in my throat, hot and acidic, threatening to spill out as the angle of my neck fought to keep it down. If the sheer knowledge of his arousal wasn't enough to make me sick, the sensation of his tongue dragging up my throat—lapping at the blood that trickled from the cut he'd made—would have done it.

My whole body filled with dread. Like water pouring in, starting at my toes and slowly filling me up. Weighing me down. Drowning me in panic.

He was going to kill me.

I knew it. I felt his intention to do it in every word he spoke, every rise and fall of his shoulders. The grip he had on me, and how he dug his nails into the skin of my scalp like if he could rip it from my skull, he would.

The only real thing I knew at that moment was that I would be damned if I went down without trying my best to take him with me.

I just needed to be smart.

"You know what's missing? *Fane!*" Declan said his name like it was vile. Like the very existence of it was something so desperately unwanted. Something he loathed.

I thought that maybe I'd been right from the start, when he approached me in the café, when he touched me at the bar, that he was only interested in me because of Fane.

But then…he'd never done anything directly *to* him. Because of that, my concern had morphed from being *for* Fane to being about what he'd do if he'd found out what was happening.

It all clicked together so clearly for me right then. I was *nothing* to Declan. A means to an end. A pawn to be used and shifted in his game.

He wanted to hurt Fane. I had no idea why, but he obviously thought the best way to do that was through me. My whole chest constricted at that thought. I'd only just gotten him back. We were meant to have more time than this. Our whole fucking lives—*that's* what we were meant to have.

This piece of shit wasn't going to take that. From me. From Fane. Who'd given up everything for me. Given up everything for everyone, his whole fucking life.

This man who always insisted on putting himself between me and the world.

Yeah, well, guess fucking what Declan? My turn.

"I think we should call him. Do you want to do the honors, or should I? Wait, I know!" Declan just kept talking, grabbing ahold of my upper arm and dragging me toward the bedroom. He shoved me down to sit on the edge of the bed before replacing his knife back at the same spot on my throat. The tip bit deeper than before as he rustled around in his pocket before presenting me with my phone. The lock screen illuminated to show a photo of Fane and Jerry when they'd fallen asleep together on the couch.

"I'll call him using *your* phone, so we can share the honors. By the way, you dropped this, Rosie." He gave a little shrug, his tone a mocking reprimand as he held it up to my face to unlock it. "You should really keep better track of your things."

I was trying to think of every single scenario in my head. Trying to think about what I could do to get out of here. To *not* think about where he had brought me. Why he had brought me there and what he was going to do.

The phone rang only once before Fane picked up, and I knew it was because he'd been waiting for my call.

"Baby." His voice rumbled through the line, warm and familiar, so solid it sent a tremor through me, like my soul was shifting. Reshaping. Preparing for impact.

That was all it took to push me over this line I'd been teetering on. Of numbness and feeling too much.

"I'm going to speak to Delilah about how long she kept you. I think we need a rule. No longer than an hour. Two, *max*." I closed my eyes, the swelling making it hard to move my face, and felt a tear fall down the side of my face he hadn't touched.

For this man who had always been my definition of safe, who'd given me the safety to be soft, just like a rose. Just like Declan had pointed out.

But roses weren't just soft, were they?

They were also covered in fucking thorns.

"What about me?" Declan's voice crawled over my body, the intent behind his words cold and heavy. "Does that time limit apply to the time that *I* get with her?"

The silence on the other end of the phone was deafening, and I felt it then, like I had the first night I'd seen him. This string, tied to every rib in my body, going right through my phone to him on the other end.

"Calista?" I heard every ounce of terror, of fury, of blazing fucking anger in his voice brewing on the other end like a storm.

"Don't be shy, Rosie." Declan moved the knife just enough to dig a little deeper, making me wince. A fresh trickle of blood dripped down my neck. "Say hi to our Fane."

"Fane," I murmured, my voice strong. Sure. My eyes trained on the imaginary piece of string I pictured leading from me and into the phone. Light, luminescent. Something made of sunshine, and drew strength from it.

"Cali." Fane's voice broke on my name. It was a plea that time, a little piece of him breaking and slicing me wide open in the process. Declan's smile widened at it.

"I wouldn't leave your hotel room if I were you, boss. The moment you do, I'll know, and if you happen to weasel yourself past my notice, then there's a really good chance you won't make it back to dear old Darling."

"What do you want?" There was no emotion in Fane's voice. It was flat and lifeless and sounded a whole lot like how he looked when he showed up at my café all those weeks ago.

"Finally what I'm fucking *owed*." Declan bared his teeth at the phone. His face shifted from one mask to another so fast I thought I was losing my mind because in the very next second, his smile was back in place. He looked so relaxed he could have been sipping fucking cocktails on a beach somewhere. "First Rosie, then everything else will fall into place, and I will finally be the one he respects." He took a deep breath, a sick, pleased smile on his face. "Well, we didn't want you to miss the show, did we?"

"I have no fucking idea what you're talking about. Don't you *fucking* touch her!" He practically roared the words into the phone. They were visceral, and that string that led from me to him pulled taut. Aching.

Declan's hand shot out, making contact with the side of my face he'd already hit. The sound of it crackled through the room. It echoed off the walls and made the tips of my fingers tingle, but I didn't make a sound.

One plan came into play, and for it to work, for me to have even a tiny shot, I needed Declan closer. I needed him out of his fucking mind.

"That's okay. You will soon, boss." Declan grinned, leaning down toward the phone, his voice smug and triumphant. "The important thing right now is for you to know that every time you tell me I can't do something to her,

Fane, I will absolutely do it."

Declan set the phone down beside me, and then his hand trailed against the side of my face he hit. His tongue darted out, wetting his cracked lips sending a spike of nausea through me again.

"She is soft, Fane. I'll give you that. I think I've learned what she likes from watching you both. I have to say, you did surprise me." Declan laughed to himself. "You don't talk much, but you sure have a lot to say to Rosie when you fuck her." His fingers trailed over the shell of my ear and elicited an involuntary shiver from me, making my organs twist and roil.

It was like slugs in my stomach. Their fat, slimy bodies worming their way up and out of my throat. My body revolted. I didn't have time to say anything before I lurched forward, the contents of my stomach emptying violently onto the floor of my bedroom. Declan's knife had been at my throat still, and the slice nicked deeper and even wider. The flow of blood now felt slow and constant.

"You fucking *bitch*," Declan spat. A hand wrapped around my throat, squeezing until my air was cut off completely. The pressure of his hand on the cut on my neck made my eyes water. I felt the tip of his blade dig in just under my collarbone, sinking in with a stinging, burning pressure that made me feel stupid for thinking the burning on my face was anything to cry about.

This felt like fire was being *poured* into me. My hands gripped at the hand that wrapped around my throat, and I dug my nails in even when it tightened. Even when my world began to narrow, the edges of my vision darkening.

I could hear Fane on the phone, but the rushing in my ears was so loud I couldn't make out what he was saying, and then Declan's hand was gone as quickly as it had reached out for me. I pulled in a deep inhale of air, the burning in my lungs dissipating slowly as I pulled in breath and breath, reigniting when it was pushed back out in a fit of coughs.

"You've let me down, Fane," Declan gritted through his teeth. "I studied you for days. Learned how you touched her." His lips curled into a sneer. "I guess you were doing it wrong."

"Cali, baby, talk to me." Fane ignored Declan's words completely, his voice breaking on my name again. "I'm right here, Rose. You talk to me." My chest pinched at the way he used my nickname, how he was taking it back as something that would only ever belong to us. It settled over me then that we both knew what was going to happen. I knew it from the moment he pulled me into this room, but I'd been alone then.

I wasn't alone now.

"Rosie," Fane said again.

"Remember the night we met?" I whispered, my voice a little raspy, but the words were clear.

"Shut *up!*" Declan snarled, hands clenched at his sides, his chest starting to rise and fall rapidly. Featured twisted into a grotesque pout.

"I remember." Fane's strained voice reached me, and I imagined that string pulling taut again. Over and over, like I could feel his breathing, the rise and fall of his chest.

"I heard your laugh and couldn't stop looking around until I found you. You were sitting at the bar." Despite it all, a little hum escaped me at the memory of that moment. "I think I knew at that moment I loved you."

"I said, *shut up!*" The back of Declan's hand cracked across my face for the third time, but the skin was so numb that it hardly even registered. I just focused on Fane.

"Sunshine." My words were a little wobbly, half of my mouth feeling numb and puffy, but I told him anyway. "That's what your laugh felt like. Being covered in sunshine. I love—"

The sound of my phone hitting the wall cut me off, its screen going black as it clattered to the floor. The call disconnected.

"You'll learn to listen to me, you fucking cunt!" Declan grabbed both my wrists and pushed me back onto the bed. He held them tight in one hand above my head while his other moved down to hold my face, making sure I was looking at him.

"Say my name," he demanded.

*Over my dead fucking body.*

My voice was muffled by the grip he had on my jaw, and he had to loosen it slightly before he repeated the demand. "Again."

So I did exactly as I was asked. "Fane," I said.

"*My* name." His face was starting to go red. The loss of control driving him feral. Unraveling him, thread by rotten thread.

"Fane," I repeated, still seeing that string taut between us despite my phone being destroyed. Despite the distance between us.

"*Fane, Fane, Fane,*" I chanted quietly, defiantly.

Declan's head lowered, his face inches from mine, his twisted smile faltering for just a second. That's all I needed.

I smashed my head into his with every ounce of force I could muster.

The impact sent a shockwave through my skull, and for one paralyzing moment, my entire world went black. My vision flickered in and out, and then–mercifully–it stuck. Declan stumbled back. Eyes unfocused, his blood streaming from his nose and painting his teeth red as it spilled over his lips.

He was stunned. I think I was fucking stunned too, because I wasted precious seconds just watching him come to the realization that I'd just headbutted him.

Our eyes locked, and then he was lunging for me. A rabid, furious growl tore from his throat that reminded me of all the worst things a person was capable of, and I rolled. The move sent my head spinning, and I landed on the floor, the impact causing a shooting pain to ricochet through the spot just under my collarbone, radiating from the spot where he'd sunk his knife, through to my chest and down my arm. But then I saw it—his knife. Right fucking next to me.

I didn't hesitate. I picked it up, the blade already wet with my blood, held it tight, and started swinging it.

Somehow I managed to stab him in the back of the leg. Well, I thought it was the back of his leg, but when I got to my feet, still stumbling, I saw that I'd embedded the blade in the middle of his ass cheek.

His roar of pain was probably the best sound I'd ever heard in my life. I didn't waste time then, I was moving. Bolting out of the bedroom door, knowing I needed to keep him away from Jerry. If he couldn't get to me I was sure he'd try and hurt him more than he already had.

I headed right for the living room, and just like when he'd chased me on my run, I felt the breeze of phantom fingers reaching for me, but this time they were tangible things. They were real, and I hadn't been fast enough.

Declan caught me and threw me to the floor of the living room before his body came down on top of mine with so much force it winded me.

The blood from his nose covered the bottom half of his face. His lips and teeth. When he smiled, he looked insane with the way his blood had settled into the dry, cracked skin of his lips. His tongue darted out, licking the blood like it was the best fucking thing he'd ever tasted.

"Oh, Rose!" he crooned with a deranged sort of laugh, his hands scrabbling to pin my arms as I fought like hell to keep them free. "You know exactly what I like."

"Get your fucking hands off me!" I snarled, managing to get a knee free and drive it as hard as I could between his legs, but all he did was grunt. Not even an eye twitch.

It was enough to throw me off my focus, and I lost our frantic battle when he managed to get both my wrists pinned above my head.

A guttural, throat-ripping sound tore from me, raw and involuntary, as he ripped the buttons from my blood soaked shirt, exposing my breasts to him. When his gaze raked over me and a vile hunger flashed in his eyes, he placed his free hand over one and squeezed violently, his fingernails digging into my skin.

He let go only to grab my face, forcing my mouth open before he pressed his cracked, dry lips against mine. His tongue slithered forward like a worm, trying to burrow its way down my throat.

All I could taste was blood, and my body jolted with nausea. The swell of panic started to rise, and the realization that the one chance I gave myself to get the upper hand had slipped through my fingers.

I started bucking my hips, trying to displace him from where he was bearing all his weight down on top of me, but all he did was grip my face harder, my jaw aching painfully at the way his fingers were digging into the bone.

I didn't stop. I kicked, I flailed, every part of me moving like I was possessed. His grip shifted slightly as he tried to balance himself against my relentless thrashing, and that was all I needed.

You didn't grow up on land with Dallas Grey as your father and not learn how to fire a gun.

Declan assumed I'd aim for his face again or maybe try another wild kick to his balls. He adjusted, bracing for the wrong attack, and that gave me the opening I needed. My hand slipped free of his hold and darted around his body, reaching for the weapon I'd seen him tuck into the back of his jeans.

The moment the gun was pressed to his side, he stilled above me. The house around us went deathly quiet, broken only by my heavy gasping pants.

The adrenaline was coursing through me so rapidly that everything turned crystal clear. Hyper focused.

"Get the fuck off me," I said, each word with precision and dug the gun into his side even deeper, enough to make him pull his hand from my face.

Declan laughed, slow and mocking. "You won't shoot me." He sounded so fucking sure of himself. I was about to tell him that I was absolutely going to shoot him when another voice pierced the air.

"Oh, I think she might."

I didn't take my eyes off Declan, but I watched him slowly lift his head to look up at the source of that voice. I didn't need to see him to know who it was.

Ashton.

I listened to the heavy footfalls of his boots walk around us slowly, lazily, until he was standing behind Declan. Watched as the barrel of his own gun settled onto the back of Declan's head.

"Get off her." Ashton's voice was sharp, deep, and nothing like the man I knew. The man who had been one of my closest friends. Someone who had come into my life fused himself to a part of me, made himself integral in memories and birthdays and *life*. Who'd only ever been kind and gentle to me, but was shaped by a past I'd never understand. A past that was dark and vicious and monstrous.

That was who was looking back at me now, and I was fucking relieved.

Declan kept his eyes on me the whole time, and I didn't lower the gun for even a second, reaching for the ends of my ruined shirt with one hand and clutching it closed.

Ashton didn't waver. "Looks like Cindy did some real damage, huh, Dec?"

"I stabbed him in the ass." My chest was heaving, but my gun was steady, and for some reason, it was the first thing that came to mind.

Ashton's laugh was so misplaced, so perfectly *not* appropriate, that by doing that one single thing he irrecoverably changed the entire situation for me. Because standing there, running through everything that had just happened, I still felt like *me*.

The terror that had been coursing through me, the life-ending panic—it had all vanished. I felt *peace*.

"I get to tell Fane." He wagged his eyebrows at me, and I knew what he was doing. He was trying to keep me focused on whatever eye of the storm this was, where I could laugh while pointing a gun at a man I was pretty sure had come here to kill me. But...*Fane*.

"He's going to hurt him." I moved my eyes from Declan to Ashton's icy-blue ones that flashed with fury at the very idea that something could happen to his friend. The same fury burned as he gave me a quick once-over, his gaze cataloging every bruise, every cut, every mark on my body.

Marks Declan had made. Against his own life, if I had to guess.

It was a strange concept to grasp that this had all happened in Darling. Sweet, safe Darling.

Love of my life spontaneously shows back up? *Check.*

Moves into my house because of a big fat lie I told for two straight years? *Check.*

Attacked by a psychopath who watched me have sex for an undisclosed number of days? *Fucking check.*

A shudder racked my body at the thought. "He said—"

"Fane's fine. He's on his way." Ashton interrupted, his voice calm but laced with steel. He dug his gun further into the back of Declan's head, his movements measured and deliberate.

"You lied," Ash gritted the words out, his tone venomous. Declan flinched, his composure cracking, and I noticed for the first time the knife Ashton had also pressed into his side. "Didn't you, you fucking pin-dick piece of shit?"

"What do you—"

"Cali," Ash said sharply, eyes cutting back to me. "I need you to put the gun down and go check on Jerry. Dial 911 on your phone, but don't call them yet."

"When do I call them?"

"You'll know."

"I don't have a phone."

"Mine's in my pocket." His instructions were clear. Calculated.

I could start to feel the adrenaline was wearing off from my system, but I forced myself to hold Ashton's eyes for a second longer.

"Between one and ten?" I asked him, ignoring the slight tremors starting to take over my body.

"I'm good. I'm a ten." His voice was unshakable. "Everything will be okay. I just need you to sit with Jerry. Okay?" he asked again.

"Okay." And I believed him.

"Remove the magazine, and leave the gun on the floor."

I did as he asked, the weight of it hitting the floor like a punctuation mark to everything that had just happened. My fingers were stiff as I reached into Ashton's pocket for his phone, but I managed.

I made my way to Jerry, my steps unbalanced but purposeful. I knelt beside him, checking him over, watching the rise and fall of his chest. Letting him know I was there, that he would be okay.

I stayed there, my hands resting on Jerry's fur, and when the sound of the gunshot cracked through the house, reverberating off the walls, off the hardwood floors, I didn't even jump.

As soon as the ringing in my ears began to dissipate, I hit call.

# 37

# Calista

**After**

The story was simple enough: Declan broke into my house, tried to kill my dog, and then attacked me.

That's what I told the officers who showed up just moments after Ash sped off in Delilah's car with Jerry. I explained how Declan had called Fane on my phone, not to ask for help but to antagonize him. To make him listen as he hurt me.

I told them how, at some point, he realized what he'd done. That he started apologizing. Repeating himself, saying sorry and how filled with regret he was. That he knew there was no coming back from it, and then he walked into the living room of my house and shot himself in the head.

I explained how Ashton had shown up shortly after, following a call from Fane. How Ash had taken my dog to the vet after alerting the authorities, who'd already been on their way thanks to the sound of a gun going off inside my house.

"And you're certain, before arriving in Darling, you had no prior contact with Mr. Thomas?"

"His name was Declan Thomas?" I winced as the nurse gave what felt like a very aggressive tug to the stitch she was putting into my shoulder.

Could I feel it? No, I could not.

But could I imagine in mind-boggling detail what it *would* feel like? Yes. Yes, I could.

"Did he tell you something different?" The shorter and rounder of the two detectives—yes, *detectives,* cue pants shitting—stepped forward and flipped open his notepad using only one hand before he settled a serious frown on me.

"No," I replied evenly, despite the tugging in my shoulder and the churning in my gut. "I just didn't know his last name. Seems too normal for someone who chased me through town, crashed his car into mine, and then broke into my house to try to kill me and my dog."

There was a beat of silence, and I got the distinct feeling that maybe, just maybe, I should have been a tad more traumatized than I was.

Before we arrived at the hospital and I was sitting, slumped and exhausted in the open back of an ambulance, I waited. Wrapped in one of those shiny blankets they give you that's supposed to help you with shock, I waited for the little fissure to form in my mental state.

I waited and waited, but honestly, there were only three things on my mind.

The first was that I couldn't tear my eyes off the bend in the street that would produce Ashton with news of Jerry.

The second was that the same bend would produce my parents, though by some stroke of luck they were in Cullen Grove, the next town over for an appointment for my mom. If they did come screeching around the corner, covering that distance in that amount of time would have been a world record.

Third, it would be Fane.

The thought of it being him made my throat tighten, and the only thing I felt was heartbreaking rage.

I didn't need to pretend the tears that were falling down my face were real. They just were. Not for myself, but for the way I heard Fane's voice break when he said my name. For the words I had missed when Declan's hand was around my throat.

How he had to, for the second time in his life, bear witness to something evil being done to someone he loved without being able to do anything to stop it. I couldn't shake the feeling that Declan knew just what wound to pour salt on. Just how to break him.

Mostly, I was sick to death of the way Fane continued to punish himself for things that had never been his fault. If I was honest, it terrified me that what had happened would change us for a second time.

I'd only ever experienced one life-altering, terrifying moment before this one, and it ended with me leaving my whole life behind in the blink of an eye.

I knew if I saw him fly around that corner that we would be fine.

I just needed him to come home.

"I'm sorry, but I still don't understand why you're here."

I winced at the first thread of the stitch the nurse made on the cut on my neck, making my breath catch in my throat. The numbing cream she applied did nothing, and based on the look of apology she gave me, I'd say she knew it too. It didn't stop her from doing it again, though.

Between her heavy-handed suturing and the stark whiteness of the hospital room around us, my head was starting to hurt. "What does this have to do with me?"

"It doesn't," said the taller detective, his mustache twitching as he offered me a tight-lipped smile. He reminded me of someone, though I couldn't place who. "We've been watching Declan for a while. He's been linked to a number of allegations."

"What sort of allegations?"

The detective's mustache twitched again, but instead of answering, he asked, "Is your boyfriend returning to town?"

"Fane?" The question came completely out of left field, so much so I jolted. That got a disapproving look from the nurse, who, in my relatively unprofessional opinion, really sucked at giving people stitches. "Why do you—"

"We really aren't at liberty to say—"

"You should get that tattooed right on your forehead, Beverly," Ash drawled, strolling into the hospital room, and for one tiny second, my heart lodged itself in my throat, thinking it was Fane.

"Mr. Manning," Beverly—the short, round detective—let out the most exaggerated sigh I'd ever heard. "Where the odor of illegal activities resides, you're never too far away."

My nose scrunched. "The *odor* of—"

Ash stopped beside me, his hand covering my mouth much to the horror of the nurse, and kept talking like nothing had happened. "Ah, Bev. You've been watching *Poirot* again, haven't you?"

My eyes bulged so wide I was genuinely worried they might fall out of my head. Ash's hand clamped down harder, muffling the "SHUT UP!" I still managed to get out.

Beverly's shoulders straightened, preening like a pigeon. Needless to say, it was one of the less comfortable things I'd witnessed.

"Fane was in Artington for a board meeting with Mackenzie Co. He'll be back soon. He left when Declan called him," Ash said evenly.

The taller detective checked his watch, muttered something about being sorry for what I'd gone through, then gave Ash a wary glance before they both left.

"*Poirot!* I freaking knew it!" The words flew out of my mouth the moment Ash moved his hand. "But, wait, why are they asking about Fane?"

Ash scratched the back of his head and dropped his eyes. He mumbled something about Fane being Declan's boss and something else about taxes that didn't make any real sense. It was a bad lie, and he knew it.

I wanted to push him on it. It was my nature to push, but the last few hours felt like something that both did and didn't happen to me. It happened to someone else, and I just had all the memories of it. So, even though I wanted to ask, I wanted a nap even more.

"What the fuck even happened today?" I dropped my head into my hands, wincing at the sharp pain radiating from my forehead.

I'd been told I had a minor concussion. The spot where Declan's face had made contact with mine was tender, but that was it. No bruising, no swelling. Nothing to show for what had happened.

The doctor told me I was lucky.

I stared at him with the fire of a thousand suns until he left with a nervous look on his baby face. That's when the detectives walked in.

"They seem to know you well," I hedged, my head tilting to the side as I studied Ash.

"They're from Artington. We've...crossed paths."

"How ambiguous."

If nothing else, at least I managed to use my word of the day from the day before. The thought made me realize I really needed to cancel my subscription to that stupid app, especially now that I was still paying for it and didn't even have a freaking phone.

He'd been poking around the little medical room we were in, a very strong indicator that he was trying hard not to lie again while also avoiding being truthful.

"You okay?" I asked, the frown on my face making the tender skin between my eyebrows ache.

His laugh was humorless. "Me? Cali, you almost died. He almost—"

"But he didn't." I cut him off because I'd thought about it too, and it still didn't make that feeling of peace disappear. "Was I scared? Sure. Will I have nightmares about that deranged psycho watching Fane and me—Oh my god, *Jerry*!"

I shot out of my seat so fast I nearly toppled over. In two strides, I gripped the sleeves of Ashton's jacket, my eyes already brimming with tears.

"Hey, no, sorry. Cali, he's okay."

"Holy fuck." My knees buckled slightly, and I braced my hands on them, leaning forward as relief hit me like a wave. "I'm the worst dog mom ever."

His snort that time was definitely full of humor. "Please, you love that dog more than you love Fane."

I stood up and palmed away the tears falling down my face. "It's pretty equal," I sniffed, trying to give him a smile, but my heart was aching.

Without Jerry, without Fane, even with Ash right in front of me, I suddenly felt very, *very* alone.

"What did he do?"

"Gave him Benadryl, and only a very small amount for his size. He woke up halfway to the vet. It was probably the best sleep he'd ever had."

My face crumpled, and I dropped it into my hands. The relief of it all washed over me like when the sky suddenly opened up, and all the raindrops fell at once. Like the second to last thing I needed to be okay clicked into place, and I felt a little less like my world was spinning out of control.

Ash was not one for physical touch, so when I felt him pull me into a hug, his arms a little stiff around me, I leaned into him and wrapped my arms around him, hoping he could feel how grateful I was that he was there.

There to save me from Declan.

There for Fane over the last two years.

There for Jerry.

Here for me, right now.

"Ash?"

"Mmm?"

"What if he doesn't come back?" My voice was small, like the deep-rooted fear of what the answer could be was shrinking me. It felt like he might be the only person in the world I could ask that question of, and who would know why it was one I even needed to ask in the first place.

"Jerry?"

I pulled back and wiped my eyes before rolling them at him so intensely I could've set him alight.

"He never left you," he said simply. "Not really."

I scoffed. "There are two years between us that say different."

Ash's expression hardened. "Two years of him working himself half dead. Of learning how to invest the shit out of everything he earned, living on scraps just so that he could come to your door and make sure he could give you everything you'd ever need and want and dream of. Two years of paying your mom's hospital bills—"

"My what?"

Ash froze, his face an instant mask of regret. Like he'd just incorrectly used an enema. "I—"

"What did you just say?" The wobble in my voice wasn't even something I could've hid if I tried.

"Cali, he doesn't even know I know," he said quickly. "Your dad said something a while ago in passing, and I did a little digging."

"I'm going to kill him," I choked, overwhelmed by the weight of the truth, the love it carried. My heart swelled in my chest, too big, too full.

"No, you're not." Ash's face softened, and he reached out, tapping his knuckles gently to my chin.

"No, I'm not," I whispered.

I clutched Ash's phone in my hand. While I'd been sobbing in his somewhat stiff but still comforting embrace at the hospital, I'd blubbered a culmination of words that he somehow managed to translate into "I need to call Fane."

I did call him. I called him four times, and each time went to voicemail.

"Something's wrong," I mumbled to myself and then shook my head. "No, it's not." Followed by another mumble a second later. "Fuck, maybe—"

"This is fascinating to watch." Ash didn't sound worried in the slightest, and I couldn't tell whether that was because he was freaking out and wanted to keep me calm or he was genuinely fine.

He released a sigh, "Cammy, he left in the middle of the night after working all day, and I would wager a guess that his phone died."

"I...hadn't thought of that." I frowned. "You're right."

"Papa's always right."

"Who's Papa?"

"*I'm* Papa?" He was smiling, and I felt like it was a public service when I licked my finger and stuck it in his ear.

"What the *fuck,* Carla?!"

"You're never allowed to refer to yourself as 'Papa' ever again. It gives off leopard print mankini vibes, Andrew. *This* is why you're single."

"I'm positive it's not," he mumbled under his breath.

"It certainly doesn't help your case." I stuck my tongue out at him and he just stuck his back.

Regardless of Fane's lack of contact, he should be getting to Darling soon. It was around a five-hour drive, but he had always been a little pedal-happy. I held onto that thought and let it soothe the swirling in my stomach.

Pulling up to my little, loving shit box felt surreal.

It looked the same as always. Well, it looked the same as it did when Fane left.

His marks on the house were everywhere. The eaves no longer sagged. The small garden that had been growing in the gutters was long gone. The single panel of wood on the second step to the door—the one too rotten to save—had been quietly replaced. Fane had fixed it without saying a word, while I'd always just stepped over it instead of stepping on it.

My eyes snapped to my front door. "What's that?"

I didn't wait for Ash to reply before I jumped out of the car and headed straight for it.

It was an electronic panel. On the wall next to it was a very fancy-looking doorbell.

"These aren't mine." I looked back at Ash, who loitered on the steps behind me with his usual, easy going grin plastered on his face.

"They are now."

"You're smiling like a weirdo."

"Just enjoying the look on your face." He pulled out his phone and snapped a photo. "I'll make this into a poster for Fane's birthday."

"I'm missing something crucial here." I waved my hands in a panic while miming punching numbers on an imaginary number pad. That's when Ash strolled up, punched four numbers into the real one, and the door unlocked with a faint beep. He stepped aside, ushering me in with an exaggerated flourish.

Everything looked the same. Everything except the shaggy rug that used to live in my living room—it was gone. And so was Declan.

"Who did all this?" I asked, my voice smaller than I'd intended.

"Fane," Ash said simply. Then he shrugged. "Well, me, but through his minimal direction and credit card."

"When did he tell you to do this?"

"When he called me."

The call that came somewhere between me stabbing Declan in the ass and running for my life.

Ash leaned casually against the doorframe. "He messaged me first. I was almost here when he called. Told me, 'I'm on my way back. Make sure you fucking kill him and install that goddamn security system.'"

"He knew you'd do it?"

"Which part?" His head tilted in the same predatory way I'd seen Fane move, but it was different on Ash. Darker.

"All of it?"

"He'd already asked me to get the security system. It just so happened to arrive this morning. I was supposed to install it while you were at work, but…things came up. It's the same system I have in Artington. My guys installed it once the police cleared the scene."

"And the whole killing him part?"

"Yes. He knew."

"How?"

Ash's face didn't flicker. "Because I never miss."

He didn't say it with cockiness, just straight truthfulness. And something else. Regret, maybe. Sadness.

He dropped my new keys into my hand and mentioned that Jerry would be ready to come home in a couple of days. Even though he was okay, they didn't want to risk any allergic reaction or the small chance of it affecting his liver or kidneys.

Those words were like another slap to the face, but I listened with no more than a tremor of my bottom lip, because I was capable of holding heavy things. That much, I knew. I nodded, holding onto the knowledge that he was in the best place for him. That he'd be home soon. That he was probably wooing all the nurses within an inch of their lives.

With a final nod back, Ash turned and walked away.

I stood in the doorway, watching as he strode down my gravel drive and disappeared out of sight.

The moment he was gone, the silence pressed in.

I looked around the house—the house that had always felt full of life, even when it was falling apart—and hated how empty it felt now.

I'd never been here, not once, without someone else under the same roof. The weight of that reality was suffocating.

When I looked around, I wasn't plagued with the ghost of Declan's presence. The horror of seeing Jerry unresponsive in the entry room. Of the glimpse I saw of Declan's unmoving form in my living room, of the blood that had ruined the carpet.

I saw Fane and Jerry sleeping on the couch. I saw Fane in the kitchen, and me on the counter. I saw the two of us carrying out all the bedding with Jerry trotting behind us, laughing until I cried at our horse of a dog trying to make a nest in the pillows and blankets while Fane was still trying to set it all up, and the moment he got so frustrated, he flipped him off with the most aggressive silent middle finger I'd ever seen.

I walked to the basket of blankets next to the couch and grabbed one, wrapping it around my shoulders before heading back out the door, and sank down onto the front steps.

The house wasn't a home without them in it.

So, I kept my eyes fixed on the bend in the street and waited for Fane to come back to me.

A poke on my shoulder startled me awake. I didn't even realize I drifted off, but the man who I looked up at wasn't Fane.

"Ash?" My voice was groggy as I rubbed my eyes, wincing at the sharp pull of the stitches near my collarbone. The motion sent a throb radiating through the bruises on my face—the patchwork of reds and purples Declan had left behind.

"Cali." The tone of his voice made my spine snap straight, and I could feel the blood drain from my face.

"What is it?" I asked, but I knew. *I knew.*

He stared at me for a while. He shook his head, barely perceptible, like he was trying to resist the truth of his own words. Words he spoke anyway.

"We can't find Fane."

# 38

# Fane

**After**

I knew there were people on the other side of the glass, watching me as I sat in the interrogation room where they'd led me before removing the handcuffs.

The sort of violence my father had lived by wasn't something I ever cared for. It had surrounded me growing up and seeped into the walls of my childhood until it became the background hum of my existence. I couldn't pinpoint the exact moment I decided I wanted nothing to do with it—maybe because it wasn't a decision at all. It was just always there, this quiet, constant vow.

The reality was, I didn't need to lay a finger on someone to make myself heard. I didn't need blood on my knuckles to get the results I wanted. Ironically, my penchant for silence had turned into the very thing that made people pay attention when I eventually did.

There was only ever one time I released the hold I had on that part of me, and that was the same night my dad left and didn't come back.

After that, I'd come close just once.

That time had been tonight—or maybe last night now—just before I entered Darling. I was ten minutes out from seeing the sign that was welcoming me back to the only place I'd ever really want to be. The place that held *everything* that was important to me. Another seven minutes or so, and I would have been home.

That thought made me desperate. It made me fucking murderous.

Instead, I was pulled over, arrested on-site for the murder of someone whose name didn't ring a single bell, and then brought here.

It was in that moment when they pulled me from my truck that the pulsing need to turn all my fury and pain and fucking unhinged fear onto them beckoned me like nothing else ever had.

But I knew better. That had never been who I was.

No, my beast was something else entirely.

Silent. Purposeful. Intentional. Patient.

So, here I sat, still absentmindedly rubbing the spot on my wrist where the cuffs had pinched, waiting for someone to come in.

I'd been here for going on six hours, and I knew that they could hold me here for another forty-two. If I were a betting man, I'd say that they were trying to get me on edge—hours alone in a silent room. Desperate to get out, to speak to anyone, that I was willing to confess to something when I wasn't even fully aware of what even happened.

Too bad they didn't know that was my fucking happy place.

Well, almost.

I'd been read my rights, but whatever lawyer I was promised hadn't shown up and they'd taken my phone even though it had died about an hour after I'd called Ash.

The only thing that delayed me leaving Artington was checking my truck. I'd been separated from it for a good portion of the day while it sat in the parking lot of the Mackenzie Co. high-rise downtown. Declan wasn't a particularly smart guy, so figuring out what he—or someone working for him—had done to my truck only took half an hour.

That was thirty minutes that kept me from Cali. Thirty minutes I couldn't get back. But after tightening the lug nuts on the tires that had been loosened and removing the wad of cloth stuffed into the tailpipe, I was on my way, driving as fast as I could.

I swallowed down the way my vision turned red at the knowledge this was exactly what I knew he wanted to happen, that he was keeping me from getting to her even now. Even after he was dead.

And I knew that he was. Dead.

There wasn't a single doubt in my mind that the second Ash set foot into that house, Declan's seconds had become numbered.

My head snapped to the side when the door to the room opened and the two men who had arrested me walked in, grim looks already on their haggard faces.

"Mr. Mackenzie, my name is Detective Dozen, and this is Detective Ambros." He stared at me like he was waiting for me to let them know what a pleasure it was to finally have them introduce themselves.

I just stared at them and waited for him to spit out whatever he was here to say.

"You were arrested for the murder of Tinsley Benshaw. Do you know who that is?" He opened the folder he'd brought in with him and slid out a picture before setting it in front of me.

The girl couldn't have been more than nineteen or twenty. Blue eyes, not as bright as Ash's but close. I flicked my eyes from the photo up to the man who had to have the stupidest-looking mustache I'd ever fucking seen.

"No."

"Does she look familiar to you here?" He pulled out another image of the same girl, except in this image, she didn't have a single item of clothing on her. Her skin was a gray hue, those same blue eyes were open, unseeing, dull. Her body was littered with bloody bite marks and bruises and there was a laceration just below her right collarbone.

I lifted my eyes from the image back to the detective's milky-brown ones. "No."

They were silent for a second before the other detective leaned forward onto the desk. "We obtained a warrant to go through your phone, to search your car, the whole nine yards, Fane. Do you know that your DNA is all over that young girl?"

"What DNA?"

"Your hair." He spoke so seriously that it took real effort not to fucking laugh in his face. "I'll admit, it was odd to see hair sprinkled all along Miss Benshaw's body, but it wouldn't be the first time a killer has left such an idiotic calling card."

"When did she die?"

"Thursday afternoon."

"I wasn't even in Artington then."

"We know."

I knew I was looking at them like they were the stupidest that Artington Law Enforcement had to offer. "You arrested me for a crime you *knew* I didn't commit?"

They looked at each other before Mustache spoke to me again. "Do you know anyone that might want to frame you for murder, Fane?"

"No." That wasn't wholly true, and the reality of it made me clench my fists. "If you know I didn't kill her, why am I still here?"

"You worked with Declan Thomas."

His name made my blood roar through my ears. "He tried to kill my wife."

"Miss Grey isn't your wife."

"Semantics." I stared at him until the little vein in his forehead started to throb in a way that looked painfully uncomfortable. The two detectives looked at one another again in a way that made it very clear that of the three of us, I was the only one here that didn't know what was going on. The only reason I could gather that they were still asking me these stupid as fuck questions was because they thought I was *in* on whatever was going on.

"We don't believe you killed Tinsley"

"Great. Can I go?"

"We actually know who did."

"Can I go?" I asked again, this time through clenched teeth, my jaw aching from the effort.

"It was Declan Thomas." He paused, watching me closely, as if gauging how I'd react to the blow he was about to land.

Then he dropped it.

"Your brother."

"My what?"

Slowly, like every page he pulled out of the folder weighed a thousand tons, the detective pulled out images of me going all the way back to when I was seventeen.

There was me at my old high school, at the gym, at the house my mom and I never left. Then me, grown up and out of that house. Working at the bar, leaving the apartment building I'd shared with Ash, me with Cali when we first met.

It was clear with those early photos that he had no interest in Cali. She was cropped out, cut off, ignored.

But then newer photos began to appear.

Photos from Darling. Of Cali and me at home, and then just Cali. I was the one cut off, cropped out.

It was like this fucked-up part of my brain knew what was coming next. It didn't surprise me the way it probably should have to see photos of Cali and me at the waterfall in Darling. Of her splayed out on the rock, back arched.

Photo after photo hit the table. Different angles, some fucking closer than the others. And then photos of us at home, through the open slats of the bedroom window.

My hand slammed down on the table, the sound reverberating off the walls as both detectives jumped, their chairs scraping back across the linoleum.

I slowly gathered the photos into a neat pile and flipped them upside down. "Look at these photos again, and it'll be the last goddamn thing you ever fucking do."

"That sounds like a threat, Mr. Mackenzie."

"Take it however you'd like." My voice was low, deadly. "I'm not leaving without these photos."

"They're evidence."

"Evidence of what? That your suspect had a fucking fetish for my wife?"

"She's not your—"

"I hope you finish that sentence."

Detective Dozen, a name that sounded more like a joke with every passing second, closed his mouth with an audible snap.

"Your brother—"

"I'm an only child." I cut him off. My stomach rolled with the idea of being related to that piece of shit.

"Declan is your father's son with a different woman."

Detective Ambros reached for another folder that he had tucked under his arm and pulled out another image of a woman I didn't recognize.

It occurred to me then that Declan was almost exactly two years younger than me. The only thing I felt at the realization that there was another version of me and my mom just two years behind, likely enduring the same things we did, was pity.

The woman stared back at me through the photo with dead, sad eyes. Eyes that were almost black, just like her son's.

It gave me a sick sort of satisfaction knowing that neither of the children that my father sired looked anything like him. Like the universe was doing its best to erase him from memory.

I also learned that where I tried to turn myself into nothing in order to escape any possibility of being anything like my father, Declan had taken to his particular tastes like a moth to a flame.

I sat there and listened while the detectives talked about how the injuries that both he and his mother sustained showed a pattern of abuse in the home even though nothing was ever admitted.

I learned that he lived down the street from me but went to a different school across town. I learned that's where my father went when I told him if he stepped foot in the house again that I'd kill him, knowing he saw it in my eyes for the truth those words held.

From the ages of fifteen to eighteen, Declan was hospitalized twice, once for a skull fracture and once for a knife wound just below his collarbone. And just before he turned eighteen, his mother died.

"How did she die?" I didn't need the question answered for me to be sure of the answer.

My head was pounding with the information they were shoving at me.

Declan's apartment in the city was a wealth of depraved information. Of journal entries and video diaries. Of detailed plans on exactly what he wanted to do to our father.

"He was curious about you for a long time, and as far as we could tell, there wasn't any serious sinister intent until—"

"Two years ago?" When I started working at *Mackenzie Co.*

"No." Dozen slid another image across the table. One of me, the image pinned to a wall with a knife through the middle of my face. "Six months ago."

"When I asked for the Darling project."

Ambros nodded. "It was a show of favoritism that Declan never received. He felt betrayed by both you and your father."

"I didn't even know him."

"Well, he knew about you. His latest entries were centered on taking things from both you and your father. He said he wanted to—"

"Get what he was owed." I could hear the words ripping from his throat through the phone. Images bombarding me of what he looked like on the other end. Of Cali, of how he was hurting her.

"He wanted to take Cali from you," Ambros said, his voice heavy. The very idea made my skin crawl, and my muscles ripple under my skin. "And from your father, he wanted Mackenzie Co."

I snorted a laugh. "There's no way in hell he would have gotten a dime from that man."

Ambros placed a third folder on the table. Where they kept pulling these from, I had no fucking idea. The contents inside grabbed my attention, though, and if I was honest with myself, they didn't surprise me at all.

Mackenzie Co. had always been a successful business. At one point, it had even been legitimate. But that hadn't been the case for a very long time.

Over the last twenty years, the majority of the company's success had come from developing towns that showed a lot of promise as up-and-coming weekend getaways. It turned out that not only were *all* of those developments undertaken using substandard materials that couldn't reach regulatory standards if they'd been propped on fucking stilts, but none of the projects had ever been legally approved.

Every single one moved forward because Mackenzie Co. paid off local town officials.

The hole of bullshit this company was in never ended. Zoning laws? Overlooked. Environmental regulations? Nonexistent. Building codes? What fucking building codes? They inflated property values like balloons at a kids' party, leaving a mess behind every time.

"And what?" I asked, voice sharp. "You think I had something to do with this?"

"At the start." Dozen leaned back, a hand going to his mustache, reminding me that these guys had arrested me for a murder they knew I didn't commit and that I'd been here for ten fucking hours. "Warrant cleared that up."

"Yippee."

"We may need you to testi—"

"No."

I stood up, my body cracking after being in one position for so long. Grabbing the stack of photos from the table in front of me, I reached for the folder Ambros held in a death grip that contained the rest of the images Declan had taken and rolled them up.

Taking evidence was definitely not legal, but they didn't do a fucking thing to stop me, namely because I was almost certain that the way they'd brought me in wasn't legal either.

They had dragged me into the Darling Police Station, which was in the middle of town, right near Sunshine, but the moment I stepped onto the sidewalk, the person standing in front of me was not the person I expected.

I had stopped being surprised by anything he did a long time ago.

"Why are you here?"

"I heard about Declan. As his employer—"

"His father, you mean." I stared at Will Mackenzie and saw the same thing I always did—a stranger. Someone I didn't know and didn't want to, and the very reason I punished myself every fucking day of my life.

I made myself believe I deserved less, that I needed to be less, because anything more meant there was a chance I could end up just like him.

No, I wasn't a violent man. But my palms were tingling with the urge to reach out and wrap my hand around his throat and squeeze until there was no life left in him.

What happened to me and my mom, Declan and his mom, none of that was my fault.

What happened to Cali wasn't my fault. It was *his*, and I wanted to kill him for it.

He took a small step back, and the delight at knowing he was frightened sent a thrill through me.

"Declan had some information about the company. Things that will need us to present a united front."

My laughter startled him. Half, I think, because the sound didn't exist in our house growing up, and half because I don't think he'd ever heard me do it.

This wasn't the kind of laugh born from joy or safety. It wasn't born from happiness.

It was the sort born of rot. Of mindless rage. The kind that grows in the parts of you meant to be nurtured but instead are neglected until they wither and die.

I stalked toward him, closing the space between us until he had to crane his neck to meet my eyes.

"I hope you're fucking suffocated by the weight of every single one of your failures," I said, voice low and razor-sharp. "And that you rot in the hell you've built for yourself."

I spat on the ground between us, savoring the way he flinched.

"You will get nothing from me."

I turned to leave, but his voice stopped me mid-step. Seems like he had more fucking balls than I gave him credit for.

"Think of Cali, Fane. Of your mother," he said, each word deliberate. Then, after a pause that bristled with his arrogance: "I'll let you consider my offer a little while longer...son."

I didn't turn back to face him, but it didn't stop the small smile from ghosting across my lips. I had resigned myself to just...let him be.

It was probably a little too forgiving of me to imagine he'd begin to fester in any type of guilt. Perhaps a long-ago wish of mine that I'd attached to the single shooting star I'd kept for myself during one of those many nights Cali and I lay beneath the night sky had been answered.

I kept walking, heading past Sunshine and toward Cali's house—our house.

The frosted, still, and pitch black night like a curtain closing on every part of my life that he had ever existed in. In its wake, a blank slate where I knew I deserved the sort of love she'd always held for me.

This person who had chosen me, over and over.

This woman I would never take for granted ever again. The truth of it settled into my bones, growing more absolute with every step that carried me home.

39

Fane

**After**

I just rounded the bend of the street, the house almost in view, when I did a double take at the person sitting in the car right across from me.

I'd never seen the car before, but that didn't mean much. What got me was the plume of cigarette smoke that poured out of the open driver's side window.

"Should I be worried about why you're out here watching the house?"

A smug grin curled his lips, his eyes a silvery shade in the moonlight. "She refused to go inside and fell asleep on the porch. I figured I'd keep an eye on her until you got home. Lest we forget the events of last night."

The mention of it sent a pang of nausea rolling through me. It made my body lock up tight, like at any moment I was prepared to bolt right back to the woman apparently asleep on the porch.

I didn't say anything, but it didn't stop him from continuing to talk.

"We couldn't find you. For four hours, I couldn't fucking find you." He took a long drag of his cigarette, the glow briefly illuminating the sharp edge of his jaw. "And then I got the news that you'd killed someone in Artington on Thursday. And that Beverly hauled you in without so much as calling it in properly." His voice had dipped, almost murderous.

"Who the fuck's Beverly?"

327

"Detective Dozen." Ash said his name like he thought the guy was as ridiculous as I did.

"I figured it was a little off when the lawyer I was promised didn't show up."

"The detectives have already been dealt with." His voice carried an edge that made me glance at him.

"What did you do?" My words came slow, deliberate.

Ashton's eyes sliced to me, sharp as the moonlight catching on glass. He didn't need to say more. I already knew.

"I told her we couldn't find you."

My stomach dropped. I pushed off the car. "What? Why—"

"Because she was waiting for you to come back," he cut me off. "She wasn't sure that you would, and still, she sat on that porch and watched for you." He stepped out of the car, grinding his cigarette under his boot. "Figured it'd be better for her to know your absence wasn't by choice than let her think you'd pulled the pin again."

"I never pulled the pin." I crossed my arms and frowned at him.

"I know that, and you know that." He gave me a little shove, but his voice softened. "She didn't."

He wasn't wrong. The fact that she thought I might not come back to her after what had happened fucking killed me, and for that I knew there was no one to blame but myself. That it would take more than a few months together to make her believe I wasn't going anywhere. To convince her to love me like she used to.

"Jared found your truck." He gestured to where it was parked a few cars back from his.

I nodded and then frowned at my boots, taking a beat before I spoke again. "Declan took photos of Cali." I shoved my hands in the pockets of my jeans. "Photos of the two of us together."

Ash's eyebrows shot up at the rolled manila folder I pulled from the back pocket of my jeans.

"I took the physicals they printed, but…"

"Consider them dealt with." His voice left no room for doubt.

"Thanks." I nodded at him, keeping my eyes locked on his. "For keeping her safe." He knew I meant more than just now, but just like Cali, it was never hard for him to understand what I was trying to say.

"Yep." He nodded, and then he pulled me in for a hug that I didn't expect. Ash wasn't a hugger. He was probably the opposite of a hugger, but the way he gripped onto me spoke volumes, coming from this man who hated to be touched.

"You okay?" I asked, hugging him back.

"Glad you aren't dead in a ditch somewhere." And then after another second, he added, "Would've been lost without your sad boy smolder."

"You should write for Hallmark," I mumbled.

Ash pulled away with a laugh that shook his shoulders, giving me a shove to the chest before climbing back into his car.

"Whose car is this?" I asked, nodding toward the unfamiliar vehicle.

"Sammy's," he said with a shrug, like it wasn't a big deal.

Well, that was new.

A second before he pulled away from the curb, he tossed my phone out the window, fully charged. The last time I'd seen it, it had been dead and slid into the pocket of one of the detectives.

"Keys are in the truck," he called, and then he was gone.

Without the rumble of his car interrupting the silence, I was left standing in the middle of the street, my breath coming in visible puffs against the October night air, but I wasn't cold.

My heart was thrumming. Pushing blood around my body so fast that it made my face tingle, and then I was standing on the sidewalk outside of Cali's house—*our* house.

She was there, wrapped in a blanket, her head resting against the banister. Her chest rose and fell in steady, even breaths.

I saw the peek of a bandage on the side of her neck. The side of her face that was shrouded in the light of the moon looked bruised, the darkest shadows pooling around her eye and jaw with a little bandage just beneath her eyebrow.

I couldn't see them, but I knew there were more from whatever happened in the seconds, minutes, hours after he'd called me. When I could hear her struggling on the other end, and I felt a crack boom through my sanity.

Picturing her on the other end, an onslaught of images had raced through my head, replacing my mother's face with Cali's. Replacing my father with Declan. The only difference was I hadn't been silently sitting in the corner, terrified. I had been fighting against it with everything I had. When I promised him, calmly and without a hint of hesitation. that he was going to die. That if someone didn't get to him before me, I'd make sure that his last breaths were painful, pathetic things. That there would be nothing left of him in the end and no one would ever remember him.

No, I wasn't a violent man. But for Cali, I would become a savage.

I would do whatever it took to keep her safe. To keep her happy. To keep her *whole.*

My boots were silent on the pathway that led to the house. She didn't stir when I dropped to my knees in front of her. When my hands reached for her, but instead of making contact like I'd been desperate to, they hovered. Shaking in the air between us because I didn't know if I *could* touch her.

I didn't know what happened, where she'd been hurt, *how* she'd been hurt. How she'd react.

My eyes darted over her blanket-shrouded body so fast it made me dizzy. When I finally dragged them back to her face, I found her hazel eyes open and fixed on me. The golden flecks in them caught the moonlight, reflecting it back like the stars of all the wishes she'd captured.

"Hey, baby." My voice was a pained croak between us. It held the way I'd fallen short in doing enough to keep her safe. I knew that what happened wasn't my fault. I *knew* that.

It didn't stop me from wishing I'd been here. Done more.

In an instant, Cali launched herself off the porch steps, her arms wrapping around me, legs around my waist, head tucked into the crook of my neck.

Her blanket fell to the ground when I stood up, carrying us up the stairs. Shifting her weight to one arm, I punched in the four-digit code to the new alarm system.

"H-how do you know the code?" she asked between shuddering sobs.

"I picked it."

I closed the door behind us and started heading for our bedroom when I stopped.

"Seven six seven three?" She pulled back, hair sticking to the tracks her tears had made down her flushed cheeks.

I swallowed thickly, reaching up to tentatively move a strand caught in her eyelashes. "Rose," I rasped.

She looked at me for a second longer before sinking her hands into my hair and kissing me. Cali pressed her body to mine in the sort of desperate way that made clothes seem like one of the worst things mankind ever created. The way her mouth moved against mine was desperate, relieved, devouring.

"Take me to bed," she whispered against my lips.

"Cali—" I started to shake my head, but she pulled back just enough to lock her gaze with mine.

"Take me to our bed, Fane." Her words were calm, deliberate. She leaned in again, her lips brushing mine as she added, softer but no less commanding, "Take me to our bed and fuck me."

Her words were irrevocably linked to a certain part of my brain that made my body fill with warmth. Made my grip on her seem too light, too inadequate, like I couldn't hold enough of her in my hands at any one time.

Her hands were still in my hair, pulling, entwining the growing strands in her delicate fingers, but I still didn't know where to touch her. If I'd hurt her.

I set her down on the bed, and slowly she pulled off the sweater she had been wearing. My sweater.

My jaw clenched so tight it cracked. My heart stopped beating altogether for what felt like eternity when I saw the bandage over her collarbone. The bruising around her right breast and the nail marks left behind. Each one of them was shadowed by dark purple bruising.

I must have made a noise. It felt like my chest was being cleaved apart, not something I could contain inside myself. Cali's hands found my face, her touch soft and warm. She kissed me, her lips brushing along my cheeks, gathering the tears I hadn't even realized were there.

"Fane," she whispered, her voice a gentle tether pulling me back to her. "Come back to me."

Her words landed softly, but they hit like a command. She pressed them into my skin—against my jaw, the hollow of my throat, my eyelids—each kiss anchoring me further.

"I don't want to hurt you," I rasped.

"I want you to." She looked at me with determination. "I want to feel your fingertips pressing into me. I want to wake up and see shadows left in the wake of what we did the night before. I want to hear you speak to me, talk to me. I want to feel the way you stretch my body when you push inside me. The way it always feels like it's too much, but you keep going, telling me how well I'm doing, how I was made for you." Her chest was heaving now, but her eyes didn't flick away from mine. She didn't hide from me the way she had before.

She told me exactly what she wanted.

"I want you to be the last man—only man—who's ever touched me." Her hands slipped from my body, leaving a cold absence that made me sway closer to her, desperate to bridge the gap.

She scooted back on the bed, laying back with nothing but a pair of black lace panties on. "Please, Fane."

With those words falling from her tongue, I was completely undone.

Reaching back, I pulled my shirt off my body, my jeans and briefs going next. I didn't take my eyes off her when I crawled my way up to her. Our bodies fitting together so perfectly as she let her legs drop open and I settled into the valley of her hips.

She was so warm, so perfect. So fucking *mine*.

"I don't want to hurt you," I said again. "Tell me what hurts." I placed a kiss just behind her ear, inhaling her milk-and-honey scent, always so entwined with the cherry blossom notes of her shampoo.

"Just the stitches on my chest," she panted. "And my neck. When they pull, it hurts. That's all."

"The bruises?" I was taking stock, making sure I knew her limits.

"They don't hurt." She lifted her hips up to meet mine. The soft, warm heat of her pussy grinding against my erection, pulling a groan from somewhere so deep in my chest it sounded unhinged. *Felt* unhinged.

"Don't lie to me." I sucked on the spot of her neck that sloped down into her shoulder, earning a gasp of surprise before I soothed the sting with a swipe of my tongue.

"I'm not. You won't hurt me. I need this. Please, Fane. I need *you.*"

Cali's hand moved down between our bodies, wrapping around my cock and snatching the breath right from my lungs. I watched her, my eyelids heavy with want while she watched the way her hand looked wrapped around me.

Just when I started to reach down, determined to rip the panties off her, she pulled her hand from me and moved it up to my chest.

I didn't need more than the slightest pressure from her fingertips to move back, and with her hands on my shoulders, she moved us in the way she wanted. Confident. In control.

God, there was nothing sexier than Cali telling me what she wanted. With her words, her actions. I didn't care.

I watched, enraptured, as she straddled me, her tits at the perfect height for me to take a nipple into my mouth, to graze my teeth over the sensitive bud in the way I knew she loved, that made her grind her hips where they met mine.  Her panties wedged just inside her pussy lips as she continued to move herself against me. I could feel how wet she was. The scent of her arousal was fucking everywhere, heady and intoxicating and mouthwatering.

I reached for her again, but the moment I did, she was moving down my body, and a choking sound of need fell from my mouth.

"Patience," she teased.

"I need to touch you," I murmured, my eyes following her every movement. Watching her leave open-mouthed kisses along my body, a path of goose bumps in her wake.

"Me first." Her mouth covered the head of my cock without warning. Her tongue flicked against the slit, collecting the bead of pre-cum before she pulled back with a soft, deliberate pop and a slow, satisfied hum.

"Fucking Christ," I panted, hands fisted. I watched her, mesmerized, as she ran her tongue up the underside, from base to tip. Her hand cupped my balls, making my hips piston forward.

Cali wrapped her hand around the base of my cock again, giving one slow pump before her other hand joined the first, and she guided me into her mouth again.

I was fucking paralyzed with the pleasure she was giving me. Watching, bewitched, at the way I disappeared into her mouth. The way her hands continued to work what she couldn't fit down her throat.

"Your mouth feels fucking perfect, Calista." I reached out, settling a hand on the back of her head, not putting any pressure, just feeling the way she met my shallow thrusts. Eager.

"Such a good girl, baby. You're so fucking *good*," I breathed. I couldn't tear my eyes from her. Stumped, not for the first time, that she existed. That she was mine.

I watched the way her body shuddered at my words, the way she pulled a hand from where it was twisting and pumping my shaft to slip into her underwear.

I tutted. "That's not fair, baby." I gripped her upper arms, pulled her off me, and dragged her up my body until she was right where I wanted her.

Cali looked down at me from where she kneeled above my face and didn't move her eyes as I gripped the side bands of her panties and ripped them off her.

A mischievous smile started to curve her swollen lips when she spoke. "I'm going to suffocate you."

My answering grin was wicked and hungry. "God, I hope so." And then I pulled her down onto my mouth.

My tongue moved along her pussy, delving deep inside of her, collecting her wetness, and tracing it up to the hard, swollen bud of her clit.

I couldn't be anything but relentless. Sucking, nipping, thrusting my tongue into her tight cunt until she was trembling above me, nothing but incoherent babble tumbling out of her heart-shaped lips. Until she started to roll her own hips, rubbing her pussy against my mouth, chasing her own release, and when it rolled through her, shock wave after shock wave pulsing through her body, I locked my hands around her legs.

I pulled her back down onto me even when she tried to lift off, continuing to thrust my tongue past the clenching muscles of her entrance. Gently dragging the flat of my tongue up to her clit before plunging back inside her, slowly, lazily, until she was moaning and lax once again. Her head tipped back in a mindless sort of extract that always brought me right to my knees.

I'd do anything for this woman. *Be* anything.

"I want you inside me," she moaned again. "I want to feel you, inch by inch. I want to feel nothing but you."

This time when she tried to move off me, I let her go, but not for long. I went with her, an arm looping around her waist while I flipped us, wasting no time in capturing her mouth in another kiss, groaning at the way her tongue lapped at the inside of my mouth, tasting herself.

I notched the head of my cock, her cunt swollen and fucking *weeping*, the moment I started to push in I had to fight against the desire to close my eyes. It was almost torturous, but it was worth it to watch the way her eyes rolled back, her mouth parting as her back arched off the bed.

"So fucking tight," I panted, continuing to push into her, feeling the way her nails dug into my arms. "But you love it, don't you?"

All she did was moan, her back arching off the bed a little further.

"You love knowing that you're at your limit, don't you?"

"Yes," she whimpered.

"Your greedy little cunt, so needy. Isn't it?" I was salivating at the sight of her.

"*Yes,*" she gasped as I pushed in the final inch, seated to the hilt. Slowly, I felt her body relax around me, her muscles softening at the intrusion, and the moment her hips gave a slow and knowing wiggle, I was moving.

One hand circled up and around her back, cupping the back of her neck, with my other at her waist, I tried to hold back. To be mindful of the parts of her body that were hurt and tender and sore.

"Fane," she breathed my name, her hands reaching up to find their perch in the hair at the back of my head. "Stop holding back. I want to feel you so deep I can't breathe."

"You're—"

"Yours." She finished for me instead. "I'm yours. I want you to show me what that means."

I waited a beat longer, eyes assessing. Then I gave in, because I always would with her. Anything she wanted, for the rest of our lives—it was all hers.

My grip on her tightened, my hips moving fast, the wet sound of our bodies meeting. And when she asked for more, when she begged for more. I pulled out of her, and with gentle hands flipped her over, grabbing a pillow to place under her before settling her down. The gentleness ended with a tender kiss to the middle of her spine and I pushed back into her without hesitation.  She let out a small, shocked whimper and a choked *"Fuck,"* scraped past my throat when I felt the way she clenched and shuddered around me. Her hands tried to find purchase in the sheets of our bed and came up empty.

"More," she pleaded, and I reached down to where I was buried inside of her, coating my thumb in her arousal and bringing it back up to the tight ring of her ass. Slowly, I eased my thumb inside of her.

"Do you have any idea what you look like right now?" I panted, moving my thumb in and out of her ass while I continued to thrust. "So fucking full of me, baby. You're taking it so well. So fucking well."

"Fane!" Cali screamed my name along with a stream of unintelligible curse words, one hand holding her up while she reached back to grab onto me.

"God, I love you," I pushed the words into her skin. Along the length of her spine. "I love you so fucking much."

She pushed back into me, meeting every thrust I made, and when I felt her erupt around me, I let myself fall over that edge of oblivion, doing what I would always do: follow her wherever she went.

When we were showered, with fresh bedding and the house still too silent with Jerry's absence, I held Cali in my arms while she absentmindedly traced the tattoos on my neck, my chest, and my arms.

"You came back." She said it with a tone of disbelief, like she'd hoped, but she'd also prepared herself that I might not.

"Always," I told her, and I meant it. Hoped she felt how deeply I meant it. I counted her breaths as they began to slow, her chest rising and falling in a steady rhythm that pulled me toward sleep alongside her.

Just before it claimed me too, I asked her the question that had haunted me from the moment I woke to our empty apartment and found her gone.

"Do you think you could love me again?"

And in my dreams, I imagined her saying, "Yes."

40

## Calista

**After**

When I woke up, Fane was already in the kitchen.

The sounds of pots and pans were clanging, and the low hum of music filtering in under the door.

I rolled out of bed and shuffled into the kitchen. My eyes were still half closed, and I didn't stop my little steps until my face was pressed into the soft cotton of the shirt stretching across his back.

The fabric was warm and smelled like him.

His hand came up to cover mine where they were pressed to his chest, and he turned to face me.

"Are you sniffing me?" His voice had that rumble of disuse it always had in the morning, making him seem all rumpled and cozy.

"I am."

I pressed my face deeper into the fabric and felt his quiet laughter reverberate through his chest as his hand settled against the back of my head.

When I looked up, his lips now curved in a small, swollen smile, still tender from last night. It flickered as his gaze swept over my face—the bruising on my cheek, the bandage on my neck, and the marks beneath the shirt I'd pulled on. The ones he'd only seen in the soft glow of moonlight

338

last night.

His hand came up, fingers light as they moved across my cheek. "I'm sorry I wasn't there."

My heart sank at his words because this was almost exactly what I had been worried would happen. I shook my head. "This wasn't your fault, Fane."

"No." He shook his head too. "It wasn't. I'm still sorry I wasn't there."

I hadn't expected that.

I hadn't expected it because it was everything I'd ever hoped he could believe—that he wasn't responsible for the actions of those around him—that it was not his job to make amends for the sins of others.

This was new for us, because when I thought of us facing big things together, the reality was that...we didn't. Not together.

I scrunched my nose at the tingling. The feeling, I knew, a result of that seed of hope that had been planted all those weeks ago reaching up to the sun. Growing and strong. Steady.

"Me too," I said, because this whole being open and honest thing was really working for us.

That thought shot a pulse of guilt through me. At the words I had heard him whisper last night when he'd held me in his arms tight, the sound of his heartbeat steady beneath my ear.

*Do you think you could love me again?*

I had to be the worst kind of person to have held those words back from him. Words that were his anyway. I wasn't even sure what it was that was terrifying me into not saying them.

Maybe it was the lingering fear that he could still leave. That even though it had broken both of us the first time, he'd still done it.

Maybe it was sitting and watching the bend in the street, waiting for him to fly around it and come home.

And he had. He'd come back to me.

Still, when I opened my mouth to say them, the total opposite came out instead. "I stabbed Declan in the ass."

Fane's head tilted back, laughter exploding out of him. Every note a splatter of watercolor dripping down the cabinets of our kitchen, and I stood there, grinning up at him in the same way I knew Jerry looked at him—like he hung the damn moon.

Maybe it was wrong, maybe it was totally fucked up to be laughing about the deceased, but there we were. Chuckling and hiccupping with laughter while the French toast—the reason I'd even managed to crawl out of bed—burned in the pan behind him. Me, incomprehensibly charmed by the boyish grin that bloomed across his face.

The silver lining here was that it was Sunday, which meant that this was the single day off I had during the week, and the moment we were fed and dressed, Fane and I walked down the street to his truck and drove straight to the vet.

Jerry was beside himself with glee at the sight of us walking through the door. He bolted toward Fane first, his tail wagging so hard he couldn't control it. Eventually, it stopped moving from side to side and started twirling in a wild circle. Then he paused, his ears flicking toward me where I sat patiently and I held back the building pressure of sobs that were desperate to be released from my chest while my big, brave boy slowly walked over to me.

His steps were measured, like he was a little unsure.

Like he was disappointed in himself for what had happened.

His cold nose pressed to the bruised side of my face before gently sniffing the bandage on my neck and the other beneath my shirt that he couldn't even see.

I knew my dog, and I knew that some people would probably think I was insane for thinking the way I did, but he was about as smart as they came. Smarter, actually.

No, we couldn't talk the way people did, or even the way dogs did to one another, but we understood each other just the same.

With both hands holding his face, I leaned down and whispered into one of his floppy ears, my tears of terror, of worry, of relief, silently tracking down my face. His tail picked up speed slowly but surely until there wasn't an inch of my face that wasn't covered in slobber rather than tears, and the vet deemed him more than ready to come home.

Fane loaded Jerry into the back seat of the truck, carefully securing what had to be the largest dog harness known to man. On the way home, he turned to me with a knowing look, one brow arched.

"You told Jerry that you stabbed him in the ass, didn't you?"

My grin stretched so wide it ached. "Yep."

For the rest of the day, the three of us didn't move from the couch, Jerry tucked between us and my hand in Fane's. When the sun went down, we didn't need to talk it through to know that when Fane got up, I would follow him into our bedroom to get our bedding and drag it outside.

This time, when Jerry started to make his nest before we'd finished setting up, we just walked back inside and got more blankets and cuddled in on either side of our four-legged giant.

The seconds ticked on, Jerry's snores grumbling between us when Fane started to tell me about what the detectives had said. Who Declan really was and what he'd done. When he finally got it all off his chest, I squeezed his hand a little tighter, pushed the hair off his face, out of his eyes and murmured, "It's not your fault."

When he replied a quiet but strong, "I know," that little flower of hope in my chest grew a little bit taller.

I still didn't have a phone, and when Fane refused to take me into work, letting me know that Ash and Sammy had it all covered, I got up and out of bed, buck-ass naked, and started trying to tie his limbs to the bedpost again. With every limb I got situated, he was up and out of my double-knotted bunny ear bows before I'd even started on the next one.

When he grabbed me around the waist and hauled me back to the bed, every bubble of laughter died in my throat when he hovered above me and said, "Time to tick off number three on the sex list," and reached for one of the lingering ties loosely hanging from one of his ankles.

My parents were still in Cullen Grove. They still didn't know about what had happened with Declan, and I put it all down to the fact that it had been two whole years since my mom got her "new phone," and she still thought the red button that popped up when she got a call was the answer button.

Every time without fail, she pressed it and muttered, "Dammit, I missed them again."

They ended up calling Fane when they kept getting my voicemail to let us know that they were going to be out of town a little longer and that they were going to extend their stay, turning it into their first vacation in over a decade.

Cullen Grove was only forty minutes from Darling, but it felt like a world away compared to the cautious baby steps they'd been taking toward their new normal after everything they'd endured.

In a bittersweet way, the distance was good for me too. I had a chance to learn a little bit more about who I was without them, after so much of who I'd been had revolved around them for so long.

I gave in to Fane's pleading and didn't work for the rest of the week. We had, however, been into the café every day, and when I noticed that Ash had been eating up all my cookie ingredient stock again, I couldn't have cared less.

I just ordered double what I had the time before, and when Fane received a message from him that said, *Tell Cora I love her so much that my body is struggling to physically hold it all in*, I didn't even roll my eyes.

Okay, I did, but just a tiny, baby roll.

Fane made us breakfast-for-dinner nearly every night, so by Sunday, I felt like a living, breathing caramelized banana.

I was quickly running a brush through my hair, getting ready for our weekly dinner at my parents' place now that they were back from their trip, when Fane called out from the front door.

"Hey, I don't think I'm going to be able to make it to your parents for dinner," he said, tugging on his boots. That made me pause because it meant he was still planning to leave the house.

"Oh." I nodded as casually as I could. "Okay."

"Do you want me to drive you, or will you take Delilah's car?"

"No, no, I can drive." I tried to smile, but he didn't even look at me as he reached for his jacket. We weren't glued at the hip or anything, though it had kind of felt like it since he'd been back. The man was hard-pressed to let me out of his sight—especially since I still hadn't gotten a new phone. I'd been enjoying not being tethered to one, if I was being honest.

So, this sudden mention that he wouldn't be coming to dinner—and the way he'd checked his phone four times in the last two minutes—made my stomach twist.

"Is everything okay?"

He looked at me finally, a small smile on his face. He just settled a broad hand on the back of my head and pressed a kiss to my forehead. "There's something I have to do."

I nodded, my fingers not wanting to let go of his jacket when he pulled back, but I did. "Okay."

I locked up behind us, and we both got into separate cars, him going one way and me going the other.

It felt weird being away from him.

It felt weird that he wasn't being weird about it, but then again, I was just going to my parents' place. Something I was, admittedly, wildly excited about.

Their absence had felt necessary when they announced their extended stay in Cullen, but by the time Thursday afternoon rolled around, I missed them enough to send a message asking if we could move our usual Thursday night dinner to Sunday.

We talked for hours, just the three of us. Before, during, and long after our plates were scraped clean. It hadn't been the three of us in a long time, and the conversation between us hadn't been as easy as it was since before Mom got sick.

I knew I had to tell them about Declan, and I did—but in the most pared-down version of events imaginable. As I spoke, I found myself absently pulling my hair across the cut on my neck, the stitches for which I had thankfully gotten out the day before. The bruising on my face had faded to a yellowy-green by now, and while it was definitely out of place for a dinner setting, a full face of makeup did the trick in covering up what little evidence remained.

They both panicked for about thirty seconds, frantic and overwhelmed, before I managed to reassure them with the same story I'd given the police. The real details—the whole truth—were known only to me, Ash, Fane, and Declan.

Their relief was palpable, but so was the lingering worry in their eyes. I could feel it in the way my mom's hand gripped mine across the table, her fingers trembling ever so slightly. It was harder than I'd thought it would be, not just sharing the story, but resisting the urge to soften it, to erase the worry so clearly etched into their faces. That worry, I realized, was universal. It existed in every parent for their children, no matter how old we got.

But, just like Fane was learning that the sins of others were not his to repent, their worry was not mine to carry.

When they hugged me good night, it was at least two hours later than it usually was when we parted ways. When my mom hugged me a little tighter and a little longer, I didn't fight it. I settled into the skin of being her daughter. A child who had grown up and no longer got the benefit of being hugged by a mother who was taller than her, bigger than her.

I let myself sink into the way she smelled like bergamot and lemon and jasmine and lilies. She'd always smelled like that my whole life. It was constant, and I let it soothe something in me. A reassurance that we were going to be okay. That we had survived so much, and somehow, we would keep going.

"Love you, kid." My dad hugged me tight, the way he always hugged me, and with a promise to see me tomorrow for his coffee, they sent me off, waving at me from the porch.

The whole drive home, I was calm and settled. I turned the radio off, rolled the windows down, and let the blistering cool air outside wrap around me. Waking me up.

Finally, it felt like I was aware of the days I was living, not just shocked at how many of them were passing by without me realizing it.

I pulled into the gravel drive, unable to stop the pleased little hum from coloring the air around me. The tires crunching creating the well-loved soundtrack of every arrival home. It was then, when I looked around, that my smile slowly melted from my face.

Fane's truck wasn't parked where it should've been.

Jerry's wagging tail thumped a steady rhythm, the sound carrying from inside the house. He was still waiting, just beyond the threshold of the door, for someone to walk through it. The realization rooted me to the spot, frozen next to Delilah's car, a knot twisting deep in my gut.

He hadn't come back.

# 41

## Calista

**After**

I stood outside the house for what seemed like a preposterous amount of time. The thumps of Jerry's tail were a metronome that pulled me into a state of hypnosis.

The moment it slowed down, I snapped out of my stare. The cold had started to bite at my skin, seeping into my thin sweater, and I tried to convince myself that the lights would be on as soon as the door swung open. Even though I could see no one was home from the darkness of the windows.

My hand hovered over the keypad, frozen as flashes of the gun pressed to my forehead and the knife at my neck replayed in quick succession. Jerry's tail picked up again, faster now that he'd heard me walk up the stairs, and those faint threads of panic started to dissolve under the steady comfort of his excitement.

The house wasn't quiet. It was filled with Jerry's loud huffing snorts of excitement, his nails clip-clapping on the floorboards, and his tail hitting the wall. But it was empty.

I stayed calm the first time I checked every room.

Maybe he'd parked somewhere else and had already gone to bed.

Maybe he was in the backyard with the pillow spread, waiting for me to join him, all the wishes he'd seen crossing the night sky collected and ready for me to use.

By the time I'd circled back to the living room, Jerry on my heels with his tail still wagging, panic had started to wind its fingers around my heart.

I walked back into the bedroom, my eyes drawn to the corner where his empty duffel bag had sat for months. The same one he'd packed up to take to Artington, and for the life of me, I couldn't remember if he'd brought it back in.

Did he even bring it inside?

The kitchen was clean, spotless, like no one had been there. Like no one had lived in it the way we had for the last week.

"Fane?" I called out, this edge of panic to my voice that I didn't recognize when all that met me was silence.

My mind felt like it was floating in a fish tank by the time I made it back to the living room on what had to be my fourth—or maybe fifth?—-search of this small, shit box house. One that he'd single-handedly turned into a home just by being in it, breathing in it, laughing in it.

My heart sank right into the soles of my feet at the fact that he'd told me he loved me, over and over, and I'd been too fucking scared to say it back.

Even when he'd shown up. Even when he came back. Even when he voiced that question into the dark of our room, his arms wrapped around me, like he thought having the love that was meant to be his withheld was what he deserved.

And I'd let him believe it.

My feet were already moving before my brain could compute. I slipped Jerry's collar over his head, and we were already jogging to Delilah's car when the front door slammed behind me, jolting me back into my body. Back from where my mind had been loitering in the memories the house behind me held.

This is what he'd felt.

I was certain of it. This had to be a fraction of what he'd felt when I crept out of our apartment, refusing to look at his sleeping, crumpled form on the couch, and left. When he woke up to find me gone.

I'd been a coward then.

The thought that I'd always known I was innately soft was trying to cover my thoughts like a blanket full of static. Whenever you tried to throw it off, it latched on to an arm or a leg.

I'd run then because I didn't think I was strong enough to withstand whatever conversation needed to follow. I'd been a coward and not what Fane deserved.

He deserved someone to show up for him, to be patient while he found the words he wanted to say. Someone to help *him* pick up whatever broken pieces he was still trying to collect, his own hands still ravaged while he'd bound mine and helped them heal.

Tears slipped down my face, silent and regretful. All this time, I'd been running back to Darling, watching and waiting for him to come home, for him to fly around that goddamn bend in the road, when I should have been running to meet him halfway.

The car zipped down the dark, empty highway, my sights set on the stretch of road in front of me that would take me back to Artington.

I'd find him. He didn't even need to meet me halfway. I'd follow him all the way to his doorstep so he knew that there was no one else in the entire world who loved him like I did.

That I was so fucking *lucky* to be the person he'd picked. Like when our eyes locked at the bar, those violet all-seeing eyes of his had looked right at me. Bright and assessing. They'd seen everything and decided that if he was going to love someone for the rest of his life, it was going to be me.

I was so focused on the patch of road illuminated by the headlights that I almost missed the truck that flew past me, heading back to Darling. Almost missed it, but not quite.

"Fane!" I yelled his name like the chance of him hearing me through car doors and wheels on pavement was remotely possible. Jerry jumped in the seat next to me, startled out of his mind.

I did a double-take at him because he was sitting right in the front seat with the seat belt pulled across him.

I knew that I had done it, but I couldn't really remember doing it.

The image of that split-second moment when our windows lined up flashed through my mind—Fane's confused, amused frown directed right at us.

I pulled the car off onto the shoulder of the road, my hands shaking because I fucking hated driving at night. My eyes still blurred with tears as I got out and stalked right for him.

I watched him climb out of the cab of his truck, that small, amused smile still tugging at his lips. His mouth opened like he was about to say something, but then he caught sight of me. His expression went blank, and we both froze, the few feet left between us feeling like a bottomless chasm.

"You left." My chest was heaving, my voice scratchy and clogged from the onslaught of tears that refused to stop. "I got home, and you were gone. All your stuff was gone, and I couldn't find you or call you or—"

He stepped forward, his hand wrapping around the back of my neck like it was instinct—like he *needed* to touch me. The rough pad of his thumb brushed against my cheek, swiping away the tears. His brow furrowed as he shook his head, a small, almost helpless gesture.

"Baby," he murmured, shaking his head again. "I was just driving home."

"Where did you go?" I felt my face crumple, words cracking under the weight of that one question.

"I…" He cleared his throat, his expression twisting into a cringe, like he hated what he had to say but couldn't take it back. "I can't tell you. It's a surprise."

I tried to step back to look at him properly, but his hand was locked onto me. "What?"

"I had an idea," he said softly with a small shrug. "I went to try and see if I could get it sorted, but it ran a little over. I texted you, and then remembered you don't have a phone. I tried calling your mom, but she declined the call."

A choked laugh blubbered out of me, and I reached up to try and swipe a hand under my nose, realizing that I probably looked fucking insane.

"I thought you left," I said again, like it was the perfect explanation for the reason I looked like...like *this.*

"I'm not going anywhere, Calista." The edge of sadness in Fane's voice wasn't acceptable, and the idea that he didn't fully grasp that still made me mad.

My hands pushed against his chest, my fists clenching and unclenching. I pointed a shaky finger at him, dropped it, lifted it again, and dropped it once more.

He looked equally as bemused as he did terrified.

"I heard you," I blurted out. I cleared my throat and swiped my tears off my face with the palms of my hands. "The other night, I heard you."

He didn't say a word. Just tilted his head in that way of his, waiting, patient as ever.

"When you asked me if I could ever love you again—I heard you." My voice cracked, but I pushed through. "And the thing is, I can't tell you that."

I watched as his body seemed to fold in on itself, like he was bracing, trying to shield whatever soft underbelly he had left from the blow he thought was coming.

"I can't," I continued, the words tumbling out. "Because there is no *again*, Fane." It was my turn to shake my head in my own helpless gesture. "I never stopped. How you don't get that is *baffling* to me."

I was waving my hands in panic now. Making the shape of hearts and gesturing between the two of us with something that resembled jazz hands. Finally, I closed the distance. I walked right up to him and pressed my palms on either side of his face.

"I am so in love with you, Fane Mackenzie. Do you hear me?"

His whole body shuddered beneath my touch, and I felt his arms circle around my waist.

"I thought I made you sick," he rasped, his eyes glassy and glowing and beautiful and looking right at me.

"I'm willing to look past it," I laughed, and it was full of sniffling and more tears, but *happy* tears. All the excess of the love I had for him that had no place else to go but out. When he dropped his forehead to mine, I pulled him tighter to me, relishing the feel of his broad, solid form beneath my hands.

This man, who was brighter than any sun.

When he kissed me, it was old and new at the same time. It was the only thing I was ever going to need, but then he pulled back and his eyes darted over my shoulder.

"Jerry's in the front seat."

I turned in his arms to look at our big, goofy dog sitting in the front seat, looking at us with nothing but adoration.

"He is."

"He's wearing a seat belt."

I nodded, "That's right."

Slowly, like an avalanche, Fane's laughter started to rumble out of him. The vibrations of it pressed into my back where he clutched me to him, picking up speed until it surrounded us, coating us both from head to toe. I turned back to face him after his chuckles had died down, the smile on my face a permanent thing.

"Fall into me, Cali," he whispered into the quiet night that pressed in on us, wrapping around me like a promise. "I'll catch you."

"I know." I didn't even hesitate, the conviction in my words was clear, and all the shooting stars and unused wishes that flew overhead were unneeded entirely.

"How?" he asked, his chest pressed to mine and our hearts beating in sync.

"Because you already have."

42

# Epilogue 1

**Fane**

**Two Months Later**

I'd always thought Artington was a beautiful city.

It had every season, and none of them were particularly brutal. It was picturesque, like something you'd see flipping through a coffee table book. That's what it felt like, living in it—from down *there*.

The crowded streets, the buildings, the trees, the sidewalks—all of it softened by a fine dusting of snow.

But from up here? The people looked like ants.

We were up so high that the penthouse was shrouded in a cloak of clouds more often than not. It made it feel like when the clouds did part, you were looking down from the heavens.

A god overlooking his domain.

My eyes shifted to my reflection in the glass, the city below blurring into the background.

The suit I wore was cut close to my body, tailored to perfection. A dark navy shirt beneath it, paired with a tie the same shade as Cali's dress.

A dress I hadn't seen yet. Hard as I'd tried to peek into the garment bag hanging in the hall, Cali had threatened to delete the entire new sex list from her phone if I so much as thought about it again.

352

The impulse had quickly dissipated.

The ding of the elevator split through the space around me at half past six in the evening, precisely as Ash said it would.

I didn't bother to turn around. My heart didn't so much as flutter in my chest when the heavy footfalls that had once stalked me, even in the fleeting moments of peace I'd found growing up, drew closer.

They didn't haunt me now. They didn't so much as make me flinch.

The fear I'd once carried—of growing into the same kind of monster as the man responsible for my existence—had long since paled in comparison to the monster I'd chosen to become.

This monster—the one standing here to ensure nothing and no one touched the people I loved? I didn't mind him.

The footsteps stopped abruptly, and I turned just in time to see the mild amount of shock he felt at finding me in his home.

It felt like an insult to the word to refer to this place as that. This was not a *home*. William Mackenzie wouldn't know a home if it slashed his fucking throat.

"Fane." He straightened, standing a little taller, like that would do anything to improve the way I so thoroughly towered over him. "I hadn't expected to see you here."

I tilted my head slightly, slipping my hands into my slacks. "No, I'd say you didn't. I believe her name was Octavia—the woman you thought would be in your bed right now."

"You're dressed a little more formally than usual," he said, his gaze flicking to my tailored suit.

I shrugged, letting the faintest edge of a smile tug at my lips. "I wanted to do justice to the occasion."

His steps were slow and measured, a performance I'd seen countless times before. He wasn't in any rush to cross the room, each step deliberate, meant to remind me that he controlled the pace of this meeting.

I fucking loved how wrong he was.

His eyes were searching, right on the cusp of locking up, when I let the faintest hint of a smile touch the edge of my mouth.

What a fucking imbecile.

Where there was power unjustly earned—stolen and wielded with the intent to create fear—there was ego. My father didn't know what a threat looked like because he believed that if there was one, he'd be able to see it. That if there was one, it would be as stupidly obvious as he was dense.

Because of that, all it took for his shoulders to relax a fraction was the hint of a smile he didn't know the meaning of.

"You did me a favor," he said, his laugh low and ugly. "She wasn't, let's say, the freshest mare in the stable."

I laughed too. Because he might as well have been turning the soil to dig his own grave, and the show was far more entertaining than I'd expected.

"Ah. Of course," I murmured, my eyes tracking his movements as his body relaxed further.

"I was starting to worry, you know," he continued, making his way to the liquor cart that sat between two plush, blood-red sofas, also just like Ash had said.

"Oh?" I hummed, nodding when he gestured toward the crystal decanter of whiskey.

"It's been weeks since we last spoke." His eyes flicked up, flashing for a second with how deep his displeasure ran at the very idea that I'd made him wait. "I was starting to think you hadn't heeded my advice."

I crossed the room slowly, deliberately, taking the glass he held out, a shallow finger's width of liquid inside.

"Oh, you mean that I should think of my mother." I nodded once, rounding the sofa with the glass in hand. "And my wife."

"Wife?" His eyebrows shot up. "I hadn't realized you'd gotten married."

The tug at the corner of my lips this time wasn't rehearsed. "Soon," I said. Thinking of how I'd referred to Cali as nothing but my wife since that night on the highway and how every time I did her eyes would roll. But there was no way for her to hide that peachy blush that colored her face or the way her eyes lingered on me when she thought I wasn't paying attention.

I was always paying attention to that woman.

"I look forward to meeting her." His smile was black tar, sticking and seeping. I forced myself not to picture the thoughts running through his mind.

*Patience.*

"Your brother really made a mess for us," he said, swirling the whiskey in his glass, his eyes flicking briefly to the one in my hand. "Take a seat, son." He gestured toward the couch opposite him with a tilt of his head.

As I walked, I made sure to take my time. Every step deliberate, calculated. Not a single ounce of the tension that word filled me with—*son*—was allowed to show. Not a single fucking hint.

The look he gave me showed all too quickly the cracks in his paper-thin veneer. The way his hand clenched around the glass he held.

"As I was saying," he ground out, face starting to flush red with the effort of pretending like we were equals, "You'll have some late nights ahead of you, playing catch-up on the plan of attack. Your first appearance as the new CEO of Mackenzie Co is next week."

"The new CEO?" My eyebrows shot up, the surprise on my face exaggerated just enough. "You're handing me the company?"

His laugh was a jarring, cracking, brittle cackle. It was something that had festered from disuse. "My boy, you've spent too much time around that girl thinking with your cock instead of your brain. In name only," his free hand shot out, snapping sharply twice in the space between us. "Keep up."

His eyes flicked to the glass in my hand again.

"You're right," I said, letting out a small, measured sigh as I sagged into the couch. I let an easy smile spread across my face, slow and disarming, shaking my head like I was finally conceding. My hand lifted the glass toward my lips, a move he mimicked, the whiskey almost touching his mouth.

"You know," I said, snapping forward suddenly, elbows on my knees. His head jerked, startled by the shift. "I think I learned a lot more from you growing up than I ever gave you credit for."

"When you were growing up?" He parroted, his expression twisting, caught off guard. It was the kind of curveball he didn't know how to handle.

"Took me a while to figure it out, but it all cleared up for me after I had time to think about it." I started to lift the glass to my lips again, and so did he, but this time there was a look of satisfaction on his face.

Wistful, like the memories he was flicking through were treasures instead of scars. He took his first sip of the liquor, a gasp of appreciation for the way I was sure it warmed his throat on its way down.

One sip was fine. One was enough.

I set my own untouched glass on the coffee table and stood up just as my phone buzzed in my pocket.

"I learned what a pathetic piece of shit looks like, real up close and personal." My voice was conversational, light even, which made his reaction just a little delayed.

"What did you just say?"

"I said," I replied, walking closer and leaning down a little so he had no choice but to look me in the eyes. *My mother's eyes.*

"You're a fucking loser, William. Has anyone ever said that right to your face before?" I straightened up, flattening a palm against my tie. "I'll be honest, it feels like a real pivotal moment for us as father and son, if I'm the first."

"You fucking—" He attempted to lunge for me but caught himself on the edge of the couch, a look of shocking disorientation on his face.

"Oops, careful, pops." I checked my watch, "You're entering the fun house stage."

I reached into the inside pocket of my blazer and pulled out a thick plastic bag, snapping it open with deliberate precision before reaching for his glass.

"Can I be honest with you about something?" I leaned in, a conspiratorial whisper. "I knew this would be easy, but I didn't think it would be *this* easy."

I dropped the glass into the plastic bag I held and turned back to where I set mine down.

"Ash thought this was about how this would go. I, at least, bet that I'd have to take a sip of my drink too, just to convince you to have one of yours." I shook my head with mock disbelief. "But nope, blow a bit of smoke up your ass and you were as good as gone."

"What the fu—"

"There is no more talking for you," I cut him off sharply, turning back to face him. All the easy-going enjoyment drained from my voice. My smile was fucking dazzling when a cry of pain left his lips, his hand flying to brace over his stomach.

"Does it hurt?" I asked, my voice laced with mock curiosity as my lips peeled back further, my head tilting slightly to the side. "I heard it fucking kills," I whispered, reaching past him for the decanter he'd placed back in the middle of the liquor cart.

I made quick work of slipping on a pair of latex gloves, retrieving the original decanter I'd stowed in the cupboard beneath the cart, and swapping it out seamlessly. The gloves joined the bag with the rest of the evidence, which I tied off with a neat knot.

My phone buzzed in my pocket again, and I rolled my eyes at the persistence of my best friend.

I walked back over to stand in front of my father, but not too close because right as I looked at my watch, he folded over his legs and emptied the content of his stomach onto the floor.

My lip curled back again but this time in disgust, "Gross," I murmured, shaking it off so I could get to my actual point.

Turns out I was a fan of the theatrics. Who'd of fucking guessed?

"Yoo-hoo." I snapped my fingers to get his attention, watching as his glazed eyes lifted to meet mine. He leaned back into the couch, his chest heaving, the words he couldn't say swirling in the haze of his expression.

"You could have avoided all of this." I gestured lazily between us. "But you had to go ahead and threaten my mother. My *wife*." I shook my head in mock disappointment. "I was actually going to just…let you go!" I scoffed, checking my watch again as my phone buzzed for the third time against my leg. "I should be thanking you, really. I imagined you like this—time and time again. But the reality? So much better than what I pictured."

I bent down and picked up the bag I'd set at my feet.

"I want you to know that no one will remember your name." My voice was cold and heavy. The fucking hand of the grim reaper reaching out to grip him by the throat. "And if they do, they will know just how insignificant you were. How spectacularly short you fell."

"You…" he wheezed, chest working exceptionally hard now.

"One more time." I cupped a hand around my ear, tilting my head toward him and frowning in concentration.

"I'm…going to…fucking…kill you." Sweat dripped down his face, his mouth twisting in pain and desperation.

"Oh." I nodded, straightening back up. "No, you're not," I said, giving him a small, pitying smile. "But I bet you wish you did, huh?" I said with a wink.

The very same that Cali seemed to be so fond of. My father, though, didn't seem to hold it in quite the same regard.

The noise he made was full of his last dispatch effort to move. A pathetic belief that he could fight the arsenic in his blood. The delusion that nothing and no one could touch him finally torn to bloody ribbons while I watched him take his final breaths.

I held up my middle finger as his chest rose and fell for the last time and then my phone buzzed again. This time, it didn't stop.

"You know," I said, my tone bone-dry as I answered, "I'm in the middle of something."

"You're taking forever. I thought he got the better of you," Ash said, his words muffled, likely around a mouthful of food.

"Your faith in me is inspiring," I muttered, heading for the elevator and pressing the call button. The doors opened immediately.

"Coraline has been calling me every two minutes, ripping me a new asshole because we're running late."

"What'd you tell her?" I'd set my phone to *do not disturb* for everyone but Ashton. I didn't want a single part of this to touch Cali.

"That we've gone fishing. What do you fucking think I told her?"

It was silent for a second while I waited for him to go on.

"I don't fucking know?"

"She thinks you're getting her something special. Like down-on-one-knee special."

My face fell. "Are you fucking kidding me? You had *one* secret to keep."

"I didn't give her specifics," he grumbled as I walked out of the elevator, leaving the bag behind. I nodded at two of Ash's guys as they passed me, their small nods returned in kind as I made my way through the lobby and out to the waiting car.

As soon as the door closed behind me, I removed the phone from my ear and turned off *do not disturb*. A flood of messages from Cali, Delilah, and Sammy filled my screen.

The last one from Delilah was a bride emoji.

"I'm going to actually kill you," I bit out, glaring at Ash.

"Well, and I was hoping you would have learned this already, but the first rule is not to tell the other person what you plan to do."

"You think you're smart, don't you?"

"I do," he replied, nodding with a little smile. "I'm also a generous lover." He shrugged, "Or so I've been told."

I lunged for him, aiming to get him into a headlock, but there was no fucking chance. He screamed like a baby, clutching his hair and whining about me ruining it.

The car started to move and the silence around us wasn't stifling, only knowing.

"So," he started again, breaking it, "What's the verdict?"

"It's done." I nodded, keeping my eyes out the window, feeling…nothing, at that sentiment.

Nothing but relief, for the second time in my life.

"And?" he pressed.

I kept my gaze out the window when I relented with a sigh, reaching into my pocket and pulling out twenty bucks and handing it to him without another word.

"I fucking *knew* it!" Ash yelled, riding the high of winning our bet, all the way to Delilah's art showing in the middle of the city.

# 43

# Epilogue 2

**Fane**
**Four Months After That**

"Is this a sex thing?" Cali asked when I helped her out of the car, a scarf tied around her eyes.

"This isn't a sex thing." I smiled against her temple, leaving a kiss there before taking her hand.

"Because if this is a sex thing, I am totally on board." The hand that wasn't clutched in mine was flopping all over the place, the only real sign that she was nervous.

"Don't be nervous, baby," I whispered against the shell of her ear. Her body shivered from head to toe, and that peachy hue I constantly craved the sight of spread across her cheeks.

Our boots crunched on the freshly fallen snow as I led her forward. She mumbled the whole way about how nerves were for toddlers and free climbers.

When we reached the perfect spot, I stopped. She stood there, oblivious and rambling, and I took a moment just to look at her. God, I was so in love with her.

The last four months had both flown by and also traveled at a snail's pace.

In that time, Cali had made the executive decision to expand the café to offer actual breakfast until ten a.m.

"I want you to be my chef," she'd announced, storming out of the bedroom and straight into the living room. A furrow of determination on her brow that was always in place whenever she had her mind set on something. When she spoke, she was also miming flipping something in a frying pan.

"Your chef?" I'd asked, amused.

"You are, by far, the most talented cook I've ever met, though if you tell my mom, I will deny it. I have essentially turned into a pancake since you came home, and now…well, I think we should work together."

*Came home.* It ricocheted off the walls of my mind, true and clear.

"I'll pay you, obviously." She threw her hands up, punctuating her words. "I'm not expecting free labor just because you're my boyfriend, and we're sleeping together." Her eyes widened. "I'm not saying that us having sex equates to you providing me with free labor…"

I grinned at her rambling. Whenever she got like this, it was entertaining as hell.

"I'd both pay you and have sex with you if you worked at Sunshine," she stammered. Her hand flew to her throat, flustered. "I mean, they're separate things! I'd pay you as an employer and sleep with you as…a person."

"What if I wanted to fuck you on our lunch break?"

That peach flush of hers started on her chest and moved up to her neck and face. Her mouth opened and closed like a fish out of water before the only thing that came out was a squeaked, "Okay!"

By then, I'd been laughing so hard I had to tilt my head back against the couch. She stood in front of me, still flustered, giving me an awkward double thumbs-up.

"Come here." I held out a hand, waiting until she finally settled on top of me, straddling my hips while her fingers fiddled with the hem of my shirt.

"I would love to work together. I think it's a really great idea, but I'd want to go into it as partners. To invest in the café with you."

"Oh." She shook her head with a small smile. "I don't own the space, I just rent it."

I lifted her off me effortlessly, setting her down on the couch. Then, without a word, I disappeared into the bedroom. When I came back, I handed her a folded piece of paper.

"What's this?"

I didn't say anything, just watched as she unfolded it. Her eyes skimmed the words, and when she looked back at me—glassiness in her gaze, cheeks flushed—she whispered, "The building is in my name."

"It is."

"The building on Main Street—the one Sunshine is in—it's in my name. Why is it in my name?" She gestured with her hands, outlining what I assumed was meant to be a building.

"When I got to town, I wasn't sure if I could stop Mackenzie Co.," I told her honestly. "I had a rough plan, but when I saw that you had a business right where the company wanted to obtain property, I bought the building under your name."

"You...what?"

"I didn't want you to worry, and if the development did go through, I wanted Sunshine to be okay. I wanted *you* to be okay—"

Cali jumped off the couch and threw herself at me, arms and legs wrapping around me like a vise. The commotion stirred Jerry from his slumber to the point he dragged his body off the couch and started nudging my ass with his nose.

She pulled back just enough to press her forehead to mine. "What did I do to deserve you?" she whispered.

"Everything," I murmured, pressing a kiss to her jaw. Without another word, I carried her to the bedroom and showed her exactly how willing I was to accept her business proposition.

For the last month and a half, we'd woken up together, headed to work together, and when the breakfast shift ended, I stayed to bake cookies and clean tables.

I used to think success was an overpriced suit and an office in a high-rise. But this—*this* was success. Doing what I loved, something I hadn't even realized I loved, with the person I loved. That's what it meant to truly have it all.

"Fane?" Cali's voice pulled me from my thoughts. She was standing where I'd left her, hands waving in front of her face like she was trying to find me through the blindfold. "Are you gone?"

"I'm here," I murmured, stepping closer. "You can take off the blindfold."

Her hands tentatively reached up to pull off the scarf, eyes squinting while they adjusted to the gentle purple hue that settled around this property as the sun was going down.

Her eyes bulged. "We're at Primrose Ranch."

"We are."

"Why are we here? This is *private property*, Fane!" she whispered, clutching to the scarf with tight fists, like someone would hear us.

"I don't think we're going to get into trouble." I smiled at her, stuffing my hands into the front pockets of my jeans.

"This isn't your ranch!" She did a small, little gallop like she was riding a horse, and I snorted so aggressively I almost blew the whole thing, catching myself from bending over and smothering my laughter.

"No, it's not my ranch." I stepped to the side, revealing the sign I'd been standing in front of. "But it *is* yours."

Her gaze landed on the freshly painted sign: *Rosie's Ranch.*

"That's my name." She pointed to it, her eyes flicking to mine, and then back to the sign.

"Yes, it is."

"My name is on that sign." She looked like she might pass out, so I walked up to her and stopped just a foot away.

"Can I ask you something?" I murmured.

She nodded, eyes glued to mine.

"I'm obsessed with you," I said, giving her a bright smile to which she just rolled her eyes, both her hands landing on my chest.

"You're the first thing I think of when I wake up, and the last thing I think of before we go to sleep."

"*Fane.*" She gave me a knowing look that said she definitely thought this was still a sex thing.

I brought the back of her hand up to my lips, brushing a kiss over her knuckles. "I want to give you everything you've ever wanted, Cali. I want to make you laugh, give you things that make you hum when you remember them. I want to cook you food and watch your face change when you eat it. I want to run behind you every single day, even though you run too fast, because I get to look at your ass."

Cali snorted a snotty laugh, wiping her face on her shoulder.

"I want to give you a peaceful life. Where you can be steady, or soft, or both, or neither."

"I love you," she said softly, and in those three words, she gave me everything I'd ever wanted.

"The thing is, when I picture life now, it feels *almost* peaceful." I continued. "But when I picture life *here*, it feels perfect. I picture you on the porch, our blankets laid out right here, Jerry between us. Maybe, when we're ready, a couple extra heartbeats."

She nodded, eyes glassy, hands gripping mine tightly.

"This house is not a shit box," she croaked, shaking her head.

"No." I laughed. "It's not."

"Fane, did you buy us a ranch?" Her voice cracked as she clutched the sides of my coat.

"This was where I was when you were flying back to Artington. I was meeting with Sammy and a lawyer here so that we could flesh out all the details of a change in ownership."

"I was coming to find you," she whispered, and it made my chest tighten—the realization that I had this person, who was made up of all the best things, willing to always run straight for me. Even when she thought I was heading the other way.

"I know." I nodded, leaning in to drop a kiss to her jaw.

"Fane?"

"Mmm?"

"You haven't asked me anything yet."

My face nearly split in two with my smile, and it stayed that way as I sank to one knee and pulled a ring from my pocket.

"Holy fuck," she muttered, her voice pitching higher with each word.

"Holy *fucking* fuck."

"Cali…"

"Sweet *fuck!*" she yelled and started bouncing from foot to foot, pointing right at the ring I held. "Is that a ring?"

"Yes—"

"Oh my god, that's a—he has a ring. He has a *ring!*" She started shaking her hands, glancing around like she needed someone to scream at about it.

"Fane, that's a diamond. That's a *big fucking diamond!*"

"Baby—"

"That's the most beautiful ring I've ever seen," she cried, covering her mouth while still pointing at the ring.

"Calista?"

"Yes?" she squeaked and then dropped to her knees in front of me, cold hands gripping my wrists and tear-filled eyes on my face.

"Will you marry me?"

She started nodding frantically. "Yes," she said. "Yes, yes, yes, holy shit, yes!" Her voice got louder with every word, and when I slipped the ring onto her shaking hand, her body crashed into mine.

I didn't care when the cold snow soaked into my jacket. My eyes stayed on her, like they always had.

Like they always would.

"Does this mean I might finally get you into a cowboy hat?" she asked, her eyes still house behind us.

"You might," I said, still absorbed by the wonder on her face, watching bit by bit as something mischievous started to bloom in her eyes.

"You know," she said, wiggling off me and dusting the snow from her hands as she came to standing. "This feels like an opportune time to try number five from the sex list."

Then, she was off. Her laughter bounced off the trees around us, loud and unrestrained. Pouring out of her in the way laughter does when you give yourself over to it completely.

And so I got up, dusted the snow off my own hands, and followed.

www.ingramcontent.com/pod-product-compliance
Lightning Source LLC
Chambersburg PA
CBHW021801190726